Jacquelyn Frank is a *New York Times* and *USA Today* bestselling author of sizzling paranormal romance novels. She lives in western North Carolina.

Visit Jacquelyn Frank online:

www. jacquelynfrank.com
www.facebook.com/authorjacquelynfrank
www.twitter.com/JacquelynFrank

FORSAKEN

The World of Nightwalkers

JACQUELYN FRANK

piatkus

PIATKUS

First published in the US in 2014 by Ballantine Books, an imprint
of The Random House Publishing Group, a division of
Random House, Inc., New York.
First published in Great Britain in 2014 by Piatkus

A CIP catalogue record for this book
is available from the British Library.

ISBN 978-0-349-40082-2

Printed and bound in Great Britain by
Clays Ltd, St Ives, plc

Papers used by Piatkus are from well-managed forests
and other responsible sources.

MIX
Paper from
responsible sources
FSC
www.fsc.org FSC® C104740

Piatkus
An imprint of
Little, Brown Book Group
100 Victoria Embankment
London EC4Y 0DY

An Hachette UK Company
www.hachette.co.uk

www.piatkus.co.uk

For Darynda, my writing buddy.
You make me work hard
to keep up with you.
Love you, even when
you karate-chop my larynx!

GLOSSARY
AND PRONUNCIATION TABLE

Apep: (Ā-pep)
Asikri: (Ah-SĒ-crē)
Chatha: (Chath-UH)
Docia: (DŌ-shuh)
Hatshepsut: (hat-SHEP-soot)
Ka: (kah) Egyptian soul
Kamenwati: (Kah-men-WAH-ti)
Menes: (MEN-es)
Ouroboros: (You-row-BORE-us) A snake or dragon devouring its own tail, a sign of infinity or perpetual life.
Pharaoh: (FEY-roh) Egyptian king or queen. This is used in reference to both male and female rulers. In this case, the rulers of the Bodywalkers.
Tameri: (Tah-MARE-ē)

FORSAKEN

THE LOST SCROLL OF KINDRED

... And so it will come to pass in the forward times that the nations of the Nightwalkers will be shattered, driven apart, and become strangers to one another. Hidden by misfortune and by purpose, these twelve nations will come to cross-purposes and fade from one another's existence. In the forward times these nations will face toil and struggle unlike any time before, and only by coming together once more can they hope to face the evil that will set upon them. But they are lost to one another, and will remain lost until a great enemy is defeated ... and a new one resurrects itself ...

CHAPTER ONE

. . . Why hast thou forsaken me? . . .

Leo Alvarez was not a religious man. He had been anything but for as long as he could remember. He had come such a long way from Sunday mass and the catechism lessons his mother had demanded of him.

Such a long way.

He was not what one would call a good man. He wasn't evil, surprisingly far from it considering the harsh realities of his life. But he most certainly was not an angel. He was not free of sin, and many of those sins were very grave indeed. But if he were to ever be judged for them, Leo would not be apologetic for the things he had done. He had a code, which he followed efficiently, and felt it would speak for him.

But however serious his sins, he didn't deserve the punishment that was presently being dealt out to him. No one deserved the cruel and excruciating torment he was swimming in.

Leo rolled in and out of consciousness, but he knew the bliss of unconsciousness would be robbed from him violently when the blade sinking into his flesh found the all-too-responsive nerves and receptors. The message was received in a burning explosion of pain, forcing him to clench his jaw until his teeth creaked under the stress of it.

But he would not scream again. He was hoarse from everything that had come previous to this new onslaught. He didn't worry about whether or not it made him seem weak. No. None of that mattered at the moment. Nothing mattered to Leo outside of one single word. One single objective.

Live.

Live, Alvarez, he demanded of himself for the thousandth time. Although, by now it was obvious that the twisted demon who orchestrated his agony had no intention of killing him.

No.

That would be far too merciful, and this evil thing—the creature that had lashed him down to the coarse cemented floor, his wrists torn to shreds inside the cuffs of heavy metal manacles—was everything opposite of mercy. But these wounds would be healed shortly. As would the newest carving that the beast was drawing into his body. Healing would come only after the thing called Chatha was through lifting Leo's organs out of his body to present them to him, just before he would begin to dissect them before his prisoner's very eyes.

This time he reached deep and Leo could feel him fumbling around inside his gut, moving lower, slick fingers having difficulty gaining purchase at first. But eventually Chatha found his kidney and ripped it out of him, giggling as he held it up, prodding at it with a finger, not caring that Leo was quickly dying of blood loss.

Maybe . . . maybe this time I will die before he can heal me, Leo thought. But he struggled to tamp the hope down, knowing that it was a part of the creature's tormenting ritual, realizing that it was contrary to his earlier directive to live. But the creature did this, liked to make him think he was going to find the release of death. Make him think that, after days of this torture it would finally be over. And he was fading. He was reaching for something . . . something beyond life. Something waiting for him. Something of infinite, blissful peace.

Then Chatha dropped the kidney, and scrambled up over his body on hands and knees. He pressed his face close to Leo's, filling his darkening vision with that innocent and maniacal visage.

"No, no," he tsked, wagging a blood-wet finger before Leo's nose. "No fair!"

And that was when tears would burn into Leo's eyes, that secret of all secret hopes dashed all to hell as the beast laid hands on him like an Evangelical preacher touched by God, and healed him.

Leo awoke with a savage shout, his body lurching out of bed, forcing him to stumble and fall as his sleeping muscles refused to awaken and do their duty. He fell to the floor, his hands barely reaching out in time to keep him from landing face-first into the luxurious carpeting. The jarring of his body shook sweat from the tips of his hair, a shower of salt and water spraying everywhere. He was soaked in it, his bare chest slick with wet and his boxers plastered to him in their drenched state.

He tried to slow his breathing, tried to make himself understand that he was awake and, for the moment, safe. This house was the home of his best friend. The friend who had seen him healed and who was patiently waiting for him to open up and talk about the horror that he had been through.

But he would be waiting a very long time because Leo would never, *ever* speak a word about it to anyone. He would not resurrect those moments in the bright light of day. He would never burden another soul with the horror he had survived . . . somehow.

No. He would go to his grave with it. He would drag

it into the afterlife with him, and this time it would be the one kicking and screaming.

She tilted her head, listening to the wind, feeling the eddy of how it flowed freely or, better yet, washed around things. The rush and sound of it acted like sonar, telling her where everything was just by the way it shifted. When there was no wind she was as good as blind to what was happening in the world, and those were the moments that she found as terrifying as humans would feel if only they knew what was out there. What was out there living and breathing beside them without their knowledge.

Knowledge. Knowledge was key and it was her job to deliver information. Her people could feel and sense things all around . . . just like she could with the actual wind right at that moment. But unlike the surety of knowing there was a cow twenty paces to her left and a church with a steeple twenty miles due south, the future had murky eddies. The wind of the future was blowing in bad directions now and if the wind blew one way tragedy and horror would reign. If it blew another, there would be tragedy and survival. And yet another would bring victory and joy. It was the first that must be avoided at all cost. The others . . . the others would fall as they would and that was as it should be.

"Whistle and blow, whistle and blow," she murmured, the phrase like second nature, her people's way of saying "What will be will be."

She pushed off the branch of a tree, letting the wind wash over her, letting it lift her up. The feel of it flowing over her skin was the most comforting sensation she knew. There was nothing like it in all the world, nothing more freeing. She had no idea how anyone could take it for granted or how mortals bore being bound to the earth. Then again, they tried to fight it, didn't they, in their great lumbering metal machines? Poor things. She supposed it was their comfortable and safe way of doing things. But the wind was not safe and as much as it buoyed up it was the sudden plummeting sweeps down toward soil that made life course through the veins. Those humans who flew on silk wings . . . yes, they were the braver sort. To know that a single tear in that silk could end their fragile mortal lives . . . it was invigorating. Those were humans she longed to know better.

But that was impossible. Contact with humans was strictly prohibited. Well . . . in true form anyway. You could hardly swing a cat without bumping into a mortal these days. It was why they lived so distant from the nearest human dwelling. But other things had the same inclination and the world was growing small.

But that would cease to be a worry for very much longer if the wind kept blowing so ill. She moved low and fast, marveling at the cacti and other strange vegetation. She had never been in this part of the United States before. Which was strange really. She loved to travel and see the world, to see how very different one place was from another. And when she had glutted on the topography of a region she would move deeper into the area, mixing with humans, learning all about the differing cultures involved and the almost rhythmic beauty of their languages. And food. God, how she loved food.

She shook the thought off. She was letting herself get distracted. There was business to be done. Sightseeing would have to wait for a different day and a very different set of circumstances.

Marissa Anderson looked up from the garden to glance over her shoulder toward the house. A little ways away from where she was kneeling in dirt, leaning against some large desert rocks with one booted foot on the ground and the other braced back against the boulder behind him was Leo.

Farther beyond him was the house. She lifted her hand to block the bright glare of the moonlight from her sight so she could get a better look at her love as he sat there staring intently at his best friend. Marissa knew just how worried Jackson was about Leo. Even if it hadn't been written all over his face at that moment. And there was clearly much to be worried about. Leo was a human man thrust harshly into a superhuman world. He had learned the hard way about all the dangers that came with it, and he had learned that the two most important people in his life were also a part of that dangerous night world. On top of being tortured, it was a lot to take in.

"Staring at them is no' going to improve the situation," a deep voice rumbled in the rolling timbre of a Scots accent from beside her. She turned to look at Ahnvil, who, like her, was on his knees in the garden she was working on. Despite her newfound Bodywalker strength he had insisted on helping her with some of the markedly heavy lifting, as he often did. But she had realized some time ago that his eagerness to help her in her landscaping tasks stemmed less from helpfulness than it did a genuine love of being in the dirt and molding nature to something thriving and living. He was a big man, and at the moment he appeared as human as she did—though his skin tone was a bit paler than hers was. But Marissa knew that Gargoyles could also appear in the shape of a flesh-and-blood human, but with a skin of stone, like some sort of built-in armor. Or they could appear, as a true grotesque Gargoyle, with frightening features and ferociously huge wings capable of lifting their enormous bodies into the air.

"I know that," she said with a deep sigh, turning back

to the comfort of the hard, colorful New Mexico desert soil. She was planting pansies, which were not indigenous to the area, but she thought they were hearty enough to make it. She missed pansies. Out east there had been such beautiful flowers, like bulbs and hydrangea and more. It was one of the little things she missed being out here.

She looked back toward the reason she had moved to New Mexico. The reason why she had decided to die and be reborn into a powerful Bodywalker queen.

We are a queen, Hatshepsut was quick to point out from deep in her soul. *You are every part the queen we are now, and do not forget that.*

Her Blending process was still so new and, she had been told, not entirely finished yet. When it was she would be extraordinarily powerful. She found that so hard to comprehend because she was already frighteningly powerful. Powerful enough to be grateful she was a well-balanced person. Someone who wasn't could go into a tailspin and use this power in very dark ways.

"The human will heal. We all heal with time," Ahnvil said.

His tone was deeper and darker than usual and she turned her full attention to him. She knew so little about him. But the one thing she knew, the one thing that was true of every single Gargoyle, was that he had been born into slavery. She didn't understand the process or how it all came about, but they had all been slaves to the wicked Templar Bodywalkers who had used their dark magic to create their Gargoyle servants and had used touchstones to keep them imprisoned and chained to their sides. After all, whoever held the touchstone held the Gargoyle's life in his hand.

But these were only general lines of information. She knew very little about the specifics of this particular Gargoyle. But her ability, her ability to feel emotions no matter how big or small, told her there was a well of trauma around him. He swam in the aftermath of it, carried it around with him every single moment of every single day. It must be exhausting, she thought with a frown. She turned her attention back to the garden and began to pull at the weeds with a vengeance, trying to hide her expression. She knew he would not react well to pity.

She glanced over at Leo and knew it was exactly the same for him. Only Leo's trauma cut deeper, ran fresher. And as much as her lover wanted his friend to open up to him, to heal with him, she knew there was no way Leo would be capable of doing so anytime soon. Marissa didn't know what could possibly change that, but she was hopeful nonetheless. For Jackson's sake as much as for Leo's own sake. But that was to be expected. Jackson's emotions would always call strongest to her. They were mated and had been for lifetimes. Every lifetime they were reborn, each into a new host, and they would find each other. They called it a love for all time, and they were not wrong. She had only known these feelings for a short time, and yet because of the Bodywalker she hosted, it was as if she had known them forever.

The idea of meeting the future without him left a cold, bitter taste in her mouth and she resisted the urge to spit into the rich dark soil beneath her. The very thought made her stomach clench with fear. And she was right to feel that fear. Last time she had been incarnated she had barely lived two weeks before she had become a casualty of this damned war with the Templars. She had been ripped away from her love for another hundred years and, though he had quickly followed her into the Ether, it had been too short a time. Was she selfish for wanting more time on the physical plane? For wanting to touch him and hold him to her every night as though it might be the last time? For urging him to make love to her again and again so she could glory in this precious physical existence?

"Leo."

Leo turned to look at Jackson Waverly. It was so strange, seeing him and his cute little redheaded woman sitting on the porch and working the garden, respectively, as if it were a lazy, sunny day in New Mexico, rather than the dark of night, and all they were missing was some cool glasses of lemonade in order to create the perfect idyllic picture. He wasn't used to living in the dark and didn't know if he could ever be. Though, he had always been better in the dark. Hidden. Shadowed. Dangerous.

But he was none of those things at the moment. His body hurt from head to toe, full of scars and gouging incisions still in need of serious healing. He had never been a good invalid, however, so he kept moving, refusing a sickbed, knowing that eventually the physical agony would fade away . . . that this healing pain was nothing compared to what he had endured. The mending carvings in his body were child's play in comparison to their acquisition.

"In a minute," he called to his friend.

He turned the word friend over and over in his mind. Maybe Jackson was still the friend he knew and loved. Or maybe he was just another evil thing wearing the skin of someone he trusted. That was all he could think of ever since Jackson had explained to him what a Bodywalker was. A soul from ancient Egypt, reborn in a host body, supposedly living a symbiotic life with that host. So his best friend was, at best, compromised. At worst . . . Leo hoped like hell he wouldn't need to kill his brother in order to get at the thing existing inside of him. He'd be damned before he would sit on the sidelines and let a thing like Chatha take over his best friend.

That Bodywalker psychopath had seized the innocent mind and body of a Down syndrome man, the ultimate wolf in easily recognizable sheep's clothing. But according to Jackson, there were the good Bodywalkers, the Politic, like the ones residing in Jackson and his significant other, Marissa, and there were the bad Bodywalkers, the Templars, who subjugated the existing soul inside of their new host and completely hijacked them.

As far as Leo was concerned, there was very little difference. And on top of it he had learned a very valuable lesson. Never turn your back on anyone, no matter how soft and innocuous they may seem. And right now that included Jackson and Marissa. Bodywalker pharaohs.

Compromised.

Leo straightened, dusting the corpses of the grass blades he had mutilated off his jeans. He remembered a little too late to do so with a measure of gentility, but a blinding sensation of pain quickly reminded him. He stood for a moment, his rear teeth clutching tightly to one another as he rode out the wave of it. He took a slow deep breath in through his nose, and then exhaled in a forceful stream. Better. It was better.

He walked over to the porch steps, but remained at the foot of the stairs, keeping his distance.

"What's up?"

"Funny, I was going to ask you the same thing."

"Nothing much. Just sitting around and healing. I think I'm a little too idle. I don't do well with too much downtime."

Jackson's eyes reflected his understanding. Nothing sucked more ass than being forced to sit still and do nothing.

"Besides, I'm not sure I can keep from stabbing your housemate through the eye with a pencil for much longer." Leo pantomimed the stab, including a vicious

FORSAKEN 13

little flurry of movement that translated into scrambled brains via an eye socket.

How could Jackson blame him? Their "housemate" was Kamenwati, the former right hand of the Templar leader Odjit and the sole means of introduction between Leo and the demented Chatha. Kamen had set Chatha on Leo like a rabid dog, supposed vengeance for the nearly dead state of his mistress. Leo had cut the bitch's throat, completely unaware of who and what she was, unaware of her import to the Templars. All he had known at the time was that she had killed Jackson.

Or so the story went. Apparently his memory had been completely wiped out of the entire encounter, a method of guarding him against exposure to the existence of the Nightwalker races—these creatures of the night with immense powers. But by robbing him of his memory, they had robbed him of the opportunity to be on guard against the revenge that had been exacted via Kamenwati and Chatha.

Leo was more than a little angry about that.

He took in a slow, soundless breath, corralling his rage, leaving his face placid.

"He's not a housemate, Leo," Jackson said with a frown. "People under heavy guard and who are being grilled nightly for information are hardly invited guests."

"I don't care if you pull his fucking nails out every night!" He rounded on Jackson with a vicious vent of ichor. "He deserves to die and I'm itching to do the deed! If you want to keep that from happening then I need to get the fuck out of here. And frankly, you should be in a rush to send me on my way because I'm not too sure you're going to make it through the next twenty-four hours either."

"Leo!" Jackson barked his name, getting to his feet. "I am *not* your enemy!"

"No, but you harbor him! Or maybe you *are* my

enemy. I have no idea what that thing squirming around inside of you is. All I know is that no one in this house can be trusted. There are too many variables at play and I'm not about to sleep soundly here while trying to figure it all out. I've had it up to my craw with blind faith and trust. I'm leaving at daylight, and from what I understand you can't follow me and neither can any of those Gargoyles. The beauty is I can move in daylight. I can get thousands of miles away from this fucked-up world of yours before sunset and believe me when I say you won't be able to find me."

"You think so?" Jackson lashed back at him. "I'll find you, Leo. You're thinking in human terms, my friend. This is a Nightwalker world. I live with Gargoyles that have wings and a smoking-hot sense of smell. Or maybe I'll get Docia and Ram's little Djynn friend to snap her fingers and bring you right back to where you are standing now."

"That just proves my point. The Jackson I know wouldn't try and strong-arm me into anything. He would have let me live my life on my own terms. But now you have all this power"—he scoffed in disgust, sweeping an acidic look over Jackson—"and no one to stop you from using it however you like."

"The Jackson you know would fight for you," Jackson said, his anger spinning away as his voice grew softer. "He would make sure you took care of yourself. He would want to see you healed before letting you run off half-cocked so you can show the world, and more importantly yourself, what a badass you are."

"The Jackson I know would never talk about himself in the third person," Leo snapped.

"Really? Is that how you want to justify all of this? Discarding me because you don't understand this world you've been thrust into? The *Leo* I know wouldn't run away like a scared little girl. He'd face his fears, face the world around him. I need you, Leo. I need people I know and trust here." He stepped forward and Leo couldn't help himself, he stepped back in instant retreat. The action made Jackson frown. "I'm facing an enemy with the powers of a *god,* Leo. A god I know very little about. The Templars are out there, just waiting for a new leader to step into the vacancy left behind by Odjit. And they don't even know that the players have changed. That the god Apep was reborn into Odjit's body. As far as they know they are following their Templar leader, and not this . . . this *thing* Kamenwati has resurrected!"

"All the more reason to kill him," Leo spat. "Tell you what, give me a pencil and five minutes alone with him and then I'll stay."

"You know I can't do that," Jackson bit back grimly. "Even if he wasn't going to play out as a powerful ally now that he's defected to our side, I'm still Jackson Waverly inasmuch as I am Menes, Bodywalker Pharaoh. I will never have it in me to sentence any man, good or evil, arbitrarily to death."

"Arbitrary? The fucker set a psychopath loose on me! I can still feel that monster's hands inside me fumbling around, trying to decide which part of me he was going to show me next! He deserves to *die*. Horribly, painfully. And soon. Because if you think I'm going to let this just slide . . ."

"Leo, you're human. You're frail and mortal, a brittle thing, as you already have learned, in the face of the power he and his kind can wield. You wouldn't even come close to him." Jackson sighed and rubbed at the tension coiled in the back of his neck. "Do you really think a part of me doesn't want to let you at him? Doesn't want to do it myself? But the knowledge Menes has of the last time this demon god sought to rule in this realm is terrifying. I've gotten no more sleep than you have since you came back, sunlight or no sunlight."

Leo quieted. Jackson had been awake? "But I thought . . . ?"

"Thought I was paralyzed in daylight? I am . . . if that daylight touches me. The windows in the house are polarized. If there was some kind of attack on this house, do you think we would want to be caught helpless? Does that make any sense?"

Jackson saw the anxious thought that flitted across Leo's features. "And yeah, I've heard you every single time you've woken up screaming like some inhuman thing. Did you really think no one would notice?"

"I don't know," Leo sneered, "you seem pretty good at ignoring the other inhuman things in your house."

Jackson sighed. He had known going into it that there would be no reasoning with his friend. He'd never really been able to influence Leo once his emotions began to propel him into something. In spite of what he would like to reflect to everyone, Leo felt and felt deeply. All Jackson had ever been able to do was try to remind his friend to be the better person. But if he took that tactic right then, Leo would most likely deck him and put that pencil in *his* eye.

"*I* am an inhuman thing," he said softly. "And that will never change. Not until I am truly dead and gone from this world. And when I think of living this life with you hating me and what I am, it's a very painful proposition. But not half as painful for me as it will be for Docia, the woman you helped me to raise from a little girl, who loves you like a father, a brother, and a mother. What about her, Leo? Are you going to jam a pencil in her eye and call it a day?"

The bald query took Leo aback, as it was meant to do. It also made him angrier because Jackson was clearly manipulating him with his weaknesses. And yet . . .

most infuriating of all . . . Jackson had a point. If he were to drink the Bodywalker Kool-Aid, then that meant Docia was every bit the girl he had loved for all of her lifetime. Only now she was *more*. More beautiful, more powerful, more wise. In fact, after watching her closely this past week, he began to notice a quiet strength and confidence that had not shined from her before Tameri, her Bodywalker, had made her into a host, housing within her like some sort of existential hotel.

Considering she'd had to die before she could become a host, well, it still made him sick to his stomach when he realized that, if not for Tameri, Docia would have washed up a bloated, broken corpse on the banks of the Esopus River after she had been pushed off the bridge straddling it. He had almost lost her. He couldn't deny that he might owe Tameri some gratitude for her intervention.

But it was hard to get past the idea that the brother and sister were different now, and that he did not trust them the way he'd always had. Then again, he doubted he would ever trust anyone ever again. Certainly not anyone from this world, this covert world that normal, fragile mortals lived in utter ignorance of.

As for Docia's Bodywalker lover . . . despite the fact that Leo had never seen her happier, more vibrant and more alive . . . he was very much opposed to that match. Back when Ram had been an "original," as they liked to call it, he had been one of the most notoriously cruel pharaohs of Egypt, the vicious Ramses II. Leo had been raised a good Catholic boy in a devoutly Catholic household, and though he didn't hold much with it anymore, he remembered his catechism and the brutal stories of Exodus. Was he supposed to take their word for it that Ram was now a good man? For that matter, was he supposed to take them at their word that they were this enlightened version of the Egyptian hierarchy? They were embroiled in a civil war, just how enlightened could they be? As if his thoughts had conjured him, Ramses II, presently known as Ram, walked out onto the porch. After giving Leo a brief nod of acknowledgment, he took a seat in a chair near Jackson, facing him. He sat on the edge, elbows propped on knees. Jackson retook his seat as well.

"Brother, we need to talk about some things," he said to Jackson, almost as though Leo weren't standing right there. It made Leo bristle with rapid fury, the anger almost virulent.

"Sure you want to do that with a lowly human around, *brother*?" he spat out. There was no familial blood between them, Leo thought angrily. Never had been to hear them talk about it. Each had been pharaoh in differing dynasties. It had not been until lifetimes later that they had become friends to each other. Become *brothers*. Just the same, this man had no idea what it meant to be brother to a man like Jackson Waverly.

Ram looked at him with a calm, assessing gaze then turned back to Jackson. "You aren't yet used to your new host body," he said. "Your power is used without control and focus because your host needs training."

"The host has a name, *pendejo*," Leo snapped.

Ram looked at Leo again, that infuriating contemplative look in his gold colored eyes. *Seriously?* Leo thought. *The guy looks like a Navy SEAL Ken doll.* Blond hair, gold eyes, and an ouroboros tattoo on his tanned forearm.

How the fuck does something that can't walk in daylight manage to get a tan?

"It is merely a reference, 'your host' is used much in the way 'your brother' or 'your sister' would be used. But if it makes you uncomfortable I will keep it to proper names." He turned back to Jackson. "Jackson can call on the power you have to react to things emotionally. He doesn't have your mental discipline."

"Jackson probably has more discipline in his little finger than the two of you together," Leo scoffed. "He's a cop. He confronts the possibility of death every time he makes a traffic stop. He faced down a meth head tweaking so bad that he shot down his K-9 partner and yet Jackson proceeded to shoot the fucker in the kneecap and the hand. Do you have any idea what it takes to remain calm enough to make those two shots that quickly? Do you know what it took for him to not kill the bastard? Outside of Docia and me, that dog meant everything to him. So don't sit there and act like he's some kind of unruly child knocking around in there getting in your way."

"That wasn't what I meant in the least," Ram said softly. "I know he has discipline. I know he is capable of a great deal of self-control and has the ability to act decisively in dire circumstances. But he trained with that firearm day after day after day and learned how to use it to the best of its ability. If we did not train him with this weapon that has the potential to level a city block, *that* would be the irresponsible thing to do."

Well, shit.

"Anyway," Ram tried again to address his superior, "we need to practice and there's no better place." He indicated the wide, flat wasteland that stretched out beyond the cultivated landscaping of their property. The house stood alone, a single road leading in to it and miles of land in every direction. Even sitting on the porch you had the sensation of sitting in an oasis at the center of a vast desert. "Nothing but the coyotes to see us."

"All right. When would you like to start?"

"Next eve. Marissa is settling into herself now.

Hatshepsut and she are Blending well together. She seems genuinely happy."

Three male heads turned to look at the woman in the garden. She was literally playing in the dirt, making little mountains of rich black topsoil from a gutted bag of it. She was smiling, clearly enjoying herself. Leo frowned. He couldn't say he knew Marissa Anderson well, but from what he'd gathered she was as uptight, polished, and sophisticated as any psychiatrist could be. She probably would have died first before being seen in jeans and bare feet, like she was right then.

Oh. Hey.

He wasn't really amused when he realized that was exactly what she had done. Died. Or just about. He was a little fuzzy on the hard details of how exactly one became a Bodywalker, and frankly he wasn't all that interested. It wouldn't change the way he felt. It wouldn't bring comfort.

"I'm out of here," Leo said, derision in every syllable of his words. He pushed between the two men and went inside the house.

Ram watched the other man Jackson considered his closest friend leave, and waited until the door shut behind him before saying, "He's going to be a problem."

"You're wrong," Jackson countered. "He's going to be difficult, but he wouldn't do anything to endanger me or Docia."

"I'm keeping a guard on Kamenwati twenty-four hours a day, but it's not safe to have the two of them in the same house."

"I don't see how we have much of a choice," Jackson said with a frown. "Leo is nowhere near ready to leave, no matter what he says, and Kamen needs to be under our close control. He may have used Leo as an olive branch to get to us, but that doesn't mean I trust his motives entirely."

"Nor do I," Ram agreed. "Let's make sure you're at full strength and skill first. Docia needs training as well. And Marissa makes three. I'm the only one whose been Blended with my host for more than a month. Frankly that makes us far weaker and far more vulnerable than I would like. Especially in light of this new danger Kamenwati says we are facing. If he is to be believed at all."

"Agreed. Do you disbelieve him?" Jackson asked.

"No. Unfortunately I do not."

"It would take something quite radical to make Kamenwati switch allegiance away from Odjit after so many lifetimes of being her first general. I often wondered if they were lovers, connected together like Hatshepsut and I. I suppose this absolves me of that notion."

"I never thought I would see the day when he would leave her side in order to join us on ours," Ram said.

"I did."

Ram raised a brow. His short laugh was obviously incredulous.

"Truly, I did," Jackson assured him. "There was always something . . . feverish to the way he sought his battles with us. And I don't mean feverish in the way that Odjit was, high with the fever of fanaticism. There was a part of that aspect, but I always thought it was to different ends. Odjit was like any bewitching cult leader, alluring and promising the true path . . . spouting that we, the enemy, were the reason why we would be kept from the light of the sun, should Amun ever rise again. But in the end she was simply hungry for power, as so many people are. But for Kamen . . ." Jackson tapped a thoughtful finger against the wood of the chair arm. "Kamen was seeking something. I can't quite put my finger on it. But I always thought that if I could just get him in a room, face-to-face, that he might listen to a voice of reason."

"Then you thought more of him than I did. The only reason he is here is because this thing he has awakened has him terrified. The enemy of my enemy is my friend sort of thing."

"Perhaps. But I suspect far more depth to him than just the shallow image of a man hiding in defeat. At the very least, we can take from this that he believes Odjit is truly gone from her body . . . or from any control of it. This god of bad mischief is in control of her now and that . . . I'm afraid that leaves us at a frightening disadvantage. At least we knew what to expect from Odjit. All we know about Apep comes from distant memories of vague stories of a long-dead version of our religious beliefs. This is going to take a great deal of research by minds far more attuned to this sort of thing than either of us."

"And I suppose you have someone in mind."

"As a matter of fact." Jackson smiled with wicked arrogance and Ram answered with a smile of his own. The intent in that expression was everything Menes. There were just some things that never changed about Menes, no matter how many lifetimes and no matter who his host was, there was always going to be that smile of utter, casual confidence. "I was thinking of whistling up SingSing, your new Djynn friend."

"SingSing?" Ram's tone was every bit loaded with the disbelief and incredulousness he felt. "She's an absolute child bouncing around in a Djynn's costume. If you bring SingSing into this mix you're asking for a can of crazy. And between you and me, nothing about her screamed scholar to me."

"Perhaps not," Jackson allowed with a nod. "But I'm willing to bet she knows quite a few other Djynn, some of whom might be thousands of years old, and who might know about things that took place thousands of years ago, if indeed she doesn't know for herself."

"Even if she did know it'd be like trying to get information out of a six-year-old," Ram muttered.

"She's lost her filter, no doubt. It's a blessing of the very old and the very young. The young are too innocent to know better. The old no longer care what people think about what they say or do."

"I suppose. Is she going to move in as well?" Not that they didn't have more than a dozen bedroom suites packed into the enormous house, more than enough room to fit a small army in with them. But then Ram realized what Jackson was doing, and this time both brows swept up high. "You want her here. Her and whomever else you can get your hands on of power from the other Nightwalker races. Jesus, Jackson." Ram ran an agitated hand through his hair. "Tell me you're not thinking of inviting Wraiths."

"I'm desperate, not stupid." Both men shook off the sensation of fear that skirted them. It was understandable, considering the subject matter. All one needed was to look into those cold, dead white eyes and you just knew you were staring down something unholy. "The day I have to go to the Wraiths for help is the day I know we are in truly dire circumstances. A day I pray never happens."

"As do I." The thought had Ram frowning darkly.

"Such serious faces," Docia tsked as she swept through the screen door. Ram's serious face disappeared instantly as he smiled up at her.

"Very likely it was due to my missing you," he said with obvious charm.

"Flirt," she accused him. But she preened under the compliment. She was still new to the idea of being worshipped for every breath she took. It really used to irk Jackson the way his sister thought less highly of herself than he did, and it pleased him very much to see that changing. She had changed a great deal in the month or so since her Blending that they had spent separated.

There was a clicking sound, the sound of doggy nails on the flooring of the porch, and Sargent, formerly of the Saugerties Police Department's K-9 unit, sat down at the heels of the woman he had followed out. Docia absently reached down to scrub at Sargent's ears.

He really should have stuck to his guns and sent Sargent back to the SPD, Jackson thought with a frown. The dog had turned out to be every bit as fearless and loyal as his former K-9 partner, Chico, had been. If he was confessing truths, he had to admit that once Sargent had stopped goofing off, his training had gone far more quickly than was normal for a K-9. Of course, it didn't hurt that Menes had something of a sixth sense when it came to animals. Jackson had been having a hard time getting Sargent to listen and behave himself, in spite of him having shown a great deal of affinity for both of those things as a pup. But once Menes had come on board Sargent had fallen over himself to listen and please his altered master. Jackson might have felt put out if not for the pleasure it gave him to have Sargent trained at long last.

But that didn't change the fact that he had walked off with thousands of dollars' worth of investment for the SPD, leaving them a K-9 unit short when they had only had two available to begin with. It wasn't as though they could ring up the K-9 kennels and instantly have a replacement. That kind of training took time . . . and even the two expensive pups Jackson had sent them as a replacement wouldn't be ready for work for over a year.

"Remind me to make a little donation to the SPD," he said absently to no one in particular.

"How much? I'll take care of it," Ram said briskly.

"I need you doing other things besides bookkeeping." Jackson frowned at him. "Do we have a bookkeeper?"

"Not on site, but there's a soft-spoken little Body-walker female named Nailah who does the heavy lifting where that's concerned. But she's not exactly a heavy-hitter power-wise so I don't know if you'd want her where she might end up in the thick of things."

"We all have our part to play," Jackson said. "And our meek might surprise us one day. As it is—"

Jackson broke off and an expression Docia had never seen before washed over his face. He lurched up out of his chair, the awkwardness of the movement tipping the beer bottle out of his hand. It hit the deck and bounced, spinning as it did so, spewing its contents over Docia's feet.

"Hey!" she cried out, dancing back away from the bottle although it had come to rest and the damage was already done.

She might have complained just then, but that unfathomable expression on Jackson's face had turned to a mixture between outright fear and unmistakable courage rising up in the face of that fear.

"Docia, get inside," he said, grabbing her arm, turning her around and pushing her roughly in that direction. "And take Sargent with you. Marissa!"

He bolted off the deck, clearing the stairs to the ground without touching a single one. By then Ram understood that something was wrong and he grabbed for Docia's arm and stood up all in the same movement.

"Ow! Hey! Why is everybody grabbing at my arm? I can walk on my—"

"Docia," Ram hushed her fiercely.

"*Marissa!*"

The way her brother shouted for Marissa sent a cold shiver of awareness creeping like icy dribbles down the length of Docia's spine. Jackson had broken into a dead run, everything about him screaming with fear.

CHAPTER TWO

Leo heard Jackson yell and immediately knew something was very wrong. He moved quickly to the nearest window, ignoring the fierce pain that came with moving too fast. There would be time later for muscle and sinew to repair, at that moment it was nothing but a minor inconvenience to him. Even as he visually tried to discern what was happening, his mind was mapping out the fastest route to the gun case in the parlor. Actually, he didn't need to map it. He'd been obsessing over getting hold of one of those guns. With that supernatural prick in the same house as he was? He'd be damned if he was going to walk around unarmed. Given their strength, their power, and their speed, it was not exactly what you would call an even match, but Leo would feel better armed than not. He'd gotten the drop on one of them before, and that was before he had even known what they were, so he'd damn well prefer the ability to do it again.

Jackson was running hell-bent for leather across the front yard, his boots kicking up a dotted line of dust clouds, his speed *everything* unnatural. It was the first time he was seeing Jackson use some of his new ability but he didn't have time to indulge in the crawling distaste the image evoked within him. Jackson was heading up the drive, toward the good doctor and her garden spot.

That was when a ragged stream of energy seared across Jackson's path, like a lightning strike from an ominous thundercloud. Dirt and rock and carefully cultivated landscaping spewed everywhere, bringing Jackson up short with a skid of his boots. Leo and Jackson looked up simultaneously. The next instant Leo bolted for the parlor, grabbing up a heavy iron bust of the god Anubis from one of the end tables as he went. He reached the case, hauled back and smashed the glass with the statue. To his consternation it didn't break. The only hint he had even hit it was from an impact fracture in a white spiderweb shape. But there was a small hole in the center of that web and that told him the glass was reinforced, but not unbreakable.

It took three more smashes with the statue before the glass gave up the ghost and created a hole large enough for him to thrust his hand through. He grabbed for the nearest gun, a black Berretta, .45 caliber with a laser sight mounted along its spine. Something that would come in handy in the dark. He checked the chamber and the clip, finding them loaded and ready. He didn't come across any more ammunition, so what he had was going to have to do and he would have to make every shot count.

As he ran to the front door, he almost collided with Docia, leaping over Sargent as it was, and exploded onto the porch. All of which cost him a great deal, making him clench his teeth in agony and wonder if he'd just reinjured things that weren't healed as yet. He flipped on the laser sighting with his thumb and with two hands pointed it into the sky. There was another belch of severe energy, the white of it blinding him and seemingly coming out of nowhere. But there was no way that was natural, and he knew that because it struck right at

Jackson's feet again, forcing him back, his leap covering enormous amounts of ground. The air between him and the dirt was incomprehensible to a man who had not seen any other displays of a Bodywalker's power other than those of Kamenwati and Chatha, and those encounters had not been anything like this at all.

No, theirs had been a very special brand of psychopathic supernaturalism.

Ram was off the deck already and the savage, ominous rumble of natural thunder filled the air. Right before Leo's eyes the sky blossomed with thick black thunderheads, whereas it had been a perfectly clear night beforehand. He knew this was Ram's doing. Leo had been told Ram could control the weather, although he had no idea what a few rainclouds were going to do to help the situation.

Another bolt of white energy burst out of the sky, the beam of it scorching past Jackson's back. The intent was clear. Jackson would be hit if he moved forward, and hit if he moved backward. He was trapped out there in the open, like a frog on a lily pad in the center of a vast lake and nowhere to jump for safety.

Leo's lack of a target frustrated him. He rapidly cleared the stairs to shorten his distance to Jackson, all the while keeping his weapon trained on that empty sky. Something was there. They couldn't see it, but all three men knew something was there.

And it was toying with Jackson.

That, more than anything, told Leo he was dealing with another sick paranormal psychopath.

Just as Ram was closing in on Jackson, a new bolt of energy lashed out of the night sky, but this one hit Ramses square in the chest and literally blew him off his feet. The impact sent him backward by at least thirty feet, the impression of his body tearing up the earth, kicking up dirt and dust. Then the Bodywalker was still. The hit was horrifying and Docia's scream came from the house behind him. Leo turned from the empty sky and tracked his aim back toward the house. There was a potted cactus, quite thick in circumference, to the right of the door. Two bullets into one side of the ceramic pot holding it made it explode and the heavy cactus within toppled over in front of the door, effectively blocking it shut, its spiny skin a natural deterrent to anyone thinking of touching it and shoving it out of the way. He saw Docia hit the door and was satisfied when he saw that she was unable to open it. That wasn't to say she wouldn't find another way out and into the fray, but it would take her more time . . . maybe enough time for them to deal with this . . . whatever "this" was.

He tracked his aim back up to the sky, hurrying over to the very still form of Ram. He bent in order to touch fingers to the fallen man's carotid artery, trying to detect a pulse while keeping his full attention trained upward. Whatever it was would show itself eventually, and he would be ready for it when it did. Leo exhaled with relief when he felt the awkward thrum of Ram's pulse. For all their power and longevity, and as amazing as their ability to rapidly heal was, these people were more than capable of dying. And while he mistrusted the bastard, Docia loved him. It shone from every bright smile and warm cuddle he had seen her give him. It would break her heart if something were to snatch him away from her.

"C'mon, c'mon," he muttered under his breath as he aimed up at the sky, "do it again. Show us what a badass you are. You can do it."

That was when a furious Gargoyle blasted up from the ground in the garden, enormous wings spread wide, skin turned to heavy stone and a face as grotesque and frightening as any gargoyle on top of a church might be. Ahnvil was a thing of power, as were Stohn and Diahmond, two other Gargoyles that had launched into the air from the direction of the house. Jackson had told Leo that these were their bodyguards, their supernatural protectors. They were strong and nearly impossible to kill and would never stop in their endeavors to protect the Bodywalkers they were pledged to.

There was nothing for them to attack, that they could see, but they all knew the general area to aim for. And then, like ducks in a shooting gallery, those massive beams of energy shot out of the sky and picked the Gargoyles off, one by one, sending them thundering back down to the earth, deadweights of stone.

But it was enough. Enough for Leo to see that the energy beam remained solid, from inception point to end point, for the beat of a few seconds, telling him exactly where the attacker might be. He blew off four shots, the recoil from the Beretta jolting through him.

Like a magician yanking a cloth away to reveal the lady or the tiger beneath it, the thing in the air winked into view. It wobbled around, and Leo was sure he had hit it.

"Leo, no!" Jackson shouted, much too late. The woman . . . and it was a woman . . . attacking from the night sky whirled to face Leo's direction. She was wearing white from head to toe, long auburn hair streaming in blowing wisps around her head, like some kind of Clairoled medusa. A stain of blood spread across the white of her clothing.

Right over her heart.

Lucky shot that, Leo thought. Right before he realized he'd shot her in the heart and she was still floating up there in midair as if it meant nothing to her at all. She lowered herself closer to the ground and Leo readied himself to fire another volley of bullets. She had to have a vulnerability somewhere, and he . . .

He recognized that face. He didn't know how, but it

was like a barely remembered snatch of a dream. A dream where he had . . .

Cut her throat.

This was the woman he had killed, slitting her throat, dropping her down on the floor to bleed out. This was the woman who was the catalyst behind Kamenwati sending Chatha to find Leo and capture him so that the Templar could deliver vengeance on him in her name.

Odjit.

The name came to him about two seconds before her laughter filled the night air.

"Very well," she said, her voice echoing and powerfully loud all around him. "If you wish to die first, I can oblige you."

"No!" Jackson shouted the word and suddenly Leo was shoved back by a powerful force, as though a linebacker had rammed into him, sending him sprawling into the dirt. His gun flew out of his hands as he gathered a faceful of dirt and excruciating pain hit him everywhere at once. He could swear he'd heard something snap, some bone in his body no doubt. But he was too stunned to feel anything in specific right then.

But he saw how Jackson's shout drew Odjit's attention and she lowered herself even farther and faced him.

"You," she said, "are dangerous."

Jackson's response was to throw out both hands and shove, as if he were pushing her off himself, had she been anywhere near close enough for it, which she wasn't. But just the same she was sent backward, much in the same way Leo had been sent flying. That was when it really sank in that Jackson had been the one to shove Leo out of the way of Odjit's attention. But unlike Leo, she didn't even come close to hitting the ground, and, outside of a midair tumble, she was almost completely unaffected by his attack.

"You," she said again, "might be troublesome, given enough time. That thought makes us most unhappy."

Us? Like, the royal *Us?* Jeez, who was this lady anyway? *What* was she? Leo was in too much pain to give it much thought. There were details, bits of conversation he'd been half listening to, that he couldn't force into sense enough to answer his own questions at the moment. His world was suddenly overrun with these kinds of creatures and he had known right from the first moment he'd become aware of them that there was nothing good about them. And he was just as certain there was almost nothing he could do to protect himself and the things he deemed important in the face of this kind of power.

But he could damn well try and do some damage at the very least. To that end, he scrambled for his gun.

"We know what you are," Jackson said with virulent anger. "A two-bit monster calling itself a god. If you think we're going to let you run amok in this world you have another—"

"Silence!" Jackson's adversary hissed. She flicked her hand, a discus of energy suddenly appearing in her fingers, right before she flung the thing at Jackson. It all happened so quickly, the move lightning fast, the distance between her hand and Jackson's throat far too short. Jackson threw up his hands in defense, but the disc whipped right through them and then straight through his neck.

Jackson crumpled to the ground, as if something had yanked his skeletal structure cleanly from his body.

"No!" Leo shouted as he choked on fear and rage. He emptied his entire clip into the woman, the satisfaction of seeing her jerk from the impact of each bullet too small and too short-lived. Bloodstains spread over the pure white of her clothing, and she turned back to Leo. Weaponless, useless, all he could do was hurl insults at her in a jumbled mix of Spanish and English. "You fucking *puta* bitch whore!"

Leo wished he could say he had never felt so helpless in all of his life, but he was definitely more than acquainted with the feeling. The thought clawed up through him, clenching around his throat. But he fought it back viciously. This was *Jackson's* life or death hanging in balance. Bodywalker or not, it was still Jackson. Or maybe it wasn't. Damn it, he didn't know, but he deserved the chance to find out! *After all I have been through, I deserve that fucking chance!*

"You are insignificant," she said in that odd, echoing tone, the sound large and overwhelming. "But you have damaged our fleshly confines." She pulled at her white dress as if she might sketch a curtsey. There was a metallic gleam over her left eye where he could see a bullet had lodged itself in her skull. Correction. A grouping of bullets. He was nothing if not a deadeye.

"Yeah, well come and get me, *puta*," he invited with a forward flicking of his cupped fingers. "Why don't you throw your little energy beams at me, huh?"

Distantly he was aware of screams. High, blood-curdling, female screams. In another life he would have reacted to that sound. Now . . . now there was nothing but him and what he had no doubt was his imminent death. On his terms. On his own two feet. Once and for all and no coming back.

Energy circled the flying woman's hand in the shape of a discus, and she reached back just the littlest bit, in order to put some spin on it, he presumed. Funny how, whenever he faced these moments, moments when his death begged for a kiss, the world seemed to slow down. As if to stretch out the final moments for as long and as leisurely as possible. Prior to his encounter with Chatha, it had happened each of the two times he had gotten what should have been mortal wounds . . . for anyone else anyway. He'd just been too angry and too stubborn to give it up. But now . . . he could go now. He'd be all right with that.

The discus flew at him and he tensed, bracing for it, wondering what it was going to feel like.

Just when it should have hit him a wall of blue energy shot up barely an inch from the tip of his nose. He could see it, like smoke blown through a blue laser light show. The discus rebounded off it in a shower of blue sparks, then whipped back on its caster, its thin edge slicing right through her left calf. If there was a wound it was invisible, but the way she screamed out and floundered in the air told him that there was indeed a damaging hit of some kind. All of that big bad omnipotence evaporated from her in a screech of pain and fury. Leo saw his breath clouding through that energy barrier and he found himself fascinated by it in some distant corner of his mind. A corner so far removed from this maniacal horror film he'd suddenly become a part of. In truth, it was beautiful, if energy could be beautiful. And for some reason, just the sight of it calmed him, strengthened a part of him that had felt so weak these past days.

The squealing bitch in the air hissed out a word.

"*You!*" It reached out a shaking finger, pointing at Leo. "You will pay for this meddling. These are not your affairs! Be warned!"

And with a new screech of frustration she ripped up into the sky, disappearing with the sound of a sonic boom.

Leo was stunned, trying to figure out what had just happened. But now that the threat was over, the sound of his own heart beating in his ears lowered enough for the rising sound of screams to penetrate.

You.

Then Leo realized what she had meant. He whipped around in an about-face and found himself looking dead into neon yellow eyes, the look of them like the way a flash caught a cat's eyes in a picture. They were something unholy and damn unnerving that close up. Especially considering there was no discernible sclera. The entire eye. Every bit of it as glowing fluorescent as could be.

They were set in black, making them stand out in relief, not that it was needed. It was a woman, black-skinned from head to toe . . . not African American black, actual midnight black as black could be. The color was so uniform she was barely visible in the night . . . except for the fact that blue laser light wings stretched out behind her, casting an ambient glow all around the edges of her silhouette. Only, lasers were not as graceful as these wings were; were not so languorous and delicate, and did not ripple with gentle, liquid movement.

Leo jolted away from her, only to bounce back when he hit the blue wall behind him. It sent him forward, forcing him up against her, their chests colliding. He reached out automatically to steady her, an instinctual response to the nature of her sex and that built-in reflex that his mother had hammered into him. And that was when he realized her soft nighttime skin was completely exposed to all and sundry. She was naked as the day she was born.

Although nothing was born with the full-bodied breasts and curves his fumbling hands came into contact with.

And then he realized she was one of *them*. *Of course she's one of them, you idiot! She has fucking wings and eyes that glow in the dark like a pothead's black-light poster.*

His next thought was that she had come up behind him and yet he hadn't sensed her at all—a realization that filled him with displeasure. No one could ever sneak up behind him successfully. It had been a game he and Jackson used to play, each trying to see if one could sneak up on the other with total surprise . . . like some kind of ridiculous tussle between Inspector Jacques Clouseau and his manservant Cato.

Jackson.

My god, how could I have forgotten? He whipped around half a turn and saw Jackson lying dead on the ground. Marissa was on her knees beside him, pulling at his shirt, grasping and shaking him by turns, all the while screaming his name down into his face as if he might hear her and suddenly pop upright as though being startled awake from a deep sleep. From the other side Docia was tearing down the drive, her bare feet flying over the white landscaping rocks of the driveway, no doubt being chewed and sliced to bits with every grinding step.

Leo was galvanized into action, pushing the strange female out of his way just in time to catch Docia around the waist, hauling her out of her dead run, her momentum swinging them full around as he absorbed the impact as best he could without hurting her. He realized then that she was screaming Jackson's and then Ram's name, both hysterically volleying out of her as if she couldn't figure out which upset her more or whom she was most devoted to. Both men appeared lifeless on the ground, but Leo knew that at least one was alive for certain.

"Let me go! Leo! Let me go!" she screamed at him, fighting with all she had to be free of him. And free she was after the third tug when she used every bit of her Bodywalker strength to set him back hard. The strength she wielded was shocking. He knew men that weren't even close to that strength, never mind a woman.

"Ram is alive!" he blurted out to her as she ran forward. He immediately hurried in her wake, expecting her to veer off and go to her lover. But his information seemed to help her choose who was in most need of her, and she slid down to her brother's side.

By the time he reached them, Marissa's screams were punctuated with panicked, devastated sobs the likes of which he had never heard in his lifetime, and could only pray he would never hear again.

"Jackson! Jackson!" Docia cried, shaking him frantically, vying with Marissa for contact with him. "Is he breathing? Tell me he's breathing!"

Leo knelt and reached two fingers to press to Jackson's throat.

"He has a pulse."

The next sobs from both women were a combination of relief and a panicky sort of hope.

"Then why won't he wake up?" Marissa demanded of him. "He's Menes, for God's sake! He's the most powerful Bodywalker living or dead!"

"His nervous system has been scorched."

All three of them looked up at the black woman, all of their breath and sound suspending at the same exact moment, the resulting silence lasting only an instant, but eerie just the same.

"What . . . how . . . what does that mean?" Marissa demanded to know. "Tell me what that means!"

"The energy the imp uses burns every nerve in the body, causing instant paralysis and a level of pain so severe there is no equal to it . . . and he has lost consciousness because of it."

"Who are you?" Marissa demanded. "How do you know this?"

"There is no time to waste on introductions," she said dismissively, kneeling down to yank Jackson away from the grieving women.

"No! You leave him alone!" Marissa hissed through her teeth, clinging to Jackson's body with all her strength.

"Touch him again, Dark One, and I will rip your arms free of their sockets and then beat you dead with them!"

"Wow, great visual," Leo said, pretty damn impressed by Marissa's believable delivery of the threat.

The woman seemed to fold her wings back, their graceful lines pulling in and concentrating in an undulation of light between her shoulders. She leaned forward as she kneeled down, her hand reaching to cover Marissa's with a gentleness that Leo could almost feel against the back of his own hand.

"Hatshepsut," she breathed softly. "You know my people. You know what we can do and the things we know." Leo realized then that a warm wind was swirling softly around them, almost as though it too were trying to soothe Marissa. "You must give him to me if we are to begin to save his life. I cannot promise you a cure, that is not within my power, but I can keep him here with us until he can be mended. He is very much needed here," the woman said knowingly, "and not trapped in the Ether for another hundred years."

"No. No, I could not bear it. I cannot bear the idea of life without him." Marissa wept, harsh gasps of her breath pulling in a staccato hitch.

"Then let me have him," she said gently.

Marissa's fingers had curled tightly into Jackson's shirtfront, but now they slowly unfurled and she sat back on her heels.

"What are you doing?" Docia demanded. "You're just going to trust her? No! No, he's my brother and I won't let you—"

"What other choice do we have?" Marissa asked her quietly, her eyes awash with brimming tears. "To let him lie here? To let him die? To fumble about trying to heal him in ways we simply aren't capable of?"

"There are spells," Docia said fervently. "I can bring my Templar power to bear. I trust myself far more than

I would trust a stranger! We know almost nothing about the Night Angels," she whispered fiercely between tense lips and clenched teeth.

So that was what she was. A Night Angel. The name suited her perfectly. Between those wings and her skin . . . and then there was her hair. Cleanly white, not a single touch of color or shading, not even a variation at the roots where a bleaching process would have been detected. She had it bound in a figure eight shaped knot on the back of her head, a thick, winding thing that told a tale of great length.

And not a stitch to cover those unbelievable swells and hollows. From the slope of her shoulder to the cleft of her backside, there wasn't a single ounce of shame. Nor an ounce of anything but well-shaped muscle beneath all of those female curves. Had she been human he might have thought she'd spent hours in the gym in order to achieve that muscular definition. Perhaps there were muscle groups required for flight. It wasn't even a thought that could have possibly crossed his mind before this week. This strange, surreal, painful week.

He watched as she bent forward, sliding an arm behind Jackson's broad shoulders and the other beneath his knees. Leo watched, utterly stunned, as those lean muscles flexed and—with a remarkable display of strength—she lifted a man who had to be at least 180 pounds of dead weight as if he were a baby. It wasn't completely effortless. He could see that as she moved quickly past him, toward the house, every single muscle in her body working hard at her task.

When they passed the spot where Ram was, Docia broke away from them and hurried to his side. He was down on his haunches, bent over as though he were trying to be prepared in case vomiting ensued. He looked pale and sick, his eyes shot through with blood in the sclera, a sharp background for the gold of his irises. At

Docia's urging he straightened up onto his feet. And even though he didn't look much better for it, Ram leaned on his love for strength and followed the entourage into the house. This rousing was also to be said for the Gargoyles, who were also picking themselves up from the deep holes in the ground left from the impacts of their stone bodies.

They all followed in the Night Angel's wake, at a loss to do anything else. She had come in and taken total command of the situation, and Leo was left without a single doubt that she deserved their hopeful faith in what she could offer them.

But she had warned that she could not give them a miracle cure. He hadn't missed that part. It sounded as though all she could offer them was a way to keep him alive for the time being while they figured out a solution.

"Where is his bed?"

"There's a couch—" Docia began, gesturing toward the parlor.

"No. He cannot be moved once I begin, so you will want him as comfortable and protected as possible."

Marissa hurried forward, showing the Angel the way to the master suite she shared with Jackson on the topmost floor of the house. Like all the rooms in the house the windows were polarized to block out the sun, the glass going blacker the brighter it became outside. Electronic blinds between the glass panes and automatic shades also reinforced that, raised and lowered as need be at the touch of a button.

Docia hit the button that did that, protecting them from the imminent daybreak, just about an hour more away. Only an hour before everyone, except for Leo, a human companion who lived with them named Max, and Marissa's sister Angelina, would be confined to the house or risk weaknesses under the sun. The humans would be the only ones able to freely exit. Which was the point of having Max for a lackey, Leo thought with a dark frown. As Bodywalkers, the owners of the house would become paralyzed at the touch of the sun. Just as the Gargoyles that stood sentry all around the property would turn to stone the very instant a single ray of sun crested over the horizon and touched them. Max would be able to carry out daylight activities and necessary tasks for his employers as they took the opportunity to sleep hidden away and protected. At least, Leo thought it was sleep. Hell if he really knew anything about any of this.

As if thinking about them brought them to life, Max and Angelina hurried to the doorway behind them as they entered the room.

"Marissa!" Angelina cried, but Max held her back from rushing to her sister's side. The man recognized the intensity of the situation, could see it was best to keep her away for now. That was probably what he had been doing all throughout this mess, keeping her inside, away from the death being dealt outside.

The Angel laid Jackson down, legs first, and then gingerly settled his head on the pillow as though she were tucking her sweet beloved grandfather into his sickbed. Marissa rounded to the other side of the bed, climbing up onto it and crawling quickly across the mattress in order to reach Jackson, take up his hand and press his knuckles desperately to her lips. Her hands and clothes were still stained with dirt, and it was obvious she couldn't care less about bringing that dirt into her bed. Leo had to grudgingly acknowledge the sense of priorities he was feeling from her. Whatever he thought of this situation, whatever he thought of them, there was no denying the fierce sincerity of her emotions toward Jackson.

"Jackson," she breathed over the backs of his fingers, her distress and sadness filling the space around the people standing anxiously in wait . . . in wait for an Angel to create a miracle.

The Night Angel stood, bracing her feet apart and facing the bed. She reached out her hands, palms down, fingers loosely splayed, like a magician about to make the beautiful assistant levitate into the air. But Leo was hoping she had something better to offer than an illusion.

"His souls are intact within him," she said with obvious relief after a moment or two . . . moments that felt like forever to everyone in the room. "This is very fortunate. Had the imp god excised either of his souls there would be nothing to be done."

"How . . . how do you know?" Marissa asked, her voice tremulous and catching softly as she tried not to sob outright, tried to keep her composure even though it was thoroughly frayed at the edges.

Yellow eyes flicked over the distraught queen, assessing and thoughtful.

"If you have Hatshepsut within you, you already know the answer to that."

"I-I can't . . . I don't . . ." She stammered, clearly at a loss and floundering. "I'm not even fully Blended with her yet. I can barely hear anything from her except these . . . these powerful, choking emotions." New tears came to her eyes. "As if I needed any more than my own."

"I am a Night Angel," she said with a quiet helpfulness as she reached over to cover Marissa's hand where it grasped Jackson's. "We see souls, both inside and outside of their corporeal bodies. Both living within the human body and walking lost upon the earth in spirit. It is our lot in life to ferry the lost ones to a portal leading them to the next stage in their lives."

"Lives? But if they no longer have corporeal selves . . ."

Leo spoke up, then wondered why that, of all questions, was the first to come to his lips.

The Angel turned her head slightly in order to look at him, her glowing eyes brushing over him from head to toe in a quick assessing look.

"You are human, so I don't expect you to understand," she said dismissively. "Suffice it to say, there are stages of the life of a soul far beyond your limited understanding."

Well. Shit. He'd just been snobbily slapped down by an *angel*. Were angels allowed to do that? Then again, were angels allowed to be naked as jaybirds? Or were Night Angels something completely different than, say, your run-of-the-mill angels? She certainly didn't look like the angels his very Catholic mother had had nailed to every wall and flat surface in her house . . . except those that had been occupied by Jesus.

Rosarita Alvarez would have been shocked to shit to see an angel like this one.

The Angel turned back to look at Marissa. "Since you are barely Blended, you are very likely unable to access all of what Hatshepsut knows about my breed. But if you turn yourself inward she will assure you that no one can care for your mate's soul better than someone of my breed can. At least, in the short run."

Marissa nodded as tears trembled on the curves of her lashes. "I can feel that."

"Then you must believe me when I tell you there is very little time for us to repair the damage done to Menes and his host."

"Jackson," Leo bit out. "His name is Jackson and he's worth ten of your Menses . . . or whatever his name is."

"Menes," the Angel corrected him, somehow making him feel like navel lint with just the dismissive tone in her voice. It was very clear what she thought of him. "Menes, the most powerful unifier in all Egyptian history. Menes, the leader of this vast race of very extraordinary peoples. Have you any idea what it takes for two souls to inhabit the same corporeal body like this? If you would look with eyes other than those filled with anger and contempt you might come to appreciate that."

Damn. Two slap downs in as many minutes. Leo felt a sudden urge to smile, but he fought it back. This was hardly the time for amusement. Still, it was a little nice to know he could find appreciation and humor in things again, no matter how small or fleeting.

"All I appreciate is that something I don't understand just tried to kill my best friend," he said sharply. "You said you could help? So *help.*"

"I can temporarily trap his souls within his body," she said, clearly ignoring his tone and the threat that bracketed it. "The power the imp used has severed his spinal cord at the midpoint of his neck, effectively paralyzing him. But more importantly, it has rent a hole in his aura . . . a hole through which his souls might escape. Our souls are tethered to our bodies quite tightly. This is necessary because every injury the body suffers opens a hole, however temporary, in the fabric of the aura that contains that soul. Think of the aura as an embryonic sack and your soul is the baby within it. Any injury causes a small tear in that sack. The greater the injury the larger the hole, and the larger the opportunity for an untethered soul to escape prematurely. This injury and the power that was used to create the rent have also severed the tethers to his souls and left an enormous tear in the aura containing them. I'm amazed he is still harboring both of his souls. It is a testament to his strength of spirit and will that his souls didn't burst free of him at the moment of injury.

"I can close the hole in his aura, keeping his souls from exiting, but I cannot regenerate the tethers and neither can he. Not spontaneously. And until those tethers are repaired he will not wake, he will not sleep, and he will not be able to recover from the injury. And, after enough time has passed with him in that kind of state, his aura will disintegrate in entirety and he will die. This is a state similar to when a human is comatose. Eventually the body withers and the person dies. In this case, the aura will wither and the souls will move on."

It sounded utterly nightmarish to Leo. He knew Jackson. What she was describing was a fate worse than death for men of action like Jackson and himself. The idea of becoming a burden on others, of tormenting loved ones instead of allowing them to grieve and then move on with their lives, was intolerable. And that was to say nothing about what it might feel like from Jackson's perspective. What if he could feel the brokenness of his body? What if he was aware of every single excruciating moment that he remained trapped in that painful sort of limbo?

"Is he aware?" Leo asked softly.

"Not as you might desire," the Night Angel said with obvious gentility. But she didn't direct the answer to him, instead aiming it at Marissa. "But there is awareness on a soulful level. He will sense your nearness. He will sense the state of your emotions. Also, it won't do you any good to cover them up. He will sense it's a façade."

"So you put this Band-Aid on him. Repair the hole in his aura. How do you repair the severing of a soul's tether?" Marissa wanted to know, her knuckles white as she subconsciously gripped Jackson's hand with all the strength she could muster, as though loosening that hold in any way would allow him to slip away.

"Let me do this first. Then we will discuss the rest," the Night Angel said softly, meeting Marissa's eyes and holding her gaze with a compassion that clearly comforted Jackson's beloved. Marissa finally let tears fall, let herself feel just how dangerous this was and just how close Jackson might be to death.

"He is everything," she said. Then as if it were something different she said, "He is everything *to me*."

Leo supposed both were true. Jackson/Menes was everything to their people, the strongest of his kind and the focal point of their political structure. Although Marissa/Hatshepsut was pharaoh in her own right, it was very clear that she had no interest in ruling without Jackson by her side.

The Angel nodded and leaned forward, resting a palm on Jackson's forehead, closing her eyes for a minute as though she were seeking for something within herself. The closing of her eyes was eerie. It made her face seem like a void of black with no relief, save for the white of her arching brows and the snowy crescents of her lashes, just as it was eerie when they were opened, a stark glow of yellow in a setting of black.

At first he thought he couldn't tell if she were pretty or ugly or strangely shaped to match her unusual coloring. But the longer he looked at her the more he began to clearly make out her features. She had full lips, like those of a child pouting with pique. However, there was nothing else childish in her graceful looks. Certainly not when those full breasts and curving hips were taken into consideration. She had an exotic sweep to her cheekbones, the rise of them exaggerated by the tautness of her drawn back hair. Her forehead was gently sloped, the line of her jaw sweeping softly into her chin, throat and neck.

She *was* pretty, he decided. Very much in her own way, and not just because she was a novelty. There was genuine beauty to her looks.

Otherwise, there was nothing delicate about her. She

was athletic and strong and it lent power to the impression of vigor she was exuding. She knew what she was doing and was confident in her ability to do it. Much in the same way that he knew how to kill a man and had utter faith in his getting the job done the way it needed to be done.

In this mixed-up paranormal world he had been thrust into, it was good to know he still had the ability to size one of these people up. And though he had no proof one way or another, he forced himself to have faith he was reading her right, even though he really had no faith in anything at all. How was he truly to judge these things he could not understand? Things he didn't want to understand. And yet, his lack of understanding frustrated him, made him feel helpless. It was a feeling he didn't like. After all, what else did they know about her? Hell, did they even know her name?

"Faith," she said, her chartreuse eyes flicking around to meet his.

He realized she was answering his question, a question he had not asked aloud. His entire body bristled in defense, his fists clenching tightly. "Get out of my head!" he bit off at her.

One white brow arched. "Who says I am in your head?" she countered.

"How else would you know I wanted to know what your name was?"

"And of course that means I was in your head." Her head tilted ever so slightly as she ran that assessing gaze over him again, as though she were figuring him into some kind of complicated algorithm.

"How else?" he countered caustically.

"Perhaps," she said as she turned her attention back to Jackson, "it is you who are intruding in my head. If humans only realized the power of their own thoughts, a great many ills of the world could be rectified, not the least of which is the constant leaping into misreading the acts and intentions of others."

Leo floundered, at a loss for a moment as he tried to figure out what she meant. "Last I checked I'm not a telepath," he said sharply. "That's an ability saved for this freaks and geeks society."

"I would argue differently. So should you."

"Why would I?" he snapped.

"Because if you've learned nothing from recent experiences, Leo Alvarez, you have learned you don't know as much as you thought you did. That there is potentially as much unknown as there is known to you. But, like most mortal humans, you persist in thinking you are the be-all and end-all of the universe. That you are the highest form of living. That there couldn't possibly be anything brighter or more vibrant than you are. And when something happens to shake that arrogance up, you're left floundering."

"What do you know about my recent experiences?" he demanded of her with blistering, barely leashed rage. And he was supposed to believe she wasn't reading his mind? *Oh god . . . what can she see?* Which of the cornucopia of traumatic and shameful events that had occurred could she see? One? A few? *All of them?* The very idea made him violently nauseous, and it was all he could do to swallow it back down.

She sighed shortly, as if he were trying her patience. She turned back to him. "To a Night Angel humanoids radiate a beacon of light, rather like if you had stepped onto a searchlight that streams up around you and on into the vastness of the night sky. Now imagine that there are words being projected onto this light, in all colors, shapes, and sizes. Projected from within the heart of your soul, Leo Alvarez. What is in your heart is there for all to see who are able to. The brighter the word, the more recent it has been stamped into your light. Your rage. Your fear. Your pain. Your light screams words like 'betrayed,' 'helpless,' 'disillusioned,' and 'violated.' The brightness of it tells me it has all been created very recently. And that then leads me to believe something happened to you, a traumatic event that showed you the measure of yourself as a man. Since the words 'Body-walkers' and 'Nightwalkers,' and such are also clearly new, I can only assume that these are all conjoined aspects of your recent experience. Am I wrong?" It was obvious she did not think she was wrong in the least. "If so, I apologize for my presumption."

She dismissed him once more, clearly not caring if she were forgiven or not. Very un-angel-like in his opinion.

His limited, human opinion. After all, what did he really know about angels? Pictures of human interpretation and expectation? Fair-haired, white-winged, halo wearers? White-skinned? It brought back a warm memory, something he hadn't thought of in years.

"Mama, aren't there any Spanish angels?" he had asked her shortly after he had turned five. He had been staring up at a white angel ornament on the top of their Christmas tree, the most recent in a long line of images of angels he had seen that holiday season.

"Oh mijo, there are many Spanish angels. Why would you think there aren't?"

"Because they're all blond and have white skin," he said, pointing to the ornament. Then he reached to wind a finger thoughtfully into his own black curls.

"Ah. So you think the men and women who make these pictures and ornaments know the true face of the angels?"

"Don't they?"

"They think they do. But the only way we'll ever really know is when we die and meet God in Heaven.

But I am very certain that they have Spanish angels who look and speak just like us."

"But if no one really knows, then how are you so sure?"

"Ah," she said, sweeping him up into her arms, her familiar oatmeal cookie smell falling like a blanket of comfort over him. "My smart boy. There has to be Spanish angels. When we die we all become angels. Tia Maria is an angel. She is watching over us even now and she most certainly is a Spanish angel."

That made him smile. He remembered his aunt. It made him happy to know she was an angel.

"Okay, Mama," he said, hugging her around her neck as hard as he could. "But I don't want you to be an angel too soon."

"Oh mijo, *don't worry about that. I'll be here for a very long time."*

Leo couldn't have stopped the soft smile touching his lips even if he'd tried. That was from a time when he had been innocent and when he'd thought his mother knew everything there was to know about anything.

Regretfully, neither had lasted past his teenaged years, his mother included.

Leo shook off the tumult of emotions this creature had sent washing through him with just a few sentences.

"Isn't that a little redundant?" he heard himself asking with a sneer in his tone. *Shut up, Leo. Shut up!* he argued with himself. "An angel named Faith?"

"No different, I imagine, than a man being named Dick," she said dryly.

He heard everyone in the room release a startled joint laugh, most of it through tight throats full of tears and tragic emotion. Then once they started laughing, they couldn't seem to stop. Well, hell. If bearing the brunt of her set downs eased the suffocating tension of fear and anxiety, he was willing to take it on the chin. And he didn't blame them for their laughter. He'd been out of line and Faith had set him back on his ass. Deservedly so. It wasn't her fault he couldn't find his footing in this ever-changing dynamic he called his life. It was probably a good thing that she refused to let him get away with it.

As he watched her placid expression, however, he could swear her lips curled ever so slightly at the corners. She was taking pride in her ability to deflect his raging bullshit. *And so she should,* he thought. There was nothing Leo appreciated more than a smart-ass.

He couldn't help himself. It made him smile as well. That made twice now in as many minutes. If he kept this up he'd be guffawing any day now. He liked a good guffaw. It'd be a damn shame if he couldn't find it in himself to guffaw ever again.

Then, as he watched, those beautiful electric wings of hers protracted. It was such a graceful sweep of glowing blue lines of energy, flowing directly toward him. He didn't step back like the others did in order to give them the breadth they needed for full extension. He should have. After everything he'd been through, he ought to have avoided letting them touch him as if she were a carrier of the bubonic plague. But there was a part of him that was eaten up with curiosity. Were they just light? Would they bump up against him or pass right through him?

Because he didn't move, they swept against him and then, before he could react with any belated protective reflexes, they passed right through his chest and body.

His first instinct should've been to be horrified and appalled at the intrusion, but it never came to fruition. Even though it ought to have been deemed no different than Chatha's brutal incursions into his body, all possible hostile feelings died a stunning death when breathtaking heat and energy bled into him, quickly followed by a sensation of peace and well-being. It was a feeling he had thought he would never again know in his lifetime, a peace that stole through him literally from the top of his head to the bottoms of his feet and toes.

But it wasn't just well-being he felt. There was something else . . . something more visceral . . . something very much like what he had felt the very first time a girl had ever touched him intimately. Although it was many years ago, he could never forget the eagerness of wanting it, the overwhelming excitement of it, and the needful readiness of his erection. There was no denying it was exactly the same overwhelming desire pulsing through him now, as well as the same glory of that first touch, thinking it would bring a measure of relief only to find out it just made things hotter, made things harder.

As he stood there he felt himself react to the memory invoked by the sensation, his body growing hard in response to it and the sensations he was awash in. He wanted to jerk away, to force himself to feel it for the violation it should be, but he couldn't bring himself to sully it. And when he saw her turn toward him with a startled, soundless gasp, he realized she was not intentionally trying to pull these things out of him. It had been happenstance. But he also knew by the look in her yellow-green eyes that she was one hundred percent cognizant to what he was thinking . . . what he was feeling. He wanted it to be a private feeling, he wanted to huddle it close in the confines of his mind and soul, not share it with someone he didn't know the first thing about. But he simply couldn't make himself hate anything about what he was feeling or her part in having brought it about.

She withdrew her wing and all its energy from him, the jerking movement almost like the too quick removal of a Band-Aid from a healing wound. But like that pain, it flew away in the next instant, and he was left simply stunned, still feeling everything he was feeling, and more than a little overwhelmed.

Seeing how uncomfortable she was, how awkward it was for her to hold that wing away from him, he stepped back at last, the movement alone reminding him he had a hell of an erection. She looked at him, her eyes partly accusing and partly . . . well, without really knowing her he could only make a guess, but it seemed like she was almost . . . curious.

But the impression only lasted a moment because she was turning away from him and looking back down at Jackson. Her left wing trembled a little, as if it were tautly ready to draw away again if he came too close. He took another step back, the shift of her eyes telling him she saw the movement. The wing slowly relaxed and he understood that she was trusting him not to come in contact with her again.

She needn't worry. He'd be damned if he was going to let it happen again.

Leo sighed, knowing instantly that the attempt to brush up his indignation was false and therefore it fell flat. The truth was that he wanted to step forward again, to feel the touch of that energy, craving the feelings the act had evoked so unexpectedly. Not the arousal, though that was a part of it, he admitted to himself, but the fresh, innocent feeling of it. The feeling so pure and untouched by the difficulties and tragedies of adult life.

Not that his youth had been a blaze of contented ignorance. There was very little opportunity for innocence in a boy from the barrio, the son of a single mother trying to do the best she could to keep her children happy and healthy, while the world thwarted her at every turn.

Bringing his attention back to the room around him and the concerns of the present day, he watched as the angel's wings curled forward past her shoulders, the left one passing briefly through Marissa before wrapping around Jackson. Leo heard Marissa draw in a stuttering breath, a sudden storm of emotions scouring across her features, one after another appearing for a brief flash of time. Bewilderment. Anxiety. Grief. Then quietness, reverence, and wonder as she found comfort in the next sensations marching through her.

And hope. The last was a welling expression of hope that made her sit back on her heels, the hands she had so tightly wrapped around Jackson's pulling in slowly until she was pressing the jumble of fingers into her stomach, just below the solar plexus, cradling his hand against her as if it were a child in need of comfort.

Whatever the Angel felt from the contact was tightly masked in her face, not even a flicker of emotion touching her, unlike when he had been touched. Maybe because she had been prepared for it this time? Or perhaps it was because she did it purposefully in order to give Marissa solace? He didn't know. And not knowing what her intentions were really bothered him.

Those graceful lines of blue energy wrapped around Leo's best friend tightly, until she was pulled in to just about being chest to chest with him, her cheek resting over Jackson's heart and her eyes closing. In another moment the lines that defined the shape of her wings became wider and wider, until there was no discerning one from the other and both she and Jackson were engulfed in a completely blue aura of energy.

Jackson body jolted suddenly beneath her, as if she'd given him a hit with defibrillation paddles. Leo tensed, his body going automatically tight with energy, the acrid taste of bile suddenly in the back of his throat. Jackson jolted again, this time his body locking hard in an arch of what could only be described as agony.

Leo lurched forward, wanting immediately to grab her and rip her away from him, but she threw up a staying hand in his direction, even though her eyes were closed and she couldn't possibly have seen his movement or his reaction.

Why he hesitated, he didn't know. Any other time, any other place, any other person and he would have shredded through the threat he perceived, neutralizing it to his satisfaction. But she stayed him, and somehow he obeyed, like a dog trained to its master. Not because the master was subjugating the animal, but like Jackson and his K-9 partner, with companionable understanding that each had to trust the other to do what they were supposed to do and believing that they would.

Having faith. Having trust.

He balked at the thought and anger raged through him. He clenched his already tight fists even tighter, his entire body equipped for defense . . . and now offense as well.

Then, as he watched, Jackson's body seemed to blur beneath the black beauty, something inside of him spilling out around him, like a yellow aura within the energetic blue glow that she had wrapped around him. Together the colors combined into a vivid kelly green. Then the blurring aura seemed to split into two distinctive halves, each straining as if wanting to fall to either side of Jackson's body. For an instant Leo recognized one half as Jackson, the man he had called brother from the moment they had first met, and the other half another man entirely, a stranger to him in almost every sense of the word.

He realized with no little awe that he was seeing the two distinct souls that were housed in Jackson's corporeal body. Anxiety clawed with raw demand down his throat and into his chest. He felt himself starting to shake, and told himself it was from the sudden dump of adrenaline in his body. He lurched forward, reaching to grab for her, to rip her away from Jackson. But this time the hands that stayed him were physical. He felt one lock around his biceps on his right arm, the other clamping onto his left shoulder. He was jerked back away from the Angel, and he rounded on the interference with a savage snarl of fury.

He found himself looking dead into the eyes of his torturer.

Kamenwati.

Leo wanted to explode, wanted to finally take the opportunity for some well-deserved payback, wanted to rip the fucking spine out of the man who had sicced that dog Chatha on him with such casual concern, as if checking off something on his to-do list.

- ☑ Go to market
- ☑ Go to dry cleaners
- ☑ Fix sink
- ❑ Have Chatha torture Leo Alvarez.

Check.

Leo didn't care that Kamenwati had defected from the Templars. Or that a great evil was coming and they needed a man of Kamenwati's power to defeat it . . . the evil that had already visited them not fifteen minutes ago. And he most certainly did not take into consideration that he was just a mortal human being and Kamen was one of the most powerful men of his breed.

He was going to kill the bastard with his bare hands. Leo wanted to see how *he* felt while being gutted, flayed apart, and filleted like the catch of the day. Only, the moment he put all of his weight into a lunge for the sick fuck's throat, all of the strength and energy in his body suddenly rushed out of him, like someone had connected a vacuum to his head, flipped a switch, and sucked up all the energy in his body like lint on a carpeted floor.

His legs turned to Jell-O. His body buckled. And now, instead of pulling Leo back, Kamen was holding him up on his feet. Weak and helpless, there was nothing he could do as Kamen levered him onto an upholstered bench sitting at the foot of the bed.

He was blind with impotent fury as he found himself looking up into those cold, assessing blue eyes.

"If you interrupt her, your friend will die," Kamen said to him. There was no emotion to the words. It was as eerie as being in the middle of the Bering Sea in a flat calm. An unnatural thing.

"Get your fucking hands off me!" Leo snarled, shoving Kamen bodily away from him, clawing at the hands that were touching him and making his stomach churn. It was all he could do to keep from vomiting on the other man's shoes. Then again, maybe he should do just that.

Of course, he hadn't been eating very much lately, so the gist of his stomach contents would be some Jack Daniel's and a bag of Fritos. Breakfast of champions.

But his efforts to push Kamen off himself were ineffectual, his body so weak he couldn't even form a fist with his fingers. If not for the bastard's hands, he realized with anger, he would have fallen over onto the floor.

"I am sorry to have done this to you," Kamen said, once again that flat, emotionlessness that kept him from sounding anything near contrite. "But you must leave the Night Angel to her business if you want your friend to survive."

Then Kamen let go of him, and Leo had to fumble out with his hands, trying to cling to the bench and not ooze onto the floor into a puddle of ineffectualness.

"Don't you ever touch me again," he spat at the other man. "You hear me? Even if it's to push me out of the way of a speeding truck, don't you ever lay another finger on me or you'll pull back a mangled stump!"

"I highly doubt that," Kamen said. "But I will do as you wish."

Leo felt his strength coming back to him, but not in any effectual way. Only enough to allow him to turn and see what was happening to Jackson. He was just in time to see those two blurring halves slowly draw back into Jackson.

The Angel sat up slowly, the movement a little bit graceless, as though she too were drained of strength. She put her hands out against the bed to hold her torso upright.

"His souls are contained, the damage to his aura repaired. But it will wear thin again and develop weakened areas unless his souls are tethered soon. They will bounce against his aura, like a helium balloon bouncing along a ceiling. Eventually the balloon will shrink and wither and finally fall to the ground. The same will happen to his souls. They will shrink and wither and eventually . . ." She trailed off. Nothing else was needed in any event. She had given them all a very clear picture of what the situation was.

"How do we fix it? What do we do?" Marissa demanded frantically. All of her composure was evaporating. Leo could see it in the slump of her shoulders and the wetness trembling on the tips of her lower lashes. Her blue-green eyes were begging and anguished. It made Leo realize that, one soul or two, Jackson meant the world to her. No matter that the time since they had come together was short and seemingly insignificant in the grandest scheme, there was sharp truth and even sharper desperation of need in what Marissa and her Bodywalker felt for Jackson and his.

"I do not have that power," the Angel told her.

She couldn't have possibly kicked Marissa's puppy

harder. Sobs began to fall out of her, tears now dropping in earnest.

"Pl-please," she begged in staccato bursts. "Do something! You have to do something!"

"Not I," the Angel said gently, moving a hand to cover the ones Marissa still had clutched around Jackson's, still pressed into her body as if it were a tether of its own and she had to hold tight or risk losing him. "But there are those who can. They are a select few and will be very difficult to find."

"I'll find them," Leo said sharply. It seemed to startle both of the women, as though they had forgotten he was even there. "It's what I do best," he said a little more gently. "I hunt people down."

It was the truth. He had hunted down thieves and warlords, cartel leaders and lieutenants. Tinker, baker, candlestick maker. There was no one he couldn't find.

No human, he realized as the women looked at him doubtfully. He was a human in their supernatural world and they knew it. They knew the truth that had been chapping his ass from the start of this mess: that he was almost completely insignificant among them.

"You cannot find these creatures easily," the Angel warned. "Certainly not with your limited human abilities."

Well jeez, lady, tell me how you really feel, Leo thought bitterly.

She narrowed her eyes on him and he had a feeling she was reading more of those words on that light thingy that she was apparently able to see. "I will go with you. I can go where you cannot. See what you cannot. But you have . . . other skills that might be helpful, however minimal."

"Gee, thanks. You're just a font of encouragement now, aren't you?" Leo said dryly.

"We need to find a Djynn. A Marid caste would be the

most ideal, but there is no way we would ever be able to find one without a specific introduction. So that means finding a lower caste of Djynn, like a Djinni or Jann. They are usually far easier to find than a Marid and far less dangerous than the Sheytan."

"SingSing!" Docia blurted out, suddenly reminding Leo that she was in the room. "We know a Djynn named SingSing. She's umm . . . Djinni level. At least I think that's what she said. It's hard to remember. She talks very fast and is a little . . . eccentric."

"Do you know where to find her?" Faith asked, the intrigued tilt of her head making him suddenly notice that her ears were gently scalloped at the lobes. It was so light a difference that it could be easily missed in the blackness of her skin. He didn't know why, but the aberration fascinated him.

Leo frowned the moment he caught himself indulging in the thought. There was nothing for him to be fascinated by, he reminded himself. He was surrounded by these *things* with power he couldn't comprehend, power he couldn't fight. That wasn't fascinating, it was utter stupidity. He'd spent years going headfirst into dangerous situations that he voluntarily put himself into, but the difference was that those situations were the devil he knew.

These people were the epitome of "stranger danger," and definitely a devil he knew nothing about.

"No," Docia said, deflating into a frown. "She just left saying something about going on vacation. Someplace warm."

"Do you have something of hers?" the Angel asked. When she spoke, Leo could see the reddish pink of her tongue behind the white of her teeth, the contrast fascinating to see, even though it was another reminder of just how inhuman she was.

"No. I don't think . . ." Docia stilled, and Leo, who

had known her all of her life, could see her mind working hard. She tended to look down at the ground when she was trying to access her memories. It was something so Docia, something so incredibly unique to her, that it made him forget about the other thing inside of her just for a moment. "Wait. She gave me a scarf before she left. But that's a gift, right? So it's technically mine and not hers."

"That depends on the state of her mind when she gave it to you," Faith said. "Bring it to me and we will see what we will see."

Docia raced for the door so fast that she tripped over her own feet, bumping and pushing through the throng of others crowded into the room. Ram. Max. Ahnvil.

"I shall hunt for the Djynn with you," Kamenwati said to the Angel. "My skills will be invaluable."

"Ego, much?" Leo snapped. "No. We don't need you. And you're supposed to be under house arrest, if I understand it correctly."

"Please," the Templar scoffed softly. "Regardless of Menes's and Hatshepsut's power, I could leave here any time I wish to. And they both know that. I remain here of my own free will."

"Feel free to *not* any time you like," Leo said darkly.

"I'll take that under advisement," Kamen said, clearly not taking it under any advisement in the least.

"How about you take my foot up your ass under advisement?" Leo spat, pushing himself to his feet and remaining upright by some miracle. *Score one for the home team!* Then, because he was damn near feeling frisky, he stepped up into the other man's face. "Come on, *pendejo*. Let's see what you've got without all that paranormal bullshit you like to throw around. Or are you going to just play god and push all us peons around like pieces on your cosmic chessboard? You know what they say about absolute power?"

Kamen took a step back, but it wasn't in any kind of retreat. Leo had a feeling it was just to give himself more rarefied air.

"I don't need *you* to tell me how far I've fallen," Kamen said quietly. "I've discovered it quite on my own. And I will not ask your forgiveness because I neither think you will give it or think I deserve it. Suffice it to say, my absolution is going to be a long time into the future, if it ever happens at all. My punishment for myself is to remain here on this earth, breathing and living this life. I don't expect you to understand, but it is by far the worst thing that can ever be done to me. So you needn't worry about me getting my comeuppance. It's well in hand."

"Let me know if you need any help," Leo said darkly.

"You'll be the first," Kamen assured him.

"I am sorry," the Angel said getting to her feet, "but you need to remain here," she said to Kamen. "You are the only protection this house will have. You and Ramses. As you see your Gargoyle protectors were insignificant to the imp god, as was just about everyone else. But together at least you can do enough to bring this house to some sort of safety. But be warned, you cannot move him unless absolutely necessary," she said indicating Jackson. "Every movement will be like water in a glass, each step risking a spill. Movement could open his aura again, allowing his untethered souls to spill free and then there will be nothing I can do for him. To be honest I am amazed I was able to keep him intact. The damage done to him was severe."

The understanding sobered everyone in the room. It smoothed down Leo's bristles, subduing his anger. *Focus,* he lectured himself. *Focus on the task at hand.*

The Angel turned toward the door, the sudden movement making her list and Leo instinctively reached for her arm. He caught her, holding her up against himself.

It was like the weak leading the weaker. He was barely steady on his own feet, but he did it just the same and it felt like a victory when he succeeded. Then he realized she was leaning flush against him, that her smooth black skin was against his palm and that she was a great deal warmer than he had expected her to be. He didn't know why. Why had he expected that noir color to be something slick and cold? Instead, it was soft, feminine, and warm.

For the first time he caught the scent of her. Again, he was surprised. Cinnamon and nutmeg. It was a bright combination and something about it was like liquid sunshine poured into his soul. His mother had made the most incredible desserts, their kitchen redolent with delicious smells on a constant basis, and it had smelled just like this Night Angel. It was as familiar and comforting as a pair of well-worn slippers. It made him smile in spite of himself. He couldn't even try to throw up a wall of suspicion and defense in the face of it. And that realization was what disturbed him all on its own. He didn't like being disarmed like this. He was already at too much of a disadvantage.

"Let's find this scarf," she said softly, looking up into his eyes. She tilted her head, her gaze vibrant and assessing. It was then that he realized there were flecks of gold and green in the lemon yellow of her eyes.

It reinforced within him the understanding that she was indeed very pretty. There was a soft innocence to her that he hadn't noticed initially. It had to be an illusion of some kind, he thought curiously. She had been anything but sweet and delicately ingenuous since the moment she had arrived. But then again, he had seen a great deal of innocence forced into roles of maturity in his time. He had seen nine-year-olds with machine guns, and five-year-olds used as land mine detectors while tethered to the soldiers walking a safe distance behind them.

"So many horrors," she said on a sudden, soft breath, her fingers reaching to touch his whisker-rough jaw. He should have been repulsed, offended by the uninvited touch as well as the observation, just as he had been offended by Kamen's.

But he wasn't. Instead he stared down into those chartreuse eyes and knew without a doubt that she was seeing a part of him that had witnessed those horrors. Whether it was just a word in his light or the emotions his memories carried, he did not know, but he didn't doubt for a second that, in that moment, she truly understood him. Something not even Docia or Jackson could claim. For years now he had been showing them only select parts of himself. He had been preserving Docia's innocence, because he had needed her quirky uniqueness to stay just as unblemished as ever . . . and not burdened with the memories he could not share. And Jackson . . . he and Jackson came from two sides of the same coin. The greater good being both of their goals, but Leo was willing to cross the line to see to it. Jackson stayed in the lines, following the laws he believed in. They had agreed to disagree on their methods toward the same goal, and had silently agreed that Leo shouldn't tell Jackson, a cop, anything he would have to, in good conscience, seek justice for.

Leo had never told Jackson that it had killed him a little every day that he had no one to truly turn to and be himself with. That even when he was with them, eating with them, laughing with them . . . he was still very much alone and out in the cold.

"You . . ." she began, but then seemed to think better on it and pressed her lips together. They were so sensual, those lips of hers. He had no idea why he found her mouth so intriguing, but the feeling was one of the best experiences he'd had since Chatha gutted him.

The thought put a damper on his appreciation of her, reminding him sternly that she was just another creature he didn't understand. And she was a woman to boot. That was like . . . double jeopardy or something.

He turned his eyes and body away from the Night Angel. Damn it, why is it so hard to move away? *It must be because of what that Templar prick has done to me.* He still couldn't feel his usual strength, still felt significantly weakened.

But he'd rather be dropped into a vat of hissing scorpions before he'd admit it.

They all, en masse, moved out of the room. All but Marissa. Ram led the way to their rooms where Docia had hurried off to. Leo, still holding the Angel's arm, motioned for her to precede him. She looked for a moment like *he* was a vat of hissing scorpions, but then moved cautiously away from him. She kept her eyes turned down as she walked and brushed a hand in a caress over her right ear. It was a habit, he realized. She was tucking back a strand of hair, even though there wasn't a single one that had escaped the severity of her twist. She probably wore her hair down under normal circumstances.

They all descended on Ram and Docia's suite of rooms. Leo was happy to see Kamen follow them, rather than staying behind with an incapacitated Jackson. Leo was certainly not convinced this wasn't exactly the kind of opportunity the Templar might be waiting for, if his defection were nothing but a ruse.

Leo gently shifted his hold of the Angel's arm to the midpoint of her biceps, and held her back from entering the rooms along with everyone else.

"Can I ask a favor?" he said when she looked at him inquisitively.

"You may ask anything you like. However, it does not follow that you will be answered."

Point taken.

"When you look at Kamen's . . . uh . . . light thing . . . what words do you see?"

She lifted a curious brow. "Why would you wish to know that?"

"Just . . . just answer the question," he said, trying to keep his irritability to a minimum, seeing as how he was asking her for help.

"Turmoil. Hatred. Loathing." She raised her brow farther. "Do you wish to know more? Or does it matter what is the brightest versus what is worn down?"

"I think you told me all I needed to know," Leo said through tight teeth.

"I do not think that is correct."

He frowned, trying hard not to let knee-jerk anger cloud his judgment. "Why is that?"

"Because all of those words are turned inward."

He blinked. "Okay, I give up. What does that mean?"

"Self. Self-loathing. Self-hatred. Turmoil and guilt . . . all pointed into him. He is not the demon you are looking for." She leaned in a little closer. "Your demon is also turned inward."

Then she pulled away and moved into the next room.

CHAPTER THREE

"Here it is!" Docia cried in triumph after having gone through every single drawer, throwing things helter-skelter over both shoulders until she came up with a long, purple scarf, shimmering with intricate silver embroidery.

"Excellent," Faith said, reaching to take the accessory into her hands, her fingertips feeling the silk and the weight of the silver in the thread.

"This is a nik." Faith knew this because she could feel the power within it and it surprised the hell out of her. "Djynn rarely give away their niknaks." Catching Leo's puzzled expression, she explained, "Djynn do not have power for themselves, per se. They have the ability to use the power they can derive from various niks—which hold magical properties. The moment a Djynn touches a nik, it becomes theirs and the power within it is now theirs to use."

"So you mean . . . they have to hold a nik to use its power?" Leo asked.

"No, no matter what, from the moment they've touched a nik, the magic is theirs, and only theirs, to draw from at any given moment whether in contact with it or not. Until another Djynn comes along and touches the nik, which transfers ownership of the nik, in effect stealing it out from under the Djynn that owned it. Djynn have great hoards of niks they hide all over the world." Faith ran the scarf through her hands. "This is an incredibly powerful nik. I'm quite amazed," she said to Docia. "You must have made quite an impression on her in order for her to entrust you with the care of such a powerful nik."

"Well, I . . . really?" Docia was flabbergasted. "I-I didn't even know it was a nik!"

"Well, that would have defeated the purpose of hiding it in a safe place. If you knew what it was, it would have made you too aware of it and might have caused you to give away its location to a rival Djynn by accident. If it were an ordinary scarf in your estimation, you wouldn't have done anything to draw attention to it. And besides, this house is probably one of the safest and most ingenious places to hide a nik. The average Djynn would avoid this house of power like the plague. Djynn dislike confrontations."

"Oh. Wow," Docia said, her eyes wide with wonder. "I didn't realize she thought that much of us."

"Clearly she did," Faith said, smiling when she saw the word "delighted" sear brilliantly across Docia's scroll, which was what Night Angels called that inner spotlight they could see. The little Bodywalker was really quite sweet and a very unusual mixture of souls. The human soul was everything innocent, impulsive, and awkward, while the Bodywalker soul was sophisticated, worldly, and confident. Both were completely harmonious, however, when it came down to their love for the injured Bodywalker in the next room, and for the one that stepped up behind her and wrapped strong golden arms around her.

Together Docia and Ram's lights combined into something far too brilliant for her to look at directly. It was the brightest light she could ever remember seeing in her lifetime. The two left in the other bedroom came a close second. But she suspected it was only the weaker of the two because the male had been so brutally damaged. That left only the female trying to shine brightly for both of them. Faith found that profoundly saddening. A light so precious was on the brink of being extinguished. As it was, she knew she should never have let them believe there was a hope of saving him. It was the longest of long shots and it would need something in the nature of a string of miracles. But Faith had watched the imp cut those souls away from their anchor without a single taste of contemplation of its actions. It destroyed because it could. Its power was vast and frightening and it liked to let other lesser beings know that. And Apep considered all beings to be lesser beings. He was perfection in his own eyes. It followed suit, of course, that he should be worshipped for all that he was. That he had adorned himself with the body of a beautiful woman was simply yet another perversion it took delight in. When Faith had come upon the scene only an instant before the god had struck the Bodywalker down, she had known she was too late and had failed in her initial mission.

So she had given herself a new mission. An impossible mission. One whose success would truly be a miraculous event.

"I can use this to track the Djynn . . . but daylight is coming . . ." She pulled her bottom lip briefly between her teeth, worrying it a little. The idea of being out in the sunlight was abhorrent and terrifying to any of the Nightwalker races. Each of them grew weak in the face of it, in one fashion or another. Paralysis. Poisoning. Altering on a subatomic level. The debilitations ran the entire gamut, including the one she was most familiar with. "I won't be able to start this journey until darkness falls."

"That's too long," Leo bit out as Docia gasped in dismay. He instinctively reached out as though to comfort her, but then drew back sharply before even touching her.

Faith was fascinated by that reaction and by this man. His emotions and thoughts vacillated so sharply from one extreme to the next that it left her completely dizzy. It was as though he were a kid with a Christmas tree full of emotions and he went ripping madly from one to the next, trying each on for size before quickly discarding it and leaping to the next. She'd never seen anyone burn through so much emotion so quickly before. The words scrawled over his scroll in a beautifully haphazard script kept changing in brightness and intensity.

What she had not explained to the mortal male was that everyone's words looked different in style as well as brightness. When she had looked at Menes's and Hatshepsut's lights they had been worded in beautiful hieroglyphs. For the woman she now stood facing, it was an energetic boldface script. For the mortal it was like that of a left-handed, impatient script, beautiful in its maleness and vivacity. The type of script she saw told her almost as much as the word itself did. Her own was a graceful Asian-styled calligraphy.

The human would be surprised, she knew, to learn just how similar his script was to the Bodywalker he loathed, the one standing on her opposite side. Although one was a little more patient and paid more attention to detail, both men's emotions were volatile, especially with regards to their feelings toward themselves.

She couldn't imagine what it must be like to live with emotions that fell away like so many shedding hairs; the next discarded before the first had even hit the ground. It had to be simply exhausting. God knows she was worn out just watching them do it.

Faith drew her attention away from everyone else and focused on the nik in her hands. It was a very powerful nik. She could sense it, feel it in the weight of the metal fused to the silken threads that made it glint and shine in the light. Since it was so clearly owned by the Djynn in question, she would very easily be able to track her using it. The trick was whether she could do it without tipping her off. If a Djynn thought it was being hunted it would run and hide and use magic to keep others as far away as it deemed necessary. As it stood right now, the Djynn's defenses were not up and Faith could very strongly feel the direction she needed to go in.

"Sunlight weakens us," she explained to the human patiently. "In some cases it can kill us."

"Us?" he echoed, hissing hard on the "s." "I am not an 'us.' Daylight does nothing more to me than give me a nice tan. So tell me how to find this thing and I'll have it here by nightfall."

Docia gasped, her eyes widening before they went wet with hurt and shocked pain. She had felt his derision and prejudice to her core, had known instinctively that he lumped her in with the "its" of his world. A dehumanized thing that he wanted no part of.

Leo realized his blunder a second or two too late. By the time he thought to apologize she had turned away from him, and buried her face into the chest of her mate. Ram's big hands engulfed her with a comforting hug, rubbing her back gently as she began to weep. It had been one hurt too many in too short a period of time, and she dissolved into tears under the stress of it all. Ram's touches and soothing words were all sweetness and comfort, but the blazing look he leveled at Leo should have set the mortal man on fire. At least he had the decency to look and feel regretful. But he didn't try to verbally apologize. He made himself listen to Docia's pain and flagellated himself with the sound of it.

"I doubt you could ever find a Djynn on your own," Faith said to him, drawing his attention. "They cannot be tracked by mortal means."

"Anything can be tracked."

"True," she acquiesced. "But unless you know of a way to track smoke and energy, your problem remains the same. You will need my help to find her. Hunting for her in daylight presents its own problems, but since time is of the essence we have little choice. Perhaps the nearness of her nik will entice her into using her magic to make it possible for her to contact us in spite of the sun. I know there are Templar spells that can create this possibility, perhaps there are Djynn abilities as well."

He stewed in those thoughts for a moment.

"So what is it with sunlight and you Night Angels anyway?" he asked. "Does it paralyze you like it does these people?"

The way he said "these people" was yet another nail of pain driven into Docia's light. He had to know how much he was hurting her, so why did he persist? His scroll read of a deep love of Docia, one that was a lifetime written into his heart. How was it possible for him to keep hurting her even though it hurt him to know he was doing so? To *feel* he was doing so. Everything about him was a wash of contradictory emotions and agendas. She sincerely felt sorry for him, because he was well and truly lost in the miasma of these feelings. He needed an anchor in this storm of emotion, and he needed one fast, or he would lose himself, drown himself in them completely.

She didn't particularly care for humans. Their minds were so small . . . so unwilling. Unwilling to learn, unwilling to adapt. Not that she hated them, but she didn't understand them. She didn't understand why everything in their eyes had to be so defined. Spelled out. Understood. For her it was the magic of the unexplainable that was so delightful. For instance, the conundrum of emotion, prejudice and love that this man was. It was tragic and beautiful and indefinable.

"If you had a vulnerability, would you wish to announce it to the world? Or do you wish to know so you can find some sort of equal footing with me?" She stepped toward him and heard him draw in his breath as she came close enough to say softly. "Will it make you happy if you know exactly how to kill me?"

"It might," he said sharply. But even as he spoke reactively, she felt him floundering, felt him question his own motives, saw him scrawl the word "bastard" across his light.

"Then I will help you, by all means." She left his side, crossed the suite of rooms to the balcony doors just outside the sitting room. "Step back," she instructed Docia and Ram, and they, as well as Kamen, hastened to do so.

The polarized glass had blocked the rising sun so thoroughly that it had seemed to be night until she opened the door and let the newly risen sunlight in. Docia and Ram pressed even farther back, no doubt feeling the numbing edges of the paralysis the light brought to them, as well as the accompanying fear that came with it. Deservedly so. Who would want to be caught frozen and helpless in the cold light of day? Certainly not her.

But for these purposes, she had very little choice beyond exposing her vulnerabilities to these strangers. Especially this one particular stranger. This was meant to help him feel equalized, meant to quell the fear she knew was fueling his suspicions of her. Of them all.

She turned her face into the sun, felt it cascading over her, the feeling like a million pricking needles along the underside of her skin. Under the light her beautiful black skin lightened to a charcoal color, then lightened again to a silvery gray. The effect continued, making her the very lightest shade of pearlescent gray before progressing into the colorless realm of white. Not human white, but the white of a human without pigmentation. The white of an albino. The blue beauty of her energy wings seemed to shrivel up until it was nothingness. The warm yellow-gold of her eyes washed away, leaving very normal looking irises . . . except for the fact that they held no pigmentation save the tender tinge of pink from the blood vessels running through them. With her white hair and brows, the effect was complete.

"Jesus Christ," the man called Leo uttered. His eyes raked over her from head to toe, stopping baldly at the barely pink crests of her nipples and the nakedness of her sex, its pinkness also showing clearly what the beautiful black of her skin had hidden away.

"There now. Does this please you?" She stepped up to him, the warmth of the sunshine burning against her right cheek. "Does this comfort you?"

He didn't deny that it did and she saw the word "human" draw itself into his light.

She said on a soft breath, "You can believe that if it gives you comfort. If it allows for us to work together. But with this human guise comes limitations you will not find so very pleasing. I cannot access my wings, so I cannot fly. I cannot access the power I used to protect you less than an hour ago. The repulsion force field. Suffice it to say, this will allow us to work in daylight together and will, perhaps, quiet your unrest about my appearance, but we're in for a hell of a time if we run into trouble."

Faith reached out and caught the door, slamming it shut in order to protect the other people in the room. There was white-hot fear written in each of their lights. She could not understand how the mortal could ever find any kind of satisfaction in something so terrifying to another. Especially to ones he professed to love.

Loved, she realized with correction. He *had* loved Docia. Then she changed and now . . . now he was too afraid of what she had become to see beyond it. But the Night Angel had faith that it was still inside of him somewhere, still a very large part of his makeup. In fact, she knew it to be a truth, however lightly scribed it might be in that moment. It was still there, embedded into his soul. But he was grieving that love as though he had lost her . . . as though she weren't standing there right in front of his face. It was, at its very heart, a tragedy and Faith felt very sorry for him. She did not let her pity cloud her caution however. Humans were, by their nature alone, dangerous to a Nightwalker being. That fear he held on to was the heart of that danger. When a mortal human feared what they couldn't allow themselves to understand, they became unpredictable and a constant source of potential risk.

But still . . . Faith found humans to be very beautiful, despite these shortcomings. This man in particular was very beautiful. Just as a male specimen alone, with his coal black hair that curled in wide, lazy waves and soulful eyes the color of warmed whiskey. There was nothing boyish or innocent to his face, nothing soft or fatty to his hard, purposely honed body. It took a great deal of work and effort to be in that kind of defined physical condition. Muscle did not sculpt itself. Denim clad thighs did not show their strength unless they were, indeed, full of strength.

He was not overly built with that muscle and she could tell from his scroll that he was not aiming for appearances. If he had cared that much his vanity would have been written all over him. No, he had much different purposes for the physical condition he kept himself in. She was not blind to the word that was deeply ingrained onto him.

Killer.

This was a man capable of taking lives. More than capable, he was an expert at it. However, she could see he was not a psychopath. Psychopaths or sociopaths had blindingly egocentric lights. Lights full of twisted thoughts and deeds. Lights without feeling and without empathy.

This man was neither of those, but that did not make him any less dangerous or deadly. She would have to be very careful if she was going to spend time in his company . . . especially while in a weakened state and considering what he thought of supernatural beings.

Faith found herself touching the whiteness of her own fingers, inspecting the pink of her nail beds with a discomfort she couldn't help. She thoroughly disliked herself when the blackness that was natural to her was robbed from her. She was also weary, she acknowledged. She had traveled far and fast in order to get here as quickly as possible, and it disheartened her that she had been too late to properly warn them. But she had not been too late to help, and she must be satisfied with that. She had given them time to do what was by far the most important thing.

"We should go," she said just as her pigmentation was starting to turn back to normal. "The imp god will only grow stronger the longer he remains in his new corporeal body. And there will be no defeating him without your male pharaoh. Many of our prophets have seen this clearly. The pharaoh will be instrumental in the curtailing of this evil god . . . but only if he survives. The injury the imp suffered at my hand is not a very serious one and he will recover quickly. When he does he will come at you all with even more vengeance. And you must assume that he knows what the prophets know, or else why would he have come here?"

"I can think of a reason," Leo said icily, shooting a scathing look at Kamen.

"But . . . but Jackson tried to use his power and it had no effect . . ." Docia said, her voice trailing away as if she realized that Faith might be insulted by the contradiction. Faith could see the stark fear on her. Fear for the life of her brother. Fear of her own inadequacies. Fear for the love that stood strong and sure at her back at the moment but had come close to meeting the same fate as Jackson. Faith watched as Ram reached out to brush his thumb over his love's cheek, his arm crossing her waist and drawing her tightly back against him, as if to say "I'm here. You're safe. I love you and we will be strong together."

Faith had to blink, lowering her lashes to try to defray the brightness of their complementary lights. Whenever they grew closer to each other or touched each other it became a blinding thing; a stunningly blinding thing.

Faith turned away when the tightness in her own throat threatened to reveal her emotions. She did not wish for them to see the envy she felt. There were much more serious things she should be considering beyond the loneliness she felt within her own life. What she could do, she thought, drawing herself back onto task, was see to it that nothing happened to tear these two asunder. Them and the two inside. They were, in a word, remarkable and it would truly be tragic if something she failed to do resulted in their loss.

"We should begin." Faith ran the scarf through her fingers thoughtfully. "I don't think she is very far."

"Then why don't you tell me where she is and just send me after her?" Leo wanted to know.

"Because the journey to *her* is not the journey that

should concern you. You should be satisfied that I am allowing you to come with me, despite the encumbrance you could prove to be."

Faith turned her back on him, unable to look at that white-hot light of fury that burned within him. She knew he would think she was dismissing him, and she supposed she was, but she couldn't be concerned with that. There were far greater things at stake than the state of his fragile male ego.

"Come along if you will. If not, I am happy to do this on my own."

She left the room without looking back at any of them. No matter which corner of the room she looked at, no matter which light, they were all far too bright and hot for weary eyes to tolerate.

And she was very weary indeed.

Kamen moved into the hallway, following in the Angel's wake.

"There must be something I can achieve here," he said to her, his hand gripping the balustrade as she paused on the first step in order to look up at him. "I am a Templar. I have a cadre of spells that could perhaps—"

"I think you've done more than enough," she said softly, baldly meeting his eyes. There was no misinterpretation. She knew just by looking at him that this was entirely his fault. He was to blame and he felt the weight of it on his soul.

"Back off," Leo snarled at him, thrusting his body between Templar and Angel. "Why don't you go hide in that room Jackson assigned to you and figure out a way to defend this house in case that thing you've called up from hell comes calling again."

Kamen wanted to argue, was used to feeding ideas to others and hearing his opinion heard with great value.

But he had no worth here, he reminded himself. Not with these people. And he did not deserve otherwise.

"Perhaps you are right," he said quietly, acquiescing with a dip of his head, readily allowing the Hispanic male to be dominant over him. He could already tell that it took large amounts of energy and self-control for the other man to keep from lunging for his throat, and in a way he had to admire his ability to maintain that control. He also had to admire the fact that it wasn't fear keeping him from doing exactly that. It was something else . . . a loyalty he wasn't all that sure of—one that Kamen could have told him was very much alive and well.

Besides that, this was Menes's house and this man, as it happens, was Menes's best friend.

Jackson. He was still wont to call him Menes, but in this lifetime, this incarnation, he preferred to be called Jackson. How odd that was, he thought absently. He had never conjoined with the soul of his host enough to want to take his name in place of his own. In fact, all Templars subjugated their hosts, pushing their second soul into dormancy and submission. It made him wonder . . . what if . . . ?

Kamen shook his head. Now was not the time for contemplating follies that would eat up his focus and his energy.

"I will keep your friend safe while you are away," he said to Leo, even though he knew the human male despised it when he addressed him directly. "If this house is attacked again I can get everyone to safety quickly."

"Remember," the Angel said, "do not move him unless absolutely necessary."

Kamen nodded his understanding, then turned and left their sight.

CHAPTER FOUR

Leo couldn't focus on his driving. They had climbed into a truck, one of the many vehicles kept available on the property, and she had told him to head east. So he was heading east. That was all she said. "Head east." And not another word since then in the thirty minutes he had been driving. Now he was distracted because *she* was distracted. She kept turning her hands over, inspecting them front and back, touching her nails, watching them go white when she pressed on them, and then pink again as her capillaries refilled.

She was also fidgeting with the knee-length dress Docia had scrounged up for her. It was a pretty heather blue one with little blue and yellow cornflowers all over it and dark blue buttons running from neckline to hem. Clearly it had come from Marissa's wardrobe, it being far closer to the Angel's height and weight than anything of Docia's would be. Docia was short and curvy, whereas Marissa was tall and . . . well . . . curvy. Though apparently not as curvy as the Angel beside him. The dress was pulled tightly over her breasts accentuating their shape and heft.

Okay, he had to admit it. She was hot. Like scorching head-on-fire hot. Albinism aside, the minute she had fully turned parchment-paper white, he had finally been able to distinguish her looks in their entirety. Before-hand, with all that monotone blackness, he couldn't see that she was . . . well . . . hot.

Gorgeous, actually. From gracefully rounded shoulders to her well-defined calf muscles, she was the kind of hot that would have kept her off all the fashion runways because she had curves and blatant female sexuality, not the stick-thin figures and drolly waiflike starvation victim look that supermodels were always striving for.

Oh yeah. She had booty. She had just enough junk in her trunk to make a man crave using it for handholds as he—

Whoops. No, no. Not that, he thought hastily to himself when, out of the cold blue tundra that had been housing his emotions and feelings lately a sharp streak of arousal began to stab through him, heading right for his heavily dormant cock and the twin brothers attached. *Do not pass go, do not collect two hundred dollars.*

Come on, man. Focus, he thought fiercely. He looked at the stark road laid out in front of them. Once they had left the city limits and caught the main highway out of Portales, New Mexico, they had left what most would call "civilization" behind. Traffic was nearly non-existent and it could make for a pretty boring drive. So, it stood to reason that his attention might wander. With that and the fact that he was tired, he excused himself. After all, he had been up all night long, having shifted his own sleeping cycle to coincide with those of the others in the house. Maybe it was like when women got together and their periods started to synchronize. It had nothing to do with the fact that every time he closed his eyes . . .

So, mix in a pretty girl with all of that and a man was wont to let his thoughts wander.

Oh . . . wait . . . she was so *not* a girl. A woman, yes. But there was nothing girlish about her. In fact, now that he'd had some time to study her and replay his short acquaintance with her over in his head, he would actually say she was a very . . . sexual creature. A sexual creature trying to *not* be a sexual creature. With her severely swept back hair and her very correct posture she was as uptight as they came, on the outside of it.

That she worked so hard at presenting a precise sort of exterior told him a lot about what she might be hiding beneath the façade. And once he had started looking, he had begun to find things.

For instance, the way she kept touching her own hands and arms, the way she brushed her palms down the length of her skirt and the fact that she did both very slowly told him she was deriving a tactile pleasure from her own actions. Her fingertips brushed absently at the nape of her neck, the small touch tugging at the short tendrils that had not been long enough to be caught into the twist of her hair. There was only the barest dusting of them, but she pulled them between her fingers and rubbed at them. Again, just for the sake of feeding herself tactile sensations.

"So . . ." Leo cleared his throat of the awkward roughness that barked out of it. "So, tell me a little about Night Angels," he said.

She immediately frowned and narrowed her eyes at him. Those strange pink irises were so disconcerting in that endless sea of whiteness . . . white skin, white sclera, white hair . . . that he found himself missing that cat-yellow color they had initially been. They had been so unique, so intriguing . . .

It was clear she was second-guessing his motives. No doubt she was studying his spotlight thing and reading words that told her things he probably would prefer she didn't know.

"What would you like to know?" she said at last.

Good question, he thought. He wanted information, but he had to be careful how he did it.

"Well . . . the foremost thing on my mind is about that light you said we all have. Is there a way someone could maybe, I dunno . . . *lie* to you or hide the words the light might show you?"

"We call the light a scroll. And everyone's scroll is different, unique, and varied. There can be no absolutes and no way to make scrolls uniform. However, you cannot lie to me if you are not lying to yourself. You can trick me into perceiving a script—the words we see—that is untrue if you put a strong effort into it. For example, if you are feeling fear you can overshadow that script by putting a huge mental emphasis on the strength you will use to face your fear. But that is something only the most disciplined minds are capable of. There are very few people, both human and Nightwalker, who can deceive a Night Angel."

"What does that mean . . . 'not lying to yourself'?"

"Let's say that you were grieving a loss. Often a stage of loss is denial. A person can lie to themselves about a given truth. If you firmly believe and feel a lie is true, it will appear on your scroll as though it were a truth. We aren't lie detectors. The ability is flawed sometimes."

"I see. Still, it seems like it is a handy skill to have. I wouldn't mind having it at my fingertips." *Especially lately,* he thought, the understanding making him frown. It would be so much easier to know where he could put his trust if he could read what was really in the hearts of those people who surrounded him.

"This is a gift that can fall into the 'be careful what you wish for' category," she said, all seriousness. "Sometimes it is better that you not know what is really in the soul of a person. It can be very . . . disillusioning."

Leo could see how that would be. For instance, he

wouldn't want Docia to see past the image he worked so hard at projecting for her. He didn't want the darkness in his life to spoil the way she felt when she looked at him and smiled. If she could read the truth on his scroll, she might never trust him again. She might look at him and see a monster. A murderer.

"I understand," he said. He quickly pushed away from that topic and all the thoughts it evoked. He felt naked enough around her. He didn't need to help her see the darker parts of himself by mulling them over right in front of her perceptive eyes. "Where do Night Angels live exactly? I mean, given your coloring, it's not as though you can walk freely in the human world."

"No. The only time we can walk in the human world is when we are like this," she held out her white arms in indication. "But even this draws unwanted attention."

He could see that, too. People were obnoxious and cruel. They would stare and whisper, even in the age when seeing weird people and the things they do to themselves might be generally expected.

"So . . . ?" he prompted.

"We live all over the world in special enclaves. Like the Bodywalker house in Portales, the homes are in the midst of a huge property, land acting as a buffer to the outside world. We tend to pick places with naturally occurring barriers, like mountains and cliffs . . . huge estates butted up against a beach and ocean or a great canyon. A dense forest or vast desert goes a long way to discouraging the average hiker. Then it's only the above-average ones we need to be cautious of, and luckily those sort are fewer and farther between. And anyway if they made it to the property they would most likely be greeted with barbed wire and electrified fences."

"Fortresses," he said quietly. "It must be difficult, living in constant fear of discovery."

She burst out laughing, the shock of it ringing against

his ears in spite of the quick hand she lifted to cover her mouth. At his inquisitive look, she tried to press back her laughter. "Do you really think so? Nature has her ways of camouflaging her creations. Believe me when I tell you that we are equipped with all the means necessary to protect the outside world from learning about who and what we are."

"I'll definitely take your word for it." He found himself smiling again. Seeing genuine humor on her changed his perception of her. It added a vibrancy to all that colorlessness, the smile accompanying it lighting her eyes as well as her lips. "Are there a lot of you? Does this," he indicated her appearance, "mean that any albino I meet is actually a Night Angel?"

"No," she said, more merriment in her eyes. "Human albinism is very much in existence. I would resist going up to an albino on the street and whispering 'I know you're an angel!' You'd probably get packed up and shipped to the funny farm if you did that one too many times."

That made him laugh, and he realized that was twice now that she had delighted him in under thirty seconds. It was such a strange feeling. For the past week he had felt like Chatha had hollowed him out, figuratively as well as literally, and that he'd been stripped of all emotion except for fear and anger. The latter caused by his acknowledgment of the former. He had never thought himself above fear, but he had never expected to be overwhelmed by it. Paralyzed by it.

When he came back from that too close examination of his demons, he realized he was rubbing taut fingers against his abdomen. Just the feel of his own hand against one of those tender spots made his entire body clench with a crippling anxiety he'd never known before. And that had little to do with the runnels of freshly made scars tracking over his belly and chest. It was more about the scars Chatha could not heal away.

That had been his sadistic power. The ability to heal. And he had used it over and over again to bring Leo back from the brink of death, making him as new as he had been in every way . . . save his mind. But the last healing had been done haphazardly, at Kamen's command moments before he had made off with Leo, running from the god he had brought into this plane of existence.

He hoped . . . no . . . he prayed that thing found Kamen one day and quartered his limbs from his body . . . and then had Chatha heal him afterward.

The thought sickened him. Literally sickened him. He veered off the road, slamming on the brakes, the tires scraping in a skid over stone and dirt. He barely had the truck in park before he lunged out of the door, got his feet on the ground and puked his guts up. He hadn't eaten much, his lunch having been a Jack and Coke, so there wasn't much to give back. That was probably why it hurt so much. That and the fact that he was still healing from Chatha's last time in the playpen so all the muscles he'd just used to reject his lunch made him feel like he'd been playing tic-tac-toe on his chest with Wolverine.

God, don't ever let me wish that on even my worst enemy again, he thought, his eyes clenched as tight as his stomach was. *I will not let him make a monster out of me!*

His ears were pounding with the sound of his own blood pressure, so he didn't hear her come up beside him. She touched him on his biceps and he jumped. It took everything he had not to grab her and throw her out in the middle of traffic. Throw her away. Just *away . . .* from him. Not touching him. He couldn't stand being touched anymore. And he was damn sick of everyone's compassion and pity.

"Leo," she said softly, ever so gently as her hand went back to rest on his shoulder, brushing a path down his arm. "Your script is—"

He exploded, rage lambasting him at the very thought that she could see inside of him, see the innards of his emotions just like Chatha had seen the innards of his gut. He grabbed her, wrenched her hand and arm behind her back and slammed her chest first into the side of the truck.

"Don't you fucking try to tell me what I am on the inside! Don't you fucking dare!"

Faith tried to catch her breath, seeing as how it had gone slamming out of her on impact. Pain lanced like fierce fire through her twisted arm and she felt the incredible strength of him up against the entire length of her back. He pressed into her with all of his weight, making sure she could feel how very serious he was.

"I wasn't," she coughed. "Leo, please . . . I'm not . . . I have no strength in my whiteform. I'm no stronger than the average human woman. Ow!"

"You are not an average *human* woman," he hissed into her ear. He leaned all of his significant strength into her, the muscled wall of his body hard and unmovable. "But you look it. You feel it. If not for your color you could pass for it." She felt his hand wrapping around her throat, tipping up her chin to make her look into his angry whiskey eyes. "But you are inhuman. You are all inhuman. Give me the lowest scum of the natural born earth over you people any day of the week," he spat at her.

"Who says humans were the ones born naturally to this earth?" she countered on a croak.

That seemed to give him pause. It made him think.

Thinking was good. What he was doing now was instinct, fight or flight, stumbling in a world he couldn't fully comprehend because of the way he had been thrust into it.

"Leo, not all of us want to hurt you . . . even if you are hurting us."

The latter observation suddenly got through to him. He jerked away from her, releasing her and stepping farther back. She spun about and lunged for him, grabbing him by his shirtfront and yanking him toward her, pulling him in just in time to keep him from getting clipped by a speeding car. There was the sound of a horn and an angry curse, but they both paid no heed. Leo had reached out for the truck, gripped it on either side of her, his head bowed as he held her caged there and looked for all the world like he was trying not to throw up again.

After a long pair of minutes that had him sucking hard for air and then slowly winding down into deep, steadier breaths, he finally opened his eyes and looked down into hers.

"Stay. Out." He said it through tightly clenched teeth.

"I can't," she said just as firmly. "You'd have to gouge out my eyes as well as the heart of me. I see with them both. Blind me and I can still see what you don't want me to see."

His eyes slid closed again and she had the distinct feeling that he was trying to keep from wringing her neck. So she figured she'd just as soon push him to it as not.

"I'll see what you think he made you," she said, taking care not to soften her voice, not to show anything he might consider to be pity. "Weak. A victim. Insignificant."

"Shut up."

"Rip out my tongue. Go ahead! Silencing me won't

stop those very same words from running around inside
your head."

"My god, have you no sense of self-preservation?" he
growled at her. "Are you trying to goad me into breaking your neck?"

"No. Because just like you, I feel pain. Just like you,
just like any of us, I can be made to hurt. All it will take
is someone stronger than I am. And that's what you've
just realized, isn't it? That there's more people out there
stronger than you are than you thought there were?"

"I'd hardly call you *things* people."

"No more than white men thought *you* people were
worth anything more than itinerant farmhands, right?
Or that slaves were real *people* with feelings. Those
kinds of people?"

"Goddammit!" He grabbed her by her arm, opened
the driver's-side door, and then shoved her into the
truck. He slammed the door shut in her wake, staying
out on the road. She figured she'd pushed well beyond
his tolerance and decided to let him have a few moments of peace.

That was when she saw a car driving slowly toward
them . . . a familiar-looking car. A small brown coupe
with about three or four people crammed up into it.
Their scrolls lit up as soon as she was in range, and ugly
script appeared on them in white-hot letters.

"Leo," she said in anxious warning. It wasn't that she
was afraid of them so much as it was that she was afraid
of what Leo would do to them in his present state of
mind. Because for all the hard, harsh truths that made
him who he was, he was not as cold-blooded as he fancied himself. But if he were pushed too far at a moment
like this, he could do something that would push him
over a moral edge he had thus far avoided. "Leo, we
have to go now," she said as firmly as possible, reaching
for the door handle.

"Stay in the truck. The day I can't handle a bunch of drunk fools is the day I hang up my Desert Eagle."

She watched him casually unzip the last two inches of his leather jacket in order to make it easier to draw the gun from the holster on his belt. He didn't hide the fact that he was armed, but he didn't flaunt it either as two of the men exited the car from other side of the road.

"Hey mister, you having some trouble?" one of the two that alighted from the car called out as they both crossed the road to approach. Leo quickly counted heads. Four of them. The one who had called out to him was skinny . . . unnaturally so. It reminded him of a snitch in his hometown named Ray-Ray who was more interested in buying his next high than he was buying his next meal.

Oh yeah, he thought, *this is trouble*.

"Anything we can help you with?" the second one asked, this one looking like he had consumed a great deal of the meals the first one had missed. He was burly and tall, easily topping Leo by a head and quite a few kilos. Leo was very sure he thought his size could get him to victory in a fight, and no doubt he was right . . . most of the time.

The first thing Leo noticed outside of their heights and weights, however, was that although they were speaking to him, they were staring in through the truck windows at Faith. An observation that was solidified with their next sentence.

"Whoo-wee! Look at that, Joey. You were right! She's as white as a ghost!"

Joey? Leo would have guessed Joe-Bob or Billy-Ray or some other Podunk hyphenate. They were clearly walking-talking stereotypes and didn't even know it.

Maybe he should apprise them of the situation. Maybe they would appreciate him pointing it out.

"We've got things fully under control here," Leo said, fighting back the urge to say "Opie." Had he been alone, he wouldn't have resisted. In fact, he was spoiling for a good fight right about then. At least fighting was something he knew, something he could get a handle on.

"Well, now, I don't think you do," the beanpole said. "Do you think he do, Joey?"

Joey shook his head. "Sure don't."

"Sure don't," the thin man echoed, as though repeating it made it more profound. As though Joey were a font of wisdom he had to access from time to time. "You were just about to fall right into traffic a second ago, boy."

From inside the truck, Faith saw a sort of stillness come over Leo. He'd been leaning back, seemingly relaxed, already appearing quite still. But there was a difference between stopping motion and just . . . stopping. Everything. He didn't so much as blink. Then he lowered his chin, the corner of his lips curling up in a smile that so clearly wasn't a smile.

"We're fine," he said. "And if you want to keep breathing, you won't call me 'boy' again."

Oh boy, Faith thought. She leapt for the window, pressing the button just in time to hear the lead man of the twosome say, "That's right unfriendly of you, Mister. Here me 'n' Joey take the time to pull over and check on you, and you go and get attitude on us. Ain't he got attitude on us?"

"Attitude," Joey agreed sagely.

"Honey! What's taking so long? I gotta pee!" Faith decided to sell it by leaning on the horn. Leo's head pivoted and he looked at her, rather like she had to be out of her mind.

It made Joey and his friend laugh.

"Sounds like you got a problem after all, boy. The girl's got to go."

Leo laughed.

Uh-oh. She'd heard Leo laugh. This was not a Leo laugh. Not a good or genuine one, in any event.

It was like watching lightning leap from cloud to cloud, the way he leapt onto the first man, bending him over in his surprise, grabbing his jacket by the back hem and yanking it up and over his head, successfully tangling him up in his own clothing. Then he sprang off him and grabbed the big guy by the shirtfront. Leanly muscled, quick and light, Leo had ducked under not one but two swipes of Joey's meaty paws and, using just the extension of his leg and a pull on that shirtfront, sent him sprawling face-first into the asphalt. By the time the thin man had caught his balance, worked himself out of the tangle of his clothing, and whirled around, Leo had his gun pulled and was aiming it . . . at the car. The two men in the backseat looked like grasshoppers on meth as they tried to hold up their hands and figure out which way to leap to gain safety, all the while trapped in that backseat.

"Here's how this goes," Leo said, with deep steady breaths and a fierce darkness in his eyes. "You get in yours, I get in mine and we all leave happy."

"But—!" The slim man was working up to some kind of protestation, Faith could see it as well as Leo could.

"Or!" Leo said sharply. "*Or* I pump two of these armor piercing rounds into your engine block and leave you four stranded out here in the desert with coyotes and rattlesnakes for company."

The thin man, now hunched in on himself, as though it might make him a smaller target, held out a placating hand.

"Now, we didn't do nothin' to you, b-uh . . . uh . . . mister!" Faith watched another smile touch Leo's lips ever so lightly. It was no less cold than the first one had been. "But we'll be on our way."

"Better hurry if you're going to catch up to your friends," Leo advised.

Faith looked in the direction he nodded the gun at and realized the other two men had finally gotten out of the backseat of the car and were running down the road at full speed . . . or at least as fast as their lumbering bodies allowed for while they struggled to keep their pants up at the same time. Apparently both were in need of a good belt.

The thin man bent to help his friend off the road and Faith could hear them cursing at each other as they hurried across the road and got back into their car. Gravel, sand, and a long, loud screech filled the air as they whipped into a full U-turn and chased down their friends. More swearing ensued, this time louder than before, as they reacquired the rest of their group and peeled off with more sand and gravel flying. By the time she looked back at Leo, he was pulling his jacket straight, the weapon already in its holster. He opened the door to the cab, and looked her dead in the eyes for a long minute.

"I can't get in until you move," he said with genuine amusement touching his lips.

"Oh!" Faith said, realizing she was kneeling on the driver's-side seat. She backed up quickly. "I'm sorry."

She stared at him with genuine puzzlement and as soon as he had climbed in he looked at her and raised an inquisitive brow. Faith couldn't help but marvel at him. Here he was, a fragile mortal male, no defenses or physical advantages . . . in fact he was shorter and a bit lighter than the average healthy man might be, and somehow he'd bested two—potentially four—full-grown men without using any deadly force.

"How did you know?" she asked.

"Know what?"

"That they were planning to attack you . . . or rather, us."

"I didn't until just now." He regarded her and took in her surprise. "I suppose you saw that on their light things?"

"Scrolls," she corrected absently. "Yes. I did. But you don't have the ability to see scrolls or read minds so . . . you couldn't possibly have known—"

She sat back in her seat in honest bewilderment.

"It was their knuckles," he said after a long minute.

"Their knuckles?" Now he was trying to confuse her, she thought petulantly. Just because she wasn't familiar with humans like some of her breed were didn't mean he could tease her as though she were stupid.

He rubbed a thumb across the ridges of his knuckles. "They both had fresh scabs on their knuckles. The kind you get when you're in a fight. Coupled with their very obviously false sense of concern . . . it's just better to gain the upper hand from the start and when they are least expecting it. Spares me having to buy more ammo." He shrugged. "And we'd be detained by the cops, explaining why they're all shot up. I figure we don't have that kind of time to spare."

"Yes," Faith said thoughtfully. "I mean, no. No, we don't have that kind of time." She looked out to the front of the truck and then frowned. "Will you excuse me for a moment?"

"What? Why?" he demanded to know. "It's not like we're taking a leisurely Sunday drive here. Weren't you the one that just said we had to go?"

"I know," was all she said before alighting from the truck. Leo watched in irritated bafflement as she began to walk away.

Man she has a nice ass, he found himself thinking almost immediately as he watched the way her body moved beneath the dress she wore. While the skirt itself had a soft flowing movement to it, the hips of it had been tailored snugly against her, accentuating the rounded shelf of her backside. Had that part of his personality and masculine cravings still been alive, had he just been in a bar looking across the way at her, he would have made his way over to her based on her booty alone. He readily admitted that he'd always had an itch where fine ass was concerned. And as pretty as she was, the albinism wouldn't have made a damn bit of difference to him.

And while he was thinking about it, she was curvy in all kinds of other places, too. It wasn't the first time he was noticing and it wasn't likely to be the last, even if he tried to lecture himself about how she wasn't a real woman. It was a damn shame she wasn't a real woman. Not a human one anyway. Certainly not by any stretch of his imagination. She was one of those things. A Nightwalker. Whatever that was supposed to mean.

Faith came to a halt about ten feet in front of the truck and promptly began to . . .

. . . talk to herself. Or, wait, not herself but the empty air. She didn't seem like she was babbling inanely, however. It looked as though she were having a conversation with someone, a gentle conversation, a persuasive one, if he was reading her body language right. And if there was one thing he prided himself on, it was his ability to size up a situation and the people in it with rapidity and uncanny accuracy.

Except for when you fell for Chatha's ruse.

Leo's hands clenched tighter on the steering wheel when the thought slipped snidely by. It always felt like he was on the tipping point of complete and utter rage lately. He kept needing to rein himself in, kept finding himself clenching his fists while he fantasized about doing violent harm to something . . . anything.

Faith smiled then and reached out as if to touch something. And just like that, in a brilliant shimmer of blue energy, he saw who she was talking to come luminously to life. It was a woman, with gaunt features and troubled eyes. She looked to have black hair, but it was hard to tell as it was filtering through blue light. But what really shocked him was that she was wearing some sort of costume, including a corseted bodice that accentuated her figure and a full-length dress with a skirt that ended in a flounce of petticoats.

Leo stared. Even though he knew he'd look like a rude sort of a moron, he couldn't help himself. As he watched, Faith took the woman's hand in hers, clasping it with warmth and vehemence up against her breastbone, all the while talking, petting, and making the woman smile.

After a minute Faith dropped the woman's hand and the moment she did so the woman disappeared, as though her visibility were completely dependent on Faith's touch. Faith turned back toward the truck, her long fingers absently smoothing back that invisible strand of hair again, even though nothing had yet escaped the tight knot. She opened the door to the truck and climbed back in.

"Okay, we can go now," she said.

Leo gaped at her.

"We can go? That's it? No explanation of who that woman was and how you did . . . what you just did?" he said with incredulity.

Faith sighed softly and then turned her body to face him. "When we die, we move our spirits from one plane to the next. It is a plane of peace and comfort that provides anything that is needed. I guess you might call it heaven, in your religion. It's called many things in many religions, but the principle is the same. And there's a reason for that. It's because instinctively we know there is another world beyond this one, and that it is a place without pain or disease or abuse." She hesitated, her clean white teeth worrying the plushness of her bottom lip as she seemingly debated what to tell him next. "When we die we immediately get sent to this place. Except . . . sometimes something happens and it keeps us from going. It traps us here." She looked down, watching herself smooth wrinkles out of her dress by running soft, slow pressure along the length of it. "Without getting into too much detail, what I do is . . . I help them find their way."

"So that," he pointed toward the hood of the car, "was a ghost? Is that what you're telling me?" He could hear himself sounding more and more shrill, but he couldn't seem to stop himself.

"Not at all," she said, "she's a soul."

"What the hell difference does that make?" he demanded of her.

She stopped all her fidgeting and went severely serious in the next moment, meeting his accusatory stare with an aggressive one of her own.

"It makes a hell of a lot of difference to the person trapped here, I assure you," she bit out. But then she seemed to rein her temper back in. "If you've learned anything about the Nightwalker world, you know nothing is what you might expect or assume it to be. Souls get trapped here in two ways. One, they won't let themselves go. They fight death so hard, resist the natural process for so long, that they miss their opportunity to cross. Like, say, a boat in the water that needs to go past a drawbridge to get to its destination, but instead of going forward with the current they throw the engines into full reverse. Eventually the drawbridge closes and the boat has missed its opportunity."

"And two?" he asked, feeling somehow disturbed by the concept of a trapped soul, a stupid sort of empathy that made him very uncomfortable.

"Someone or something purposely holds them here. There are spells and such that can achieve that. But there are also . . . there's another force that can do it very easily. They are called Wraiths. If they kill someone and are touching that person at the time of its death, they will trap the soul and use its pain and torment to fuel themselves, to fuel their power. It takes someone like me, a Night Angel, to lead them through portals that only we can find. The wind . . ." She trailed off. "I guess you don't really care about all of this."

Leo wished he could say that he didn't. But he did. In spite of himself he was eaten up with curiosity as to how things in this other world worked. Actually, *she* made him curious. Maybe because she was a Nightwalker in a pretty, bearable package, or because listening to her made him want to know more if for no other reason than to continue hearing the soft sweetness of her tone of voice. She was strong and vibrant when needed, but moments like this, when she turned gentle and almost a little sad . . . it made him lean in and want more. More of . . . something.

"The wind?" he prompted after a long moment.

She looked at him sideways through the corner of her eyes, her brow wrinkling a little bit as she tried to decipher his intent. He kept his expression carefully neutral, nothing discouraging and nothing encouraging. He hoped that whatever she could see on his scroll didn't interfere with her responding to him. But there was nothing he could do about that, so he just let her decide how to dictate the moment.

"The wind blows over everything. There's nothing it doesn't touch, almost no corner it can't get through to. Angels can get the entire topography of an area for miles around in any direction just through our sense of the wind. But it also allows us to feel the cusps. The cusps are small alcoves in the edge of normal perception . . . and they are the thinnest point between here and the next plane. We can find them and lead the trapped soul to them."

"Is that what you did? You led her to the afterlife?"

"No. I merely promised her that, if she remained here, I would come back for her and help her then. I realize time is of the essence for Jackson, and this soul has already been here for over one hundred years. She can wait a little bit longer. I will come back and I will take care of her," she said with determination.

"But why not now? How long could it possibly take?"

"Not long at all, actually," she said. "But I can't help her like this." She indicated her appearance.

"You mean . . . because you're in sunlight?"

Faith nodded.

Then, for a bright and shining moment, he really understood that this state of being was very unnatural for her. That in its own way it troubled and hurt her.

"Are you all right like this? Is . . . is this going to cause you pain?" he asked, unable to keep himself aloof. He wasn't that much of a prick . . . was he?

"Eventually, if I stay in daylight long enough . . . yes, it will become increasingly more painful. Physically as well as . . . well, it's very painful to see a tortured soul like that and know I can't help her. Leaving her behind where she isn't really safe disturbs me."

"I don't doubt that in the least," Leo said thoughtfully.

Not even realizing he was going to do it, he reached out and brushed a thumb over the powder-soft cheek closest to him, momentarily marveling over how dark his Hispanic complexion was in contrast to all of that white . . . and yet, when she was out of sunlight, she would return to her black coloring and then it would be he who would seem paler than she was.

But coloring was not what compelled him to touch

her, and when she startled at the contact and looked at him questioningly, he should have snatched his hand away. He didn't want to engender a sense of connection between them, a sense of camaraderie. He wasn't in this to make a new friend, only to save what was left of an old one. But the more he felt the fragile softness of her, the more he wanted to stay in contact.

What the hell is wrong with you? he asked himself meanly. *Keep your goddamn head on straight.*

What she had told him only proved what he'd been thinking all along. These things were dangerous and they were carriers of their own unique brand of absolute power. Power that could crush humans by the hundreds—perhaps even thousands—if they put their mind to it. And he knew he and every other ignorant son-of-a-bitch human out there was going to get caught in the crossfire and there was nothing they or he could do about it.

Soft to the touch she might be, but he had seen her powerful side. She was strong, self-assured, and did not need someone to point her in a certain direction and give her instructions on what to do next. She just rolled up her sleeves, turned her brain on to maximum and began to plow through one moment at a time. Being a mercenary, when a plan went south, it forced him to work off the cuff and . . . well, that was his forte. He could appreciate the skill for what it was. But it was easy to dive right in if you'd been born with the power to back it up.

Or . . . at least he thought she'd been born with it. When it came right down to it, he didn't know anything at all about any of them, and that really kinda scared the piss out of him. Being out here, chasing more Nightwalkers down with only her for backup . . . yeah, it really did scare the piss out of him.

Leo pulled away from her, though not as quickly as he

probably should have, his fingertips lingering just a moment or two too long. It was hard to pull away from something that soft and, well, comfortable. That was the word for it. In the face of all her strangeness, there was just something about her that made him feel comfortable.

And comfortable was the last damn thing he needed to be around any of her kind.

He threw the truck into gear and moved them down the road. Faith was glad to have his focus and his hands pointed in another direction. There was no way of explaining how much his touch, as unexpectedly tender as it had been, had disturbed her. The brush of his thumb had swiped a streak of heat across her cheek, the sensation startling. It was all she could do to keep herself from touching the still-tingling spot. She'd never been touched by a live human being before. They'd always been souls . . . apparitions with no corporeal state. And while she'd met her share of Bodywalkers before, this was somehow different. He didn't have half the ability they had, but he did have something incredibly dynamic about him. And it wasn't just the anger and rage he kept bludgeoning her with. It was . . . indefinable, really. He just seemed so alive.

"Better grab your belt."

"My . . . ?" Faith looked down at the dress she was wearing. It didn't have a belt. She hadn't seen the use for it.

He abruptly leaned toward her, one muscular arm shooting out so close to her face that she pressed farther back into her seat and drew a startled breath. But instead of hitting her which, she had to confess, she'd thought he was about to do, he grabbed hold of the seatbelt over her right shoulder. Keeping one hand on the steering wheel, he used the other to drag the belt across her and snap it in.

Once she was latched in he eyed her with a peculiar expression.

"Did you think I was going to hit you?" he asked her, breaking eye contact briefly to check the road.

"No. No, of course not," Faith said hastily. She fidgeted nervously with the belt strap.

She was lying. Leo could see that. And she was painfully bad at lying too, he noted. But he let it go. He wasn't out to get to know her better. They had a job to do. He would see this thing through because he owed Jackson at least that much. Whether he was the Jackson he'd loved like a brother or . . . or something else, he needed to do this for him. Him and Docia.

He tried not to think about Docia. He didn't want to examine that closely. No more than he wanted to examine the Night Angel that closely. Turning to watch the road, Leo frowned and made himself pay attention to his surroundings.

Faith was a strong woman, he reasoned with himself. There was absolutely no reason to think she would be abused in any way. He stole a glance at her, doing a quick perusal of her delicate whiteness. He had seen no marks on her, no telltale warning signs. No. He must be mistaken and reading too much into it. Hell, he probably would have flinched too if a man of his caliber had practically shoved a fist under his nose.

"Tell me something," he said after a minute. "Is there anything else your people can do besides read script and the other things I've already seen?"

"It all falls under the same categories, more or less. Why do you ask?"

"You mentioned not being strong in this form. Did you mean just the fact that you can't use your power?"

"Oh. The sun leaches away our strength along with our pigmentation. Our reflexes slow down. Even our thinking becomes weary. If I stay out in the sun, I will eventually lose the ability to see script, and, like I said, I can't do anything else I'm used to doing."

"I see. So in essence it makes you human."

"It makes us less than what we are," she said in a combination of sternness and irritability. "Would you want to be exposed to a condition that made you feel alien to yourself and robbed you of your skills and healthful condition? For instance like now. You've been injured and it's slowing you down. Do you mind it or do you find it frustrating?"

"How do you know—?" Leo cut off the demand when he realized he already knew the answer. It was all he could do to keep himself from grabbing her, shaking her and demanding she mind her own goddamn business.

"Your anger speaks for you," she said. "I will take that for your answer." She reached down to the floorboards of the truck, where the scarf had slipped away to. Her lashes fell to half-mast as she seemed to focus on it for a second. "The Djynn is closer now. I can feel the connection to her nik growing stronger. With any luck she will feel us coming and will hopefully think we are Docia and Ram and will find a way to meet us. Otherwise, we might have to wait until night to track her down."

Leo's hands clenched on the steering wheel for a moment, and Faith could tell he was angry. She could also tell he didn't want anything to do with her. Which was fine, she told herself, because she didn't want anything to do with him either. He was an obnoxious and dangerous individual. With all the anger he was keeping contained within him added to the aggressive skill he had just displayed, it made him a powder keg. He was able to hold back during this last altercation, but would that hold true in the future? He was clearly fraying at the edges. It was only a matter of time before he lost all cohesion and started reacting irrationally to things. Not unless he got some sort of help, be it a doctor or a friend.

"May I ask you something?" she asked.

"No way to stop you, really," he said, his hands tightening once again on the steering wheel.

"You are willing to do this thing, this task that could be very dangerous, but you hold a great deal of distrust for the Bodywalker Pharaoh. I am curious as to what your motivation is. There are so many words evoked whenever you think of him, that I find it very confusing."

"A very good reason why you should mind your own business," he said caustically.

"Perhaps you are right. But since I have asked the question, perhaps you might answer."

"I'm not particularly inclined to," he said.

"Very well," she said, settling back and contenting herself with the wild-looking scenery, all its varied browns and russets broken up by the odd green patch of cacti.

To her surprise he huffed a breath out his nose and said with obvious reluctance, "I don't trust that *thing* inside of him. How do I know any of the Jackson I know has survived the possession of him? If he's usurped the Jackson I know . . . I want to know. I want to know so I can do the right thing by my friend."

"I don't understand. The right thing?"

He paused for a long minute and she saw the fiercely bright scrawl of a word on his light.

"Because if that thing inside Jackson has destroyed the soul of my best friend, I'm going to do everything in my power to kill the fucker."

CHAPTER FIVE

Marissa and the Bodywalker inside her, Hatshepsut, were grieving. She touched Jackson's face, squeezed his hand tightly within her own. Hatshepsut had loved Menes for lifetimes, since they had first met in Hatshepsut's first host. By then Menes had been reborn twice already and was very familiar with the nature of the Ether and the way to live in harmony with a host after the Blending. It had been long before the Templars had separated from the Politic. Long before the Bodywalkers had even had enough cohesive numbers to organize a working government.

They had known from their first touch that there was something powerful between them. They had known they would be together from that moment until the day they experienced the actual death, if such a thing were ever possible.

But these last few incarnations had been so painfully short, the war robbing them of the time they craved to spend with one another. In her last incarnation Hatshepsut had only lived a week before Odjit had caught her exposed and slaughtered her. One week. And that had been a cruel and painful death, Odjit truly showing the color of her nature as she had tortured Hatshepsut and her innocent host. It had been a horrible way for that innocent to die and that was why, although she had craved Menes with all of her heart and soul, she had not wanted to be reborn. Reborn to what? To another painful death? To a time much too brief? For her ability to put physical hands on her beloved to be robbed from her far too quickly again? And what of the innocent soul she would share her body with? How could she willingly put that soul in the line of fire?

And then there was the grief. The grief the lover left behind would be blinded with. A grief so insurmountable that, in spite of how badly their people needed them, they could not see their way to living another hundred years before their mate could be returned to them. Last time she had been the first to go, but Menes's grief had been so total that he and his host had preferred to take their own life rather than go on without her.

And now she was facing that same mourning, facing that same chasm of time without her soul mate. And as deeply well worn as Menes's and Hatshepsut's love was, the love between their hosts had been just as white hot and undeniable . . . but so new, so untried. And unlike their Bodywalker souls, Jackson's and Marissa's original souls would not be reborn in a hundred years. They might not be reborn at all . . . ever. As far as the Bodywalkers knew, they experienced the actual death.

This time . . . this time they hadn't even had a week together. They were being wrenched apart, again, much too soon. The senselessness of it was more than they could bear. She could not stop the tears that ran from her, sometimes in great, painful sobs. She could not breathe . . . not without him.

She felt more than heard Docia enter the room. She wanted to scream at her to get out. Wanted to throw herself over his body and keep anyone from touching him. She had knelt there in that stupid garden and had simply watched while that savage thing had cut her lover down. And where had Ram and Docia been? The Templar soul inside of Docia, Tameri, had extraordinary power at her fingertips. Why had she done nothing to save him? How could they have simply watched?

Just as she had simply watched. Watched him put his life at risk in order to protect hers.

"Shh," Docia said softly, reaching to rest comforting hands on Marissa's shoulders. "We can't give up hope." But Marissa could hear the shaky doubt infecting the other woman's voice. "We have to have faith in . . . well, Faith. You know as well as I do that the Night Angels are capable of extraordinary things."

"I do understand that," Marissa said quietly. "But I am afraid that nothing can fix this. What if . . ." She trailed off, unwilling to give her fears voice. Obviously she didn't need to. Docia sighed shakily.

"I know." It was all she could say. "I know."

Apep frowned as he looked in the mirror, studying his new corporeal body for what had to be the thousandth time since he had been called into it. He always found being a female so much more complicated than being a male. The most confounding and superfluous parts of it being the breasts and the uterus. He had very nice breasts, he admitted as he ran his hands over then, hefting the weight of them in his hands. As far as that went, he amended. But other than their aesthetic loveliness, they served him no purpose. It wasn't as though he would suckle a child. And yes, that led him to think of the other troublesome item on his body. A uterus. How complex it was, how inconvenient it could be, to engage in carnal activities when there was always the risk of being infected with a child. It was really a thorough annoyance. Perhaps he should be content to engage in lustful relations with only other females. That would eradicate the threat of infection. Yes, he thought with satisfaction. That was an ideal plan.

Of course . . . there was something to be said for the idea of procreation. He could perhaps section off a part of his godly energy and imbue an infant with it. Then that infant would grow into a beautiful scion of himself, an ally of equal power.

Yes. There was something to be said for *that* indeed! In fact, the more he thought about it, the more curiously appealing the idea became. But he would have to choose a physical sire and that was no small feat. It couldn't be just anyone. It would best suit his purposes if it were another being of power.

He turned and looked at Chatha for a thoughtful moment. Chatha was such a beautiful creature. Not his physical form. That was most certainly sub par in his eyes and therefore took him completely out of the equation. His aberration was called Down syndrome. A limiting factor indeed. No. As beautifully wicked, as scrumptiously perverse as Chatha was, a child of his must be sired by an ideal physical specimen.

Any one of the Nightwalkers would do, he decided. There were twelve breeds, each with their own strengths and limitations. Some more so than others. Their weaknesses could very well be inherited by their offspring.

Well, except for the Bodywalkers. Neither their power nor their weaknesses would convey. Like the one rattling around inside of him, the one called Odjit and the even more obscure human soul that had originated with this body, they were merely visitors to these bodies. The power was conveyed by the soul and if that soul were ripped away the power would go with it. There was no genetic alteration, they could not portion off their power and their souls like he could and put it into what would be a very human, mortal child.

But with part of his soul and power within him,

Apep's child would grow beyond its mortal shell, would be a demigod in his own right.

"But the inconvenience of pregnancy," he whined aloud. "All that bulk and awkwardness. But I suppose it is a sacrifice that must be made in order to bring about a desired end. And yes, there is none more benevolently self-sacrificing than I." Yes, this was turning out to be an excellent idea. But again . . . who to father such a child?

"A Djynn, perhaps?"

"Smoke, smoke. Weak, weak," Chatha said with a shake of his head.

"Well, it's better than a paralysis in the sunlight," Apep argued. The Djynn breed had a weakness in the face of the sun just like any other did. They dissolved into smoke at the touch of sunlight.

"Wraiths," Chatha offered with a giggle.

"Oh dear." Apep shuddered. "No, that won't do at all. Lycanthropes?"

Chatha turned to him with a face full of curiosity.

"What's that?"

"You know, *Lycanthropes*. Come to think of it . . . my son no better than a lowly beast?" Apep scoffed. "Disgusting. And Shadowdwellers are out of the question. One touch of any light and poof!" He made a clouding gesture with his hands, then was distracted by the polish on his nails. Such a pretty lavender color. Yes. He rather liked these modern embellishments.

"Lycanthropes?" Chatha asked again, truly perplexed.

"Oh yes. I had quite forgotten about the curse," Apep said with no little impatience.

He had toyed with the idea of dispelling the curse, shocking the nations into awareness and entertaining himself with the fallout, but then thought better of it. He would save that for a later amusement, if indeed he could dispel such powerful magic. He would certainly have to try at some point. If for no reason other than to prove his own power.

Or maybe he would imbue his son with the potential for that power! Yes! An exciting idea!

Oh, but then to wait so long for him to come of age.

"So many complications," he tsked aloud. "Demon?" he suggested to himself, perking up at the idea, but then he immediately wilted again. No. Growing increasingly weaker with every moment left in the sun? Comatose and helpless? No. Certainly not. Although, the power to be had when accessing the elements, a Demon's source of power, could be vast. It was without a doubt a worthy candidate, but not without its flaws.

Night Angel.

Again, Apep perked up. Yes. A Night Angel. Like that wicked little bitch who had set him back, seared him with his own power.

"I didn't like that at all," he muttered aloud.

All the more reason to have a son and ally, he reinforced the idea to himself. Together they could have destroyed that impudent thing! "My mind is quite made up," he said with a nod. Then he leaned in to inspect the arch of a perfectly groomed brow. "We're comely enough. We have very nice breasts. I could seduce a male to my side quite easily, I think. And now that I'm thinking on it, their weaknesses are really quite minimal. I hardly consider changing color in sunlight to be a weakness. Paired with the genetics of this body, and my own manipulations, the possibility is quite promising."

"Yup," Chatha agreed, and then he went back to his autopsy of a small white rabbit.

"Honestly, your obsession with the innards of things is almost worrisome," Apep tsked as he took down his

hair from its coif and arranged it softly around his graceful shoulders. "Yes. This should do quite well. Chatha,
I'll be back. I'm off to get impregnated. Do keep an eye
on things, won't you? There's a dear boy."

Faith sat upright suddenly. She had been dozing off,
the alteration in her form a very taxing thing and the
quiet of the company she was keeping a very boring
one. Not that she expected him to entertain her. It was
probably for the best all around, she had decided. The
less contact she or any Nightwalker had with mortals,
the better off things would be.

Her eyes had drifted closed not too shortly after that.

But suddenly the energy of power radiated into her
body, setting her hands alight with a bright tingling
sensation; the hands that were wrapped up snuggly into
the scarf. The Djynn's nik was becoming excited by the
nearness of its master.

"Slow down!" she cried out, unthinkingly reaching
out and placing a hand on strong, warm biceps. His
arm flexed beneath her touch and she could feel the rejection that went along with it without even looking at
his scroll or his face. She lifted her hand away as he
slowed the vehicle down and pulled over to the side of
the road. There was nothing. There was nothing to be
seen except the vast scrub of the wilderness and the
backdrop of the distant mountains.

"I can feel her nearness," she said when he looked at
her quizzically. "We're practically on top of her."

"Maybe that's because you are."

The voice came out of nowhere and was punctuated
with a tremendous clap of thunder. Storm clouds raced
across the sky, blotting out the sun so thoroughly that it
was ominous and dark.

Leo and Faith both jolted in surprise when a head full
of blond corkscrew curls popped up between them from

the rear window. The Djynn waved, her hand on the other side of the solid glass, her neck bisected by it as though the glass had chopped her neck clean through.

"Jesus Christ!" Leo exploded in shock. He reached for the door, throwing himself outside of the truck, his boots scuffing on the sand and gravel that had accumulated on the road. Faith followed him outside, watching as the Djynn pulled her head back through the glass, then stood upright in the bed of the truck and waved at them again.

"Hey there! It's nice to meet me, I know. Now give me my nik." She held out her hand, then thought better of it, jumped out of the truck bed and held out her hand again. "There, much easier to reach me this way."

"SingSing?" Faith asked.

"The one and only. How'd you get my nik? Give it here." She emphasized the extension of her hand with a little wiggle.

"The friend you left it with needs your help. She sent me with this," she held out the nik but kept it firmly wrapped around her hand, "to find you."

"George? You took this from George?"

"Uh . . . you left it with Docia," Leo spoke up, inching a little closer to the two women. But Faith could see he had the butt of his gun seated firmly in his hand . . . though he had not unholstered the weapon yet. Good thing, too. Djynn didn't take too kindly to threats. He narrowed sharp eyes on the Djynn. "But you know that," he said astutely. "You know exactly who you left it with. You're just testing us."

She grinned and shrugged a shoulder. "Can't be too careful these days. So what does Docia need? Does she have a *wish*?" The Djynn's eyes had widened with eagerness.

"No! No wishes," Faith said hastily, making sure she shot Leo a warning look.

"Oh c'mon," she whined a little. "This one's full of wishes. I can just smell it on him." She stepped closer to Leo and gave him two obvious sniffs. "And fear. I can smell fear."

"Fuck y—"

"SingSing!" Faith cried over Leo's potent verbosity. "We need a Djynn who can tether a severed soul back into its body. Can you do that?"

SingSing chuckled, seemingly unaware of the tiny dragon head that peeked out from among her curls. Faith hoped like hell Leo hadn't noticed it because he would very likely have a stroke.

"Oh no. I'm only Djinni caste and I'm nowhere near that strong. Only Marid could do that. Or Afreet. One or the other. Say, are you holding my nik hostage?"

"I'll give it to you," Faith said.

"Good!"

"As soon as you tell me where I can find a Marid Djynn."

"Not good," SingSing deflated with a frown. "Marid don't exactly advertise their locations, you know. There's a reason for that. They'd be like . . . constantly getting clients knocking on their piggy bank. Not that you don't want a client, because, then, what's the point of being a Djynn, right? But still, if you're kicked back in your hookah pipe and ding-dong, ding-dong! 'Hey can you grant me a wish?' I mean, that's not even including more intimate pasttimes that could be going on inside your canteen. I mean, who wants to be interrupted in the middle of *you know* . . . you know? Don't come a-knockin' if the canteen's a-rockin'!"

"Piggy . . . ?" Leo began, having a hard time following the rapid-fire deluge of thoughts that were spewing out of the diminutive little Djynn.

"What?" SingSing demanded, her face scrunching as she narrowed her eyes on Leo, "did you think we all lived in bottles or lamps? Bottles can be recycled these days and believe you me, there's nothing worse than waking up in a refuse reclamation facility. And lamps, of course, are so passé."

"O-of course," Leo agreed, looking a bit shell-shocked. Faith had to press her lips together to keep from looking too amused, but she realized her eyes had given her away when he looked at her and then immediately scowled. She supposed she should have warned him that Djynn were all a bit . . . quirky, each in their own way. But even for a Djynn, SingSing was absolutely effervescing with quirk.

"Are you saying you don't have any Djynn connections? You don't travel in Afreet or Marid circles?" Faith asked.

"I absolutely know several Marid and several more Afreet! Well," she deflated a little, "I know one Marid. Maybe two or three Afreet. Well, maybe *know* is stretching it a little, but all Djynn of all levels know their local Marid Sultan or Sultana. They're sort of like the king over all less powerful Djynn in their empire . . . or, well, *you* might call it a territory. Stop that!" She reached to gently flick the green-and-blue-headed dragon that had begun to wrestle and chew on one of the springy coils of her hair.

Yeah, Leo had definitely seen that.

"Is that a dragon?" he asked, pointing accusingly at the beast that had ignored its owner's wishes and was now enthusiastically tangling itself up in her hair.

"Dragon*let*," the Djynn said. She rolled her eyes. "A real dragon wouldn't play with my hair, it'd floss his teeth with it. You know, like, on the way to swallowing me for lunch? Actually, more like an appetizer. As a whole people are like sushi, you eat some and get hungry again about an hour later."

"Could we just stay focused?" Faith said hastily when

Leo went pale beneath his natural tan. She didn't blame him. Anyone who had never believed that anything magical or supernatural existed, only to be suddenly thrust into this world and watch it expand in all directions all at once, was bound to be a little intimidated. What was more, she could see that Leo was used to being in control of himself and being able to tackle anything thrown his way. For him, his reactions to these things, his paralyzing sense of fear, would be far more frustrating to him than anything else. "Considering what we're up against, it would probably be most efficient for you to point us in the direction of the Marid. We don't have time to hunt down a less powerful Afreet only to have him not capable of the task at hand."

"Well, that's going to be a little tricky. The best thing for you to do is to wish for it, then I could send you straight there." She smiled brightly, as if she were the most benevolent Djynn of all time.

"No wishing," Faith said firmly, knowing full well that wishing always came with a price to pay. Either in the right now or the later, there was *always* a price. And it was never a good idea to owe a Djynn from a wish.

"Then no Marid," she said, folding her arms over her chest and humphing loudly with exaggerated pique.

"Then no nik," Faith countered, holding up the scarf. She could only hope the power in the scarf made it a big enough bargaining chip.

"Fine. I don't need it." SingSing turned up her nose and spun her body away with another punctuating "humph!," as if to leave. But a quick, longing sideways glance at the nik gave her away. It was only a second before she turned back around. "It's just one little teensy tiny wish! I promise you won't owe me a thing."

That was a bald-faced lie. Djynn always lied about the quid pro quo of a wish. They couldn't help it. It was in their nature to bargain with all they had in order to close the deal on a wish. Sort of like a used-car salesman knowingly trying to push a lemon off his lot. Only in this case it didn't make her a bad person. It made her a Djynn acting one hundred percent in her nature.

"Thank you, but we'll find another way." This time Faith was the one to turn away. She sent Leo a look, and he took the cue instantly. He turned as well and they walked back to the truck.

"But that's mine!" the little Djynn whined. "It's not nice to take things that don't belong to you!"

"Then you shouldn't have left it lying around," Faith called back. "We'll just find another Djynn," she said in conversational tones to Leo. "I'm sure this nik is something they might like. Sorry to have bothered you!" she called out brightly to SingSing.

"Okay, stop!" the Djynn said as she materialized with a bounce right under their noses, startling them both. Now there were *two* dragonlet heads sticking out of her hair, as well as a tail. Whether it belonged to those two or any one of potentially dozens of others, there was no way of knowing. "What if I traded one of my dragonlets for it? He can show you the way to the Marid and I get my scarf back. There. Everyone's happy now, yes?"

"No deal," Faith said. "As soon as we turn our backs he'll just fly home again."

"Oh God. It has wings?" Leo said.

"Of course it does! It's a *dragonlet*, duh!" SingSing huffed in frustration and both dragonlets immediately folded their arms over their chests and huffed as well. "Fine. You drive a hard bargain," she said, frowning intently. "Now give it to me." She held out a demanding hand.

"Yeah, right," Leo said. "I don't think so. The minute you get it you'll go poof and disappear. Or you'll send us to a hut in the middle of the Gobi desert. Or you'll keep your word, send us to the Marid, but yank us back again a second later."

Faith smiled. Leo Alvarez was a very smart man. He was definitely getting the picture now. She had to concede that he was very clever when he next addressed the Djynn.

"How about we hold on to your nik," Leo said, "keep it safe and sound, and we'll give it to you when we get back."

Faith had to admit, he was pretty good at thinking fast on his feet. But she had to consider that men like him didn't survive the things he had been forced to survive without having some pretty ballsy skills.

"Yes. What he said," she said, backing him up completely.

"No way. If you bring a nik with you in the presence of another Djynn he'll totally take it away from you."

"He's already a Marid," Faith argued. "Surely this little nik would mean nothing to him." She dangled the scarf again.

"If you believe that, then you don't know Djynn very well," SingSing groused.

"Well enough to keep this safe," Faith said. "I know that he cannot forcibly rip this from my hands, and he cannot use magic to take it from me. A nik has to be handed over voluntarily as long as someone else is in physical possession of it. If it's found lying around that's another story, but as long as we're holding on to this the Marid Djynn can't take it from us."

SingSing chewed on her lip thoughtfully. "Okay, I'll do it. But don't you let him have my nik or you'll have one seriously pissed off Djynn to deal with. And I might not be a Marid or an Afreet, but I'm definitely stronger than a little human," she pointed to Leo, "and even a Night Angel." Her pointing finger shifted accordingly.

"I don't doubt that in the least," Leo said, his tone

and expression conveying serious agreement, his glance going pointedly to the darkened skies. Only Faith could see the word on his scroll that told her he was being mostly patronizing.

Then again, there was definitely a part of him that was all too serious about knowing how weak he was in the grand scheme of the things he was navigating of late. She could tell that he had experienced the world of the supernatural in a very unfriendly manner. It was very much the seat of his hostility toward her. But she hoped he would come to realize that there were the good and the bad in the supernatural races just like there were the good and the bad in the human race.

"Well then, we're agreed. But I feel the need to warn you. The Sultan of the Western states is, well, very old and very clever and very . . . bored. And a bored Djynn of any power is a bad, bad thing. They thrive on their urges to entertain themselves at the expense of others. And believe me when I tell you there are hundreds of ways they can think up to do that and there's no telling exactly which he'll use on you if he does. Just don't say I didn't warn you."

Faith looked over at Leo, the question in her eyes long before she said, "Are you sure you want to do this? I can do this by myself if you don't want—"

"No, I'm very sure I don't want to deal with any of this," he said sharply. "But it's here and I'm in it and there's nothing I can do about that, so count me in."

"If you want, you could maybe make a wish," Sing-Sing wheedled. She narrowed her focus on Leo. "You could maybe wish not to remember ever having met a single paranormal entity. You would forget everything that's happened to you, to date, that is associated with a paranormal creature."

"No!" they both cried in unison. Faith looked at him in surprise. She wouldn't have thought he would resist a temptation like that so quickly and definitively. She could tell just looking at him that this world had been the crux of whatever trauma it was that he had suffered. Djynn had a knack for ferreting out what someone wanted most in the world, and she knew that somewhere in there was the ultimate in temptations for Leo.

"All right then. As long as you're sure. Tie that nik around your neck or wrist or something. He can't take it from you, but he can trick you into dropping it if he wants to."

Faith did as instructed, looping the pretty thing around her neck and tying it on in a low knot that rested on her breastbone.

"Okey doke!" SingSing said, dusting off her hands and wriggling her fingers dramatically. "Off you go!"

And off they went.

CHAPTER SIX

Leo felt himself dissolving in a tingly numbing sensation. It was as though he had become a carbonated beverage, popping little bubbles of himself into the air. And then he resolved just as slowly, just as sparkling, until he was solid again and feeling incredibly heavy in his normal weight and body after having felt so light.

The first thing he did was look for Faith, to make certain she had arrived just as safely and that she was nearby. He exhaled a silent sigh of relief when he saw her. He was reluctant to admit it, but having her near him made him feel a little safer somehow. She had certainly proved her supernatural expertise as she had navigated the tricky dealings with the diminutive little Djynn. His reluctance came with letting himself think for a single second that dealing with these creatures was safe on any level. He was determined to keep his guard up and do whatever he could to keep his head above water and protect himself, for what that was worth considering he was seriously outgunned.

He looked around and was absolutely shocked to find himself in front of a gingerbread house. Well, not made of gingerbread and candy, but it was a large, colorful house with clapboard siding painted pastel colors. Purple on the casings of some windows, pink on others. The main breadth of the house was sunshine yellow, but the garage was sky blue and the upper floors were minty green. There were white scalloped edges framing just about everything, especially the roof, every window was tinted with color . . . and it was obvious from an up close position that you couldn't see inside the house through the glass. He could only assume it was polarized like the house in New Mexico. The driveway was made of white stone kept one hundred percent in a perfect stripe. There was, literally, a white picket fence about two feet high all along the front edge of the property. However, it did not escape his notice that the fence to the backyard was over six feet in height, but picketed just the same. The other difference was while the pickets in the front fence were wide apart from each other, the pickets in the back fence were set so close together that there wasn't a single hint of light passing through them.

Leo heard Faith sigh in a hard exhalation and he looked at her. Instantly he reached out for her, a helping hand because it was obvious she was unsteady and, he suspected, in pain. It was hard to determine with her universally white pallor, but he could somehow sense she was sickened and hurting.

"What's wrong?" he asked, moving closer to her so he could lean her up against his body. She was a tall, strong woman, and he felt that eddying into him in spite of her weakened state.

"Night Angels don't teleport well. Most Nightwalkers don't in my experience. Magic is such a tricky thing."

"As opposed to what *you* can do? That's not magic?"

"No," she said, exhaling another soft sigh. "What we do is innate. In our genetics. Born to us. What Djynn do, that ability to tap into magic, that's innate . . . but the magic itself is in the niknaks. They draw the power from them, accumulating it and using it. I've always

thought that they were the only Nightwalker for whom
magic is not a negative aspect to be avoided at all costs.
Not to themselves anyway. It's almost like they can filter the negative properties out somehow."

Leo found himself nodding even though he wasn't
sure he fully understood. He was still getting used to
the idea that all of these things . . . genies and dragonlets and *all* of it were *real*. And to make things worse,
having been fascinated by mythology and mythical beings when he had been younger, he had a vast recollec-
tion of hundreds of creatures and their abilities. Were
they all real? What was fact and what was fiction, he
wondered, his gut tightening even more than it already
was. An interesting feat considering he felt like a head
to toe knot of tension.

"Better now?" he asked after a minute of letting her
catch her breath. "I don't know how long we'll go un-
noticed standing here. We kind of stand out. Well," he
smiled sheepishly, "I do in any event."

She shot him a look that said "And I don't?"

"I'm just a lowly mortal, and you're, well, not. Besides, you're white. It goes with the motif." He lifted a
brow toward the house.

"Ha. Ha," she said dryly. But she smiled in spite of
herself and gave him a chuckle. Leo looked farther
around, noticing that they were in what one might call
an average suburban neighborhood . . . if the neighborhood was made out of gingerbread houses. The lawn
ornamentations alone were going to put him into sugar
shock. Everything was just so . . . sweet. Little kittens
frolicking in the lawn, gnomes and lawn jockeys standing to stalwart attention. It might as well have been
made out of candy after all. Then again, there was a
house a little ways down the road that looked very
gingerbready. Good thing he hated gingerbread or he

might have been tempted to take a bite . . . just for shits and giggles.

"Well, let's start the next leg of the magical mystery tour," he invited her, gesturing for her to precede him. She leaned her weight into him in a silent indication that they should head up the drive together, side by side. Their proximity to each other made him realize a few things. One, she was just about as tall as he was, and two, she radiated that delicious smell of cinnamon and nutmeg. Christmas, he thought suddenly. She smelled like the scrumptiousness of Christmas desserts.

A few other palatable observations struggled for his attention, but he pushed it all away. He could never forget what she was, he reminded himself sternly. Even though the powder soft white of her complexion screamed how different she was, he felt he needed reminding just the same. As it was, looking at her was no longer followed with a feeling of shock, that sensation the limited human psyche felt whenever it saw something so far out of the norm that it had a hard time processing it. It was the next step in desensitization, he realized. Get bombarded with something extraordinary for long enough it would start to feel quite ordinary.

Wherever they were, it was windy and cold. Like, on the brink of snow cold. He could smell it on the air and because neither of them was wearing coats, they most certainly felt it on their skin.

"Where the hell are we?" he asked aloud.

"I'm guessing the Northern states?" But it was more a question than it was an answer.

"Maybe. It's still winter. On the tail end of it, but still enough to account for the cold. But there's no snow on the ground."

"Yet," she said looking up at the sky. "Soon."

"I'd kill for my cellphone right now," he said.

"Why didn't you bring it?" She was all curiosity,

nothing accusing or insulting in the question. Another woman would have whined or possibly outright bitched about a cellphone being left behind, as well as whatever else struck their minds. It said something about how much of an impatient, intolerant world it was that they lived in, and how much being used to complaining was a part of it. But *she* didn't complain. She took everything in stride . . . even his erratic behaviors; of which there had been many in their short time together.

"I . . . lost it," he said, not bothering to explain how it had been lost. That it had been in his hand the day Chatha had jumped him. He hadn't gotten around to replacing it just yet.

"What would you do with it anyway?"

The question seemed to take him off guard. Why did he want it? Was he looking for some kind of lifeline before putting his neck out? Even if it wasn't to call anyone specific, but just the sensation of being connected to the outside world? He answered her question with a shrug, and as usual she simply accepted it.

They stopped and both of them looked at the door, then at each other.

"So . . . we ring the bell and say what?" Leo asked. "Hey, are you a genie? Can I see your bottle?"

She pressed back a smile, but it shone in her eyes just the same.

"They don't like being called genies," she said. "Especially not at this level."

"But I thought SingSing was a genie level Djynn."

"It's a caste system. And its Djinni, spelled D-J-I-N-N-I with a blend of the d and j at the beginning."

"I get it. How about I leave all discussions with magical beings to you?" he suggested grimly.

"Oh, I don't know," she replied, that smile in her voice again. "You held your own against SingSing admirably well."

He didn't reply, reaching out instead to ring the fuchsia-colored doorbell.

Fuchsia? Really? Come on now, he thought with a mental eye roll.

It took a minute, and another ring of the doorbell, but someone finally came to the door. When the door opened there was no one there . . . above four and a half feet. Looking down they discovered a tiny old woman, so small she hardly looked more real than the garden gnomes at the end of the drive. She wore a blue and white gingham dress, a string of pearls, a pair of reading glasses on her nose, and a garish red lipstick on her lips. In one aspect it was exactly what he would have expected to find behind the door of a house that looked like this. On the other hand . . . no one could possibly predict anything in this world he was flailing to tread water in. He refused to be taken in by innocent sheep's clothing ever again. He had turned his back on Chatha because of his Down syndrome appearance, and it had cost him dearly. It was a mistake he would never make again.

"Yes?" she asked, her voice sounding disused and gentle. "May I help you?"

Leo didn't know what to do next, a feeling he was becoming increasingly familiar with. Something inside of him remembered his mother smacking him in the back of the head for mouthing off to old Mrs. Wheederman down the street, but it was severely contrasting with a long adulthood of knowing anyone could be the next threat.

"Where is he?" Faith asked.

The question was flat and cold, brooking no nonsense, and for once he was grateful to have someone else take the lead. Which was funny because one of the problems he'd had when he'd been an Army Ranger had been the chain of command. A total moron who had somehow put in enough tenure to become a major was giving orders, often with bullying connotations, just so he could feel like his erection was the biggest one in town? Yeah. Not Leo's idea of a good time and certainly not his idea of how to take care of business.

"Who do you mean, dear? There's no one here but me."

Leo could read people really well, and he'd have been tempted to believe her, but that was his mother and that sting on the back of his head talking.

"Let's not play games. I really don't have the time," Faith said, her hand coming to rest on the door. She leaned her weight into it pushing the woman back a few inches.

"You better back off, missy," she said sharply to Faith, "or I'll be calling the authorities!"

"I said—!"

"That's a pretty shade of lipstick you're wearing."

Faith's head veered around and the look she gave him was stupefied, pure and simple.

"Really? You like it?" The old woman preened. Literally preened. Then a rattling sort of chuckle erupted out of her. "It's called Hussy Red!"

"It goes well with your dress and your . . ." He paused when he realized she was wearing red shoes. Ruby slippers, to be exact. ". . . shoes. My friend didn't mean to be rude," he continued, "but we are in . . . someone's in trouble and we were told we could find some help here."

"Well, I could call the authorities," she said helpfully, but she stepped back and let the door open wider. "That's about all I can do for you. Can I get you something? Some sweet tea maybe?"

"That sounds lovely," Leo said, but he was talking to her back and they were stepping into the foyer. A quick look around showed a home exactly like one he would have pictured for a sweet little old lady. A little china tea set on a low table. TV dinner trays . . . one with medications lined up neatly on it. A recliner that clearly got a lot of use with a doily on its back. There was a fat gray cat snoozing on top of the doily.

"What are you—?"

"Shh," he said softly, reaching to squeeze Faith's hand in a gentle signal that she should trust him. He realized what he was doing an instant later and after a startled look into her slightly widening eyes, he drew back from her. Strangely enough, her warmth didn't disappear from its place against his fingertips as quickly as it should have. He found himself wiping his palm surreptitiously down over the thigh of his jeans.

"Here you go. Some sweet tea," she said, a glass for each of them in her hands.

"Thank you," they said in unison as they reached for the glasses.

Sweet tea.

"Is that a touch of the South I hear in your voice, ma'am?" he asked her. Of course, he didn't hear anything of the kind, but sweet tea was the knee-jerk drink of choice in the South and he suspected there was some import to her offering it, even if he didn't exactly know what he was dealing with. But this was clearly a series of hoops they were meant to leap through, and he was willing to play the game for the moment. And this hoop, it seemed, was based strongly in their politeness to this old woman.

"Why yes, yes it is!" she said, a southern drawl magically appearing in her tone. "Now what is it you nice people want from me? Shall I call the authorities?"

Not police. Authorities.

"Would you do that for us? Call the authorities?"

"Why yes. Of course. Let me get my phone. Now you drink up!"

"Don't drink it," they whispered in unison to each other once she'd left the room. Leo met her eyes with surprise, finding her just as astonished as he was by the way they seem to be hitting the same notes together.

Leo looked over his shoulder for the fifth time since entering the house, the crawl of nervousness over the back of his scalp a constant sensation it seemed. He had learned the hard way not to turn his back on anyone, and ever since then it had been a constant thing for him, this hyper vigilance. He wanted to see it as a good thing, an added awareness that would keep him from ending up . . .

Leo pushed the thought away before it was birthed. Now was not the time for self-reflection. There was a great deal of danger in what he was doing. He had no idea why he was here, why he was risking his neck for . . . for what? For whom? Did he even know? Did he really know if the man he had left in that bed was the friend he had known since boyhood? Or was he just holding on to something that was already gone?

"There. The authorities are on the way," the old woman said. "You haven't drunk your tea," she noted with a frown.

"I'm not thirsty, thank you," Faith said, leaning to place the glass on a nearby table.

"I wouldn't do that if I were you."

Faith froze as the threat in her words and tone came through loud and clear.

"I beg your pardon," Faith said just as sharply.

"I've had about enough of you, missy," the old woman said with obvious agitation. "You're rude and ungrateful, that's what you are."

"We're sorry," Leo jumped in. "We're just very worried about our friend."

"Now that's not entirely true, is it?"

This time it was Leo's turn to still. He narrowed his attention on her, the feel of his gun itching against his spine. It was an instinct, a reaction he had always trusted.

"You're not even sure you want to be here. Not sure you would even call him a friend."

Leo swallowed. The anxiousness that crawled up his chest was painful and once again he felt the need to look to his back.

"That may be true," he said, his words a little forceful as he made them leave his mouth, "but it doesn't follow that he doesn't deserve to be saved."

"Interesting. Now, why don't you drink up," she suggested again. "I doubt you'll find what you're looking for otherwise."

Leo looked to Faith and hoped she could see the word that indicated his feelings of the moment. Capitulation. Alice, he realized, would not have gone on her adventure if she'd never given in to the request of a simple bottle. However, as he raised his glass to his lips, he could not make himself drink. He broke out in a cold sweat, his breath suddenly hard to catch.

"Fuck," he said in a wild burst. He was about to slam the glass down and walk out, but Faith reached out to him, touched his wrist, met his eyes. He didn't know why it should matter, didn't know why it should make him feel a sense of calm, make his heart slow, his breathing even out, but it did. She did. Something in that simple touch and the look of understanding in her eyes made him relax in a way he had not been able to since this whole fucked-up journey into the paranormal had begun.

He watched her lift her glass to her lips, and barely take a sip before she suddenly dissolved away from before his eyes.

And, still not knowing why, he followed suit.

Faith felt like she was falling. A dizzy, sickening feeling. Falling slowly at first, then more quickly, gaining speed. Like Alice and her rabbit hole, potentially the truth to the myth of that story. Maybe Lewis Carroll had fallen down a similar rabbit hole and it had been an experience retold in a child's tale. But this time she was the one falling, falling into the past where so much had shaped her through the years, and then falling into the future. A future of laughter and pain. Of delight and desire. A future of infinite possibilities.

CHAPTER SEVEN

Faith awoke in bed next to her lover, feeling his heat along the length of her body, his naked skin smooth and warm in places, hot and furred with crisp hairs in others. The hair on his body surprised her every single time she saw it. Every time she felt it. Before him she had known only Night Angel lovers, and Night Angels were free of body hair. She reached out and touched his chest, touched the springy curls.

"You're obsessing about my hair again," he said with a sleepy smile, making her laugh because he knew her so well. He reached for her, drawing the full length of her tighter to his body. Her skin was instantly seared with his heat. Night Angel lovers were so much cooler to the touch, or so it seemed in her retrograde memory. Maybe it was just the way she burned so hot for him, the way just the anticipation of him made her soft and wet.

"Leo," she breathed as his mouth brushed over hers. How was it that every time felt like the first time? How was it that she felt that curl of anxiety and anticipation every single time he was going to kiss her, wondering if he would, hoping beyond hope that he wouldn't change his mind. It didn't matter that he was only human. It never had. Not for her. And though, in the beginning, he had mistrusted her and her innate power, that was long past them now.

"Faith, give me your mouth, I find I'm famished for it this morning." He suddenly rolled over her, sliding her beneath him, placing himself right between her thighs as she braced her feet against the mattress. He was hard and hot against her, cradling himself into everything that was wet and warm that she had to offer him. Her hands ran down his sides, the play of the muscles under his skin breathtakingly powerful. He was no Nightwalker, but he was a prime physical specimen of his own species and that was more than enough for her.

Then, finally, he kissed her. The long, sweet, toe-curling kind of kiss that could bring tears to a woman's eyes, because she knew that it meant he loved her with every fiber of his being. The kind of kiss that erased all doubt, if there ever was any, and solidified confidence. He was hers and he wanted no one else but her.

Then she was gasping for breath as he lifted away from her, cradled her face between his hands and looked at her in the way that told her he was just as floored sometimes by his feelings for her as she was for him.

"I think you're going to have to let me marry you," he said, the thought obviously surprising him as well. "I never thought I'd see the day I'd say that, never thought I'd trust anyone enough or find anyone who could understand a bitter, worn-out mercenary like me, but from the moment I met you you've been putting me in my place and proving me wrong. So . . . I think I'm going to have to make you marry me. And I may even want kids," he said with wonder. "Holy hell."

"You always said . . . but . . ." Faith was utterly floored by his declaration, "you always said you never wanted to be that close to anyone . . . to put anyone in the line of fire that could be used against you." And to venture into the possibility of a child? She hardly knew where to start when it came to a suggestion like that. There would be a lot of bravery required on both their parts in order for that discussion to take place.

"Faith, if there's anything I've learned, anything I've come to understand, it's that you would give anyone who threatened your loved ones a ferocious fight. You're not human. You're not under threat by humans. You face much worse than that every day from other species. What I mean is, I can't spend my freedom in a cage of fear. You've taught me that. Everything I fight for, the code I live by, it means nothing if I can't reap what I sow."

Faith couldn't help herself. Tears entered her eyes. He'd finally realized that he had to let someone, anyone, close to him or nothing would be worthwhile. He'd had that once. With Jackson and Docia. But that had all changed when they became Bodywalkers and he had felt that he had to keep a cautious distance from them. That had cost them all very dearly, and now there was no way of going back and fixing it. But he could move on into a new future. Maybe now he would stop hurting himself with his cautious aloofness and finally let others in. Let the need to trust come back to life within him.

"Don't make offers you don't plan to follow through with," she said, caution of her own shining through. It was a lot to take in, seemingly so sudden. But the more she raced through her thoughts, the more she realized that it wasn't all that sudden after all.

"I never make an offer I don't mean to follow through with to the very end," he said with no little intensity. "Just like I never take a job without finishing it. You know that."

"I know that," she agreed with breathless wonder and a cautious dose of fear as she looked up into his serious dark eyes and knew her life was about to change forever. "I think I'm going to have to marry you," she agreed, "just to make you prove it."

"I'd rather you do it because you love me . . . *and* because you're hot for my body," he said with a grin she barely caught sight of before he lowered his head to her chest and pressed an open mouthed kiss to her breastbone, a soft, wet touch of his tongue on her skin stroking her as if he were kissing her on her mouth. He moved a few inches lower and did it again, then lower again, to the point between her breasts, and did it once more.

She felt the touches soul-deep, felt her breasts go taut and tight in anticipation. She knew what she wanted, what he would give her, just as he always did, always as if *he* were able to read *her* scroll and the words burning across it. She could see the words burning across his right then, and it made tears sting her eyes. It was one thing for her to know what he was feeling via his scroll, and something else entirely for him to admit to it.

He moved to the point of her breast, breathing over her once, twice, glancing up at her with mischief in his eyes as he taunted her and didn't follow through.

"You always finish what you promise to do," she reminded him breathlessly. "So if you're trying to make me fret it won't work."

"Oh, I'll finish it. The question is . . . when."

He smiled, mischief curling up one side of his lips and lighting his eyes. He lowered his attention back to the smooth violet blackness of her nipple. Even though he was somewhat dark-skinned himself, he looked shockingly light in contrast to the blackness of her. It was a contrast that always took her breath away for some reason. Perhaps because it was a reminder of how different they were, and how much that didn't matter to either of them.

His lips touched her nipple, his tongue fluttering out against her. He knew she was ten times more sensitive there than a human woman might be. It was one reason why she disliked wearing clothes and avoided it whenever she could. So he knew that just the gentle sucking sensation he was gracing her with was like pouring a sweet acid into her body, the burn scorching her straight from her breast to her already wet sex. He was already pressed into that wetness, his hard erection lying there hot and ready and dormant of action. Frustratingly so. She tried to lift her hips, tried to encourage him into her body, but he reached a strong hand down and pushed her back down against the bed.

He tsked. "Don't rush me. It's hard enough keeping my head on straight around you as it is. I don't need you wriggling around toying with my self-control."

And to teach her the lesson, he snatched up a brightly colored scarf from the table, wove it around her wrists and tied her to the spindle of their headboard in record time.

"There, that should keep you from rushing me." That said, he slid his mouth back down over her throat, came around to the sweet spot beneath her ear where he knew the barest touch of his tongue made an erotic heat go tumbling through her, playing her like a well remembered instrument. He brushed his lips along the line of her shoulder and then directly down to her other as-yet unattended breast, making her groan with desire and frustration. "Leo, please," she begged him.

He ignored her, replacing his mouth with the toying of his fingers as he slid down her body, moving himself away from the heated core of her body.

"You're going in reverse," she all but whined at him, her body undulating beneath his in frustration. But again, he would not be rushed. Instead, he replaced the weight and heat of his erection with the darting heat of his tongue and the teasing touch of his mouth. But the teasing didn't last long. He pressed into her, his tongue swiping hard over her sensitive clitoris. Even though her clit was set farther back . . . closer to the entrance of her vagina . . . than a human female's would be, he had known how to find it from the very start. He had delighted in the difference, remarking on what a clever design improvement it was because it meant that every stroke in or out of her would drag him across the sensitive flesh.

Very sensitive flesh. It was as highly sensitive as her nipples were, so the swirling tease and tasting of his tongue was driving her mad, driving her to the brink of an orgasm . . . and then beyond. She whipped into the orgasm, crying out, her hands ripping free of her light bondage and diving into the thickness of his short hair, her fingers trying to clutch at the strands and finding herself frustrated as usual. He was moving back up her body now, coming back to her mouth and showing impatience at last as he settled himself against her once more.

"God, how I love to hear you cry out my name when you come," he said roughly as he kissed her for all he was worth. She hadn't even realized she'd called for him, hadn't remembered what sounds she had made. It made her head spin, as did the feel of him easing into her. They groaned in pleasure together at the intimate relief of the connection. She was tight around him, as usual. It was another difference, her channel made more resilient than that of her human counterparts. Whatever his use of her, she would come back to virginal tightness every single time. A flaw in the design in some aspects. It was one reason why childbirth in her breed was so incredibly difficult.

But for now he was using her tightness to excite himself, stroking hastily back and forth within her, immediately finding a rhythm. She clutched his shoulders, hugged him tightly to her, opened her mouth against the strong column of his neck and held him with the light pressure of her teeth. Lucky for her he had never minded her urge to nip and gnaw at him during sex. In fact, she'd dare to say it excited him all the more now.

And she knew something else that excited him, too. With each thrust forward into her she let her wings surreptitiously extend through the mattress, and then she reached forward and curved them around him. Then with his next inward thrust, she wrapped them up against his skin.

"God!" he ejected harshly, his pace changing, becoming rapid and hard and a little bit wild. Oh yes, she knew how powerfully arousing the contact with her wings was for him. It had been that way from almost the first time they'd ever touched.

Good! She thought feverishly. She wanted this. Wanted to feel him whipping into a frenzy, losing control, loving her that much. He cried out again, this time all sound and no coherent words. He forced her back into the pillows, made her look into his dark, beautiful eyes, made her see the love and fire he felt for her. And just as tears of joy burned into her eyes, he came in an explosion of heat, holding himself to her tightly, his body locked hard into the commotion running like a riot through them both.

When he released her, it was like the release of a great sigh, their bodies relaxing in unison, their breath coming hard and fast and without hope of slowing with any immediacy. He was back to looking into her eyes, back to dragging his fingertips through her hair at her temples, back to making her feel like she was the only woman in the world.

One year later . . .

Faith screamed, the agony ripping through her killing her slowly, convincing her that her flesh was being torn apart. She wanted it to end more than anything in the world, tears weeping freely from her eyes. She wasn't ashamed to cry. Anyone would cry under such agony.

"Easy," Leo said softly, his eyes snaring hers, making her look into him just as he had always done. It had always been her focal point, her peaceful place. The comfort of knowing she was no longer alone in the world . . . would never be alone again. "You're almost there," he assured her. But he could not hide the worry ghosting through him from her. He looked up at the woman kneeling between Faith's feet, her hands against her in counter pressure, trying to ease some of her pain.

"The child is almost here. The way is clear and I am not worried," the midwife said, reassuring them both. So many Night Angel females died from childbirth. It had been a source of fear for them both throughout the long months of her pregnancy, however much they had tried to reassure each other otherwise. It was the weakest moment, the most exposed a Night Angel female could possibly be.

Faith screamed as new pain tore through her, this one worse than all the ones before. Her fear returned in a rage of emotion.

"It doesn't feel right!" she cried, panic hurting her heart and laboring lungs. There was another possibility. The child inside her might not survive the birthing process. Whatever happened to her, losing her child absolutely couldn't happen, she thought feverishly. Leo would never be the same if something like that were to happen. After all he had been through, after so much pain and loss in his life, she wasn't sure he would be able to open himself up again after an additional loss of that magnitude.

"You must relax and trust me. I would tell you if

there was trouble. What you are feeling is the child erupting past your cervix. It is the most painful part of labor, but now it is time for you to push."

"I feel it!" she cried. Leo moved behind her, helping her to sit up and push into the labor pain. He leaned into it with her, his breathing just as fast and worried as hers. The midwife grabbed the purple-colored scarf they had rested at her feet, looping it around Faith's wrists and through her hands and pulling her forward and into her first push. Together the three of them pushed forward, bending her toward her knees, helping her to push with all of her might.

After nearly another hour of that hard, pushing labor, the child slipping free of her body was the most relieving sensation Faith had ever known. She cried out with the reprieve of it, tears of pain and relief warring for release. But the tears did not fall until she saw her child in the midwife's hands, being lifted toward her, screaming with the angry indignity of being ejected from the safe confines of her uterus.

"Oh," she wept and cooed, reaching to take her daughter in her hands. "Oh now. I know. I know it was so hard. But you're here now." She cradled the baby to her breast and felt Leo hard at her back. She heard him sob softly, and then his hands reached to cradle the top of the baby's head.

"Jesus, Faith. Look what we did." He fought for composure and lost, tears dropping over his whisker rough face and onto her shoulder. Onto their child.

"I know. I know," she agreed, holding their daughter up farther into his hands. She was a black wriggly little thing, but it was a fair black, like a dusty charcoal. She was clearly a Night Angel and would one day grow her wings, but she was also part human, part Leo, and who knew what that would mean for her.

Six months later . . .

Leo panicked.

There was no other way to describe the feeling when he walked into the house and found his wife and his baby missing, the signs of a fight everywhere. He tore through the house looking for them, but already knew he would not find them.

Good. Good, he thought. If they weren't there it meant they were still alive. Whoever had them wanted them for a reason. To control him, he acknowledged grimly. It was his worst nightmare come to life. He went back into their bedroom, breathing hard, trying to make his mind work. He found her scarf on the bed and swept it up into his hands. He twisted the silken fabric, the bright color of it almost garish as he struggled to tamp down his fear. He tried to think who it could be, then realized suddenly he knew exactly who it was, exactly who would sink that low.

Marissa. She had been the bane of their existence ever since they had failed in their mission to save Jackson's life. She had blamed them both and her vengeance had been virulent. She had promised to never rest until she saw them hurt the way she had hurt when Jackson's life had bled away, one soul into the actual death, and one into the Ether, consigned there for another hundred years, leaving her alone and desolate.

In a way part of him understood her grief now. He understood it most keenly that very instant. The loss of either his wife or his child would be something he couldn't imagine surviving. Just the thought of it sent fear ripping down the center of his soul. And this was exactly what she had wanted him to feel.

Keep it together. Keep your head, he warned himself fiercely.

But what could he do to battle someone of Marissa's

power when he was merely human, utterly defenseless and without recourse in the face of her wrath?

He realized it didn't matter. He would offer himself up to her, which was exactly what she wanted. He knew one of them would die today, but he would be damned if it was going to be either Faith or the baby.

Tying her scarf into his belt loop, wearing it like a knight would wear his lady's colors before entering the field of battle, he went into the basement, taking the stairs three at a time. He walked past the reloading press and the digital gunpowder scale he used to make his own bullets, then headed straight to his gun safe. He'd never had a safe before the baby had been born, but things had had to change along with a lot of his ways of dealing with the world. Ever since Faith had come into his life. But one thing that had not changed, that would never change, was that he knew with cold truth what evil there was in the world. Evil that had almost destroyed him. And not just on a physical level. He would have been able to tolerate the physical destruction of his body. Had even anticipated it, never once thinking he would die a natural death after a long lifetime and a tenure as an old man.

But Chatha had nearly obliterated his mind, nearly eradicated who he was at his heart. If not for Faith, there was no telling what would have become of him. He would have descended into a dark hole, become something else. Become something he would have hated.

He keyed the safe, pressing his thumb to the scanner for the fast release fingerprint combination. The safe clicked open and he pulled the heavy door forward. Not many people had a gun safe big enough to walk into, but then again, he was not many people. They had built the house around this safe. It couldn't possibly have been brought into the basement otherwise.

In a rack, above the assault weaponry, were his handguns, both the collectible and the serviceable. He passed over the shiny stuff and went right for the cold stone killers. He grabbed his gun belt, the weight and style of it almost exactly like the ones most law enforcement used, but with a few personalized tweaks. No cop would be walking around with seven spare clips along his back. Handcuffs were in their usual place, but in a loop at the rear of his hip was a bunch of zip ties. There was nothing handier that a strong zip tie, he had discovered over time.

He changed out the spare ammo on the preloaded belt, however, to armor-piercing ordnance. They would get through just about anything, and then cause as much damage as possible once they hit flesh. As powerful as she was, Marissa still had a human, mortal body. She could be killed. It was just a matter of whether he would be able to get some rounds off before she saw him coming. But with Faith and the baby in the mix, she would definitely be expecting him. After all, that was the whole point, wasn't it?

He slung the belt around his hips and put his Desert Eagle into the holster. But that was just his first backup. His second backup, a Glock G29 10mm, was strapped around his ankle in a holster. Then he shrugged into his shoulder holster and grabbed his primary weapon. It was a Smith & Wesson 500. It used 50 caliber bullets and he had made damn sure four of his spare cartridges were loaded with the beastly armor-piercing rounds he had made for it.

Yes, she could die just like any other human if enough damage was done too quickly for her extraordinary healing processes to work, but he was more worried about the Gargoyles that protected the property. Their ability to turn to stone made them nearly invulnerable.

Nearly. Fifty caliber bullets would take a hell of a bite out of them no matter what they were made of. They too could be killed, he'd learned some time ago, it just took a lot to pull it off.

He didn't care. He'd use every skill he had, every bullet he'd ever made, to get his daughter and wife back.

Then he grabbed his assault rifle and a flack jacket with flash bang and tear gas grenades attached to it, and left in search of his family.

"I swear to God, Marissa," he said, his breathing heavy and his whole body shaking with the agony of the injuries he had sustained. "I'll kill you where you stand. *Give me my family.*"

His family was locked behind glass in an enclosure about thirteen feet by thirteen feet, a few mere strides away from him. But Marissa stood between him and them, in spite of a bullet wound that had hit just to the left of her heart. He'd used the 10mm to do it, having burned through all but half a cartridge for the S & W 500, and he needed that half cartridge to blow that glass apart and get them back off the property. All he could do was pray no more Gargoyles materialized. And they would in time, so he had to hurry and get this done.

"I'll kill you where you stand first," Marissa hissed at him, the fever of her rage and hatred burning in her eyes. He knew the feeling well. She looked utterly unfazed by the promise of death he held targeted onto her forehead. One clean headshot and it would all be over.

But he couldn't kill her because she held a remote control in her hand, her thumb pressing down on a dead man's switch. If he shot her, the instant she let go his family would fall victim to whatever it was that she had rigged up to murder them. Faith was kneeling on the floor of the glass room, their child clutched to her bosom. She was weeping . . . no, sobbing uncontrollably and rocking forward and back in some kind of attempt to comfort herself. He had never seen her like this, not even during the terrifying and long labor she had endured while in fear for her and her baby's life. It wasn't like her to fall apart like this. It made his mind race with fear and anger, made him wonder what had been done to her.

"Just give me my family and we'll both just walk away from this," he lied. There was no way he was going to let an open threat remain alive, especially someone with her position of power and endless resources. There would be no rest for him and his, no safe harbor, unless he ended this here and now.

"You're going to know what it feels like to lose everything you love," she said, "and I'm going to watch while it happens." She held up the remote tauntingly. "Prepare for the worst moment of your life."

"*Puta,* the worst moment of my life has already happened, believe you me. And if you throw that switch you'll never have the chance to enjoy my pain, which I know is why you're doing this."

"My enjoyment is in the knowing. My delight is in using my empathy powers to feel the raging, painful emotions you are both suffering this very instant. And I can watch your agony from the Ether as well. I do not need this body for that. Do you think I'm afraid of death? If you kill me you will send me back to my beloved who waits for me in the Ether. I will win this day no matter what you do, Leo. Now say goodbye to your wife."

Leo exhaled and prayed with every fiber of his being. *Please, God, let me be fast enough.*

He pulled the trigger three times. Once to blow up her hand and the remote within it, once to send her brains blowing out the back of her head, and once to shoot the glass keeping him from his family. All within a single breath of time.

Glass shattered and fell. He had been afraid it was

bulletproof, and was relieved to find it was not. But he did not take even an instant to enjoy his victory because until he got them out of that room, until he could pull Faith and the baby out of there, he couldn't so much as blink. Shooting a dead man's switch was no guarantee that the signal would not be sent. He had to get them before they could be harmed by whatever it was Marissa had planned for them.

He leaped over the sea of broken glass and grabbed for his wife and baby. But Faith was not moving, not reacting in the least. Instead she just knelt and rocked, and clutched their child.

"Faith, move! Get up! We have to get out of—"

She opened her eyes, tipped her head back and looked up at him, devastation written all over her face. Then she turned her attention back to the quiet baby, hushing softly to her, as if she were just as upset as her mother was.

And that was when he knew.

"No," he rasped aloud, falling to his knees as all of his strength left him. He reached for his daughter with a trembling hand, his soul shredding apart, his whole essence sucked clean out of him in a savage rending that left him gushing out his life from every pore of his body.

At first Faith cried out and jerked the baby away from him, then she doubled over, her body bending into her devastation.

Leo reached out once more, and this time he touched his cold child.

CHAPTER EIGHT

Leo roared out with agony. It was an agony of the heart and soul that left the bitterest of all tastes in his mouth. He choked on blinding, pent-up sobs, gasping for his breath, clawing at the ground with both hands as if trying to root himself to the spot.

It was the feel of soil in his hands that made something inside him pause a moment, made him realize on some minute level that things were not as they were supposed to be.

He opened his eyes and found himself kneeling on hard-packed earth, not shattered glass, the room nearly pitch black as opposed to lit brightly in order to best show him the plight of his family.

Family? As his furious gasps for breath finally sent enough oxygen to his mind, he became aware of more things. There was no gun belt around his hips, no shoulder holster under his arm, no gun resting tightly to the inside of his left ankle. He was not injured from the pounding of a stone fist into his ribcage.

The only thing that was as it should be was the colorful scarf tied through the front loop of his jeans. He touched the thing with shaking fingers, feeling the silky texture of it, watching the silver in it shimmer, grounding himself further with it. Confusion warred with the white-hot grief that was still dragging at his heart and soul.

And then he heard a feminine outcry, the wail of it filled with the same insane grief his soul was bubbling over with.

"No!" she shouted out, and he recognized her voice instantly.

"Faith!"

He crawled over the floor to reach her, not caring about what dangers he might find in the darkness. All he wanted was *her,* to touch her, to ground himself with her.

"Leo?" she cried out just as they made contact with each other. She threw herself into his body, her arms locking like a vise around his ribs just under his arms. He held her just as tightly in return, her head cradled in one of his hands, the other on her back. The skin at her back was electric, turning blue, the eruption of her wings imminent.

"Where are we?" she asked, her voice hitching with her emotions. "Where is . . ."

She floundered, searching for something, and he knew it was about the baby. Their child. Floundering for . . .

A name. What was the name of his daughter? Why couldn't he remember?

"I-I don't un-understand," she stammered, her grief faltering. He stroked a hand over the sugar white of her hair, the loose and tousled sheet of it the only thing visible in the dark.

"Extend your wings," he instructed her gently. "The light will help."

She did so, the blue energy unfurling right through his hand and wrist. The sensation was like receiving a thousand electrical shocks conducted through the tips of a thousand needles spread out all over his skin, but more stimulating rather than painful. It had a surprising quality to it. A newness. As if he'd hardly ever felt it before. But how could that be if they had been lovers for over two years now? If they had been wedded to each other? Surely he would have felt it over and over again in that time? Hadn't she wrapped up his whole body in her wings during their lovemaking?

The light from her wings was blinding at first, but then lightened the entire room as they stretched to full breadth. The blue light cast a strange, ghostly illumination over everything.

. . . Like the iron bars and locked door that was caging them.

"How did we get here?" she asked, loosening her hold on him enough to look around, but not even coming close to letting him go. He was as much an anchor for her as she was being for him.

As he looked around he absently brushed his thumb over his left ring finger. The ring that should be on it was gone. As if it had never been there at all.

All of it was as if . . . as if he had never been married to her at all.

And the more he thought about it, the more he realized he didn't actually remember their wedding ceremony. Not because it was a lost memory, he realized, but more like it had never been. How could that be? How could he remember asking her to marry him, remember all the feelings that had gone with it, yet not the wedding? He remembered when he had asked, remembered that they had conceived their first child that very same day, and yet . . . nothing about the wedding itself. He remembered the birth of their child, all the pain and fear, all the excruciating joy but remembered nothing beyond that event. Had she been christened? Given a name? Why couldn't he remember dressing her or changing her or playing with her? All the things that should have been burned into his memory and onto his heart were missing.

"Leo . . . what's happening? How did we get here?" She was growing stronger in his embrace, her body tensing with her strength. He could feel it eddying into him, feel it under his hands. This was the woman he had changed his entire life for, who had somehow made him heal from the trauma Chatha had subjected him to . . . and yet he recalled nothing of that process. How had he begun to feel his attraction for her? At what point had he confided in her about the deep-seated, horrific things Chatha had done to him . . . all the things he had stolen away from him.

It was as if it had simply never been.

"Jesus," he said as understanding finally began to dawn. "It was . . ."—he was choking on his own words— "it was a lie. All of it was . . ."

He looked down at his clothing, and then shifted his attention to the blue dress with the blue cornflowers that she wore. He remembered that dress. Remembered her coming into the room at the manor house with it on and being stunned at the contrast between it and her black skin. It brought him back in time, brought him back to a gingerbread house made of brilliant pastel colors and a little old lady who had served him sweet tea.

"What the sweet Mary fuck is going on here?" he roared out into the room. He should have shoved away from Faith and all the false emotions he had been made to feel for her, but he simply could not make himself do it.

False or no, a lie or no, it had felt really goddamn real to him. Even now, as the smell of her wafted into his senses, he found his body reacting to it, found himself longing with the urge to bury his face against the side of her neck just under her ear and touching his tongue to the erogenous spot he knew was there. He felt his blood pressure change, felt himself growing hard even in the face of their circumstances. It was as though it had been ingrained into him to feel this way, the way a deep repetitive memory would do. All of it in spite of the fact that he was coming to realize he hadn't ever so much as kissed her lips.

And that was when he realized that, once again, some sick Nightwalker bastard had fucked with his head. Hadn't he been through enough? Couldn't the fucking cosmos be happy with the screams of horror, pain, and rage Chatha had wrought from him? Wasn't it enough that every last ounce of trust he'd had left had already been burned to dust and ash?

A victim. A weak, powerless nothing. A toy for the universe to play with, like a child ripping the hair out of her Barbie doll's head just to see what she looked like bald. Chemotherapy Barbie.

"Sweet God," he heard Faith whisper. And that was when he knew she had also realized what was going on. She too was realizing they had been taken on an imaginary journey, no doubt to entertain the sick delights of a bored Djynn. The Djynn that they had come looking for. A web they had willingly thrown themselves into.

And yet . . . Faith did not let go of him. She still grasped him for comfort. Still held her warmth against him and drew from his strength in order to embolden hers. And as much as he knew it had all been a lie . . . he couldn't change the way it made him feel. Needed. Depended on. Loved.

He pushed himself out of her hold at that thought, cursing himself for being twice a fool. It was an *illusion*! There was no *love*! It was smoke and mirrors and more fucked-up torture from another fucked-up paranormal piece of shit!

Yet when she gasped in shock from his withdrawal it

dragged on his soul, the idea of causing her pain, of setting her adrift in the world. God knew that was what had happened to him. He had been forsaken, cut away and cut into, nothing and no one reaching out to catch him.

She reached for him then, catching his hand in both of hers tightly as she knelt at his feet. Her upturned face was ravaged with emotion, but most of all he saw pain. She was exposed to her core, just as much as he was.

"Please don't feel that way," she begged of him, her voice rasping roughly from her throat. He opened his mouth to shut her up and shut her down.

"You don't know a damn thing about what I *feel*. And whatever I feel, whatever I *felt,* was obviously a saturating deception. Your familiarity is inappropriate. You act as though you have a special insight into me, but I can assure you that you don't. That, like everything else, is a lie. It was all a *lie,* Faith. I wouldn't even consider touching one of you people if it could at all be avoided." He pulled his hand out of hers sharply, coldly. "Never mind becoming a lover to one."

He watched her wings wilt, dropping slowly until their neon lines were piled onto the floor. Her hands drifted down into her lap. She turned her stricken expression away from him. It baffled him that she was so affected by this. Surely, as intelligent and strong-willed as she was, she could shake this nonsense off and get back to business, couldn't she?

Her limp hands slowly curled into fists, her wings shuddered a little then snapped into shape, the gracefulness of them missing, however, as they stood straight and stiff.

"Of course," she said, slowly gaining her feet. "You're right."

She turned sharply away from him and he had to pull back in order to avoid getting smacked with the energy of her wings. He was disconcerted enough without the radical sensations coming in contact with her wings caused. "The Djynn was toying with us for a reason. This was a very intricate thing, and he no doubt expended a lot of energy. There must be a reason he would—"

She was whipped out of existence right before his eyes and he felt the shock of it, as if she had been connected to his solar plexus and then was suddenly yanked free of the connection. The feeling infuriated him and he balled his fists tightly.

"I swear to God, if you do this to us again," he shouted into the sudden darkness, "I'll rip your fucking heart out!"

And see how you like it, he thought viciously.

That same instant he felt himself get yanked aside, as if he was about to be thrown over the back of a sparring partner. He hit the ground and light exploded all around him, as though someone had suddenly thrown on every light in the world. Of course, that could just be because he'd been in darkness up until then. Not liking being blinded and on the ground, two craptastic defensible positions to be in, he rolled up onto his feet and narrowed his eyes to try to defray the power of the light. The first thing he saw was Faith. It was impossible to miss her, since she was the darkest thing in the room. That and she was standing in front of him. He swept the room for enemy bodies, but was so shocked by what he was looking at that it took him a minute to get his head right.

Gold. Everywhere everything was made of gold. Treasure. Coins in trunks that were overflowing, lamps and jewelry and boxes all made of gold and encrusted with jewels. The walls were covered in beaten gold, the floor tiled with it.

"You gotta be fucking kidding me," he uttered.

"I hardly think this could be conceived as a source of humor, seeing as how it's my home."

Leo's head whipped hard to the right as he turned his gaze face-front. There was an elaborate throne of gold before them, the back high and curved at the edges like a wing chair. Its seat, a plush red velvet cushion, had been empty mere seconds ago, but now a man was sitting there, lounging indolently, a knee hooked up over the right arm of the chair. He was tall . . . very tall. Tall enough that Leo could see it in spite of his slouching posture. Also, the muscular build of the man belied the projected image of laziness he was trying to exude as he filed a nail gently and with care for detail, using a file that was, of course, made of gold.

Even his clothing and his hair were as gleamingly rich as all the treasures around them. Leo had never seen anyone with hair color so akin to true gold. Not even out of a bottle . . . though many women had no doubt tried.

But the matching gold of his brows and lashes and beard attested to the fact that no bottle had come into play. He was not clean-shaven, but his beard had no significant length to it, maybe one to two weeks' worth. It was neatly trimmed, the line of it perfection, accentuating the strong angles of his face. Leo couldn't guess at the Djynn's age, not knowing exactly how or if his species even aged at all. But in appearance he looked no more or less mature than Leo's own age. The Djynn's eyes were not the same gleaming gold as the rest of him, but rather a dark honey color.

But Leo couldn't care less about his appearance.

"Listen Midas, if you're behind what just happened to us—"

"Of course I am," he cut Leo off, pausing in his manicure to wave a dismissive hand at him. "Let's not start this off by lying to each other."

"And what do you call what you just did to us, you manipulative son of a—"

"How do you know it's a lie?" the man of gold interrupted once again, punctuating the query with a single raised brow. He tossed the file aside, a little click, like coin against coin, sounding as it hit the nearest pile of the precious metal.

"Because I would never even think of touching someone like her," he pointed at Faith, "never mind become her lover! Believe me when I say I will be happy the day I excise all of you sick, deceptive sons of bitches from my life!"

"Well, we both know that's not true," his opponent said as he got to his feet, delicately brushing an invisible piece of lint from his shoulder. "No matter what you do, we will still be here. And no matter what you do, you will never be able to forget that we are here and could possibly be in any one of the faces you look into in the future." He came to face Leo, standing about six feet away from him.

Fine. I can do a six-foot leap for the bastard's throat no problem, Leo thought heatedly.

"And as for being sick and deceptive, we Nightwalkers, as races in general, are no more or less sick and deceptive as members of the human race might be. We have our liars and our truth speakers. We have our saviors and prophets and we have our psychopaths." He leaned forward a little, "but you already know about that last one, now, don't you?"

Leo stiffened, ice and rage clawing down his spine. He forgot why he was there, forgot what he was dealing with . . . he forgot everything but the white hot blinding rage that smacked into him. He leapt those six feet in a single instant, punching up into the Nightwalker's chin with the meat of his palm.

Only by the time he would have struck, he found himself striking through a cloud of gold with the fineness of sand and glitter. He whirled around to search for the object of his rage, but instead found himself crashing bodily into Faith.

"Leo, stop!" she commanded on a hiss as she grabbed him by both wrists, bringing his angry eyes to hers. "What we've been through will be for nothing if you anger him! Do you think he will grant us any favors if you attack him?"

Leo didn't know why, maybe it was his own logic centers coming forward because of what she'd said to him, but the touch of her hands and the lean of her body into his calmed him. Focused him. He realized the truth in her words and was forced to remember why he had come there in the first place. He looked down into her creamy chartreuse-colored eyes and found himself unable to resist touching his knuckles to her face, running them along her jawline from the tip of her chin to the touch of her hair.

The caress brought them both into feelings and memories shared, false though they may have been. He found himself seeking solace in her soft eyes and was shocked when he found it there. The rage and turbulence that had been his steady partner for all of the days and nights since his return from captive hell just dissolved away. He took a deep, clean breath, feeling her rest a hand onto his chest. Instead of feeling the revulsion that he had felt whenever Jackson or Marissa or any self-proclaimed Nightwalker had touched him since he'd learned of their existence, he warmed, as though she were transmitting a balm of heat and letting it range throughout him, spreading from that focal point where she touched him.

He tried to stir his anger back up, to remind himself that the reaction was in response to the falseness of the Djynn's manipulations, but it didn't work. The shape of her lips as she formed a silent "please," her eyes imploring and worried, filled him with an inexplicable impulse to run his thumb over the extreme fullness of her bottom lip. He drew back before he gave in to it, but he left her gently, rather than with the harshness of the rejections he had been subjecting her to. He reminded himself that she had been just as used and abused by the Djynn. Maybe even more so. After all, he had not been made to feel a child slide from his laboring body and into the world. He couldn't imagine how that must have felt for her. And here he was, only focusing on himself.

When had he become so selfish? he wondered.

Right about the time that sick fuck was using you like a pincushion.

He took another breath and looked for the Djynn. He was standing, once again, about six feet away from Faith's back. It made Leo think. That specific distance had to mean something, though he doubted he could figure it out logically. Normal logic was completely suspended in these circumstances. But what it could all boil down to was response time. He needed those six feet of warning in order to move or react in time to thwart any type of attack they could muster up.

Faith turned to face the Marid, but her fingers gently touched the inside of Leo's wrist, a silent, staying gesture.

"Why have you done this to us? Why have you abused us?" she asked, her tone hard.

"Abused you?" The Djynn chuckled. "Sweet girl, what I've given you is a gift. A very generous gift at that."

"A generous *gift*?" she hissed through suddenly clenched teeth. "You gave me a child, made me feel what it meant to birth that precious life into the world, and then you ripped it away from me! Ripped it away along with my soul! How is that a *gift*?"

Faith's surge of emotion made her start to shake and

Leo could feel her hurt and anger radiating into him.
He reached to slide comforting hands over her shoulders, rubbing her gently against her collarbone. Truth
or not, her pain was fierce and bright and he had to do
whatever he could to defray the blinding agony of it.

The Djynn leaned forward a little, making sure Faith
was looking him in the eyes. "Because what you have
seen is the future you will know unless I do what it is
you are here to ask me to do. I wanted to make it very
clear to you just how crucial this favor will be so that
you can understand how deep your debt to me will be in
return."

"You . . . you know why we're here?" she asked.

"I know the Djynn that sent you to me, the one who
owns that scarf," he pointed to the fabric tied to Leo's
belt loop. "She isn't as weak as she likes to let others
believe. If she sent you to me then it means you need a
magic she couldn't provide. And sending you to me
while in possession of one of her most powerful niks
tells me that the need is so great she was willing to trade
away the nik for the favor. She knew that all I had to do
was touch that scarf and that would make it and its
power mine.

"But as lovely as the gesture of the nik is on her part,
I don't need anymore niknaks. I have them aplenty. In a
nutshell, you need me far more than I need anything
from you."

"That isn't true," Faith said softly. "You do need
something. Otherwise, we wouldn't be standing here at
all. You would have slammed the door in our faces and
that would have been the end of it."

"Hmm." The Djynn turned to pace away from them
and the room of gold dissolved around them, bleeding away until they found themselves standing in the
middle of a vast, elegant private library. There were literally thousands of books in the hand-carved wooden

shelves. Wooden rails were polished to a shine, bracketing a sweeping staircase leading from the lower level of the library to the upper . . . and then again to a third floor. The room was circular, floor to ceiling windows on the eastern side. They could see the inky night sky beyond them and they realized that a great deal of time had passed. How much was anyone's guess. From Faith and Leo's perspective they had lived at least a year and a half since starting out that morning.

"Forgive the theatrics," the Djynn said as he threw himself into an actual wing chair, settling down into it comfortably. "This is much better, isn't it? Much more *real*." He took a breath then said, "All Djynns need the same thing. We need others to make wishes. We need to grant those wishes. It's like eating or breathing. If you neglect either you die pretty quickly."

"Are you saying you will die without being able to grant wishes?" Leo asked incredulously.

"Something like that," the Djynn said with a nod. "Please sit down for a minute." He indicated the small, cozy-looking sofa across the way from him. Leo and Faith exchanged wary looks, but then mutually, silently agreed to humor the Djynn. "Let's do a proper introduction. I am Grey. You are Faith, the Night Angel. And you are Leo, the very special human. There now, we're all familiar and friends now. So tell me what is this favor you wish to ask of me? I only gleaned an impression of it from watching your future with you. Let's work in specifics." Grey crossed his long legs, beringed fingers drumming thoughtfully on his thigh.

"The Pharaoh of the Bodywalkers has been severely injured by Apep, the imp god, come to earth in a mortal body."

"Apep!" The Djynn sat up sharply. "Who the devil let that beast out of its cage?"

"Does it matter?" Leo asked darkly. "It's done and people are paying for the ramifications of it."

"True. But this is a very deadly development. Whenever a god awakens in a mortal body cataclysmic events can take place. Especially a god as destructive as Apep is. He is the psychopath of the Egyptian gods. There's always one in every pantheon, but he is particularly dangerous because he can see beyond his impulses. Not that he isn't victim to them, because he is, but he is also quite capable of weaving a web and waiting very patiently for things to get caught in it, watching them struggle until they die. He draws his power from the destruction he causes. Take your Pharaoh friend, for instance."

"He's not my friend anymore," Leo said coldly.

"Oh, but that's not true now, is it? If you really believed your friend was not a part of this you would not feel the sense of loyalty to him that drove you to volunteer for this duty." He smiled thoughtfully. "And for whatever my word is worth to you, I can assure you that the man you know and love is very much intact inside the new man he has now become. Or at least he was before Apep got his hands on him. But we should, perhaps, focus on that a bit."

Grey seemed to get lost in thought for a moment, allowing Leo a small opportunity to see how he felt about the information Grey had just imparted. Shouldn't he feel a sense of relief? Or should he even believe yet another untrustworthy Nightwalker? Wasn't that what it boiled down to? He was being toyed with and there was no one he could trust.

Except perhaps . . .

Leo looked down at his hands, surprised to find himself caressing Faith gently. Even more surprising was the sense of comfort that came with the touches. Even though it was based on a tremendous falsehood, it still felt nice.

"It boils down to this," Grey said after a moment. "In order to repair Jackson's souls it will take a great deal of very powerful magic. I cannot access that magic without a wish. So one of you is going to have to wish for what you need." He looked at Leo a moment. "It should be you, Night Angel," he said. "Our special human should save his wish. There is something he wants very much that would require another powerful draw on magical resources."

"I don't have a wish," Leo bit out.

Grey merely chuckled. "Oh, you do, you just haven't come to it yet. You'll leave here and you'll start thinking and eventually you will realize what you want. And I'll be right here waiting." He looked to Faith. "So will you do it?"

Faith frowned. "If there was one thing my father taught me it was to never make a wish from a Djynn."

Grey laughed, a deeply rich and rolling sound. "Wise advice . . . for most Djynn. Don't be fooled by what just happened, which, I remind you, is not a falsehood at this point. It is very much the future ahead of you. But despite what you think I have no need for trickery and deceptions. Firstly, I am much too old for such childish amusements. Secondly, I would much rather have you indebted to me. If I have learned anything in my 888 years on this earthly plane, it is that I will one day be in need of something and I will know exactly who to get it from. And if that someone is already indebted to me, that will make it all the more easier for me. I rather like things to be no fuss no muss."

Grey stood up, brushing his hands down the front of his pants. He chuckled at himself, then his golden clothing melted away into an Armani suit with crisp well-tailored lines and fashionable elegance. Then he shook his head in negation and the suit dissolved into jeans and an oxford shirt.

"I sometimes forget to discard the whole genie in a bottle guise. The tourists expect the whole Aladdin's lamp and golden treasure room effect. I never know whom to take seriously. Clearly you are no tourists."

"Thanks, I think," Leo said dryly. But then he turned to Faith, a strange trepidation writhing into him. "Faith, you don't have to—"

"No. It's fine," Faith cut him off. "I'll make the wish. But if you trick me," she said darkly to Grey, "you better believe I will find a way to rain hell down on you." She rose to her feet and Leo stood next to her. Before he could check the impulse, he caught her hand into his and gave it a comforting squeeze.

The Djynn watched him do this. He smiled.

"You know, it truly wasn't a fabrication," he said to Leo.

"It?"

"The future that makes you lovers. But, of course, if you make your wish it will change everything."

"You can try and lord it over me all you like," Leo said in a clipped tone, "but you're not going to get to me."

"Very well," Faith spoke up abruptly. "Will you give me a moment to construct the wish?"

"Take your time. Have a bite." He indicated the coffee table and a tray of food appeared. It wasn't until he saw the tray that Leo realized how hungry he was. But he hesitated, looking at the food suspiciously.

Grey laughed at him.

"The tea was never drugged. It was what you expected so it allowed me to make the magical transition into the precog experience that much more easily. You should be careful with the thoughts you think. This world has stranger things than I in it, and your thoughts can be your downfall should you meet up with them."

"One more question," Leo said with a frown as he once again dismissed Grey's explanation of things.

Grey raised a permissive brow.

"You keep calling me a special human. How am I special?"

Grey leaned in and gave Leo a slow smile. "Don't you think you are special, as far as humans go?"

"Not especially," he said with a frown.

"Don't demur. It's unattractive." Grey drummed his fingers against his thigh. "Even before all of this," he encompassed the room and themselves in a broad hand gesture, "you knew you were something outside of the average human being. You are stronger than most. Faster than many. Sharper and wiser and, by far, more deadly. If this does not make you special, then what would? I'll answer that," he said quickly. "A human who can navigate the world of the Nightwalkers and not only live to tell the tale, but be crucial in the shape and form of that tale."

Leo had to give in a bit when he realized that everything Grey was saying was very much the truth.

"Tell me one more thing . . ."

"Young man, if you want to know anything else, you'll have to wish for it. And since you only get one wish per Djynn, I would use your wish very wisely. Especially when wishing from the most powerful Djynn in the Americas. I'll know when you are ready, so you better get to it, Faith." With that, and in a shower of golden dust, the Djynn disappeared.

Leo turned to look at Faith. She was looking at him, her hands clasped tightly. He moved closer to her and reached to cover her hands with one of his. "Are you sure you want to go through with this?" he asked. Somewhere inside of himself he realized he knew she always laced her fingers tightly together like that whenever she was nervous. It was almost like cheating, knowing these intimate details without having learned them the right way. *I wish I could have discovered this in my own time,* he thought.

Leo shook the thought off. It didn't matter. Not any of it. He shouldn't even be interested in knowing *anything* about her. And he didn't trust Grey as far as he could throw him so the odds of them becoming lovers . . .

He looked into her eyes, the bright lemon color of them so breathtaking in their own way. When first he'd seen her, describing her eyes as beautiful would never have occurred to him. Alien. Strange. Deadly. Yes, all of those . . . but not beautiful.

But they were. They were crisp and bright and expressive and the more he thought about it, the more he had to agree with himself.

"I don't trust this guy," he said, moving closer to her. "And I can tell you don't either."

"Djynn are notoriously not trustworthy," she agreed. "But there are exceptions to every rule." She cocked her head to the side. "I am wondering why he's so sure you'll make a wish."

"I could give an ant's fart what he thinks I want to wish for," he said sharply, even though he'd just been asking himself the same question. "What I'm worried about is . . ."

You, he thought. *I'm worried about you.*

She smiled at him, a soft, warming expression. A knowing one. "Well," Faith said, "it's nice to know you don't think me entirely contemptible."

Damn. He'd forgotten she could read that scroll thing. He wondered what word had been scrawled across it. He wondered if she knew things about him that he didn't. Maybe she knew something and just didn't feel inclined to share.

Jesus, Alvarez, you're starting to sound paranoid!

"When it comes to wishing," she said instructively, as if he might need the information in the future, "simplicity is to be avoided. The more specific you are the less likely the Djynn is able to find a loophole."

"Loophole? You mean like . . . 'I wish I lived in a palace' so he gives you a room at the Palace Roach Motel?"

She grinned. "Exactly like that."

"Great. Or like 'I wish I was surrounded by some hot bitches' and he makes you a dog walker of female dogs in heat."

She laughed, a short little snort of amusement. "That's a good one. Or 'I wish men would fall at my feet' and then every time you touch a man he'll pass out cold. It's called the Midas effect. Midas wished everything he touched would turn to gold. He couldn't eat, couldn't drink . . . and eventually he touched his beloved daughter and turned her into a gold statue. That isn't just a fable. There really was a man named Midas. But over the years it changed into a cautionary tale rather than a true historical accounting." She smiled softly. "Did you know that a Djynn started the Revolutionary War? Well," she nodded her head in allowance, "maybe not started . . . but all that tea getting dumped in the water had more mischief behind it than it did protestation."

"You're kidding me, right?"

"You know I'm not prone to lying," she laughed.

"Except when you're trying to make me own up to my feelings."

"That's not lying! It's merely encouraging you to see the error of your ways by any means necessary."

"You mean lying." He snickered. "Justifiable fibbing."

"I like to call it creative solutioning."

"Is that even a word?"

"You'd be surprised what makes a word. Especially when it comes to you. Just because it isn't in the English *or* Spanish dictionary doesn't mean it's not—"

She broke off, her eyes widening suddenly. And then Leo realized, just as she had, what they'd been doing. They had fallen into an easy familiarity, like long-time lovers might do, teasing each other, goading each other . . .

"I'm sorry," Faith said quickly in a soft voice. "I didn't mean to . . ." She trailed off, unable to put too much effort into her regret. Truth be told, she liked laughing with him. He had a nice laugh and his eyes smiled alongside that charismatic curve to one side of his mouth. He seemed somehow more handsome to her when he was enjoying his own indolent charm, when he flirted with her as if there were nothing different about them at all.

But the truth of the matter was that they *were* different. Worlds apart, nearly literally. And that flirtation was as knee-jerk to him as brushing his teeth in the morning might be. There was no real intent behind it.

And though it shouldn't, it hurt her. It hurt her to know he didn't feel anything for her. Nothing positive in any event. To him she was the "them" to his "us."

But for a moment there they had felt like an "us." That feeling, she knew, was Grey's fault. Whether what he had shown them was the truth or a lie, it had felt real . . . still felt real. No amount of telling herself otherwise seemed to be working.

"Don't apologize," she heard him say quietly. Surprised, she looked up at him. "We've been manipulated. I recognize that. It wasn't your fault."

Now that really did surprise her. Freeing her from blame was as good as picking her for his team. Until that moment he had made it very clear he wanted nothing to do with anyone that fell under the category "Nightwalker."

"I can't help what I am," she heard herself saying to him. "And I don't want to."

"No, I don't suppose you would. No more than I would. I carved my identity a long time ago, learned to take responsibility for who I was. It wasn't always that easy, being a young Hispanic man running around the barrio trying to look like a badass. It was hard not to get caught up with all the gangbangers hustling the neighborhood, always trying to claim it like a fiefdom. But I loved my mother and I'd never do anything to lose her faith in me. And then along came Jackson and Docia. I could have really gone the wrong way at any point in my life I guess is what I'm saying, but I didn't. I'm all right with who I am, too."

"How did you meet Jackson?" she asked him curiously.

"Well, one day I was hanging out with some of the neighborhood boys trying to be a badass like them, coming really damn close to shaming my mother with my behavior . . . until this white kid, young and strong, walked by and became a target for the older boys. They blocked his path, got in his face, puffed themselves up like peacocks.

"That was the day, the moment, I decided not to be what they were. Not to be the same old story, or the stereotype. When the first punch flew, I leapt into the fray like a wild thing, putting my back against Jackson's. In that moment I had changed the encounter from one against four to two against three. Jackson dropped one of the three with a single punch. Not bad for a kid as young as he had been. I found out later on that Jackson's father was a highly trained martial artist and had demanded the same from his son. Of course, Jackson was nowhere near comparable to his dad at that age, but he had it far and above over the lazy shit-talking bullies who had confronted him.

"I didn't realize until later that I had been very lucky in picking the right side. I blame it on my mother, blamed it on hearing her voice in my ear, feeling her hand against the back of my head, teaching me to respect her above the easy choice, respecting her above the lemmings I lived around. That day was the closest I came to becoming a gangbanging jackass like all the rest of the boys from my neighborhood."

"And Docia?" she asked gently, amazed that he was offering all of this information up to her. Grey may have put them through hell with those visions, but it might just be worth it if it meant it let Leo lower his guard a little. Let her in a little.

"My mother had died. There was nothing tying me down. My brothers were fucking useless pieces of shit who did nothing but give my mother grief every day of their lives. I had always envied Jackson's world, the love of his father, the steadiness and the balance Jackson had been raised with. I was genuinely shocked when Jackson's father took me in like a second son. By the time Docia had been born I'd been slated for the Rangers and Jackson was already dreaming of being a cop. It was all he had ever wanted . . . and he'd almost lost it all the day his parents were killed just a few short years later. With a baby sister to raise, Jackson was watching his dreams wash away as he was forced to make ends meet rather than take his turn at the academy. He was struggling to keep a roof over their heads. He barely graduated high school.

"That was when I told him we were going to do this right. We were going to raise his kid sister, give him his career and give me mine as well. I worried about the bills and Jackson went to school. We sort of split the duties when it came to raising Docia. We each had our strengths and weaknesses. But I think we did a pretty good job overall."

Leo sighed and looked away from her. "I don't know why I'm telling you all of this. It doesn't really matter in the grand scheme of things."

"Yes, it does," she said heatedly. "It matters a great deal! Now I understand why you are sticking your neck out for your friend, and why you are so afraid of him being somehow less than the friend you knew. I mean, my god, he's your best friend and she's as good as your flesh and blood daughter . . ."

She trailed off and their eyes met, both of them remembering another daughter . . . one that hadn't been real . . .

Leo resisted the urge to get his temper up all over again. He was tired of feeling so much hatred. It had never been who he was, no matter how jaded he had become and how far off the path he had strayed since his mother had left him. He'd never doubted his moral compass. Even though he had chosen to cross the line in order to see justice done, he had never lost focus on the right and the wrong of things.

Until now. Now he was blaming her for things she hadn't done, condemning her based on her race alone. It made him laugh with the irony of it. How many times had he hit a wall based on nothing but his race?

"What's done is done," he said quietly. "We can't change what we know and we can't help what we've been manipulated into feeling. I recognize that you are a victim here as much as I am. And that's all the more reason why I get a sick feeling in my gut when I think of you trusting this guy, this Djynn, after the tricks he's pulled on us."

"I didn't say I trusted him. I just . . . I don't see how we have any choice in the matter so we have to just proceed at smartly as we possibly can."

"For whatever that's worth." Leo sat down across from her with a sigh. "I'm navigating in a world I don't understand, playing by other people's rules." The look he shot her was a mixture of irritation and anxiety. "I don't like it."

"I don't blame you," she said. "I only ask that you realize I'm doing the exact same thing. What I know of the Djynn begins and ends with warnings never to make a wish. I was always told that there's no such thing as a smart wish because they are *always* smarter. But I have heard that there are a lot of Djynn, mainly Afreet and Marid like this one, who are not interested in the trickery the less powerful Djynn seem to take delight in. I can only assume that he wouldn't have reached this position of power and import if he'd wasted his time and magic on unimportant things.

"Think of the amount of magic it must have taken for him to take us on that journey just now," Faith said, leaning toward him with energy. "I can promise you that it was a lot. Djynn don't just throw their magic away for no reason. If he showed us a possible future it was very probably for the reasons he stated . . . though I'm sure he'd had other ulterior motives as well. Odds are he doesn't have an altruistic bone in his body, that's true, but I have to hope that he doesn't want to screw with us. Maybe he's trying to curry favor like he says. Djynn like it when others owe them favors. Especially people as important as . . . as Jackson is."

Leo had been divining things about people for too long not to notice that hesitation. His attention perked up and he narrowed his eyes at her, trying to access whatever he could from those pseudo memories they had shared. If he knew about her anxiety tells, maybe there were other things he'd learned from those vignettes that he could use to his advantage.

He realized then that she knew a great deal more

about him than he did about her. His only sense of it was that she had somehow turned her back on her heritage, her people, in order to be with him. She had known that he'd had little tolerance when it came to Nightwalkers, so she had tried her best not to remind him of their differences . . . in spite of the fact that it stared him in the face every time he looked at her, every time he'd touched her black skin.

But you've never really touched her, a voice inside his head whispered to him fiercely. *Never really made love to her.* And he couldn't escape the thought that that was a damn shame. He didn't want to think it, didn't want to give birth to even an instant of curiosity over it, but he couldn't help himself.

Leo shook himself from the inside out. *Focus,* he told himself. *Stay on point.*

"Who are you?" he asked, watching her face very closely as he did so. "How is it that you ended up at the right place at the worst time and were able to do what you did to help Jackson . . . and me?"

She hesitated, taking just a moment too long to look up at him. But when she did he could tell she wasn't going to lie to him. He could tell because he knew her. Thanks to that Djynn, he knew her.

"I'm a Night Angel," she said simply. "Djynns need to grant wishes, and we need . . . we need to help others. I don't know a better way of explaining it. It revitalizes us, the knowledge that we've done something to help someone. Ferrying a soul into a cusp is not totally selfless. We reap a great deal of pleasure from it. It satisfies us. I suppose all of that is where the ideas about angels come from, although they're a teensy bit off on the coloring." She held up her fingers with a pinch of air between them.

"That didn't even come close to answering my question," he said, pinning her down with a hard stare. "Who are *you*?"

"A messenger," she said quietly. "Just like any other society we have a hierarchy. We have hierophants, messengers, and saints . . . and none of those things are what you might think they are. They're not what humans think they are. Our hierophants are our oracles. A hierophant very close to me saw what was going to transpire on the lawns of that house in New Mexico and I, being a messenger, was sent to try and prevent it, or at the very least control the damage afterward. Some think it's not our place . . . but others feel that we are bound by what we see and what we can do, that we have a moral duty to try and make things right."

"A messenger. What you did . . . it packed quite a punch."

She nodded. "Messengers are sent for a reason. We're the strongest of our breed. We have the power to do certain things that not everyone has. I was chosen, and rightly so, because the hierophant knew my specific abilities would come into import in the situation. And he was right."

"And what is your ability? What is it that I saw you do?"

"I am a reflector, you could say. I have no real ability, per se, except that I can reflect back to others whatever power it is they choose to use against me. So long as I am aware it's being used against me, that is," she said with a grim expression. "I wasn't aware of what the Djynn was doing to me. I can be just as easily deceived as the next person. But I should have known better. I should have been on guard against . . ." She trailed off and he nodded.

"You couldn't, could you? You had no way of knowing he could do that, so you couldn't reflect it back against him."

"I know now. He won't be able to do it again. Not without my consent, in any event."

"This makes you very powerful, doesn't it? It makes you just as powerful as anything you come up against."

"Yes . . . and no. There is a downside to what I can do. I can reflect things back, but it doesn't stand to reason that I will have any control over the power that I'm wielding. I got lucky against Apep. I took him by surprise. I won't have the luxury of that advantage again. He will see me for the threat I actually am next time we meet, and believe me when I tell you he won't be very happy with me."

Leo did believe her. He had a feeling that they had barely scratched the surface of what Apep could do. And when it finally came down to brass tacks, no matter how she tried to underplay it, she was going to be a crucial and dangerous weapon they could use against Apep.

"I feel like you still haven't answered my question," he said. "You've told me what you are and what you can do, you've told me your mission in this world . . . or your mission as you see it, but there's something you're avoiding telling me, and that's who you are. It's an important detail, or you wouldn't go to so much effort to hide it."

"I'm not hiding—"

"Don't lie to me," he said sharply. "I'll give Grey that much. He made it so I can tell if you're lying to me. I know your tells, Faith. I know you can't look me in the eye when you're being deceptive. I know you run the pads of your thumbs over your nails when you're anxious. Please I have a hard enough time trusting as it is and I'm making an effort here. Please don't lie to me."

She looked up at him, met his eyes, and realized he was right. Realized what a mistake it would be to break this fragile trust with him. He truly was making an effort. She could see that. And she could feel just how difficult it was for him. She suspected that, if not for what they had just been through together, he wouldn't even be trying. He certainly had not been inclined to before Grey's interference.

"I'm . . . well, you know how the Djynns have castes? How the Afreet and Marid are the upper crust of their society? I . . . my branch in the Night Angel tree is considered . . ." She cleared her throat. "Royalty."

Leo blinked. Stared at her. Blinked again.

"Are you telling me you're a frickin' *princess*?"

"In not so many words, yes."

CHAPTER NINE

Apep could have used his power to transform himself into a Night Angel female, thereby making him more appealing to any candidates he might have found that were worthy of providing DNA toward his get.

But he did not. His power resources, at the moment, were quite puny. Or so it seemed to him. He was used to having much more power than this. But he was still newly reborn, still trying to force the Bodywalker, Odjit, to show him how to use the power she could provide for his use. She was being very uncooperative for some reason. He would eject her soul, along with the insignificant human soul that also housed itself in this body, if he could, but the truth was that he couldn't. If he ejected the soul naturally born to this body, the human soul, then Odjit's—which was deeply Blended with it—would flee along with it. And if he ejected Odjit, all of her potential and power would disappear with her. It did make for a terrible overcrowding inside one sack of flesh, but until he was at full strength and until he no longer needed Odjit and her power to help him get what he wanted, he would simply have to put up with it.

So he didn't change form or alter his appearance. It would take far too much energy. But that did make things a bit trickier. It wasn't as though he could blend into Night Angel society, considering he was like a fair-skinned beacon when in their midst. So it required some creative thinking on his part. He would have to hunt one of them down after he had left his herd.

Which was exactly what he'd been doing.

He'd followed more than one trail, studied more than one candidate. After all, not just any Night Angel would do. He wanted someone very powerful. Someone strong. But powerful and strong meant he was putting himself at risk. He didn't want a repeat of what that Night Angel bitch had done to him. He was lucky he hadn't lost one of his three souls in that little unexpected skirmish.

The other tricky thing was that it was very difficult to deceive a Night Angel. They could see words written across the light of a soul, words that told them whether or not to trust, whether or not they were seeing or hearing the truth.

Now that *was* something he had to expend precious energy on. He had no doubt that the light of all three of his souls would be easily seen, like three separate beacons, and that alone would warn off any potential suitors. Whereas two souls in a single body might be expected and announce that he was a Bodywalker, three would be something never seen before and therefore something to be avoided at all costs.

He couldn't rid himself of any of those lights, but he could toy with an Angel's perception of those lights. He didn't have to do it for very long. Just long enough to reel a little Angel fish in.

And he was pretty certain he had found his candidate.

His name, he had learned, was Dax. A single name, a strong name. It suited him, Apep thought. He was of beastly proportions, wide, impressive shoulders, muscular arms thicker than most people's thighs. He didn't lumber about, but instead had a way of holding his bodily strength in a manner that was incongruously graceful. He was a dark-haired redhead, the color just as stunning a contrast against his black skin as the white hair of the bitch Angel had been on her. The Angels seemed to wear clothes or go without according to personal preference, as opposed to it being a social norm. Either way, they had no sense of shyness and wasted no time or energy on their physical appearances. It was hard for Apep to understand that. He was constantly catching his reflection in glossy surfaces and considering how he might make himself more attractive. It didn't matter that he was male and his physical body was female. It only mattered that he was attractive to any and all sexes, to any and all creatures.

And he had indeed succeeded, he thought as he touched his hair not in self-consciousness, but in self-assuredness.

His attention returned to his target. Dax. The great and powerful Dax. Apep didn't understand the hierarchy of Angel society, but it was not necessary that he did. All he had to do was watch as this Dax gave commands to others, called for and gained attention with a quick ease, and held himself in a way that left very little space for things like fear and self-questioning behaviors. He had no doubts about who he was and what his purpose was. That fact practically oozed out of his every pore. And the way those around him gave him deference and made so much effort to please him told Apep that his displeasure was something these people were avoiding at all costs. Apep couldn't tell if it was because he reacted easily with wrath or not, only that others bent over backward to do as he commanded.

Yes, that would do very nicely. Physical superiority. Personal superiority. The question was whether or not his power was also superior to all others. It could be assumed so. Only those with great abilities could hold positions of power in a paranormal society. Achievement of the fittest. So Apep was willing to assume personal power was also to be extrapolated from his observations.

The only thing that mattered was whether or not he could control that power, whatever it was. He had to find a way of binding this Dax, of neutralizing any threat he may pose.

But of course there was nothing that could threaten *him,* Apep reminded himself. He was, of course, superior over all things. Most certainly over a Night Angel. That one bitch had merely been a fluke. He had been unprepared for her. He would not make that mistake twice.

Not that it could be called a *mistake,* he thought, merely an unfortunate happenstance.

Apep waited for the Night Angel to quiet, to find himself alone with his work. He slowly entered the room, or rather, materialized into it. He had been watching in a noncorporeal state for several hours now. With a thought he sealed off the room, made it soundproof, making it inescapable. He had barely taken a step when he heard . . .

"What can I do for you, Bodywalker?"

Dax's question caught the god by surprise. He hadn't thought to be detected so quickly. When Dax looked up at him and narrowed lime green eyes on him, he had to admit he was impressed. It was a reminder, however, not to let his guard down. At least Apep could be assured that his hidden soul was just that . . . hidden.

"It's more a matter of what I can do for you," Apep said, his body moving in flirtatious, feminine sexuality.

"I don't need anything from you," the big male assured him with controlled politeness, looking back at his work in a dismissive manner. Honestly, it put Apep out. Was he not beautiful? Was he not delicious to look at? How was it this lesser being did not recognize that?

"I can offer you a great opportunity," Apep continued in spite of his momentary pique.

"Again," Dax said without looking up, "I am not interested in anything you have to offer me."

"Not even if it creates a great bond between our peoples?" Apep asked archly. He moved to the male's desk, sliding onto it and taking a seat at one corner. He rested a beautifully manicured hand over the paperwork the Night Angel seemed so intent on and leaned in toward him, making sure he could smell the perfectly delectable scent of him. Any being of any race should be quite aroused with just one breath full of his scent.

Dax looked up at him, very hard eyes narrowing just the littlest bit. "Your people are embroiled in a bitter civil war," Dax said. "I will not choose sides. I do not support one side over another. It is on you to resolve your differences, make yourselves a unified society. Then, perhaps, we can discuss diplomatic relationships. Until then, I will thank you to leave me to my work and ask you to please stop bothering me."

Dax reached out and lifted Apep's hand from over his work, pushing it aside as though he were discarding it.

Apep began to get angry, but, he thought, he would impress himself with his own self-control. He would not let this lesser creature disturb him. He would explain himself more clearly.

"I don't think you understand," he mused, making certain his voice was musical and light. Pretty. "I've decided to give you a gift. A very generous gift."

Dax looked back up at him, one brow arching up as amusement seemed to pull at his lips.

"Is that so? Very well, give me your gift."

Apep laughed.

"You first!"

"Me? I have no gift for you, and my patience with this game is wearing very thin, I warn you."

"Agreed. This truly is most tedious."

Apep reached out and grabbed the male by his thick throat, propelling them across the room together at lightning-fast speed, the impact crushing the air out of Dax's body, not to mention snapping several of his ribs. Apep made sure to squeeze his hand tightly around Dax's neck, preventing him from drawing a breath. Surprise laced the Night Angel's expression. Shock. No doubt he was trying to figure out how something so delicate and beautiful could be so gloriously strong as well.

"Yes, yes," Apep agreed with himself. "I know. I am to be thanked for deigning to choose you. No doubt you will express your gratitude accordingly."

Out of the corner of his eye, Apep saw Dax clench his hand into a mighty fist but was too surprised to so much as duck when the fist came crashing into his face. Apep was surprised to find himself traveling back an entire yard under the strike. It only reaffirmed his excellent choice in a sire for his child.

"Okay, now that was just rude," Apep noted, lurching forward and once again smashing the Angel against the wall. He was pleased when the male's eyes once again went wide with surprise. Clearly he had not been expecting him to roll with that punch so easily. Then his eyes slid shut, as if he were going to give in, which of course he would have to, Apep thought. Continued resistance would only be a waste of time and would just make things so . . . unpleasant.

But instead of acquiescence, the male punched at Apep's face again, only this time there was a commitment of strength and power that had not been there before and to his surprise Apep found himself hurtling across the room. He slammed into the opposing wall so hard he crashed through the drywall, his spine striking the framework beyond it with such force that the wall cracked in two other places.

Apep pushed out of the wall and back onto his feet. He looked down at his beautiful clothes and frowned at the dust that was soiling them. He reached up and felt chalky chunks of wall in his hair.

Now Apep was truly angry. "You've damaged me!" he cried out, taking a moment to try and shake the dust off himself, trying to return himself to perfection. "Damn," he said with a sigh. "I'm quite ruined and will have to start all over again."

And now that he was angry, he was through playing games. He launched himself at the rude male Night Angel, grabbing hold of him and driving them into a wall yet again. This time the whole room shook from the impact. Apep recaptured Dax's throat beneath his hand, then slammed him down into the ground. Wrenching the ungrateful wretch around Apep propelled them into the ceiling as a single, grappling entity. Another twist and they barreled back to the ground so hard that the tiles in the floor cracked for a good ten feet in every direction.

"Now," Apep hissed into the churlish rogue's face. "You will father my child and you will be grateful for the privilege!"

"I'd rather die first," the big Night Angel choked out before grabbing hold of Apep and throwing him back across the room. Apep went skidding through broken tile, the sharp edges doing irreparable damage to his pretty burgundy dress. "You can keep coming at me," Dax growled as he drew for breath and tried to gain his feet. "But I will fight you with your own power, Body-walker! My ability allows me to gather your strength whenever you expend it and then use it against you. You cannot win this!"

Apep got to his feet and chuckled.

"Oh, now it all makes sense! I was wondering how a puny little Nightwalker could cause me so much damage! Now I see it is because I am literally fighting myself!" Apep giggled. "Thank you for telling me how to defeat you. That has made things infinitely easier."

Dax was snatched off his feet, as though being grabbed up by an invisible dog, and shaken violently before being spit out onto the ground again. Then that invisible hand flattened against him, crushing him down onto his back and into the floor. The pressure was so massive that the broken tiles beneath him were being ground to dust, and, one by one, his ribs were snapping in two . . . then three . . . then four pieces. From across the room a small decorative stool flew over him and slammed down onto him, the legs stabbing through the muscle and bone of his body until it erupted through and drilled into the ground beneath him.

Dax bellowed out in the sheer agony of it, but immediately regretted it because he could not draw another breath inward. His adversary came over to him and sat gingerly down on the stool, as if concerned about hurting him. The female Bodywalker looked down at him and smiled beatifically.

"You should thank me really," she said conversationally. "You're about to father a demi-god."

Dax wanted to rage with his anger and impotence, but blood was filling his throat and lungs and it was all he could do to just draw in the smallest amount of breath. So in lieu of anything else, he spat a mouthful of blood at the bitch and wheezed out: "Fuck you!"

"Well now, that's the spirit!" She clapped her hands together like a gleeful child. "I tell you what, you don't have to lift a finger." She giggled. "Actually, you do have to lift something. But I'm going to do all of the hard work, never you fear." She fluffed at her hair. "Yes. You just sit still and this will all be over before you know it."

And that was when Dax truly realized that he had lost. That there was nothing he could do. He could feel his strength ebbing away on the tide of the blood spreading beneath him into the tile. He found himself looking up at the ceiling, at the lights shining there, and through all of his agonizing pain he felt her reach out and touch him along the fly of his pants, cupping him, feeling him. And in spite of the agony he was in, in spite of the fact that there was nothing but revulsion running through him at the sensation, he felt himself responding in a way that shouldn't be possible.

That *wasn't* possible.

That was when he realized he was going to be raped and there was nothing he could do about it.

Leo was floored. Not because she was royalty, but because, if Grey had been showing them a truthful version of the future, it meant that she had turned her back on all that she was in order to be with him. And from the sound of it, it was a very expensive price to pay.

"Jesus," he said softly, not knowing how to feel about that. "What . . . so explain how this thing works . . . with your people."

Your people. Not you people. It was a gentle sign that he wasn't looking at her like some kind of massive negative entity that needed to be guarded against. Needed to be regarded with prejudice.

"There are seven Night Angel prefects. One prefect for each continent. Each prefect rules his continent under a sketched-out series of laws, we call them principles, but otherwise each prefecture is run as a monarchy. A prefect can do whatever he wishes, with only

the other prefects able to make him answer for any actions he might take outside of the principles. A prefecture is not inherited, it is earned, but children of prefects
always get first opportunity to prove themselves worthy
of the seat if something should happen to their parent
or if their parent chooses to step down."

"And you are the daughter of a prefect?" Leo asked,
although he realized he already knew the answer.

"Yes. Actually . . . two prefects," she lowered her eyes
and Leo could swear that if she hadn't been black she
might have blushed just then. "Australia and North
America had what you might call a . . . uh . . ."

"Summit meeting?" Leo couldn't have possibly
passed that one up, even if she was clearly uncomfortable.

But she laughed, a good hard laugh that made her
eyes dance and shine.

"Yes. They had quite a torrid affair, from my understanding. But eventually . . . eventually my mother
brought an end to it. I tend to think that . . ." She
stopped and Leo looked at her with a discerning eye.

"You blame yourself for it. You think you were responsible."

"In a manner of speaking, yes. My mother found out
she was with child and ended the affair. I wish I could
tell you why, exactly, she felt it necessary to do so, but
she has never given me a satisfactory answer. I could
speculate, but it only gives me a headache." She frowned
and looked down at her hands, which were sliding together in nervous activity, as if what she was discussing
made her feel cold inside and she was trying to warm
herself up.

"You know, I actually find it comforting," Leo said.
"to know that your kind have the same complex emotional pitfalls as any human might have."

"Of course we do," she said, jerking herself awkwardly to her feet and away from his reach. "We're not animals. And even if we were, animals have emotions, too! If not, then explain the devotion of a beloved pet, or . . . or the way a wolf mourns the death of its mate. We're not cockroaches just scurrying about concerned with nothing but the finding of food!"

"I didn't say I thought you were an emotionless cockroach!" Leo erupted, standing up and reaching for her arm. But she moved out of his reach and backpedaled away from him.

"You don't have to say it," she hissed at him, her fiery eyes burning like two yellow flames. "Your contempt oozes out of you like a tide. From the instant I met you you've done nothing but batter me with your obvious derision toward me and all of Nightwalker kind! But never you fear," she said, her hands balling into fists. "As soon as this wish is made you'll be quit of me and you'll never have to set eyes on this *thing*"—she indicated herself with a jerking hand gesture—"any longer."

She turned her back on him and stalked angrily away. He opened his mouth to recall her, to argue with her that she was overreacting and being too sensitive, but instead he went quiet and felt a forlorn sort of regret birth inside of him. He couldn't argue against the truth. But neither could he help his feelings nor the horrifyingly overwhelming distrust that seethed through him whenever he came close to any one of these breeds.

And it was for the best that he hold on to that, he told himself. It was best that he never forget to be cautious, that he never turn his back on any of them. There was no telling if he, a simple mortal man, would ever survive if he did. He did not belong in this world of titans and demigods. He didn't even want to know such things existed.

But it was better that he did, he argued with himself.

His ignorance had cost him dearly, had scarred him in a way he might never recover from.

But as she stopped at a desk across the room, shuffling through the books that were laid upon it, he found himself remembering things about her, things that told him what an honest, valiant heart she had. He remembered how she had wept in devastation as she had clutched their dead child to her breast.

No. It was an illusion, he whispered fiercely into his own psyche as the memory of the agony he had felt in that moment threatened to overwhelm him. *It was all pure fantasy. Pure fiction.*

And yet he couldn't seem to stop himself as he crossed the distance between them. He stood behind her, struggling with himself so hard it was exhausting him.

"I was tortured." Leo jerked with surprise as he said the words aloud. Why should she know that? Why would he want her to know that? She could just use it against him . . .

Faith turned around slowly, her surprise written all over her face. But he thought she was more surprised that he had confessed the thing to her than she was about the nature of the thing itself. Then he remembered she could see those words being written onto himself over and over again, and he knew there was no way she could have missed something so deeply ingrained onto his scroll . . . onto his soul.

"A Bodywalker named Chatha. He's . . . on the outside he looks like a Down syndrome man. I don't know if you know what that is . . . but suffice it to say, it's sheep's clothing. I let my guard down because I thought he was harmless. He got the drop on me and he . . ." Leo trailed off, his heart racing and sweat breaking out over every surface of his skin. "Anyway . . . it's just going to take some time . . . I can't be expected to just forget it."

"No. I don't expect you to forget it," she said quietly. "But I do expect you to realize that one Nightwalker made of pure evil does not mean all Nightwalkers fit that same definition. And I expect you to be intelligent enough, evolved enough, to understand that."

"That's not fair," he snapped. "Why don't you run across that sick fuck and let him fillet you like a fish for a few days and then we'll see if . . ."

Leo's anger slipped away on a sheet of cold shock when he heard his own words ringing out into the room. He would never, no matter who and what they were, *never* wish Chatha on anyone for any reason. And suddenly the idea of her being at Chatha's mercy blossomed horrifyingly within his imagination and he thought he might be sick onto his own boots. He staggered away from her, dizzying nausea trying to win the day.

But then she was there, stepping up against him, her warm, vital body burning its strength into him. She felt like a tether, a lifeline. He didn't know why he would see her as such, but just the same he found himself wrapping his arms around her. He hugged her to himself brutally hard, his face against the softness of her neck, his entire body quaking under her touch. God, he had never known such weakness. Such fear.

"I'm sorry," he said on fast breaths. "I'd never want you to know even half of what I was forced to learn at Chatha's hands. I don't even want to speak his name aloud in your presence because I'm terrified it would conjure him up."

"It's all right," she said softly against his ear, her breath spilling over every curve and hollow of it.

"No. It's not." His shaking hand traveled up to the back of her delicate neck. She was strong and she was powerful, but she would be just as fragile as he had been under Chatha's vicious blade. The thought was obscene as he stood there bathed in her warmth, the sweet scent of her filling his senses. "It will never be all right for as long as that thing lives. I will never rest easy as long as it's alive."

She drew her head back just far enough for her to see into his emotion-ravaged eyes.

"I'm going to say something, and you might hate me for it, but I want you to think about it. Okay?"

He felt a wary sense of dread, but he nodded awkwardly just the same.

"When a Politic Bodywalker is reborn, it Blends with the soul of the human that hosts it. Then they see the world together with joined eyes. But when a Templar Bodywalker is invited into their host's body, they do not Blend in the same way. They subjugate the host soul, forcing it to lie in complete and utter helpless submission. The originating soul must simply stand by and watch everything the Bodywalker says or does." She drew a breath. "So somewhere inside Chatha there is a sweet, innocent soul, the soul of a Down syndrome male, who has been watching everything this psychopathic Bodywalker soul has been doing. He will feel it all, smell it all, and remember it all. He will suffer under it every single day until someone puts Chatha down like the rabid dog he is. As much of a victim to Chatha as you were, that innocent is a thousand times more a victim because he has to watch as his very own hands and eyes do to others what he did to you."

Leo didn't want to hear this. He didn't want to know it. Anger and outrage warred within him, sick disgust their companion. He wanted to sit down, his legs weak beneath him, his body shaking uncontrollably as his mind struggled to reconcile what he had been feeling every minute of every day about that monster that had brutalized him with the image of innocence and sympathy she was forcing onto him.

"No. No, God, I can't do this. I can't do this!" He

shoved himself out of her hold, staggering to the desk, his hands gripping at it as if it might suddenly be snatched away from him and along with it all of his strength and composure. "Don't do this to me!"

He felt her hands on his back, felt her warmth ebbing into him as she slid her touch to his shoulders and gripped him tightly there. She didn't speak. She didn't need to. She'd said it all already, hadn't she? Hadn't she forced the idea onto him that was currently ripping away at him?

The idea that there was a victim out there suffering a thousand times more than he was.

"He should be killed," Leo rasped out, his neck tight with tension. "I already thought so . . . already knew that I wouldn't rest until I had destroyed him, but now . . ." Leo fought back the burn of tears as he forced himself to keep breathing. "That kid. Andy. The real Andy . . . he's stuck inside that thing. Isn't there something we can do? Isn't there some way we can rip Chatha out and leave Andy intact?"

"No," she said gently.

"What about what Apep did to Jackson? He severed his souls, right? What if we sever just the one and leave the other intact? Couldn't that—"

"That's too simplified, Leo. It doesn't work that way. The Blending, however much or little has taken place, makes it impossible to separate the souls. Although there are two separate tethers for Jackson's souls, the souls themselves are like conjoined twins. Each twin has its own umbilicus, but they can't be simply pulled apart. There isn't any way of ejecting Chatha without killing Andy. It's been tried before and it's never succeeded."

"Are you sure?" he said, turning toward her, knowing his every emotion was stricken across his face . . . written across his scroll for her to see.

She nodded, gentle fingertips reaching to smooth through his hair at his temple. His eyes slid closed for a moment as he fought to understand why, in this sea of horror and misery, that single touch had the power to soothe him. She did it again, like a mother comforting her child, like an owner petting a beloved companion. It exuded strength and affection, bringing them together to provide a shield to fortify him and armor to protect him.

When he looked into her eyes he was not offended by the sympathy he saw there and that was surprising. The idea of someone feeling sorry for him should have enraged him. But he knew it was not pity she was feeling when she looked at him like that. It was understanding. It was commiseration. She knew it was a hopeless situation, just like he did. She knew that she had taken away the clarity of his hatred for Chatha. She knew that it was no longer so simple for him to want Chatha at his cold mercy.

He had imagined thousands of ways he wanted to visit revenge on Chatha, but now . . . knowing what he knew now . . . he could no longer have the satisfaction of the fantasy of it. It was no longer black and white. Good and bad.

"I need to walk," he said, his voice sounding rough to his own ears. He moved away from her, looking quickly around the room for an exit. He'd not seen one as yet, but maybe . . . maybe he had missed it. He needed to get out of there. He needed silence and solitude . . . just for a few minutes. Just long enough for him to wrap his mind around all of this and come up with . . . something. A new answer? An altered version of plotting Chatha's death? Chatha still had to die to set Andy's soul free. To give him peace.

And part of the problem was that he knew . . . he had always known that, as a simple mortal human being, there was no way he could have gone up against a being as powerful as Chatha. Not if he expected victory. It would be just like being mauled by a lion, and then getting up and walking into the lion's den. It was madness. Suicide. Asking for more defeat and more horrifying agony.

"Leo."

He looked at her and saw her pointing to the back wall. A door made of stained glass with an elegant brass handle stood where no door had been just moments ago. It told him that, while he was not present physically, Grey was watching them closely. He had heard Leo's need and had provided for it.

Leo didn't have the focus needed to be angry about that. He just walked to the door, opened it and stepped out into . . .

Sunshine. Although it had been full night a moment ago inside of the library, the moment he opened the door he was looking at a vast sunshine filled garden. It was tranquil, peaceful and, Leo thought as he began to walk along the garden path, it was a place where no Nightwalkers would be.

CHAPTER TEN

Leo sat outside for what felt like a very long period of time, but it was not time wasted. The sunlight seemed to sear a kind of strength into him, a kind of quietude that softened the raging thoughts and emotions inside of him. He was so tired, he realized. Tired of being so angry so much of the time. He had never been the bitter sort, though he had been known to hold a grudge. But he never let those grudges fester. He went after the source with a vengeance, satisfying it however it needed to be satisfied. What quickly came to mind was Benitio Montalbano. He'd been a powerful man, living on the Mediterranean coastline in the town of Cinque-Terre, Italy. But his home in that idyllic setting belied the monster that Benitio was. He was wealthy and powerful and he had been one of the most notorious pedophiles ever to walk free in Italy. But his power and position had kept him free of the long arm of the law and he had continued to traffic in little girls, both for himself and for others, destroying their psyche's thoroughly before discarding them when they grew too old or developed things like breasts and other accents of adulthood.

Benitio had captured the daughter of a woman, the widow of David Rabinowitz, one of Leo's best buddies from back in his army Ranger days. She had come to him, beside herself looking for her missing child, begging him to help her and get her daughter back . . . by any means necessary. Leo had known David's daughter since the day she'd been born. She had been nine when she had disappeared from her very own street in the bright light of day.

It had taken every resource he'd had, every favor he could think of. He'd been stunned to learn she'd been not only kidnapped but sold and shipped out of the country. Eventually he had traced her to Italy, and then to Montalbano's home.

To say he had exacted revenge had been an understatement. But it had taken time and very careful planning. He had needed to remove his emotional attachment to the situation in order to see David's daughter safely retrieved . . . and to see to it Montalbano would never touch another little girl again.

And that, he realized, was what he needed to do now. He needed to excise the emotion connected to the way he felt toward Chatha. No easy feat that, but he satisfied himself with knowing the time for emotion *would* come. There would be satisfaction one day. He didn't know yet what method or face it would have, but it would be done. He and Faith would see to Jackson's safety and then together they would find a way to make Chatha pay—

Wait. What? When had Faith become a part of his fantasy of dealing with Chatha?

When she had made you see there would be more to it than just vengeance against a psychopath.

She had robbed him of the rage he'd been wallowing in, robbed him of the single-minded revenge he'd been fixated on. Why would he want to include her in his plans?

Because she can see things you can't. Because she

will keep you honest. Because she will make certain your rage doesn't make victims of innocent collateral damage.

And because he somehow felt more centered when she was around. He felt calmer and stronger now. Sure, it was likely because of Grey's manipulations, but he knew that there was a vein of truthfulness to the whole thing. Not so much that they would end up lovers, but that they each had new insights into the other and could understand each other on a more visceral level.

That they could trust each other.

The thought calmed him. Come what may, Faith was the only Nightwalker he knew of that could be considered an ally.

Except for Jackson.

The thought leapt into his brain before he could stop it, before he could force it down with his newfound prejudices. Leo sighed and rubbed at his temples. Jackson. What was he supposed to make of all of it? And Marissa . . . capable of becoming a murderer? How could that be? The woman he had been coming to know had not seemed anything like the monster he had seen.

But it wasn't until he had lived a future where there was no Jackson in his life that he really felt fear of losing him, whatever he might be. He'd been around him for over two weeks and everything had seemed so . . . Jackson, but was that a truth or was it a facsimile? Jackson or just something that wore his face?

Jackson. It was Jackson. Leo realized it so suddenly and so sharply that he felt wetness in his eyes and tightness in his chest. He *had* to be Jackson because Leo couldn't imagine life without him. He was everything good that Leo was not. He was Leo's anchor and moral true north. Jackson kept him honest, and he needed to be kept honest. He walked the edge too often to run around without that anchor.

It was a leap of faith. Believe or don't believe. Like Santa Claus. Only Jackson wasn't a myth. He was real. And Leo had been pissing on what had been the deepest relationship he had ever had.

And how had he come to realize this?

Faith. His ally. A trustworthy ally. And he would need that ally not only for dealing with this Jackson thing, but when dealing with his mode of recourse against Chatha. He would need her power . . . and her levelheadedness. He would need her to keep him honest and on the right side of good. Just like Jackson.

Leo was not an evil man and he would not allow Chatha to make him one. He would much rather have Faith and his friend to keep him from becoming one.

Leo exhaled, soft and long.

Good, he thought.

Good.

By the time Leo returned to the library, Faith had finished constructing the wish she was going to make. It had taken a few drafts and a lot of careful thinking, but eventually she had come up with something she could tell herself was reasonably satisfactory. A Djynn as clever as Grey could find a loophole in any wish, she was sure, no matter how careful she tried to be. She just hoped that the Djynn was a man of his word and that he was above such petty amusements. But she did worry, just the same. Usually the older a Djynn was, the more powerful he was, *and* the more easily bored he was. If Grey was looking for a way to divert himself, Faith could very well be making herself the perfect entertainment.

All she could do was pray that, for all their sakes, this was not the case. Leo was struggling enough as it was with trust and his understanding of the world around him. He didn't need a Djynn reinforcing his mistrust of all things Nightwalker.

Leo looked significantly more settled, having had the time and the peace to put himself back together. She had known that he had been putting a lot of energy into fantasies of how he would take his revenge out on Chatha. For all he was human, he was a man of action and deeds, and if he was imagining doing it . . . then it would most likely get done. The problem had been that he was thinking in linear human terms, totally disregarding that there was a great deal more complexity involved than what met his unpracticed eye.

She had not wanted to be the one to rob him of his illusions, but neither had she wanted him to throw his life away without seriously thinking about what he was doing. In a way, Leo was going through a massive grieving. He was grieving the loss of himself. The loss of the man he had thought himself to be and the power and control he had once thought he had. In the blink of an eye he had gone from being a badass mercenary to a victimized, insignificant, mortal man. That couldn't be an easy thing to cope with. And on top of it the trauma itself? She couldn't begin to imagine what it must have been like, what he must have suffered. All she had was the scrawling, fiery words that had streaked across his scroll in a wild, acidic jumble as he had struggled with her earlier.

"Are you ready?" Leo asked her. He was absently running a hand over the scarf still tied at his belt loop. Watching him get comfort from it, she found herself hiding a feeling of . . . it was hard to explain what the feeling was. Intimacy? A part of her realized that she and he and their pseudo relationship was tied tightly into the silk making up that scarf. Just looking at it reminded her of . . .

"Yes," she said, shaking off the thought and trying to stay focused on the moment.

But it was hard to stay focused when, every time he slid the scarf against his palm she was remembering the feel of his hands on her body as she'd lain there tied and helpless, unable to do anything but feel the pleasure he was giving her.

Faith gasped softly and turned away from him, giving herself a mental shake. Now was not the time or place for such thoughts. And knowing how he felt about Nightwalkers, there would never be a time and place. Not involving him, in any event.

"Are you all right?" he asked, laying a hand on her back, moving it in soothing circles. "You can still back out of this before it's too late. I don't care what Grey says. There's nothing for me to wish for other than . . . anyway, I'll do it instead of you."

"Other than?" she repeated back to him, unable to keep her curiosity from devouring her self-control. What was it, she wondered, that he would wish for? Revenge? A power with which to fight the Nightwalkers? A way of protecting himself against them?

He was silent a long minute, long enough for her to think he wasn't going to answer her. Then he looked at her and reached for her nearby hand, giving it a squeeze.

"I would wish to forget it all. It sounds cowardly to my own ears when I say it, but there it is. I'd wipe myself clean of remembering what Chatha did to me. I . . . I wouldn't want to forget there were Nightwalkers and such out there in the world, I can't protect myself with that kind of ignorance. But my wish . . . my wish is to cleanse myself of these memories and of the paralyzing terror that it causes to run through me."

"I can grant you that wish. All you need do is ask."

Faith and Leo turned to face Grey, who had apparently materialized on one of the couches, his long legs crossed while he picked a microscopic piece of lint from his pants, then brushed the area smooth.

"Thanks, but I'd rather swallow a bucketful of hot needles."

That made Grey chuckle. "That's fine," he said with an amused expression. "But should you change your mind, all you need to do is find some sand and write my name in it. I am allowing you the ability to summon me."

"Gee, you're a real peach," Leo said dryly. "But I wouldn't hold your breath. You'd die of asphyxiation."

"Leo," Faith warned softly.

"No," Grey lifted a conciliatory hand, "he's perfectly entitled to have his opinion. I won't take it personally. So your wish?"

Faith cleared her throat and, holding the paper she had written the wish on in her hand, she recited it very carefully, word for word.

"I wish for Jackson's and Menes's souls to be retethered into Jackson's body, as they were right before Apep's attack on him."

Grey relaxed even farther back into the couch, his mouth curving into a smile. "I'm really quite impressed. It was detailed yet succinct. And, as you know, left little room for creative interpretation."

"You mean trickery," Faith said with a dark frown.

"Yes. But I assured you I wouldn't do that and I'm a man of my word. But I am also to be taken seriously when I say there is a price to pay for this wish. There is always a price to be paid, however small the wish might be. But this one is quite complex and will require a great deal of magical expenditure." He paused for a thoughtful moment. "I believe I am going to require payment for your wish immediately."

Leo stiffened so hard and so fast that Faith could feel the energy of it hit her like a shove. She hastily reached out to catch his hand in hers, squeezing it tightly in warning, a reminder that he wasn't dealing with a mortal person here. This was a being of great power and his mood might turn on a dime if he was mishandled.

"What kind of payment?"

Grey smiled again, meeting Leo's angry gaze.

"I am going to need you to retrieve a certain item for me."

Faith narrowed her eyes on him. "You mean you want us to get a nik for you," she said, her tone sharp. Leo turned to look at her, a mixture of surprise and tension swirling over and through him.

"Yes. I'd like for you to nick a nik." He chuckled and leaned forward. "Steal it, to be blunt."

"All right," Leo said carefully, outrage crawling across the light of his scroll, belying the calm tone of his voice. "Let me get this straight. You want us, a Night Angel and a simple mortal, to steal a nik from what I'm assuming is a very powerful Djynn, even though you are reputed to be the most powerful Marid Djynn in North America?"

"Inaccurate but close," Grey said rising to his feet.

"Why don't you just go get it yourself and leave us out of it?" Leo snapped. "If you're so damn powerful just take what you want from the other Djynn."

"I would, but there is only one problem with your assumptions. The nik isn't being held by a Djynn, it's being held by a Wraith."

CHAPTER ELEVEN

Leo could tell by the way Faith suddenly clenched his hand within hers that there was something very, very wrong. He didn't have to be a rocket scientist to figure out that they were jumping straight out of the frying pan and right into the fire.

"I'm going to take a wild guess here and say that Wraiths are not very nice people," he said.

"Wraiths are . . ." Grey trailed off to hunt for a way to describe them. "They are very powerful and very dangerous. I find them to be a xenophobic, inflexible, and noncooperative species as a whole."

"And you can't get this nik yourself because . . . ?"

"Wraiths can kill other Nightwalkers with just a touch," Faith said quietly. "Their death-touch is useless against humans, but to Nightwalkers . . ." Leo heard her swallow noisily and he could just about taste the fear on her. "For the most part they stay to themselves, keep themselves away from other Nightwalkers. Wraiths are the boogeymen Nightwalkers tell their children about in scary campfire stories."

Leo blinked. "You go camping?"

The question was so unimportant that it made her laugh shakily. Then when she looked at him she real-

ized he'd made the joke in order to calm her fears . . .
and she was grateful to him for it.

"So I get it. You need a human to go into some
Wraith's house and steal this nik," Leo recapped. "Is
that death-touch the only thing they can do? Any super
speed or strength or any other physical or metaphysical
aspects I will find myself up against?"

"No! Leo, you can't do this! It's a death wish!" Faith
turned a fiery gaze on Grey. "He doesn't understand the
nature of what he'll be dealing with!"

"It's no more or less dangerous than bringing him
onto the territory of the most powerful Djynn on the
continent," Grey countered firmly. "In fact, *you* are
going to be the one in the most danger. A mere touch
and a Wraith can kill you. You would be wise to send
him in alone."

"Absolutely not! I won't send him into a Wraith
dwelling with—"

"I'll do it," Leo interrupted her.

"Leo!" Faith was breathing hard, her hand shaking in
his, her eyes wide with fear.

"Faith," he said softly to her, using his tone and the
strength of his touch to center her, to calm her. "I have
made it in and out of heavily guarded fortresses with no
one the wiser more times that you can imagine. I've
killed a man . . . a monster . . . in his own bed while a
phalanx of guards waited right on the other side of the
door. This is what I do. This is what I'm good at."

"Except Nightwalkers have reflexes, senses, and
powerful abilities that you have never gone up against
before," she argued fiercely.

"You're wrong," Leo said grimly. "I *have* been up
against it before and I know exactly what I might be
getting myself into." He turned back to Grey. "So tell
me, what else?"

"My god, you're insane!" Faith hissed before pulling

her hand out of his and pacing anxiously away from him.

"To be very honest, we don't know very much about the Wraiths. All we know is we must avoid touching them skin to skin at all costs. I know that they are incredibly strong and fast when in their noncorporeal states, but when they are in the corporeal state they are at their most vulnerable, no different than any other Nightwalker."

"Got it. So the best thing to do is to go after this thing in daylight."

"Wraiths are not stupid," Grey warned him. "They most likely use humans to protect what they feel requires protecting. Mortal creatures and mortal technologies."

Leo chuckled. "Now that's music to my ears. So the Wraiths can't operate in sunlight I'm assuming, like any Nightwalker. Will they be awake? Able to see me and warn whatever guards they might have?"

"It's possible. Like all Nightwalkers daylight is their time for sleep. When sunlight turns a Djynn to smoke we are able to see and feel everything around us, but without corporeal bodies there is nothing we can do about it. The same might hold true for a Wraith. But I will warn you, do not let the Wraiths see you. They won't forget an insult like this and it is likely they will not let a theft go unpunished."

"Like I said, stealth and precision extractions are my specialty. But I don't want Faith coming with me. If just one touch can kill her, she can't be anywhere near these things."

"I am not letting you go by yourself!" Faith snapped at him. "I don't even want you to go at all! If this is the price we have to pay then you can keep your wish! We'll find another way!"

Grey regarded her patiently. "The wish is already

made. It will be done, but only when that nik is in my hands."

Leo frowned. "What is this nik exactly? Because if it's a life-sized marble elephant, we're in a world of trouble."

"Actually, it's not a niknak. It's a nikki."

Leo sighed. "Okay, you lost me."

"Niks hold our power, yes?" He waited for Leo's nod. "There are two kinds of niks. Inanimate niks are called niknaks. However, living niks are known as nikkis."

"This thing is *alive*?" Leo asked. "Please tell me it's not Bigfoot."

"Leo, this is no time for jokes!" Faith said in a burst of emotion. She couldn't understand why he seemed so damn delighted by this! They'd been tricked into doing something deadly and dangerous. Even the thought of being within a mile of a Wraith left her cold and sick inside.

"It's the perfect time for jokes," he replied, a lazy sort of smile crooking up a corner of his mouth. "When things are already funny and happy, jokes are just redundant."

Faith fought back hot tears. She wanted to scream at him and shake him and make him understand what he was doing! After being faced with what Chatha could do, she would think he would be more wary, more cautious . . . just as he had been since they'd started this journey. Grey wasn't to be trusted!

Leo turned and saw the expression on Faith's face. He reached out for her hand but she jerked it away from him. He followed her with a step and this time caught her hand, pulling it by the wrist until it was pressed against the warmth of his chest, until she could feel the beat of his heart.

"Look at me," he ordered her when she turned away and stared hard at a row of books some distance away. "Look at me," he said more firmly, squeezing her wrist tightly until she did. It was not meant to hurt, only to acquire her attention. "Not my eyes, Faith. Not my face. Do what you do and look at me."

He meant he wanted her to look at his light, he wanted her to read his scroll.

And there it was. All the answers to all of her questions and confusion. Strength. Power. Confidence. Potent words, robust words. Words that had been faded from his scroll . . . faded and missing from the places they used to inhabit. This was what made him who he was. This was what gave him power. This had been ripped away from him, left him floundering, left him afraid . . . and now it was back. It was his element, and it was where he belonged.

"All right," she said quietly, not willing to take any of that away from him. It was dangerous, yes, but he needed that danger, needed to prove to himself that he could win against one of the Nightwalker breeds, the creatures he'd turned into personal boogeymen. It was crazy dangerous and her heart was still in her throat, but she wasn't about to tell him no.

"I need a floor plan, I need to know what I'll be carrying and I'll need to know what I might run into," Leo said. "And I'll need weapons. The best you've got."

"If there is one thing I excel in," Grey said with an amused smile, "it's in having the very best of everything."

"I am content," Apep said with a satisfactory sigh. "Yes. This was an excellent idea and a job well done. He was quite powerful, you know. An excellent choice."

"You didn't bring him to me? I wanted to play." Chatha pouted as he fussed over his surgical tray. The highly polished metal on the tray gleamed from all angles. His tray had been acquired over time, this blade from one place, this from another and so on. The hunting knife with the serrated spine and wickedly sharp edge had come from his last toy. Chatha knew that toy from the inside out. He had studied every part of him over and over again. It had been such a wonderful experience. They had become so close with each other.

He had been very disappointed when he'd realized Kamen had stolen his toy from him. Actually, he had been very put out. Kamen should have been his friend. Instead he had betrayed him and taken his favorite toy away from him. It was really quite fortunate that his mistress had awakened. His mistress but not his mistress.

A god. His god. His god promised him a free hand. Promised him any toys he liked. But he had not brought him the stud to play with, and that made Chatha feel cheated.

"I think it best we leave that dog to lie. He will meet his death. But take pleasure in the fact that he was suffering the entire time. There's a good boy. Now, I think I'm craving something. Maybe chocolate. Ice cream, perhaps? I like ice cream. What clever things mortals invent."

"I want Kamen."

Apep lifted a brow. "Is that so?"

"He stole my toy . . . so, I want to play with him. Yes. Very much so."

Apep could tell Chatha was itching for the release he got through his experimentations on his victims. It really fascinated Apep, to find another being of such like-mindedness. He had never thought to find such harmony with someone.

"We will get Kamen back. He is, after all, my summoner. If not for him I would not be here among the living." Apep moved to look out a window. They were living in some kind of commune, these Templars, milling about and craving direction from their mistress,

who Apep now inhabited. They were deliciously sub-
servient to him, respectful really. They had been well
trained. But Apep wanted more than absolute mindless
respect. He wanted devotion. He wanted them to love
him. And more important, he wanted them to fear him
with every fiber of their souls.

"We must call in my followers. Tell them the news."
Apep rang a nearby bell and an acolyte hurried in.

"Yes, Mistress?" he said, bowing very low because
the last time he had bowed to his ruler it had not been
low enough and now he was healing from a broken nose.
His might be a hardy breed and very quick healers, but
not so quickly as all that and the pain lasted for a good
long time as well.

"Gather all of these . . . creatures," Apep said, making an encompassing hand gesture. "I have glorious
news to share."

"Yes, Mistress, at once." The acolyte scurried off.

Apep had to wait an interminable amount of time before the acolyte returned to inform him of his gathered
disciples. A whole ten minutes! He was lucky, really,
that Apep was in a good mood.

"I am now in a delicate condition," Apep announced
from his position on a balcony above them. He rubbed
his belly, though it was completely flat with no outward
signs of any pregnancy as yet. But there would be soon
enough, and he was most pleased by the night's efforts
and rewards. He had used his godly powers to see to it.
Had inbued the rapidly separating cells with part of his
godly energy. "I will need volunteers to help me deco-
rate my son's nursery. Preferably a carpenter or interior
designer."

When they all stood awkwardly for a full thirty seconds, Apep felt a thread of anger weave through him.
He knew he should not waste energy on such annoy-
ances, but just the same they should be leaping for the

opportunity. Clearly they did not love him as much as they should.

Perhaps this was an opportunity to make them love him. They were not yet cognizant of his magnificence. They still thought he was their puny little mistress, for all he had altered her appearance. For the better, he might add. Certainly this strong, enlarged Amazonian figure was superior to that soft puniness that she had once displayed. Why could they not see that?

"Those who volunteer will be greatly rewarded." Then, to prove his statement, he conjured a chest of gold. It was piled so high that coins were sliding off and hitting the ground with little clinks. "Or perhaps a greatest fantasy?" He chose a male in the front of the crowd and with a snap of his fingers created two buxom blondes who immediately started to fondle him and rub up against him. "Whatever your heart desires, I can fulfill." He turned to them with a beatific smile. He was ready for the wave of adulation.

"Mistress," a small male voice spoke up, "if you please, won't this affect our ability to fight the Politic?"

"Oh. *Them*. Believe me, I am as strong as ever, and I can prove that whenever you like."

He reached out toward the one that had dared question his master plan, fisting his hand in the air until the dissenter was yanked off his feet and left dangling there, obviously being choked to death by an unseen force. But before he lost consciousness, Apep reached his other hand out then yanked his hands apart, as if tearing something.

A great tortuous force ripped the man in two, dousing the gathering in an explosion of blood.

And then came the screams.

Oh yes, Apep thought. This was much better. He would have his volunteers . . . and he would have their love . . . and more important, he would have their fear.

CHAPTER TWELVE

Leo was feeling a bit weary. It wasn't a physical weariness. He had endured a great deal more physically challenging things than what he was dealing with at the moment, so a little loss of sleep was hardly the issue. No, it was strictly a mental weariness. They had been through a lot, and knowing that they would be going through even more still had him tense and ready, but tired and aching at the same time. He was not fully healed as yet and probably shouldn't be taking this on. Especially not as half-cocked as it was. It was better to have a full knowledge of your enemies capabilities and the time to draw up a plan that took in all variables and possible difficulties.

But he didn't have the luxury of any of that. And to be honest, behind that weary feeling was a tide of excitement, an eagerness to take control of this and have a strong hand in solving this problem with the speed and succinctness he was known for. And beyond that was a powerful surge of loyalty for a brother who possessed all of the strongest connections to Leo's emotions. He had been through so much already that he didn't think he could take losing Jackson as well.

Leo racked back the slide to the Glock nine he'd been given, checking the chamber, making sure it was clean.

Then he released the slide, letting it close. He grabbed for the clip to his weapon and shot it into the butt of the pistol with a push. He chambered a round and, for now, put the safety on.

He might not trust the Djynn, but Grey certainly knew his weapons. He'd conjured a veritable arsenal for Leo, including a flack vest and a plethora of weapon holsters to chose from. And as he loaded the pockets of his vest with spare bullets and small ordnance, he realized the Djynn had also provided him with something else. A reason to trust. To trust Jackson, and to trust Faith. Something he was desperately in need of. He had to admit that he was beginning to feel more secure in that knowledge with every passing second, or he wouldn't be risking his neck like this, wouldn't feel so compelled to do this. Overall, it was a very different feeling than he had first started out with.

He stole a glance over at Faith. She was pacing the library in a short, agitated circuit, her arms folded tightly beneath her breasts, her upset more than obvious. He realized that she was in part responsible for his changing perspective toward Nightwalkers. Well, some of them anyway. He had asked himself several times now why she was doing this. It was clear she was putting herself in the line of fire, setting herself up for being victim to things far more powerful than she was, yet here she was just the same. She had no stake, that he knew of, in any of this. So either he hadn't uncovered her true purpose, or she was just doing this selflessly for the greater good.

"So now we wait for daylight," he said, looking down at the equipment laid out before him and ready to go. After another quick mental inventory, he came around the table and moved toward her. He reached out to catch her arm, stopping her short march and making her look at him. Her luminescent eyes fixed on his and he could see the desperation of her worry written in them.

"This is insane," she breathed. She caught her breath and he realized, with no little surprise, that she was on the verge of tears.

"Hey," he said softly, pulling her close and touching her distraught face near her right cheek. "I'm going to be fine." He frowned then. "You're the one who shouldn't be going."

"If you think I'm going to let you—"

He cut her off with the gentle touch of his fingers against her lips. It made him realize just how full and lush her lips were. She had a beautiful mouth which, if not for the stunning presence of her eyes, might well have been the most arresting feature on her face. At first he had thought her universally black from head to toe, but now he realized that wasn't the case. Her general skin tone was an even, unblemished ebony, but her lips were actually a deep, dark purple . . . so dark it could fool you into thinking they were also black.

"Why are you doing this?" he asked her abruptly. "What's in it for you?"

She looked absolutely startled. Then she looked at him as if his hair had suddenly caught fire.

"You really don't get it, do you?" She laughed, a hard, scoffing sound. "This isn't about me. It's not about you. As corny as it might sound, it's about the fate of the world. And maybe that doesn't mean so much to you, but it means a hell of a lot to the rest of *us*." She said the "us" with a very sharp emphasis, reminding him how very often he had labeled her with "*you people*" or whatever he could conjure up to devalue her species and all of the Nightwalker breeds.

The truth was, he didn't know very much at all about Night Angels. That information had not been included in Grey's little fantasy scenario. But other things had.

Things like her capacity to love. Things like how passionate she could be. And just thinking about it drew his attention to the way she smelled, that divine scent of soft, sweet woman and the spices of Christmas; and the warmth of her, standing so close to him they were almost touching bodies. Actually, with every agitated inhale of her breath, her breasts did touch him. It was oh so slight, barely able to be felt, but he felt it just the same. He realized then that she was hotter to the touch than a human woman would be . . . or so it seemed. He knew he couldn't chalk it up to her upset emotions, because thanks to Grey he knew that she naturally ran this hot. He knew that sleeping next to her was like cuddling up to a delightful little furnace.

He tried to shake the image away, needing to stay focused on their conversation.

"I still can't fathom you," he said softly, his eyes searching her face slowly. "You appear out of nowhere and jump into this . . . this *quest* with both feet and with no regard for your own well being. Why would you do that?" Before she could speak he added, "I mean besides the saving the world part. Why would *you* do that. Why have *you* volunteered for this and no one else?"

"Because with position comes responsibility," she said, her tone softening, "With strength and power comes the obligation to protect those without. Human mortals like you have no idea of the dangers and the battles being fought just beyond their periphery. It needs to stay that way in order to protect them."

"And not to protect yourselves?"

"I won't lie to you. There is a heavy element of that as well," she conceded. "Can you imagine what people would do if they saw someone like me? If they could see my wings and see my ability? But regardless of that, think about an all-out war . . . a universe rending battle with a deviant god. Who do you think will get caught in the crossfire?"

"Why not let them know? Why not give them the opportunity to protect themselves?" His tone turned more than a little bitter. "I was kept ignorant 'for my own good' and was nearly killed for my obliviousness of the danger I was in. Had I known—"

"You would have what?" she demanded of him. "What do you think you could have done against a Bodywalker? Cut their throat? Shoot them?" Again, she scoffed, and he knew she was right. There was nothing he could have done to keep himself safe from the likes of Chatha and Kamenwati. Kamen had been determined to extract his revenge from Leo, and he would have stopped at nothing to get it. He would have hunted Leo down, sending his dogs after him from all quarters. He might have been able to dodge it for a little while; he was good at making himself disappear, but he would have eventually been caught and made to pay for what Kamen had perceived as a slight to himself and his precious mistress.

And even if he had been successful in hiding he would have paid for it in other ways. He would have lost his connection to Jackson and Docia, the only family outside of his mother that he had ever cared for.

He would have died a little if he'd had to turn his back on the Waverlys. And he would have suffered as a person. Jackson had always been his moral compass. Always a fervent boy scout, Jackson's drive to do the right thing and to demand Leo do the same kept Leo honest and reminded him not to let the dark underworlds he traveled in drag him down with them.

And maybe that was why he was so terrified of what Jackson had metamorphosed into. Maybe he was afraid of navigating the world without his true north.

"You're right," he conceded. It was a concept he understood all too well, actually. And then there was another aspect. By keeping all of this hidden, they were protecting the minds and spirits of the mortals around them. Right now they lived in the bliss of ignorance. It would be nothing but terror and stress for them if they were to learn of the darkness slithering around so close to their exposed jugulars. "Though there are some, like me, who could perform well under the pressure of knowing the truth and protect themselves in spite of the extreme difference in capability, most cannot. I am by far an exception."

"But even then . . . you weren't," she reminded him as gently as possible. And she was right. As cold and hard a truth as it was, she was right. All the skill and strength in the world could not have protected him in the face of beings as powerful as Kamenwati and Chatha.

"I know," he said softly, searching her eyes for something, anything to secure him as he faced that terrible fact. He saw sympathy swim across her features, the look so soft and gentle, so understanding, it tightened his chest and throat with emotion. He knew she understood what it meant to be weaker than an opponent. He didn't need to wonder why. The creatures they were about to go up against explained it easily. One touch and she would be dead.

"I don't want you to come," he said, his breath coming hard and fast the more he thought about her vulnerability.

"I have to. You need me."

His fingers reached to touch her forehead, drawing a gentle line from one side to the other, and then falling back onto her cheek. God, the urge to kiss her came out of nowhere. But when it came, it came with raging force. However, before he could accept or reject the command, she surged up onto the tips of her toes, pressing her mouth up against his and reached to plow her fingers through his hair. His breath caught in his throat and he expected revulsion to streak into him, but he had forgotten what the Djynn had shown him. He had forgotten they already knew each other as passionate lovers.

Whether it was true or not, it simply was. He caught her head between his hands and pulled her up into the kiss even more tightly, letting the lushness of her mouth pervade his senses. He did not introduce his tongue to her, did not seek the same. He wanted to know her, without deception or fabrication, for who she really was and how she really felt.

And he had never known such an electric sensation in all of his life. Having kissed a great many women, of all shapes, sizes, personality, and creed, none had evoked that startling sensation. It made him draw back in surprise, made him leave her if for no other reason than to see if the sensation continued on separate and apart from her. To prove to himself its origin.

"What the hell?" he breathed across her mouth.

She smiled. "I guess Grey left that part out," she mused.

"Fuck right he did."

"It's just . . . my chemistry. Night Angel chemistry. I'm told that the sensation for a human is similar to licking—"

"A nine-volt battery," he finished for her, "only a hell of a lot more powerful."

"In a bad way?" she asked, a frisson of anxiety stealing over her features.

"No. No, not in a bad way," he said before pulling her back to his mouth and letting that sensation wash over him anew. Good god, what a feeling it was! And it didn't stop at the physical connection of their mouths. It streaked electric awareness through his entire nervous system. It was amazing how quickly addicting it was.

How he wanted more and more of it with every passing instant. To that end he dragged her up close and tight, fitting her lean strength to his, reveling in how she was soft and potent all at once. Her fingers bled out of his hair, trailing down the side of his neck, and he started a little when it felt like a static charge had leapt from her skin to his.

"Jesus," he breathed against her lips. And then he wanted more again. More then just this surface connection. He began an onslaught, opening his mouth over hers, coaxing more of the same from her. He heard her make a small sound of pleasure and it went through him like that static charge. That was the instant he knew he had to have her and he would take her with all due haste. What lengths that desire reached to, he didn't know right then. All he knew was that he craved every aspect of her that she was willing to give. And she seemed very willing as she opened her mouth for him, inviting the invasion of his tongue and meeting it with an invasion of her own. If he had thought her kisses to be electric before, they now seemed chaste in comparison to the whipcord heat and desire racing through him.

Now they were ribcage to ribcage, her breasts pressed against him, her belly flush to his. And still he pulled her in tighter. He didn't understand why it didn't feel like enough, why it felt as though he were starving for the feel of her still. Maybe because the taste of her was so incredible. Maybe because though she felt like it, she certainly didn't taste like licking the top of a battery. No, that was a tart, acrid thing, and she was everything sweet and delicious. He had never been one for fine dining, but he could recognize it when he tasted it.

Somehow his hands had found position on her body, one on her upper back and the other sliding down over her backside. He'd always been partial to a girl with a nice ass, and maybe that was why he was more than a little turned on by hers. He used his grip to connect their lower bodies along with their upper and that was when he realized just how hard he was. It should be funny, the idea that he would be unaware of something like that, but it was just another shock to him, just like the way she kissed him shocked him.

Then he found himself remembering things. Remembering the way she had felt beneath him, the way she had felt around him . . . and just by remembering that hard state became even more so. A thousand thoughts and impulses seemed to race through his mind all at once, but what it all boiled down to was him wanting her, and her acting very much like she wanted him in return. She was like holding on to a live wire, dancing and wriggling in his grip, her body curving up against him, rubbing up against him. She moaned, and he felt it right to the bottom of his being.

Christ. Christ almighty, was it safe to want this power-fully? Was it normal?

No, it wasn't normal, and that was exactly the reason why it felt so damn good. Even if she wasn't of his kind, hell . . . not even of his *species,* she was very clearly in his blood and it was an intense experience just begging to be had.

But just when he would have pushed even harder, she jerked away from him. She wrenched herself out from between his hands, leaving him feeling shockingly bereft.

"What?" he demanded, surprised to hear the exasperation of the query. He'd never been the type to ignore the signals a woman was giving off, and pulling away was a huge signal. But instead he was feeling cheated, feeling impatient to get back to where they'd just been.

"You don't even like me! You hate my entire kind!"

she blurted out, her breathing just as labored as his was, her fingers pressing against her mouth as if to placate it for what she'd taken away from it.

"I . . ." He hesitated, trying to think clearly enough to respond. She was right, wasn't she? At least, as far as she knew. He'd had nothing but ichor oozing out of himself toward her kind from the moment they had met . . . longer even. "Believe me," he said with no little bewilderment. "I'm just as shocked as you are."

"Fine," she said, her eyes filling with anger. "Let's chalk it up to momentary insanity on your part and leave it at that."

She went to turn away, to leave him, and he didn't know why, but he grabbed her by her arm and turned her back to him.

"I'm not going to do that," he heard himself saying. *Really? So what now, genius?* "I don't hate you," he said, and the moment he said it he knew it was true . . . and by the expression on her face he could see that she knew it, too.

"This . . . all of this," she said indicating their closeness, "is because of what Grey did to us. It's not real."

"Felt pretty damn real to me," he argued. "Felt better than real, for that matter."

Now that statement seemed to give her pause, so he took advantage of the opportunity and moved in, taking her mouth with his once more, but this time slower, more gently. Savoring that sparking sensation and the simple warmth of her. When the kiss ended he could see the hesitation in her eyes and he didn't blame her for not trusting him.

"Put it all aside," he said quietly. "Forget what Grey showed us. Forget whatever suggestions we might feel is motivating this. Strip it down to the skin and you'll realize, just like me, that there's something very intriguing here. Something . . ." He kissed her lips with aching softness and breath stealing slowness before speaking again. "Something that's just *us*."

She let him kiss her again and he felt victorious for it. He had coaxed another kiss from her and it fed the seething hunger building inside of him. For every moment she let him stay he wanted another two, for every four he wanted eight. It was beyond exponentials. It was beyond anything he'd ever known . . . or cared to know. Usually something like this . . . something outside of the norm . . . was something to be avoided at all costs. The kind of life he led, there was no room for extraordinary things when it came to women. In his experience they simply couldn't take him in serious measure. No average woman could ever cope with the mercenary way he lived his life and the deadly games he played. So that meant lying. And anyone worth having wouldn't deserve the stack of lies he'd have to tell just so she would find comfort and peace of mind. It was exactly what she had been saying. They were better off not knowing.

This time he was the one who broke away from her. He backed away, stunned by the turn of his thoughts. It was like a new shoe in the wrong size. It didn't fit him. And it would be painful to wear besides. It must have shown clearly on his face because she sighed, a deflation of her energy that told him she understood him all too well.

"It will be daylight soon. Perhaps we should take the opportunity to sleep."

"Okay," he said, as he tried to cut off this seemingly new urge to examine his motivations.

But it wasn't okay. Feeling her move away, feeling her growing more distant . . . it was everything but okay.

Why? he asked himself. Why was this frustration and confusion present like this? This should be a clear-cut understanding that he was better off keeping a fair distance from her. And frankly she was better off keeping a fair distance from him. This physical connection . . . it was all wrong.

So why couldn't he just walk away? Why couldn't he file it under the "get out while you still can" category and feel lucky for the escape? He'd done it before. Dozens of times. Probably more times than was right.

But she was different. Just by virtue of being a Night Angel, she didn't fit neatly into all the little categories he usually put women into. She was a puzzle and a wild card and he simply didn't know what to do with her.

"Tell me, what does a Night Angel princess do besides run around saving the world?" he asked as he followed her over to the comfortable grouping of sofas. He watched her sit down, curling her legs beneath herself, her head tilting to the left a little as she quietly took his measure.

"Isn't saving the world enough?" she asked. But he could hear that light brush of amusement in her voice and it made him shoot her a wry grin.

"It's a pretty decent occupation I suppose. I've done it one or two times myself."

He took a seat on the other end of the sofa, turning himself toward her so he could continue to study her. And there they sat, side by side, each trying to grasp what made the other tick.

"My father rules the North America Night Angels with a very careful hand. He has expectations of his people. He makes it very clear that there is a code we must live by and he won't settle for anything less. It's a code we enjoy fulfilling, otherwise my father would not be ruler to one of the most powerful Nightwalker races on this planet."

"And what is this code?" Leo asked.

She tipped her head again, just as she did every time his questions made her recall a memory. It was as if the movement helped her to access her thoughts. It made the fine white strands of her hair brush softly against her skin.

"We're Angels. We're called Angels for a reason. We are meant to take care of this world we live in and all of its inhabitants. The world has a natural course to take, and we see that it's not destroyed by unnatural, evil things. Things like Apep. Although, as I understand it, it's been a very long time since something as dangerous as Apep has threatened the world."

"So you're telling me that you are just . . . do-gooders. Just for the sake of doing good?" He tried not to sound disbelieving, but it was very hard not to. In his experience no one did anything without hoping for some kind of quid pro quo.

"We have an altruistic bent, yes," she said. "But we're far from perfect and far from being purely good. We are a people like any other people. We have our good, our bad, and our indifferent. We have our heroes and our criminals. But law-abiding Angels approach their nights, each and every one of them, with the will to make the world a better or safer place in whatever way they can. If it means capturing a criminal, then we set out to capture that criminal. If it means giving aid in a place torn by disaster, then we give that aid."

"To humans? Looking like this?" He indicated her white hair and black skin, both of which would make her stand out like a sore thumb . . . never mind the electric-blue wings.

"There are those of us who can alter people's perceptions . . . make humans see us as just a group of normal humans trying to help. Just like there are those of us who can sometimes see into the future and know when dangers are lying in wait for us . . . and if we are lucky they will even know what we can do to alter that chain of events from happening."

"Like you did when you kept Apep from killing Jackson. So someone saw that was going to happen and your father willingly sent his daughter to get in between a wrathful god and his victim? And why only you? Why not a phalanx of Angels?"

"My sister is a hierophant and saw that something terrible was going to happen there, but she didn't know precisely what. She told my father it was very dangerous, but all that was needed was a single Angel. My father sent what was needed, and only what was needed. I don't always know what motivates my father, I don't know why he chose to send me in particular, but he is rarely wrong with his actions and those actions have always helped the greater good. I trust him with all my heart and all my soul. There is no one wiser, stronger, or better skilled at navigating the world."

"How old is he? For that matter," he said, thinking on the fly, "how old are you? I couldn't even begin to guess how to tell a Night Angel's age."

She smiled then, her deep violet lips curving with genuine amusement.

"You can tell by our wings," she said. "We aren't born with them. They develop at puberty, rather like a young girl develops breasts. Our puberty, however, doesn't occur until we are nearly fifty years old."

"Fifty! You're fifty?"

"Angels with brown wings are fifty. Angels with green wings are just over a hundred years old. Angels with red wings are about the two-century mark. My sister's wings are red."

"Blue. Get to the blue," he encouraged her. She chuckled at his impatience.

"Blue is about three centuries old. I'm three hundred and eleven years old. But there are angels much older than I am. Angels with white wings are our ancients and are our most revered members of our society."

"Your father?"

She nodded. "He's not the oldest of us, but he is among them. And when he leaves us, his daughters will stand in his stead."

"Really? Even though there are older and potentially wiser Angels out there?"

"Older, perhaps . . . but we are our father's daughters and we like to think that has made us very wise as well. Anyway, it is the law. The rule of our people is first offered to the blood kin of the previous ruler."

"So a bona fide three-hundred-year-old princess. I suppose to you I must seem like . . . I don't know. A child?"

"Hardly that. My age gives me no more or less value than yours does. It only matters what we are at our souls. I am a woman who put herself between a god and his victim, you are a man who is putting his life on the line for a friend. We are not so very different."

Leo reached out to her, catching several strands of her sugary white hair between his fingers, letting it filter softly through them.

"You know something, the more I talk to you, the more you make me feel like I'm a judgmental ass."

"You *are* a judgmental ass," she said with a light laugh. "But it's one of your more endearing qualities."

"Well, I'm glad you're so enamored by it. I have very little else to impress you with."

"You don't need to try to impress me, you've done that quite a bit already," she said.

"I'm afraid to ask in what way."

"In many ways, both good and bad. But if you think I'm going to sit here and judge you like I am holier than thou, you'll be sorely disappointed. You are who you are. You are what the world has made you. Do you really think I consider myself flawless in comparison to you?"

"No," he said. "No, not at all. But unlike myself, you don't cast blanket judgments on others and, somehow, you seem to see the good in others. At least, in my experience so far. You're cautious, but willing to believe the best. Look at Grey. Had I been here alone I probably would have gone for his throat. I wouldn't have succeeded, but I definitely would have tried to kill the fucker."

She quieted and looked away from him and he knew immediately he had stuck his foot in it.

"That's not to say it was a wholly unpleasant experience. Except for the end . . ." He was feeling awkward and when she looked at him, her eyes conveyed her sadness completely. As did the way she absently rubbed her chest above her heart, as though it were physically painful for her to remember. And he knew it was. Just as real as that passion had felt, the tragedy of the death of their child had been blindingly devastating.

Leo reached out for the hand at her heart, taking it between his own and pulling their joined hands against his chest. It drew her forward, closing the distance between them just as effectively as the emotions of the moment were drawing them closer.

"Are you okay?" he asked her gently. He had no idea of knowing what she had experienced from her point of view. Had she witnessed the violence of the act itself? He knew she had experienced what it had felt like to hold her lifeless child against her heart.

"It's better when I tell myself it wasn't real . . . but you know it . . . it felt so real and in some ways it still does." She looked away from him, and he could see the painful tears of loss filling her buttery eyes. They seemed paler in luster and just looking at her sent stabs of remembered devastation through him.

"We can't do this to ourselves," he said quietly.

"Well, excuse me if I do!" she bit out at him. "I can't

just turn off my feelings and responses to things like you can!"

"I never said I was . . . that was just as devastating to me as it was for you!"

"Really?" she said snidely, pulling at her hand. He refused to let go. "Because it seems to me that's it's so easy for you to ignore all of the things we felt!"

That quieted him, forcing him to acknowledge what she meant. He still held her hand to his heart, could feel the warmth of her spreading across his chest like a thick, sweet molasses.

She meant the passion of the kisses they had shared. She meant the overwhelming physical attraction he now felt for her when there had been nothing before Grey had—

That's a lie.

The inner whisper was fierce and acidic, full of self-contempt. He sat there staring at her dead-on as he realized he had been feeling an attraction toward her from the very start. Everything about her had seemed so electric, and that was way before he had even kissed her.

The moment he recalled the crisp, hot passion of their kisses he had to close his eyes. If he accessed those memories while looking at her he'd . . . well, there was no telling what he'd do.

That's a lie.

Oh yes, it was a whopper of a lie. He knew exactly what he would do.

So he opened his eyes and looked at her.

"I'm not ignoring it. In fact," he said, "I'm so far from ignoring it that I really want to throw you on the floor and make like the birds and the bees with you. Exactly like the birds and the bees. One bird with wings and one bee with a vicious stinger of an attitude. Inter-species mingling. Or"—he cleared his throat—"well, I don't even really know if it's possible, but I'd be giving it a damn good try."

Faith's lashes drifted down, hiding her eyes from him, but there was no hiding the way her breath quickened. It was the worst thing that could have happened because the moment he saw that first sign of response, he knew he wanted another. Wanted more. More of her than he'd had, even including what had been conjured in a dream.

If Grey had gotten the details of kissing her wrong, what else had he been cheated of? She was so extraordinary. So deeply layered. She was destined to one day rule an entire species, and that species couldn't have been more lucky. She was sensitive and fair, passionate and sharp. So many things that made her way out of his league before even considering the sexual. When he had stopped earlier it hadn't been because of what she was, it had been because of who she was. Because the one thing he was sure of was that she was far more human than he was.

Leo leaned closer to her, his attention fixing on her deep blackberry-colored lips. "You don't get it, Faith," he said softly, his breath rushing over her lips just as hers was rushing over his. "I'm not pushing you away because of what you are. I was pushing you away because of who *I* am. You deserve someone who can share himself with you completely. How can I give away pieces of myself when they're lying broken on the floor all around us? When I'm not even sure if I know who I am anymore?"

"And I would have thought," she said breathily, "that you of all people would simply ignore that and seize the opportunity."

He bristled at that and pulled back an inch to give her an angry look. "I'm not that much of a prick and I'm sorry that you think I am. You deserve better than me, but hey, if it doesn't matter to you then let's get to it."

With every hour that crept slowly by, Marissa felt her hope draining away in swift rivulets of fear. She had wept all she could, her body now drained of tears, her heart too heavy to even take a breath. Docia kept coming in, kept intruding on her time with him. Didn't she get it? Every minute could be the very last minute she would feel his warmth in her hands. With every minute the specter of death and loneliness threatened to take over.

She didn't expect Docia to understand. The rare and special connection that Marissa felt with Jackson, the love that had endured lifetime after lifetime after lifetime, made them two halves of a whole heart . . . it was so powerful that the removal of one half meant the other half could no longer continue working. Yes, Tameri and Ram had found that same connection, but they had not experienced their first deaths yet. Not since they had found each other. This was the first time they had connected like this. All they knew now was the pleasure and the joy of it. Unlike Hatshepsut who had suffered through Menes's deaths too many times to count. They had yet to know the excruciating pain of it. The rending of the heart and soul that came with it. The borderline insanity of grief that overwhelmed and drowned the survivor.

Marissa was done begging the universe to spare her lover's life. She had poured out every prayer in her heart more than once, and she knew that if it had not heard the wailing of her spirit by now, it never would. And the hope that those prayers would be answered was bleeding away, minute by minute. Like a heart that had been stabbed through with an ice pick, leaving blood and life to ooze away one heartbeat after another.

"I can't breathe," she gasped out softly to her comatose lover. "I can't breathe without you. If they fail me I will suffocate on my pain and grief. Please," she found herself begging the universe once more in spite of her resolve not to. "If you take him, I'm afraid of what I might do. Afraid of what I might become." She swallowed noisily, once more shoving away the blinding rage that threatened to swamp her. But it was as if she were scooping water from a sinking ship using only her hands. It was useless, and eventually . . .

Eventually, she would drown.

CHAPTER THIRTEEN

Leo yanked Faith to him, captured her startled mouth with his and pressed a ravaging kiss on her. Not cruel, as he might have thought he was being. Faith knew to the bottom of her soul that he was capable of deep depths of brutality when it was called for, but the only way his kiss would be cruel would be if he stopped it before it culminated in its promise.

It was sweet and hot, dominant and powerful. He turned with a sharp movement, dragging her underneath himself on the couch. And still he kept his lips seared to hers . . . as if they were conjoined and could not be separated. His tongue swept into her mouth even as his hand swept up the left side of her body. His legs were tangled with hers, but she could feel the heat and strength of a hard muscled thigh pressing directly against her sex, the push of it against her telling her that it was very much on purpose.

The moment he let her take a breath, she quickly said, "I only meant that after having such a brutal brush with death you, of all people, would grip life in both hands! That you'd want to live every moment to its fullest and without regret." When he didn't rush back into his attack, she slowed down for a breath and met his dark, troubled gaze. "I thought . . . I thought if you really wanted me, you wouldn't have let all the rest of it get in the way."

But now she saw that he'd been trying to protect her from himself. She saw it in his sable eyes, settled deeply in with the hunger of desire. He hesitated only a moment before catching her mouth back up, but this time the kiss was slower, almost achingly sweet, most certainly full of a gentle craving. He kissed her like that until her head was spinning and her whole body was humming with need.

This time when he separated from her, both of them breathing as if they'd run a passionate marathon, he said, "I've always thought I should never subject myself onto a certain kind of woman. I always . . . I chose very carefully. Decent enough to tolerate, indecent enough to not care when I disappeared the next morning without so much as a goodbye or thank you. I'm a killer, Faith. I have a lot of blood on my hands and it's not going to change. I'm not a bad man, I just do bad things to bad people. And you know . . . from what Grey showed us . . . you know it took a lot for me to let someone in. When I kiss you that's what it feels like. Like I'm letting you in. And I don't know if I can handle that. I don't know if I'm going to fuck it up and end up fucking you up in the process."

"You won't fuck me up," she said breathily. "I'm a big girl. If you tell me you don't want me to make long-term plans, then I won't."

"It's just . . . it's hard to separate the feelings of . . . I'm not that man, Faith. I'm not the one Grey showed you, the man who can love you."

She didn't think it would have hurt to hear him say that, but it did. And it was a deep hurt. As if he were already her lover, as if he'd already told her he loved her with all his heart and soul, and then told her he had changed his mind.

But unlike a Night Angel male, he was unable to read her scroll and see the depth of that pain. She somehow managed to keep it out of her expression too, otherwise he would never have believed her when she said, "I'm okay. I promise you, I'm going to be all right with that."

It was like setting him free. All of the confusion between them that had caused their passion to seem stilted and jerky evaporated. The minute he returned his mouth to hers, the minute she absolved him of any responsibility, he became a different being.

The electricity of kissing another Night Angel was something familiar and expected, but somehow Leo's kisses began to convey an even more powerful current. There was so much hunger behind it that she could hardly breathe. His hand slid down her side and thigh, quickly sweeping beneath the skirt of her dress. When she tensed, afraid he was going to skip all the niceties now that she'd devalued herself to the worth of a brief one-night stand, she was amazingly mistaken. He merely pulled her leg tight against his hip.

No. He didn't skip any of the niceties at all. He kissed her with the hot, fiery need of a new lover, like when the flirting and mating dance was done and the physical act was on the cusp of resolving. She found her arms hooked beneath his, her hands latching on to his broad shoulders, just touching him there, just touching him *anywhere* was giving her the complete impression of the strength he harbored in his body. He breathed hard and hot into her mouth, his craving for her more than thoroughly announced by the deep masculine groan he let roll out of him.

"My god," he said against her lips, his tongue punctuating every word he said with a lustful stroke. "I can feel your heat against me."

To emphasize what he meant, he pressed his thigh

tightly against her sex. The pressure sent off a wild rush of arousal and she gasped.

"I can't wait to get my hands on that," he said heatedly. "Not to mention my mouth."

She went utterly and absolutely wet. The promise was unbearable and she moaned deeply under the onslaught of it.

"Seems like you're pretty damn eager too," he said with a chuckle, dragging his kisses away from her mouth and burning a path down her throat. She felt his teeth catching her skin in the smallest little impressions of a bite. She felt his hand rushing up the line of her body and streaking from thigh to hip to waist to ribs and then . . . then he caught the weight of her breast in his hand just in time to hold her up to his mouth.

He could have unbuttoned the bodice of the dress easily and exposed her, but he didn't. Instead he mouthed her through the thin fabric, the stroke of his tongue muted and dampening the cloth, but electric and unbelievably arousing. Her nipples distended, as though yearning for the promise of his bare mouth. She moaned softly as her hands crawled up restlessly into his collar and hair. There was just too much fabric between them. She was frustrated by it and it must have transmitted because he gave her a chuckle.

"Trouble?" he asked, his breath warm through her dress as it tumbled over her.

"Take your shirt off," she commanded him, tugging at his collar for emphasis.

He went very still. As still as a wild animal crouching in the grasses, waiting for a predator to pass them by. But it only lasted a moment, such a brief moment that she thought she had imagined it by the time he pulled away from her.

He rose up on his knees and, grabbing it by the collar at the back of his neck, he stripped off his shirt. The shock of what she saw was like a cold-handed slap across her face. On his right side, splayed over his ribs and wrapped halfway around his body was a massive tattoo. But that wasn't what made her breath catch in her throat. No . . . it was that everywhere, streaked left and right, vertically and horizontally and diagonally, almost every single inch of his chest was covered in angry red weals of flesh. He had been injured and was healing, but it was more than obvious that he had not healed enough.

"Oh my god! Leo!"

This, she realized as her shaking hands went to his injured skin, touching it with fierce fragility, this was what had been done to him. It looked horrifyingly like someone had cut strips of flesh from him, and just looking at the grim set of his jaw she knew that it had been exactly that and that he had been awake for every last one of them.

It was no wonder he hated them all.

His scroll was lit up with brilliance as a storm of emotions marched through him. Passion and rage. Craving and hate. Wanting and resolution. Need and vengeance. It was a battle between what he was feeling with her right in that moment and what he had swimming in his heart and the memories connected with the injuries he had suffered. He caught her shaking hands in his, made her look into the dark chocolate of his eyes.

"This is not all of who I am and it doesn't matter in this moment. I need for it to not matter between us, Faith."

And she saw that it was very much the truth. He wanted something new and good to wash away the muck and poison of the rage and impotence he felt every time he remembered what had happened to him.

And she wanted more than anything to give that to him. Using her captured hands to pull him back down to her, she reached for and caught his mouth. She swept her tongue over his lower lip in an erotic invitation, drawing his focus to her mouth. He let go of her hands to brace a hand beside her head, kissing her as deeply as breathing would allow, yet holding his torso up and away from lying against her.

She was sorry her shock had interrupted their passion, but she was determined to win it back. It really wasn't difficult at all. Her entire body still burned for him, against his denim clad thigh she was still wet for him. She reached for the buttons on her dress, determined to rid herself of the frustrating clothing she wore. Faith almost never wore clothes, especially as it was a little painful to use her wings through the confines of clothing. Of course, she made the exception where clothes were concerned when she had to travel in the human world of daylight. But she had chosen this dress because of the light, breezy fit of it so she didn't feel as confined.

Now it was frustrating her, an obstacle in the way of her desire to be touched. And Leo, damn him, was clearly laughing at her expense.

"Stop that and help me," she growled at him impatiently.

"Your wish is my command," he said with amusement. "Consider me your personal Djynn." He moved her hand away from the stubborn buttons, pausing a moment to cup the swelling shape of her left breast before finally reaching for the first closed button. "But if I grant you this wish," he said as he popped the thing free with an easy brush of his fingers, "you know there's going to be a price to pay."

"There's always a price to pay for wishes," she agreed breathily. Watching him undress her with such excruciating slowness felt like dying a little from deprivation.

"Always," he agreed, the second button slipping free. "And I'm going to ask a very high price for this wish."

"Oh?" It was less of a word and more of a sigh as it escaped her.

"Yes. Do you want to know what it is going to be?"

She nodded as the third button was undone. She couldn't have formed a coherent word if it was required to save her life, because now, with every unbound button, he was pausing to stroke ever-so-light sweeps of his fingers over whatever flesh was newly exposed. It was mostly the line of her breastbone, and she arched her back a little to try to let her breast come into his sight more fully. But the bodice was too snug and her breasts too full to allow for it. He continued to work the buttons free, and it frustrated her that they ran the entire length of the dress. She was quite certain they weren't meant to be undone completely. Didn't he remember they were working with very limited time? She could feel the approach of daylight creeping along the follicles of her hair.

"Surrender," he exhaled against the skin of her upper belly. "Complete and total and utter surrender."

Faith felt yet another button give way and now his tongue was drawing a heated circle around the outside of her navel. At that point she had no choice but to lose patience. If he was working to frustrate her, he was doing a bang-up job of it, but she'd had just about enough of it.

Apparently, so had he. Impatience blared through his scroll, and suddenly he was surging up onto his knees, reaching for both halves of her dress and with a yank that oozed barely repressed ferocity, he peeled apart the bodice, jerking the dress down her shoulders and arms, forcing her to wriggle them free or else find herself tied down by her clothing. She couldn't stand the idea of that so she let him strip her to her waist.

"Jesus," he said on a quick breath as he looked down at her. "How did I not see it before?"

"See what?" she asked shakily as she watched him reach toward her with fascinated fingers. He touched her along the bottom swell of her left breast.

"That you aren't as universally black as I first perceived you as being. That, like your lips, you're actually a very deep violet at your nipples and . . ."

He went back to her buttons, this time working quickly. She knew what he was looking for and it made her entire body flame with a flush. In another instant she was naked beneath him and he was reaching to touch searching fingertips to the nude pillow of flesh protecting the entrance to more darkly violet parts of her. He moved his touch down and separated the lips of her sex, spreading her wide so he could inspect the color variation more thoroughly.

"Here," he finished his sentence at last. "Such a pretty, dark color." He let his fingers slide into the very wet folds of her flesh and she heard him growl with pleasure. She knew it was because she was so obviously aroused by him. And as one hand explored her there, the free hand came back to the task of shaping and toying with her breasts. The full strokes, touches, and the plucking of his fingertips on her nipples felt incredibly glorious and astoundingly frustrating all at once.

Then, as if knowing a complaint was brewing behind her lips, he lowered his head to her, the dart of his tongue caressed and painted her nipple, catching the beaded tip of it between his teeth then sucking her hard against his palate.

It was like throwing gasoline on a banked fire. They went from idling desire straight to virulent passion. Their mouths crashed together, tongues tangling. Leo forgot about keeping her from touching his chest as he lost himself in her savage mouth. He stroked her sex with swirls of movement until she was taut with expectant nerves.

"Please," she panted when she next came up for air. *"Please!"*

He could have teased her or tormented her some more, she supposed. She was, after all, an easy mark at that point. But it spoke volumes of his own impassioned investment as he left off from touching her in order to unbutton and unzip his jeans. Freed from its cruel prison, his erection made a sudden and stunning appearance. She reached for him even as he pulled her hips down a little farther on the couch cushions.

"Sweet mother of God," he groaned when she wrapped her hand around him tightly. He thrust forward into her fingers, a heated curse erupting from him as she made thorough work of learning him by touch. He was doing the same, his fingers drenched by her saturated intimate flesh. The next instant he was thrusting an impatient finger up into her body, and then he made it a pair. She gasped, raising her hips toward the invasion of his touch.

He was so hot and heavy in her hands. She'd never had a human lover, and knew of very few Night Angels who ever had in their long lifetimes, but she'd always thought they would pale beside a lover from her own species. How wrong she had been. His fervor alone was something so different for her. Night Angel males were so cool, aloof to the point, sometimes, of looking like they didn't really care one way or another. But this was so not true of Leo. He ran hot and made her run at equally blistering temperatures.

He thrust his fingers up into her again and again until she was calling out her increasing pleasure again and again.

"I could make you come just like this," he said hotly against her ear. "Over and over, let you burn yourself up like a little melting candle. But I'm not going to. Not this time."

And before she could stop it, her heart took flight at his words. Not *this* time. Which meant he wasn't planning on doing this just once. She tried to rein herself in but she was running on pure adrenaline and couldn't control herself. He pulled his hand free of her, pushed her thighs apart with a dominant surge of his hips, putting himself in bald contact with her heat. So eager was she that her back arched and pleasure swam through her. Pleasure as close as she could possibly get to orgasm but not quite. But the fluid movement of her own body made a stark contrast to the sudden inflexibility of his. He was very still again. Breathing hard, his muscular body tense and defined with need, he cursed.

How could he be so stupid? It had never entered his mind, not once, until he felt that stark touch of intimate flesh to intimate flesh. It was something he never did. Never once. Not bareback that is.

A condom. He didn't have a goddamn condom. It wasn't as though he had ever thought for even an instant when setting out on this little adventure that he would need one. But he'd always had one in his wallet because, you know, you just never know. He was always up for unexpected pleasures. But he had been stripped of everything because of Chatha, and that included his wallet, his I.D., and his emergency condom.

Fuck.

"Faith," he rasped roughly near her ear. "We . . . I can't . . ."

But she felt so incredibly good. Good enough to outweigh his fears and his sense of self-protection. And because he could feel that, because the temptation rode him that hard, he pulled away from her. He was off her and on his feet in the next heartbeat, stumbling with an awkward lack of coordination. He was a coward and turned his back on the shock written across her features. *What the hell do you have to feel so bad about?*

You're doing the right thing, his conscience whispered fiercely to him.

He heard her move and he grabbed his shirt up from the floor shielding himself with it as he tried to explain to certain body parts that there was no relief or fun in the immediate future. Why didn't he explain himself? He didn't know. Maybe because he was just as disappointed as he knew she was?

When he was finally able to redress himself he turned to her, running an agitated hand through his hair. She was sitting up, knees primly together, hands clasped loosely on her thighs. She had not buttoned her dress back up, and he found it incongruous until he remembered she was wearing clothing as an afterthought.

But it was her stricken expression that hit him to the quick, and it made his heart ache.

"No, no, no, no," he soothed, hurrying to kneel before her, grabbing up her hands and squeezing them tightly. "This isn't about you. This isn't a rejection in the smallest of ways. Look at me," he commanded, making her look into his eyes. He saw they were wet with unshed tears and he realized . . . for the very first time he really saw her for the gentle, emotional soul that she was. What Grey had showed him was only the surface, but it all rang loudly in his head. She wanted to be loved. She wanted to be passionate. She wanted to be a mother one day and have a family and be . . . be happy.

"It's just an inconvenience," he said softly, bringing her tense fingers to the kiss of his lips. "It's just the wrong place at the wrong time with the wrong circumstances. Come here," he said. Pulling her close and wrapping his arms around her. He whispered into her ear. "There is nothing I want more than to make love with you right now. Don't you dare doubt that. But . . . I'm not the kind of guy who has unprotected sex with anything that moves and turns his back on the possible consequences. Especially not with you."

He felt her tense and he pulled back to see her wounded look.

"Faith! Look at me! I mean I won't risk getting you pregnant knowing what I do about how damn dangerous pregnancy is for a Night Angel woman. Christ, do you think I'd be that careless? That thoughtless of you?"

She shook her head, but still she was silent, and then he realized it was because it was taking everything she had not to give in to tears. He had handled this badly, had insulted her unintentionally, and he'd confused her before making himself clear. In short, he was a dick.

He sighed, deflating as he rested his forehead against her knee.

"I suppose 'I'm sorry' isn't going to cut it?"

"No. I mean, it's fine," she said at last. "There's nothing for you to apologize for. This was a crazy idea all around. I mean, I'm a Night Angel. A Nightwalker. And you don't . . . well, it's different worlds, isn't it? If not for Grey's tampering, we wouldn't even have considered . . . anyway, it's like you said. It's for the best."

She stood up and walked away from him, leaving him there on his knees. What she was saying was very true, Leo acknowledged.

So why did it sting like a rejection so damn bad?

CHAPTER FOURTEEN

"This form is so limiting," Apep observed, once again inspecting himself in the mirror. "I can't sense things as well as I should. It's seriously curtailing my omniscience. However, as time goes on it should improve. I am, after all, *me*. But it does leave me with a little bit of a problem."

"Oh?" Chatha asked. He had taken a break from his dissecting amusements. Because he had the power to heal, he could do his experiments to a certain point and then heal his object of study; at the moment the little white rabbit was hopping around the room in confusion. What he found the most fascinating was finding the point where healing could no longer occur. What, exactly, was too far? When was that invisible line crossed? It was an art form, truly, to know exactly when that crucial moment was. That was why he had to practice on the smaller life forms. To perfect his craft.

"Yes, it does. I can't see clearly what is happening at that little farm in New Mexico. I went to retrieve Kamen, that foolish man, so he could come back and worship me like he ought to have done, but then that Night Angel interfered. Come to think of it, I owe her a bit of comeuppance," Apep said, straightening his spine at the sudden inspiration. "Yes. Let's find that little bitch of a Night Angel and show her that she can't be rude to a god and expect to get away with it. It's my duty to do so."

"Yup," Chatha said. He had learned that agreeing with the god was the best course of action. And Chatha was happy to stay where he was as long as the god fed him new toys to play with. That idea made him perk up. "Play?"

Apep sighed in exasperation. "Very well, if you *must*!" he said. "I'll bring the Night Angel here to you and you can play with her all you like. That should definitely teach her a lesson. I don't know why I didn't think of it sooner."

"You had to make a baby."

"Oh yes! That's right. I have to have my priorities." Apep was quiet for a moment, and then quickly grew bored. "This gestation process takes an incredibly long time."

Apep sighed again. He would simply have to pass time entertaining himself with the Night Angel and whatever else turned him on.

"So let me search for her a bit." Apep closed his eyes and reached out with his godly senses, looking for the signature, or ka, of the creature that had attacked him. It was easy, actually, because once *his* power had touched *her* power he had learned what her ka felt like and would, from that moment on, be able to search for it with ease.

Only, there was no ease, Apep learned with a stormy little frown. As far as he could tell, the Night Angel wasn't in that more immediate dimension. She had disappeared. She couldn't be dead, could she? That would be terribly disappointing. Especially for Chatha. He did want to make Chatha happy. After all, he'd grown quite fond of the little deviant.

Apep decided to section off a small part of his energy

to keep an ear out for her in case she returned. It was possible she was in one of the scapes, as the Shadowdwellers liked to call them. There were several, although certainly more than the three the Shadowdwellers were aware of.

Thinking of the Shadowdwellers made Apep think about the curse that was keeping one set of Nightwalkers from seeing the other set. It had been a very long time since he had constructed that little gem of a curse.

Once upon a time there were several gods—all of whom were less powerful than Apep, of course—and they had come together to fight a great war against other gods, also not as powerful as Apep was, but a nuisance just the same. Each created a race of Nightwalkers to act as their champions. There had been a terrible war and eventually they had been victorious. Apep grudgingly had to admit the Nightwalkers they had created had played a very key role in that. As a reward for all their hard work, the gods had set the Nightwalkers into the mortal world where they could live in peaceful retirement . . . and be available should the need arise.

Over time peace had grown frighteningly boring for Apep. To amuse himself he was reborn in mortal form and decided to play a delightful game of mortal chess. He captured cities, decimated armies, violated women. Yes, it was all great fun. But soon his nemesis, a god named Amun, had come and warned him to evacuate his corporeal form or he would forcibly extricate him from the mortal world. Apep had not liked the ultimatum, but he knew Amun was very good for his word and that he would enlist the help of the other gods to see it done. And, while no single god was more powerful than he was, a joined group of gods would certainly be something to take seriously.

Well, at the time he'd been having much too much fun to leave, so Apep had chosen to stay. But he had realized that that meant the gods could send the Nightwalkers after him and while he was omnipotent, his mortal body could be destroyed under the right set of circumstances and he would then have to start all over again. He had not been in the mood for that and had been determined to adhere to what he already had.

So in order to prevent that from happening, Apep had constructed this gorgeous, deeply involved curse that had made it so the Nightwalkers would be split in half and the two sets would be completely ignorant of the existence of one another. It had been very complex. It had taken a great deal of talent and power to make it so that, for instance, the written word of a Night Angel could not be read by a Demon. The words would be incomprehensible, the words shifting continuously. This way, if the Demon should stumble across a Bodywalker tomb or scroll, their minds would be blind to it. Then, if, say, a Shadowdweller physically bumped into a Night Angel, they would be none the wiser for it.

So the split had been right down the middle. Six, the Demons, Lycanthropes, Druids, Shadowdwellers, Vampires, and Mistrals were ignorant of the existence of the other six, the Bodywalkers, Night Angels, Wraiths, Djynn, Phoenixes, and Mysticals, and vice versa. Therefore it had made it impossible for them to join forces together against Apep, and eject him from his mortal form.

Apep had even given the Wraiths, the race *he* had created, their death-touch so they could lay waste to the other Nightwalkers with ease. But in that way the curse had backfired the teeniest bit because it now protected half of the races from the Wraiths. Of course, if he dissolved the curse that would instantly open the field. Definitely something for him to think about.

Anyway, in the end it had all been for naught. Amun had rallied the other gods and had ripped the mortal world away from Apep. Then, they had added insult to injury and had used their significant power to create an ethereal prison for Apep, which had insured that he could not be reborn again. He had been trapped there for eons. But then his liberator had come along and had somehow, delightfully, freed him from his prison! Now he was mortal again and able to play games once again. And with no sign of Amun or the other gods, this time he could run amok without interference.

So it was best, he resolved, that the curse remain tightly in place. It was now only the joined forces of the Nightwalkers that could cause him threat. And that powerful Bodywalker Pharaoh had been one of the key dangers in need of eradication. So although he had failed to retrieve Kamen, he had succeeded in eliminating that particular threat.

Now Apep was making a list of the most powerful creatures in each Nightwalker race. He would pick them off one by one and weaken the Nightwalker ranks considerably. Just in case they thought to try something. It was purely precautionary.

Perhaps he would start with the Demon King. Then the Ancient Demon medic named Gideon. The Lycanthropes did not concern him, but the Vampire Prince was a great source of power.

Perhaps what he should do next was go to the Wraiths and recruit them to his side once more. He would remind them from whence they had come and out of sheer loyalty they would be on his side once more.

So which should he do? The Night Angel bitch or reclamation of his Wraith forces?

"I've such a busy schedule," Apep sighed.

"Can I help?" Chatha asked eagerly. "I need new toys, remember."

"Yes, yes," Apep said with dismissive impatience. But then he perked up. "Yes! An excellent idea! Chatha, my love, I will send you out to retrieve the Night Angel toy as soon as she returns to this scape! You can play with her while I hunt down the Doyen of the Wraiths. An excellent plan! I'm so clever, really. It's almost unfair."

Smiling, Apep went about making himself pretty so the Doyen could not mistake his magnificence and would know from the very start how amazing he truly was.

Grey was watching. He sat in a chair set in the upper left corner of the library he had left his guests in. The chair was floating near the ceiling, and both it and Grey were invisible to all eyes. Well, except to a Phoenix's eye, but that went without saying. Phoenixes could see anything. Right through magic, right through glamours. It was called true vision. And like a Wraith's death-touch, it was a force to be reckoned with. That was probably why he avoided both species like the plague.

He supposed it was a bit cowardly of him to set this task on these two individuals, but he didn't have much choice. He could not risk his own life at this juncture. He knew he was one of the most powerful Djynns alive and that he would be crucial when the time came to face the danger that was brewing, but for all his power, a single touch from even the weakest of Wraiths would kill him.

He wasn't a coward so much as he was aware of his limitations. Just as Leo was aware of *his* limitations. Grey had considered, for a brief moment, conjuring a condom for the poor fellow and dropping it down on them in its nice little packet. But then that would have given away that he was observing them, so he had restrained himself. He knew that if they wanted to be together, be it physically or emotionally, they would have to find their own way.

What he had shown them had been one of many possible futures. And now that the wish had been made, Grey was able to tap the magic that would help him to save the life of the Bodywalker Pharaoh. And it was crucial for that to have happened. But first . . . first he needed this nikki. If for no other reason than to get it out of the hands of the Wraiths, the nik needed to be got. He had been trying to come up with a possible solution for quite some time now, and it had never occurred to him to simply send in a mortal human.

Mainly because while they were immune to the death-touch, it didn't mean they wouldn't still be outmatched by the supernatural strength and power of the Wraiths.

What amazed him was that the Night Angel was very obviously planning to go with the human man. She had to be terrified, knowing that all it would take is a single touch, but she was bravely determined to back him up.

It was strange to Grey, this sexual tension between such disparate beings. When he had seen a future with such a strong possibility of a union between them he had realized it was something that must be engendered. There were ramifications to such a union. In fact, it was necessary if they wanted to have the strength needed for the coming storm. Both Leo and Faith would be essential to defeating the evil that would come upon them.

Grey waited until they were all clothed and the majority of their autonomic functions had calmed down, then decided it would be best to disturb the thickening tension in the air. The best thing for all involved would be to get this task started.

* * *

Faith was trying to figure out how she was feeling. Numbness for one. Was she hurt or was she relieved? Was she insulted or was she complimented by the idea that he wanted to take care of her? He wanted to make certain she was kept safe. And she could respect that he was being responsible.

Still, there was a sense of rejection involved in this. She knew she shouldn't feel it, that it was irrational, but it was there all the same. She opened her mouth to say something to Leo, to seek some kind of reassurance, but just as she did, Grey appeared between them.

"Let's begin. Daylight has come. I will teleport you to the Wraith's stronghold. I can bring you right to his door, but not to the room where the nik is. Wraiths have protections that keep beings like me out of their homes. So it will be up to you to make your way to where the nik is. And I am sorry but I have no floor plan. But I do have this."

Grey produced a small electronic device about the size of a cellphone. It was a flat screen and it had two dots on it that were blinking. One blue, one red.

"It's very straightforward. You are the red dot, the nik is the blue. Head straight for it and get out as soon as you can. I'll be watching. The only way I can rescue you or get you out of there is if you exit the walls of the house. You must make your way free of them or I can't help you."

"Got it," Leo said, tucking the device in his back pocket and quickly girding himself with the gear he'd been given.

After a moment Grey turned to Faith.

"Going with him is suicidal, you know."

"I know. But he'll be dealing with supernatural beings and will need my help. What I need is an outfit that covers me head to toe, wrist to wrist, and up my throat. Can you give me that?"

"One catsuit coming right up."

Grey snapped his fingers and Faith found herself covered exactly as mentioned. She felt like the fabric was suffocating her, but it was better than leaving her skin bare to the touch of a Wraith. She was happy to see he had thought to give her gloves as well. The material was black and a light, thin spandex, so it wasn't as bad as all that. It still allowed her to move freely.

She tugged at her gloves and the edges of her sleeves nervously, making certain they overlapped so none of her skin was exposed. The only part of her left bare was her face and the long white tail of her hair. She had worked it into a thick plait and it swung freely down her back.

She looked up and found Leo staring at her with a hard look. She looked at him askance.

"One wrong move and they could . . ."

"I won't make a wrong move," she promised him. "In fact, I plan on us getting in and out of there without seeing a single soul."

"I can do that," Leo said. But he was still not comforted. He was incredibly anxious about her coming and it was a risky distraction. But she was right. She was his ace in the hole if he came up against anything powerful. Her ability to deflect power back to the caster was invaluable.

"Okay, Grey. Get us out of here."

CHAPTER FIFTEEN

The sun seemed almost garish as it beat down on them. To Leo it seemed strange to be moving clandestinely in daylight rather than night. The principal was the same, but it was sort of like wearing a swimsuit in the snow in his mind. He was used to navigating in the dark and in the shadows. He was used to sneaking around, using stealth, and dozens of tactics employed strictly in the dark in order to keep from being detected. He was used to slipping in like something cold and quiet, something unexpected and dangerous. But this was a whole new set of rules and he hoped he could adjust accordingly.

He hadn't worked with a team since his Army Ranger days. And back then he had been completely well versed on what all of the other soldiers were capable of, seeing as how they had trained together so much that they knew one another like the backs of their hands. He only knew part of what Faith could do. Of course what he did know about her was pretty amazing, but he knew that was only the tip of the iceberg. He knew that there was so much more to her.

Well, he knew one thing about her for sure; he knew that she was a very passionate creature. In fact he had to make himself *not* think about what a passionate creature she was or he wouldn't be focusing on the moment. And God knew he needed to very much be focused on the moment. But once he started to think about it, it was damn hard to stop. He could still remember the taste of her. The warm, delicious smell of her. The way she made little sounds and moans when he touched her at just the right spot.

And the more he thought about it, the more he began to realize that there were other things he could have done to give her the pleasure she had deserved. He had just been so out of his element, so off kilter ever since this whole journey begun. And he didn't just mean the journey since they had left New Mexico searching for Grey; he meant the whole kit and caboodle, including his lovely vacation at the hands of Chatha.

Shaking his head he reminded himself of the danger that they were facing. He reminded himself that all it would take was one touch and Faith would be dead. And that was more than enough ice-cold water to keep him on task. Grey had cleverly planned their insertion by materializing them right at the front door or, rather, the back door. At least that's what it looked like. It was hard to tell which part was the front of the house and which part was the back from their position.

They immediately backed up flush to the house and looked around to make sure that there were no human or daylight immune guards. Grey had said he could insert them at a prime moment and he would know if there were any guards in the immediate area and could protect them from a precipitous appearance in a guard's path.

It looked pretty quiet but that did not mean that there were no technological observers, as well as whatever magical ones they were using to protect the stronghold. The sooner they got inside the better.

In his back pocket Leo had lock picks. It was actually

a very nice set. But hey, you can get the best when you had a Djynn providing all of your equipment. But before Leo opened the lock pick pouch, he had to inspect the door very carefully.

Faith was no stranger to working in a clandestine manner. She did not exactly feel like a duck out of water. She did not feel frightened, although there was a heightened sense of nervousness. But who wouldn't be nervous if they were about to enter a house full of an indeterminate amount of people who could use a mere touch to bring about the end of your life? But mostly her fear was all centered around Leo. He was only human. She didn't care how skilled he thought he was. It would be nothing in the face of a race of people with extraordinary strength, amazing reflexes, and a really bad attitude. It was said that Wraiths despised humans. But then again it was said that Wraiths despised everybody.

The house that they appeared behind was a two or three story colonial; or so it seemed from the outside. Just like any other house you might see on any other street in any other suburb. But there were no streets. There were no neighbors, and for all they knew they were hell and gone from America. There was an enormous field as far as the eye could see in all directions. She could easily picture what it might look like in summertime, waist high wheat grasses or corn, no matter which way you turned it would be a wall of uniform vegetation.

Leading directly up to the house itself was a little footpath made of crooked bricks and oddball stones that curved and wobbled and wended as if it were an afterthought rather than a planned walkway.

"Hey, Faith," Leo said softly, "get down low and wait for me right here. I'll be right back."

"Wait! Where are you going?" The last was said in a low hiss of a whisper, but she may as well have been talking to herself because he was already gone. If she wasn't nervous before, she most certainly was when he just left her there to her own devices. For some reason, having him next to her had made her feel more secure. Safer. Protected. Wasn't that funny? That she should feel safer because he was around when, in fact, she was the stronger of the two of them? At least physically speaking. She briefly thought about the scars on Leo's chest and realized just how tough of a person he really had to have been in order to make it through something like that. She was pretty positive that she would not have made it out of that completely intact. But then again it was quite possible that Leo had not made it out of that without significant mental damage. In fact, his hatred of all things Nightwalker was very indicative of the damage path that had been torn through him.

There was a bush to the left of the door. It was a low scrappy little thing with barely any leaves on it and would provide absolutely no coverage, but she found herself crouching down behind it just the same. Her breath came nervously, her chest felt as though a length of fabric had been wrapped tightly around it and was being tied tighter and tighter and tighter, until there was no more room for breath. As she waited anxiously for him to return it was as though time began to crawl, limping along, and everything she did, every minuscule breath she took, was as loud as a scream.

Suddenly he was back beside her, touching her shoulder and shushing her when she gasped in surprise.

"My god, where did you go?"

"Just had to take care of a little alarm," he said. He reached up to the doorknob and as if he were using a key in the lock rather than a couple of lock picks, he quickly unlatched it. The door swung in without a sound.

He ushered her in with a light touch on her back and

she moved quickly ahead of him. It was throttling, the way her entire self tried to pull her back to the exit, back to the relative safety of daylight. Leo checked the area quickly, then looked back at her.

They had agreed that the best plan of action was to find a safe spot as soon as they entered the house and wait for her to resolve into her normal color and revert into a powerful state. Since it took time for her color to change it would be a dangerous few minutes. What was in their favor was that she had not been in the sun for very long and so she would revert more quickly.

They had entered into a small vestibule with a door opening a few feet up to the left, and hallway walls leading a good distance away. She couldn't see what kind of room it was, and it didn't matter to her. What mattered was the fear climbing over her. She was fighting it with every part of her spirit, wrestling with it so hard she broke into a cold sweat.

She watched Leo move forward a few inches and glance into the room. He shook his head hard, indicating that he wasn't happy with what he saw.

"Kitchen," he whispered on the barest push of sound.

The kitchen in any house was a central hub of traffic. The one thing everyone had in common was the need to eat. The second thing would be the need to eliminate so the bathrooms were guaranteed to be just as busy. He moved forward down the hall and she followed quickly, both of them moving in a low silent crouch. Her heart was pounding, the swish and flow of her blood noisy in her ears. A short way up the hall they found another doorway on the right. He glanced into this one too and must have liked what he saw because he gestured her in. The smell in the room, redolent with perfume and damp heat, would have told her it was the laundry room even if she hadn't seen the washer and dryer within. As she moved in she felt his hand touch briefly along her spine, a seemingly innocent gesture that both soothed and added to the tension of the moment.

There was no door to the room, so all they could do was stay there, quietly crouched, studying her skin as it began to darken to a fair charcoal-gray color. She could hear the rush of her breath, panicking that it was too loud while at the same time marveling that she couldn't hear his breath at all. In fact, he seemed calm enough to dig in and take a freaking nap! He reached out to her then, obviously reading her state of mind, and laid a hand on her neck, his thumb touching her on the only exposed skin she had, that of her face. He guided her to look straight into his eyes and she did. He didn't speak a single word with his lips, but volumes with his eyes.

I'm here. I'm right here. I won't let anything near you.

Finally her skin was black again and she could feel the energy of her wings at her back. The comfort it gave her was boundless, but it couldn't touch the comfort she had gotten from Leo's eyes.

He nodded when he realized she was ready and moved around to the door, keeping her safely at his back. Before she could catch her breath he was moving out of the room, forcing her to hurry after him or find herself alone and exposed without him. As they moved she was aware of Leo, aware of his strength and the catlike beauty of his movements as he took point, moving with confidence, and a perceived sense of fearlessness. Every so often he'd reach back with his left hand, touching her hip as if he were corralling her into place and the relative safety behind him.

She saw him glance at the electronic device Grey had given them, using it as a guide to move through the hallways. She followed him from one to the next, never knowing what they were going to see, never knowing what they were going to find around the next corner, but going just the same. It seemed like the most perfect act of insanity.

He stopped her and she found herself holding her breath again. She watched him reach for a hunting knife that he had in his flack jacket. He slipped the black blade out of its sheath with perfect silence. There wasn't a single ray of light in the entire house, the windows obviously polarized just like most Nightwalkers would use in their private houses. She had no idea how he could move in so much blackness or how he could see. She had eyesight meant to see through the dark because she was meant to live in the night. But how did he manage to move and to know where next to step?

She could hear somebody coming. There was no doubt about it, no mistaking the sound. A live being was walking in their direction. A white-hot streak of terror went through her. She suddenly felt completely exposed and wanted to hide her face, the one place on her body where her skin was showing. She was paralyzed with fear and couldn't move but she knew it was the worst thing she could possibly do.

The next thing she knew the coiled line of Leo's body moved, sprang forward like an absurd little jack-in-the-box. There was the sound of contact and the sound of a knife moving through flesh and bone. She could hardly believe what she had seen as a now-lifeless body fell to the floor. Leo had thrust his knife up through his victim's upper throat, through its mouth and the rear of the tongue and into the brain stem. The knife was just as quickly removed as it had been inserted, leaving the body to fall at her feet. Obviously she could not touch it to check and see if it were still alive, but why she would ever want to do that was completely out of the realm of considering. It lay at her feet way too close for comfort, and she could see its face. Its pallor was a complete gunmetal gray, the skin of it like a muted, matte finish. The hair was equally gray, done in a combination of short and long dreadlocks. It had no eyebrows, but his jaw and chin were lined with a short black stubble that accentuated its hollowed-out cheeks.

She had never seen a Wraith before, and she didn't even think she knew anyone who had. She wondered if her father, who had been alive for eight hundred and twenty-two years, had ever crossed paths with one. It was said, however, that witnesses were few and far between strictly because they never lived to tell the tale. It was rail thin, as if it had some sort of wasting sickness. And the smell . . . the smell of it was the foulest thing she'd ever known.

She covered her mouth and nose, gagging from the stench and from the fear that it was going to reach out and touch her, even though she knew it was dead, that it couldn't possibly have survived.

Suddenly she felt Leo reaching down for her hands, the strength of his fingers wrapping around hers, giving her comfort and reassurance. Once again it was a support that she needed more than anything in that instant. And it meant something to her that he was giving it to her in the middle of all this deadly madness.

He pulled her close to his back. Close enough that she could feel his warmth. She suddenly felt the urge to cuddle up to him, just so she could feel the vigor of him. It was a ridiculous impulse to have at the most ridiculous time.

They went past several more doorways and went down several more hallways. They seemed to go on and on, and it felt like they weren't getting any closer to their goal. Faith's heart was beating like a drum, every once in a while missing a beat when she thought she heard something over the clamor of it and her breathing. *Why oh why do I have to be so loud? Can they hear me? Are they able to sense me?* She had no idea what their skills or weaknesses were, had no way of preparing against them if she could.

As for Leo, it was as though he were taking a walk in the park; every step was made with ease, every move was succinct and sure.

"We're close," he told her in that nearly airless whisper. "I think what we're looking for is either through this door, or the other one off the hallway parallel to this one. Stay very close."

As if he had to remind her. Leo knew she was scared because every time he touched her to bring her closer in he could feel her whole body shaking. But he was much more relaxed now that he knew he could kill them using the methods he was most comfortable with. Guns were good and all of that, but nothing beat a good, dependable knife when it came to moving through a place in stealth. The maneuver he'd used to take out the Wraith was one he had practiced hundreds of times and utilized more times than he could count. It allowed for a quick death and prevented an opportunity for the target to raise up a vocal alarm.

Leo gently tested the knob to the door. He began to doubt this was the right room the minute it turned easily in his hand. If this was such a powerful nik, why wasn't it being guarded with more than a juvenile alarm system and carelessly unlocked doors? The tongue of the doorknob slid out of the latch with the smallest of clicks. With a single finger he gave the door a small push, letting it swing open by several inches. The room was as black as pitch, just like all the others before it. Grey had offered him night vision goggles, but he had declined. The fewer encumbrances he had the better off he was. Besides, they cut off his peripheral vision and he needed eyes in the back of his head for this mission. He signaled Faith to stay with another gentle touch of his fingers, and moving as silently and lightly as was possible he slid through the door and did a fast sweep of all corners of the room as best he could in the dark. But for Leo, it had never been about just what he could see. It had been about instinct. The instinct to sense when there was another body in the room. He wouldn't have been able to explain it to an outsider. There was just a different feel to a space when something living was in it.

As far as human bodies were concerned, that is. He had no idea what he was up against in this setting. Like Faith, he would be the first to admit this was a poorly prepared plan. Not knowing everything about their enemy was the largest deficit. The second deficit, he realized, was that Grey hadn't told them what the nikki looked like. He'd only said "You'll know it when you see it."

He hated cryptic bullshit like that, but when Leo had pressed him Grey had refused to respond. And since Grey was the one with all of the power in the situation, he'd had very little choice open to him. They had to do this. So it had just been about gritting his teeth and hoping for the best.

The room was not very large, but he knew right away that there was nothing of import in it. Nikkis were alive. They would move or breathe or something to that effect. He pulled his gun, flipped on the laser sight and quickly ran it around the room. It was only a thin red beam of light, not meant to be a flashlight, but he could see what the light looked like as it hit the target of the wall and it helped him make out the molding and indentation of another door.

And then, suddenly he felt it. Knew something was there. He jolted to the right just as something hit him with a screeching growl. It plowed into him, sending him crashing down into the floor. He felt the impact clawing across every one of the partially healed wounds in his chest and he couldn't help the low, gravelly sound that escaped him. The gun went skidding across the floor, the knife did not.

The thing was incredibly strong, no doubt about that, he admitted as he was jerked up and then slammed back into the ground. His head struck and a numb ring echoed throughout his skull. It was the last free shot this thing was going to get. He went to go for its neck when he felt it jerk away from him. To his shocked witness, he watched Faith pull something that had to weigh at least 225 by the feel of it right off its feet, flinging it into the wall. But instead of hitting the wall it went right through it, phasing completely through as though the wall wasn't even there. Then before Leo could fully regain his feet the Wraith came barreling back through the wall with another rasping screech of anger. But instead of a physical attack, this time a cylinder of yellow energy whipped around it before barreling toward them. Again, Faith stepped up, throwing herself between the energy blast and Leo, the power she harbored deflecting the attack right back onto the attacker. Like a nuclear blast, the thing was struck and became an instant, momentary pile of burning ash in the shape of a man . . . before collapsing into a heap of disintegrated cinders.

"Okay, no more skulking. That thing was screeching loud enough to wake the whole damn house," Leo said, not having the time to be utterly impressed by Faith . . . or utterly terrified by the power these things were wielding.

He crashed into the next door, knowing that it was going to be locked. He didn't bother checking for forms of life because if they all could phase through walls like that, then it was a waste of time.

He was reaching for his flashlight, but the moment they were fully in the room they could see the nikki.

"Oh, you gotta be fucking kidding me!" Leo ejected.

It was a horse. A winged blue horse with a sparkling pink mane like some kind of overgrown My Little Pony. That was when he got hit by the stench of horse manure in the room.

"They must have phased it in through the walls," Faith said breathlessly. "It'll be hard, but we can walk it out the way we came or . . ."

"Or?" he prompted, somehow already knowing what she was going to say.

"Or I can grab hold of a Wraith, deflect its phasing ability into the walls ahead of us and, as long as we're connected together, we should all move through just fine."

"Are you out of your mind?"

"It's all I can think of!"

"Great . . . just great," he grumbled, trying not to feel sickened and terrified as he retrieved his weapon. "You're going to commit suicide and I'm supposed to stand and watch? Stand and hold on to a *blue horse* and watch?"

The demand was soundly punctuated by a very long, very low sound of flatulence.

The horse nickered.

"Jesus, when did my life turn into a goddamn carnival?" Leo asked no one in particular. "Lead the horse through the doors. Follow my light. We'll walk it out. I don't want you touching another one of these Wraiths if you can at all avoid it. Now *hurry*."

But just as they were about to drag it through the first door, the horse nickered again as it splayed out an impressive thirteen foot wingspan and struck a shoed foot against the tiled floor so hard sparks flew from the contact. If Leo had to interpret horse-ese, he'd say that definitely equated a desire to stay put. There was no way they were fitting the horse through any door if it kept its wings spread out.

"We're so going to die," Faith said weakly. She looked around the room, trying not to panic. Then her face lit up and she leapt for a burlap bag stamped with the word "apples" on it. She grabbed as many as she could and quickly held one out to the horse.

"Stands to reason there's a bag of apples," she said cooingly to the horse, "because you *like* apples. Now don't you?"

Like a cobra, the beast shot forward and snatched the apple from Faith's hand. It bit into it, half of it falling to the floor, the other half chomped juicily between its teeth.

"Just keep them away from me," Faith said, as she backed out of the door, holding an apple out to the horse. The horse retracted its wings, folding them down tightly to its body, and clip-clopped through the door in pursuit of its next apple. It was going to be slow going, Leo thought with virulent fear clutching in his gut. The alarm was already raised. It made sense that Wraiths would descend on the room with the most valuable commodity in it first to check and see if all was well there. Leo took point again, turning his back on Faith, his shoulder touching hers as they walked back out the way they had come. A Wraith literally came out of nowhere. Jumping out of a wall and leaping onto Leo. Or trying to. Leo raised his weapon and put it down with a shot through its left eye.

"Keep doing brain shots," Faith told him. She was breathless with her fear. But he could see the light of life in her eyes, even through the darkness. He knew exactly how she was feeling. Nothing made you feel more alive than when you were facing the possibility that these were the last few seconds of your life. "They'll keep coming otherwise. If they're like any other Nightwalker they can heal fast and have incredible stamina."

"Incredible stamina, eh? We'll have to test that one

out after we get the hell out of here," he said with a grin.

Leo felt something snare him around his ankle, and he went down on his knee as it tripped him up. He turned his weapon downward and could see a Wraith's hand phased up through the floor from the basement, through his booted foot and gripping painfully tight at his ankle.

That was when he realized that Faith's head to toe clothing was about as effective a protection as a layer of baby powder might have been on her naked skin. These things could phase right through her, touching her from the inside out.

"Faster," he said after raking the knife across the back of the hand holding him. It released with a muffled scream coming up through the floor. "Thank Christ we're on the first floor."

"We just have to make it out the door. Grey said he'd be able to get us as soon as we get out the door."

"Let's pray he's a Djynn of his word."

Faith didn't reveal how much she thought a Djynn's word was worth. She could only hope as much as Leo was hoping. She held out another apple as they turned another corner. Was it her, or did this place seem bigger on the inside than it was on the outside?

It probably was. Like Grey's little gingerbread house, there was some kind of spatial distortion that allowed them to pack a lot of rooms into a small space.

Leo grabbed hold of her arm, hurrying her along after him. She had to resist in order to make sure the horse was still engaged by her lure. But she needn't have worried. It was following eagerly along. And, apparently, apples gave the poor thing terrible gas. Even if they weren't making a racket clomping their way out of the house, the sheer stench of the horse's farts would have led everyone right to them.

"Back door!" Leo called out triumphantly. He jerked the door open sending a stream of bright sunshine into the hall. A series of screams made them start as the light revealed a crowd of four Wraiths coming through the walls. But the moment the sunlight hit them their bodies solidified mid phase and they were left screaming in agonizing pain, heads and torsos writhing and smacking around in a desperate flail to be free of their agonizing prison.

"Sunlight makes them solid!" Leo realized, even as he watched Faith turn from black to pale white at the touch of the sun. "They can't phase! That's their weakness!" For good measure he shot through the glass of two windows on either side of the door, allowing them to coax the Pegasus out into daylight in relative assurance that no more Wraiths were going to endanger their mission and, most of all, none were going to endanger Faith. The horse nickered and shied, clearly unaccustomed to the light.

"Christ, is this thing able to go into sunlight?" he thought to ask a little too late.

"We don't have any choice!" Faith pointed out. Faith moved forward between flailing hooves to grab its mane and shush and soothe the frightened beast and Leo felt his heart lurch with fear, thinking any second she was going to be trampled to death or kicked in the head.

But after some more sweet cajoling and two more apples the horse willingly followed them onto the stony path. And true to his word, the moment they were free of the house they were teleported away, horse and all.

"My god, she's beautiful," Grey said with truly obvious admiration after standing a moment in awe after they had materialized in front of him. He moved forward, reaching out with a tentative hand, as though he were afraid to touch it. But then Faith remembered that it took only a touch for a Djynn to claim a nik as his own, and Grey had clearly waited a very long time for this nik . . . and the nik quite obviously was a source of great power.

"Hello, my love," Grey said softly as he approached, nodding in gratitude to Faith when she handed him an apple to offer the beast in friendship. Faith was amazed by the change that came over Grey, by the incredible softness in his demeanor. "You're safe and now you'll be able to run free and eat all the apples your heart desires."

They had materialized in a dark stable, no sunlight streaming into it. They could see doors that would lead out into the promise of a large corral or pastureland. Now that they were once again in darkness, the Pegasus's wings had reappeared and she was stretching them out as wide as possible in the roomy stall. Faith had to admit she was the most beautiful horse she'd ever laid eyes on. There was something . . . something about a winged horse that called to the child inside of her. It told her that amazing, fantastical things were truly possible, and that she had only just begun to see the beauty in the world. There was so much more for her to see and learn, so much more than her secluded and often sheltered life in her father's house.

She reached out to touch the horse's wing, the powerful bony joint of it more than strong enough to lift the weight of the beast into the air. But it could only fly at night or in sunless weather, she realized. In its way, it too was a Nightwalker.

"Maybe one day you will trust me enough to show me who you really are," Grey said to the horse, once again speaking as gently as he could. "Trust is the issue here," he said to Faith and Leo. "She is a Mystical. Like no one you've ever known in your lifetime or ever will again.

But she won't show me who she is. First, she has to know she can trust me."

"A Mystical?! I thought you said she was a nikki!" Faith cried out.

"Wait. What? What's a Mystical?" Leo wanted to know.

"A Mystical is a *Nightwalker* breed, not a nikki," Faith said darkly.

"Mysticals are both niks and Nightwalkers," Grey explained calmly, all the while gazing lovingly at the Pegasus. "They hold tremendous amounts of power—but because there are those like the Wraiths who would trap them and use them like car batteries, a source of power to be tapped into rather than a being that craves what we all crave—to be loved—they do not often show their true selves to anyone other than fellow Mysticals. But maybe," Grey said to the calming beast. "Maybe you will show me who you are when you learn who I am."

He finally touched the horse on its forelock and a brilliant light bled into Grey, lighting him up under his skin from the hand he used to touch it with and slowly all the way down to his feet. Faith could see the blood vessels in his body as the light moved through him and she could feel a thump of force against her, like a static charge had been released.

"You know, any minute now I'm going to wake up with a hell of a hangover and I'm going to think to myself, 'Dude, we are never doing that much tequila ever again,'" Leo said.

Faith laughed at him and he smiled at her. She realized then that there was a life and energy and all-out joy in that smile that had been missing at the beginning of their adventure. He had come a very long way in a very short amount of time. He'd had to cope with things, to see things that he had never even conceived of being real in the life he had been leading before. It was no wonder he'd had trouble adapting to all of this. This was a lot to take in even for her, and she was used to moving in supernatural circles.

The Pegasus farted again.

"Oh god, what have they been feeding this thing?" Leo asked, waving his hand in revulsion.

"She's a her, not a thing," Grey snapped at him. "And they've probably been feeding her eggs. Eggs suppress her ability to change."

"That explains why she didn't just change form and walk out," Leo said. "That house was pretty wide open. But she couldn't open doors and couldn't simply walk out as long as she was in this form. I'm amazed she survived in there. All it would take is one touch and they would have killed her."

"I find that intriguing myself. So little is known about the Wraiths," Grey said. "Perhaps they can control the use of their death touch. They can decide whether or not to kill. A conscious choice."

"Which makes them all the more evil," Faith said bitterly. She shivered in revulsion.

"Do you know her name?" Leo asked, reaching a tentative hand out to touch the horse. "How did you even know she was their captive?"

"Are we *wishing* to know the answers to those questions?" Grey asked archly.

"I think not," Leo said, holding up both hands as if touching any of them might equate a wish.

The horse nickered and moved forward, shoving Grey aside in order to head-butt Leo affectionately.

In spite of himself, Leo chuckled and went back to petting her. "You're welcome," he said, reaching to scrub at her forelock.

"Let's get a decent meal into her and then . . . then I have a wish to carry out for you," Grey said.

CHAPTER SIXTEEN

Grey, Leo, and Faith appeared in Jackson's bedroom so suddenly that Docia, who was standing at the foot of the bed, released a shocked little cry. She had been watching Marissa as she lay curled up in the bed next to Jackson, her body wrapped around him, holding him tightly, as if by will alone she could keep him in this plane of existence with her.

Docia took one look at the trio and burst into tears. She knew very well what their arrival meant and all the strength she had been using to keep herself together suddenly abandoned her. As if they had a magic of their own, Docia's emotions triggered Ram's almost instantaneous appearance. He was hurrying to her side the next instant, pushing past Ahnvil and Stohn and Max and Angelina, who, for some reason, were all in the room. The reason became obvious when Ram, who had given Docia the expanse of his chest to weep against, looked up at Leo and Faith and Grey.

"I don't know if you're in time," he said quietly, even though he clearly wished he could say anything else. "He's grown pale and cold. He may be without one or both of his souls already, his body only lingering."

Grey moved around the bed, and as he approached Jackson's side of it Marissa came awake. She sat up in a

wobble of confusion, forcing herself out of the depths
of her exhausted sleep.

"Is he gone?" she demanded, her hands clutching at
her lover's shirt. "Did he leave me while I slept?"

The panic bordering on the edge of despair rang
through her voice. She looked at the stranger approach-
ing the bed and out of some innate instinct she threw
her body over Jackson, protecting him from this unknown element.

"Who are you?" she demanded of him.

"My name is Grey and I am a high-level Marid Djynn.
I come with the magic necessary to repair your loved
one's souls."

"H-how do we know w-we can trust him?" she
needed to know, looking helplessly at Ram. "What if
he's here to hurt him further?"

"There is nothing worse that can be done to him that
time isn't already doing," Ram pointed out. "He's dead
if we don't extend our trust and dead if we do and the
Marid's motives are untrue. But he will have to keep in
mind what I will do to him if he does kill Jackson."
There was even more threat in his tone than there was
in his words. If the Djynn was cowed by it in any way,
he certainly didn't show it. Probably because when it
came right down to it, Grey's power could be endless,
and Ram's, significant as it was, could probably do very
little to countermand that power.

"Madame, if I may?" Grey asked with politesse before reaching out with a hand, leaving it to hover over
Jackson. He waited until she moved past her hesitation
and gave him a permissive nod before letting his graceful, long-fingered hand lower to touch Jackson on his
broad bare chest. Somewhere along the line, Faith realized, Marissa or someone had stripped Jackson, bathed
him clean of the mess Apep had made of him, and re-
dressed him in a simple pair of fleece drawstring pa-

jama pants. Jackson had grown paler in color, his lips almost porcelain beige, his eyes looking like twin bruises in the face of his sickly pallor.

"It's not too late. I can still reattach his souls," Grey said quietly. "But they will be injured and the attachment will be tender and raw at its best. I need an outsider, someone with a single soul who is close to him, to act as a surrogate. I will attach the surrogate aura to his weakened one and the healthy aura will keep him energized and strong while his souls continue the healing process. It will also fortify his aura against any further injury." He let his eyes sweep the room, taking in the plethora of single-souled Gargoyles and humans. "Volunteers?"

Leo stepped forward a heartbeat before anyone else could react, putting himself directly in front of the Djynn's sight. "I'll do it," he said quietly. "You need a soul to ground him? Someone close to him? That's me. There's no one closer to Jackson than I am."

Grey seemed to absorb that for a moment, his head tilting to the side a little as he debated within himself.

"No. I'm sorry, but for these purposes the volunteer must stay close to his side for almost a month. Perhaps this human"—he indicated Max—"is the better choice, considering your desire to leave this place in the dust. I can't attach him to someone who might walk out on him at the drop of a hat or when they find themselves so uncomfortable they think taking off is the only solution."

"Are you calling me a coward or something?" Leo demanded, his entire aura bristling with his outrage. "Are you saying I would just walk out and leave my friend—my *brother*—to die? Because if you are I'm going to have to remind you pretty freakin' fast that you don't know a damn thing about who I am and what this man means to me!"

"If anyone would be there for Jackson," Marissa said,

grabbing Leo's hand and drawing him even closer to the bed, "it would be Leo. They have been through so much together. Jackson has always saved Leo, and Leo has always saved Jackson. That's just how it is."

Grey smiled with a small measure of satisfaction lighting his eyes, and Leo drew in a tight breath as a tide of understanding washed over him. It didn't matter what had happened to Jackson, his feelings toward him, his loyalty, would never change. And the reverse was also true. Perhaps that had been the crux of his fear. Perhaps he had been afraid that Jackson would no longer be there for him as his life and new world began to take up a place of importance. Where would Leo stand in all of that?

Right here. Beside his friend. Always.

"Very well. All you need to do is come closer to the bed. I will begin."

Everyone seemed to hold their breath for a twofold reason. One, to make sure Jackson was still breathing. Two, to wait and see if the Djynn could pull off a miracle they were in desperate need of.

Grey drew a breath, closed his eyes, and leaned his weight forward on his hand, pressing Jackson down hard into the bed. It was as if he were trying to snap Jackson's breastbone in two. Grey began to tremble from the exertion, as though a great battle was being fought where he and Jackson were connected. It went on for a minute . . . two . . . then three. Grey broke a sweat, his handsome face coloring red under his dark complexion. Then suddenly he dropped, his hand plunging into Jackson's chest, through skin and bone and muscle, but not a drop of blood to be seen. Grey pushed harder, as though feeling around inside of the man, the very idea of it making Leo cringe inside from memory. But this, he tried to remind himself, was for healing. That had been for torment. All he could do was pray Grey wouldn't need to put his hand inside of him as well, because frankly, while he wanted to be there for Jackson, he didn't know if he had it in him.

Grey's other hand came to join the first, it too struggling to breach Jackson's outer surfaces.

Elbow deep inside of Jackson, he continued to search and fight. Faith could see the severe concentration in him, and she could see he was grabbing at the twin scrolls inside of Jackson. Normally the scroll of a person was a single bright cone of light that began at the feet and streamed upward in a cylindrical shape toward the heavens. Jackson had two scrolls, one for each soul, and they had been bouncing about in the confines of his body, trapped in his repaired aura. An aura she could see had thinned greatly. It was because of that thinning that the Djynn had been able to gain entrance. Now he held each soul by the tail, as it were, and was holding them in place as he poured healing magic into them. He was murmuring something, the words a tumble of exotic inflections, clearly his native tongue that was quite similar to those of Indian or Pakistani bent. Neither, and yet similar.

Faith could see the scrolls slowly settling in, reattaching and beaming widely in the proper direction. By the time Grey withdrew, everything was perfect. Exactly as it should be . . . except the hole in his aura left by Grey's intrusion. Grey then rested a hand atop Jackson's chest once more and beckoned to Leo.

"Take off your shirt," he commanded.

Leo and Faith both froze, their breath locking in their chests. Faith watched as Leo hesitated, his eyes sweeping the crowded room with a current of sheer anxiety emanating from him. But then he looked down at Jackson, grabbed his shirt, and whipped it off his back.

If he was waiting for a reaction, he was sorely disappointed. But it took only a moment for her to realize that their lack of shock at the sight of his gouged chest was like telling him they did not pity him, did not think him too weak or too subpar for the task he'd volunteered for. He exhaled, dropped his shirt to the ground, and lifted a brow toward Grey.

"Your surrogate guinea pig awaits," he invited.

Grey smiled and without hesitation or a tremor of concern that the contact might cause him pain, he used his free hand and pressed it against Leo's chest.

"Jesus," Leo said, his breath coming fast, reminding Faith of when she had been in the Wraith house, sounding loud and frightened to her own ears.

"Night Angel, if you will?" Grey nodded toward Jackson and she quickly moved forward to repair his aura while Grey attached Leo for the surrogacy.

"Don't worry," Grey said to Leo when he saw the man had broken a sweat. "I don't need to go fishing for your soul. It's already where I can find it. I won't need to breach your body, merely connect you at your aura." Grey took Leo's hand and brought it into contact with Jackson's, then returned his hand to Leo's chest.

Faith suspected Grey could have done the aura repair on Jackson himself, but wisely, after such a tremendous expenditure of magical energy, he was delegating the task to her so he wouldn't burn himself out completely.

The moment his aura became intact and reinforced, Jackson woke up, sucking in a startled breath, as though someone had been holding him under water all of this time. It was very likely that was what it had felt like. He had been slowly suffocating to death without access to the souls that gave him life.

Marissa and Docia both cried out, and flung themselves against him, heedlessly knocking Grey and Leo out of the way. Jackson automatically caught them up against him. He was confused and didn't know what to make of all of the attention and tears. He looked up and met Ram's eyes first but in the end it was Leo whom he turned to for clarity. Leo reached out and put his hand on his friend's shoulder.

"It's very good to see you, brother," Leo said.

Jackson tilted his head and said, "Brother? I thought the last time we spoke I wasn't your friend any longer."

"Well, I wasn't quite myself," Leo said sheepishly. "But I'm better now. And you are better now, too. You suffered a lot of damage in the attack by that thing."

"That god," Grey said. "And that god is going to be a lot of trouble. More trouble than it has already been."

"I know that." It was Faith who said that. "That's the whole reason that I came in the first place. I suppose one reason was to protect Jackson and the other was to warn you all about the trouble that was coming. Not just for the Bodywalkers, but for all of us. All the Nightwalkers. My father sent me," Faith said, "when a prophet saw some terrible futures ahead of us should we lose Jackson or Menes. I was sent to help divert that possible future from happening. And I can see now that I've done exactly that." Faith smiled, her teeth brilliant against the blackness of her skin and the violet of her lips. Leo looked at her and saw just how beautiful she was when she smiled, just how beautiful she was period.

Leo backed off from the gathering of weeping, laughing women, watching them from a distance. He couldn't help himself from joining in with their smiles.

That is, until Kamenwati walked into the room, drawn by the commotion. Kamen stood in the doorway, his tall, dark presence a strong, overpowering source of hatred for Leo, and he found himself swamped once again by the negative emotions and state of mind that had been crippling him since Kamenwati had "rescued" him from Chatha's demented mutilations. But Kamen had not rescued him out of any sense of right and wrong. He had only done so in order to have a bargaining chip to convince Jackson that his intention was to defect from the Templars and join his side.

But what he was, what he would always be in Leo's eyes, is a sick fucking son of a bitch. He would always be the reason why he had come into Chatha's hands in the first place. He would always be the reason why he couldn't find it in himself to trust anyone any longer.

Including Faith.

Leo's attention swung to Faith, who was still laughing and celebrating with the others. An awkward jumble of feelings washed over him and he simply couldn't cope. He couldn't bear it all. The joy of Jackson's revival, the hatred of Kamen's arrival, the vastness of possibility that he felt whenever he looked at Faith.

Leo turned and escaped from the room, shoving angrily past Kamenwati, slamming the other man into the doorjamb on purpose as he passed. Kamen could have taken umbrage, but he did not. Leo was unimpressed by his show of hands.

Leo was such a powerful force of negativity and he knew it, just as he knew it had no place among the celebrations going on in that room. He would just drag everyone else back down into the hole he had found himself in once more.

He threw himself out of the house, suddenly feeling like there wasn't enough air in the entire world to help him breathe. The New Mexico night was sharp and cold, the cold of a desert gone dark. He walked out into it, letting it penetrate his skin, letting it remind him that he was still, somehow, alive. But that had been the problem all along, hadn't it? He had never died. Chatha had mutilated him again and again, each time bringing him to the very edge of death's door, and then using his power to heal to drag him back and ready him for the next bout.

"Leo."

Leo turned when he heard her call for him. She closed the distance between them and he suddenly found himself fighting the urge to cry. To all out sob on her shoulder and spill his tears of pain into her hair. The need for succor was so powerfully overwhelming that he fought it, threw himself in the other direction, let himself flounder alone in the cold instead.

"Leo," she said again, her tone so soft, her use of his name so beckoning, as she laid gentle hands on his back and shoulders.

"I can't do it. I can't stand to be in the same house as that . . . that fiend. That demon that cast me down into hell."

"Kamenwati," she said knowingly.

"Yes."

"He is just a man. A man who made mistakes and knows it."

"Am I to feel sympathy for him?" Leo raged at her suddenly. "Forgive me if I don't!"

"I never meant that you should," she railed back at him. "I only meant that he is just a man. Not a demon. Not this great force of evil. Just a man like any other man. And he will never be able to harm you again. Not while you are loved and protected by these people who are your friends."

"These people are the ones who have taken him in and given him safe haven. They might be able to forgive and forget, but I am not so able!"

"And no one expects you to be. Do you really think everyone wants you to pretend you haven't suffered through this terrible thing? I know the only reason I know about any of it is because of Grey. I know it's not fair that you didn't get to choose when to share your pain with me, but I know what it is just the same. And I want you to know . . ."

He watched as the laser blue of her wings slowly unfurled from her back, stretching far and wide, the beautiful grace of them curving forward and then surrounding him in the protective circle of her power. "I won't ever let him hurt you again, Leo."

"I don't need your protection," he rasped angrily, but he couldn't seem to make himself turn away from her. He couldn't back away when she stepped up closer to him.

"It's all right if you do," she said gently. "It's not so horrible that you need others to help you. Aren't you tired of being out there on that island all alone? Isn't that the way you've been doing things all this time, even before Kamen and Chatha? Is that really what you want?"

"It's not fair that you know all of this," he said hoarsely. "You know things that I've never shared with anyone . . ."

"Including your best friends," she agreed with him. "Because you were trying to protect them. And that's all they were doing when they erased your memory. You hold them responsible for what happened afterward, and maybe they are responsible, but they were just trying to protect you. No more or less differently than what you've been doing for years." She reached out and laid hands as gently as butterfly wings on the expanse of his chest. "But now they are strong and solid and no longer in need of protecting. Instead of looking at it like you are weaker than they are, why not look at it like they are finally strong enough to know . . . to really know you."

"I don't know," he said quietly, his anger bleeding away as he looked down into the chartreuse of her eyes. "I don't know if I can be this better person you seem to be expecting of me. I am who I am . . . bullshit and all."

"This isn't who you are. You are not the sum of your

anger. It's just what you feel. All I am hoping for is that it will fade in time. Hopefully in time for you to keep from alienating everyone who gives a damn about you."

Leo reached up, unable to curb the impulse, and traced gentle fingertips over the rise of her right cheek. "We did it," he said, a smile touching his lips briefly. "Didn't we? I didn't think we were going to pull it off, but we did it."

"We make a pretty good team," she agreed.

Leo felt the reflex of her wings coming even tighter around him. He felt utterly surrounded by their energy, felt it flowing into him in strong, potent waves. He reached out with his free hand and passed it through the laser edge of one wing, making them both gasp at the fiery connection. Leo looked down into her face, his expression full of curiosity. "What does that feel like to you?" he asked her. "Does that happen all the time with just anyone who does this?"

She shook her head, the sugary fall of her hair sweeping against his hand as she did so. When had she unbound it, he wondered? "No. There's feedback yes, but no one . . . nothing like I feel when you touch me like that . . . or like this." She reached out and stroked gentle fingers along the back of the hand touching her face. He had to admit that it was very different for him, too.

"I wonder why that is?" he asked absently as his fingers drifted up to her forehead. "I wonder why you make me feel like . . ."

"Like?" she asked when he paused for several long moments.

"Like I want to grab you, dip you, and kiss you till your toes curl like some corny romantic movie. The orchestra comes up with a sweeping, grandiose score and we just . . ."

"Kiss." She laughed at him. "That *is* corny."

"I know. But I'm going to do it just the same."

And he reached for her, ringing her shoulders with one arm and swinging her around and down into a bona fide romantic dip before touching his lips to hers. The movement drew her wings tightly around him and it was like setting him on fire, the way their energy passed through him. But as electric as that was, none of it could compare with the static essence of the feel of her mouth against his. Somehow he had forgotten how much like kissing fire it felt like to kiss her. And he realized he always would forget it at least a little bit. There was just no way he would ever be able to get used to the power of the connection. After a long minute of simply tasting her, he swung her back up onto her feet and took some hard breaths as he stared deeply into her eyes, trying to figure some kind of resolution in his mind. Part of him was thundering out instructions that warned him to push her away before she got too close, other parts were conceding that it was already too late for that.

"One thing's for sure," he said softly to her as he found himself tracing the curves of her face once again. It was as though he needed to map them both physically and spiritually. "I'm thinking I need to make love to you, Faith."

"Oh," she breathed. "Really? Because I'm thinking I'd really like that." Then she seemed to second-guess herself and withdrew from him. "But . . . I'm not a human woman, Leo. I'm not what you'd look for in the long run."

"I don't look for anyone in the long run," he said with a frown. "I'll be straight up about it, Faith. Outside of that kiss, I'm not a romantic guy. I'm not looking for Miss Right, I'm just fine with Miss Right Now."

"Oh," she said. Leo knew that what he'd said caused her some kind of pain, but he ignored it in order to make himself clear.

"We're all grown-ups here, Faith. Am I right? You being what you are and me being who I am, it's not like there's sunsets and forevers in our future."

" 'What you are'? *What?* Not who? Am I still a . . . a *thing* to you? Am I still not worthy of consideration in your eyes? I thought we'd gotten past that. I can see I was wrong." She jerked away from him, her wings pulling back with a snap. "You might not be looking at me for the long haul, Leo, but you're not looking at me for the short one either. You want to make love to me? Are you sure about that? Because it sounds to me like you just want to conquer this thing that is stronger than you are in whatever way you can possibly manage. Well, I'm not about to make it easy on you, Leo. I've got news for you. I have standards, too. And my standards say stop and no way when it comes to pigheaded, prejudiced jerks who don't even think I deserve equal measure as a person. I know you've wondered about what I have been suffering from at home. That there's been abuse?" She scoffed. "I flinch because there was a man once . . . a man who thought a princess was the fast track to power. And that controlling that princess by any means necessary would guarantee it. He didn't think I deserved equal measure as a person either. Maybe you need to examine that parallel a little bit while you're sitting there judging people."

"There's no way I'm like that sick son of a bitch!" Leo roared at her. "Not even close! I've never laid a hand on you!"

"The methods are different but the result is still the same! You hurt me, Leo! You really hurt me!" She stepped back when he reached for her. "Don't you dare get pissy with me when you know it's the truth! Until you can talk to me with respect for who and what I am, I don't want you to talk to me at all!"

She turned her back on him sharply, the laser blue of

her wings cutting through him like electric saw blades. They both started and gasped at the feedback, but then Faith shook it off and stomped away from him.

"Fine! Go off and have your tantrum!" he barked at her back. "Call me when you grow up a little!"

The fact that she kept going, that she didn't turn around and fight him over that statement, made him a little sick to his stomach. Faith not fighting was a frightening thing to think about. She had kept him honest and kept him on his toes since the minute they'd met. For her to just give up . . .

Had she fought or given up before? he found himself wondering. What had she done and how had she eventually escaped that abusive situation? He hadn't found that out and, damn him, Grey had left that little part out of their imagined future together.

But why should he even care? he asked himself. *She obviously doesn't want you bothering her, so let it go, Alvarez.*

He watched her go back into the house and when the door closed behind her he felt an overwhelming sense of panic. He couldn't explain the reason why. Couldn't give it voice right then.

"So," Grey said, suddenly appearing at Leo's side. "Have you realized yet what you should be wishing for?"

"I told you. I'm not making any wish."

"No, it wouldn't be just any wish, now would it? It would have to be for the thing you want most in the world, yet you realize there is no other way on earth for you to achieve it."

Leo's frown darkened and for a moment he entertained the idea of taking Grey up on that offer. Faith was a beautiful woman. One of extraordinary strength and impressive force of will. And once he began to think of one or two attributes, it opened a floodgate of others. She was honest and trustworthy. If he'd learned nothing else in their journey, he had most certainly learned that. And that honesty was clearly rooted in her compassion and her need to do the right thing at any cost to herself. She had proven that by making that extraordinarily dangerous wish . . . and sticking to it even when she had been faced with the ultimate terror of a powerfully deadly enemy. Her bravery in the face of the Wraiths was something he would never forget.

He stole a glance at Grey. What he wouldn't give, he thought in that moment, to be a different man. To be the kind of man who could truly, deeply love a deserving woman like Faith. Outside of Suzy Bigelow in the eighth grade, he'd never fancied himself to be in love. He hadn't had the time or the luxury of being worthy of that kind of relationship. Besides that he would be doing the woman a terrible injustice, taking into consideration his mercenary work and the amount of time it took him away from home . . . and the constant knowledge that he was always in mortal danger, putting himself into situation after situation that would risk him not coming home . . . leaving her heartbroken.

But if he had ever thought to fall in love, it would have been with a woman like Faith. Independent, understanding of what it really meant to be the love of a soldier, and even able to fight by his side in the very thick of it. God, how tempting that was, he thought, running an agitated hand over his hair.

"I suppose you think I should ask you to make me be able to ride off into the sunset with her," he said, his tone irritable . . . a perfect match to his feelings. Though he couldn't understand why this felt like he was shoving pins under his nails.

"I wouldn't presume," Grey said with a low chuckle. "Women are a great difficulty in the lives of independent men like you and I. Without a woman we can live our lives on our own terms, live exactly the way we want to, absolutely no apologies given or expected. A woman makes things . . . complicated. Suddenly we find ourselves bending and compromising in order to make her happy. We alter our true selves in some kind of ridiculous effort at trying to live up to whatever image it is that she deems makes us the perfect man. It's utterly exhausting work. I would in good conscience have to try to talk you out of a wish like that, and that says a great deal coming from a Djynn."

"I suppose it does," Leo said absently. Of course Grey was right. In fact, he had hit on all the key points he had used in any and every argument he'd had in his head when he had found himself toying with the idea of settling down in the arms of a single woman. So why was that irritating the crap out of him? It was a much needed reality check, and yet . . . "There's nothing wrong with Faith," he found himself saying defensively to Grey. "She isn't really all that complicated. She's probably the most straightforward and honest woman I've ever met." Funny how it took an inhuman woman to make him feel that way. "I'm the one that's complicated. I wouldn't wish me on the most virulent bitch on the planet."

"So maybe you can think of a way to change that," Grey said archly.

Again, the wish thing, Leo thought irritably. *Doesn't this guy ever give up?* "Like you said, I like me fine just the way I am."

"And you are so delighted with yourself and your life that there is nothing you can think of that needs changing?"

"You know, you're starting to annoy me," Leo growled darkly.

"Because of my mere presence or because my observations are hitting too close to home for you?"

"Screw you. Why don't you just go and grant a wish somewhere like a good little genie and stop pestering me?"

"I would, but I have a feeling you'd just be recalling me soon, so why make the trip only to have to return again?"

"I'm not making a goddamn wish! Will you please just back the fuck off me?"

"As you wish. Jackson has been kind enough to offer me a suite of rooms for a day or two of rest. He knows just how exhausting using that much magic can be, even for someone as old as I am."

Leo eyeballed Grey's youthful visage, ready to scoff at him . . . though he didn't know exactly why he might want to. It wasn't until that moment, however, that he realized Grey was looking very pale, his handsome, patrician features showing a weariness that took Leo by surprise. It had never really occurred to him that Grey would have to pay a heavy personal price in order to carry out the wish. He'd just thought . . . he'd thought it would be easy for him. He'd thought he was this all-powerful Sultan Djynn that had more power at his fingertips than he knew what to do with.

"And yet you're here, waiting for me to make another wish? You should quit while you're still on two feet." Leo frowned. "Can that happen? Can you overextend yourself?"

"Magic is finite. I can only use magic from niks. The more niks, the more power I can channel into other tasks. However, manipulating more power than you can deal with can have detrimental ramifications. The older we are the more easily we can manipulate vast magics. But no matter how old we are, we can still burn ourselves out if we are not careful."

"And that's what happened here, isn't it? You came close to burning yourself out?"

"Mmm . . . not quite. Not with this wish, although I promise you it was no easy task. But your wish . . . I sense your wish, whatever it ends up being, will be that dangerous for me."

"Then why do you keep coming at me about it? Why not cut bait and run while you still can?"

"Self-preservation advice?" Grey chuckled. "I suppose you are uniquely qualified to give it to me."

"What does that mean?" Leo demanded of him.

"It means you are an expert at self-preservation at all costs. And I do mean *all* costs. Because my advice, which I'm happy to impart for free, is that you might have a care for what you are doing. You're going to wake up one day and realize you've done such a good job at protecting yourself that you've managed to isolate yourself from anything that makes a life worth living. And that, my friend, makes you very much like that Templar priest you despise so much. He is only now coming to realize what folly it has been, his search for his holy grail at the cost of everything else. And in that way he is one step ahead of you." Grey leaned in closer, ignoring the rage simmering in Leo's eyes. "He, at least, has come to realize what his mistakes have been and is willing to work on improving himself. You . . . not so much." Grey shrugged a dismissive shoulder. "And now I'll take my leave of you before my lambasting, I thank you. As I said, I'm quite worn out. I'm not quite up to a sound tongue-lashing."

And just like that, he winked out of existence, his usual theatric shower of gold dust drifting to the ground in his wake. Leo, left with no avenue for his anger, was at loose ends. He began to pace the walkway with urgent, heated steps.

"I am nothing like him!" he shouted out into the cold night air, his voice echoing until it sounded hollow and lost. *I am nothing like that sick Templar son of a bitch,* he reiterated in his own thoughts. Or whoever it was that hurt Faith.

Unlike that Templar bastard, Leo was a man of conscience. A man of thought. He would damn well think twice before hurting anyone else. In fact, he was constantly trying to protect those around him from the harsher truths about himself. Docia and Jackson, for instance. He'd always kept the finer details of his life to himself because he didn't want them to worry or become anxious for him.

Leo stopped pacing so abruptly that the rocks under his feet skidded.

Or maybe you were just protecting yourself? No. No, he wasn't selfishly motivated. He honestly didn't want anything he did to end up hurting them. He loved them more than anything else on this earth.

But now they no longer need protecting. *Now they are the ones protecting you.* The thought sat ill on him, but he wouldn't let his anger come into play so it could cloud the issue. Cloud the truth. And the truth was . . .

They had been protecting him. When they had erased his memory of his attempt on Odjit's life, they had been protecting him from exactly what was happening . . . a crisis of his self. Having been a victim to, and having become painfully aware of this Nightwalker world, he had been floundering in anger and loss. He had lost his opinion of himself. Lost his . . . identity. Yes, that was it. Leo the badass was no longer the best game in town. No longer able to be the strongest, the wiliest, and the best at what it took to come out on top. Now he was low man on the totem pole and frankly . . .

It sucked. It hurt. It made him angry.

God, what a colossal waste of time this all was! He had never been a wallower, but it seemed like all he had been doing was wallowing. Walking around and feeling sorry for himself. Using anger to keep himself righteously separated from a world he had so little say in. And if he kept it up he was going to . . .

Lose. Everything. Anything that was important to him was going to fall away from him. *Christ*. He didn't want that. Fighting the Wraiths with his gutsy little Night Angel had proved to him that he could hold his own with these paranormal badasses. He didn't have to be afraid of that any longer. But he did have to admit to himself that his ability here was limited and had to be used carefully. If his interaction with Chatha had taught him anything, it had taught him that.

Actually, Faith had taught him that. Faith had never once told him he couldn't pull the job off when they were gearing up for the Wraiths. In fact, she had seemed to be worried about her own part in it. She had thought *her* fear of being touched would cause *him* trouble.

In that scenario he had been the key to defeating the Wraiths, and she had been the low man . . . and yet she hadn't been angry, pissy, or threatened . . . unlike him.

But he had a legitimate excuse, he tried to reason with himself. He'd been victimized . . .

Christ. A victim. When had he turned into a victim? When had he allowed that to happen?

Leo marched into the house, making a beeline for Jackson's bedroom suite. There were a lot of people crowded in there, Gargoyles, Bodywalkers, humans, and, of course, a Night Angel, most of whom were full of excited talk and gestures of delight. There were two notably silent presences. Kamenwati and the much subdued Faith. Kamenwati was standing off to one side, arms folded across his broad chest, head bent pensively as he observed the ruckus going on all around him. Jackson was in bed still, apparently not yet able to move because of the press of femininity weighing him down. Though he did still look gaunt and weak. Leo had no doubt it was going to take some time before he was fully up to par.

"Excuse me," Leo said after noisily clearing his throat. All eyes turned to him quizzically. "Can I get a moment alone with my friend?"

Marissa's hands tightened on Jackson and by the look on her face she was about to tell him to piss off. But Jackson beat her to the punch.

"Sure," he said. "There's something I wanted to ask you, too."

Everyone realized they were being summarily dismissed and began to move toward the door and into the outer suite of the master bedroom. The room emptied out, both Marissa and Docia dragging their feet and continually looking back at Jackson as though he might disappear the minute they let their attention stray. That being said, it was Kamenwati who was the last to leave the room, clearly wanting to avoid coming into physical contact with anyone else.

"Hold it. I want you to stay for a minute," Leo said, even the neutral "you" coming out of him sounding derogatory.

Kamen raised a curious brow, but stayed behind, closing the door in the faces of a lot of baffled people. Once the door was closed Kamen sighed.

"I imagine you are looking for your pound of flesh, if you'll pardon the figurative," Kamen said quietly. "Or perhaps you'd enjoy the literal."

Leo was still and silent for a minute, but Jackson could see the tension in his friend's body. What was more . . . he could feel it. In fact, he could feel the entire screaming jumble of emotions Leo was trying to sort out in his head. It was as though he were an empath like his wife was, but never before had he experienced anything like this.

Grey had told him there might be some side effects

because of the way things had been processed, nothing to worry about because it wouldn't last. Dumbfounded and curious, he looked at Kamen. Nothing. The only thing he could feel was what Leo was feeling. It was easy to know whose feelings it was because all the emotions were directed toward one person. Leo despised Kamen and it showed on all levels. Not that Jackson blamed him.

"First, since I have to stay here a whole month with you under the same roof," Leo said pointing to Kamen, his tone hard but not envenomed, "I would prefer you stay out of my way. Otherwise, you'll be making it too easy for me to give in to my instinctual urges to kill you."

Kamen's expression, placid as it was, was clearly marked with his surprise. It was very clear he had been expecting the full force of Leo's rage. And while he wasn't shaking hands and backslapping the other man, it was clear he wasn't as interested in starting up a physical ass-kicking.

"I will endeavor to do so," Kamen promised him.

"Good. Now leave, I need to ask my friend for something."

With a nod, Kamen left the room. He offered no apologies, no side of an olive branch. He knew Leo was not ready for it . . . and that he might never reach that point was also a strong possibility. Neither was Kamen ready to deserve it, in his mind.

Kamen saw Ahnvil at the back of the group that was milling about the door, wondering what was transpiring on the other side of it. He had flung himself into a chair near the fireplace, his big body dwarfing the chair and, it always seemed, taking up far more space than anything else in the room. Kamen walked up to him.

He stood there silently for a moment, watching Ahnvil cock his head at his approach.

"What the bloody hell are you wantin'?" he asked roughly, his Scottish burr, thickened with hostile emotion, rolling hard off his tongue. Here was yet another man in this house who had a bone to pick with Kamenwati.

For Ahnvil's part, he had just as good of a cause. As he rubbed an absent hand over the ouroboros brand over his chest, he reminded himself of why. All Gargoyles had been reborn as slaves to Bodywalker Templars. All bore the mark of their Templar masters, and all of them carried the energy of their maker within them wherever they went.

In Ahnvil's case, he carried Kamen's.

"I am concerned. There's good cause to believe Apep will return to finish what he has attempted."

"Tell me something I doona know," Ahnvil said, scoffing at his maker.

"I'm only trying to figure out how we might defend ourselves in that case. You and I . . . right now we are the first line of defense for this house. All the other powerful players are weakened or spent."

"Again, you've a talent for stating the obvious. Doona fret, lass," he chuckled mirthlessly, "we Gargoyles will do as we've always done. Protect your hide and do your dirty work. After all, is that no' what you created us for?"

"Yes. Yes, it is," Kamen agreed, not shying or demurring from what was fact. Ahnvil had to grudgingly accept that. "But I think we are safe for a while, in any event. Gods do not injure easily, and when they are wounded badly they do one of two things. Either they retaliate in full fury immediately, in the moment, or they go off and heal . . . and plot. Apep will not come at us until he is certain he can win. And as long as we have Faith here . . ."

"True. Still, I willna be relaxing."

"No. I didn't imagine you would."

"I wanted to apologize," Leo said to Jackson, moving closer to the bed. Jesus. The closer he got the worse Jackson looked. It made him truly cognizant of the fact that they had probably been just minutes away from losing him completely.

"That isn't necessary. You've been through a lot, and I recognize that. I also knew that you were much too strong to let Chatha get away with robbing you of yourself. It was just going to take a little time. Although I have to admit I didn't expect it to happen this quickly."

Leo looked Jackson in the eye. "Someone showed me . . . showed me what I'd be missing if I let hate and bigotry consume me," he said quietly, feeling the understanding like pain under the marks on his chest. "I just realized . . . I don't want to miss out on it. I don't know if I can even pull it off, but I know I am not going to give up without even trying."

"You're being very cryptic," Jackson mused.

"It won't seem so once I ask you for a favor."

"And that is?"

And for the first time since his ordeal had begun, his friend smiled his patented Leo Alvarez smile of mischief.

CHAPTER SEVENTEEN

Leo emerged from Jackson's room and Faith watched him scan the room quickly. His dark, intense eyes landed on her and she could tell instantly she was his target.

Feeling momentarily trapped, she found herself looking for a quick exit. There were too many people in the room and, realistically, he would only go after her or just find her later, so it was a ridiculous idea. Unless, of course, she simply left. Flew off home and never returned. He couldn't follow her then.

But she was reluctant to leave while Jackson was still so weak. If either Jackson or Leo needed their auras repaired or strengthened, she was by far the best choice. Her skills in this area even rivaled whatever the Djynn could come up with . . . provided he was willing to do it without asking for compensation. His obligations to Faith's wish had ended the instant Jackson had awakened.

When Leo made it past the crowd of people pushing to reenter Jackson's room, he came up to her and took her arm in hand.

"Come with me," he said. Not a request in the least, not a demand. Just a statement of fact. She was going with him. So she did. She was feeling a little numb as she let him lead her away. It was hard to know what to expect from him. His emotions seemed to vacillate so wildly . . . as did her own. Tears of hurt and anger stung in her eyes as she tried to remind herself that she'd only known him a pair of days at best, but she couldn't make herself understand that in any way other than the logical. In her heart she had known him so much longer than that.

Damn Grey anyway. Why did he have to do this to them? Why had he felt it so necessary to manipulate them? But she knew the answers before she even asked the questions. Grey was a Djynn. A Djynn that had wanted something . . . a nik . . . and when a Djynn wanted a nik there was nothing they wouldn't do to get it. She had known that going into this, had been willing to put herself on the line in spite of knowing that. If anything she should be more understanding of Leo. He had been through so much even without Grey toying with their emotions and perceptions of reality. And unlike her, he'd had no idea what he was getting himself into.

And maybe that's what made this so hard for her. Knowing what a good man he was simply because of the sacrifices he'd so readily made in the name of a man he loved like family . . . even when he hadn't been certain he was the same man he knew at all.

No, she was being too hard on him. She had to tell him she was sorry she had laid into him, judged him . . . been so harsh with him. But she couldn't help the fact that she had feelings, too.

Leo drew her down the hallway and she followed, dragging her feet a little. She didn't think she could bear him being so cold to her again. Not when she knew the love he was capable of. But still she let him lead her into a room off the main hall, the suite set up similarly to the master suite. When he let go of her to shut the door, she stood awkwardly, waiting for him to throw more anger at her, ready to watch with an aching heart as he skidded around looking for traction in a world covered in ice.

Just remember, she thought fiercely, *he's in pain. He won't mean half of what he says. If he needs a whipping boy as he lashes out once more, it's better if I am his target than anyone else.*

Because she knew that as long as he couldn't come to terms with the changes that had occurred with his beloved friends and family, he would have no one to trust . . . and no one to lean on.

He needed desperately to—

The thought was cut off when he abruptly turned to face her, took the steps that were between them with a breathtaking speed, cupped her face in his hands and dragged her up to the strength of his mouth. She gasped as he unleashed the sudden, passionate intensity, unable to move or react for all of ten seconds. And then she felt the warm persistence of a fine, strong male mouth that radiated just how determined he was to have her kiss.

Faith melted into the kiss, all stress and pain forgotten because she wanted it so badly. She felt as though she were starving for need of him, for who he was now and who he had been when Grey had brought them together. Because of Grey she had been able to feel what a passionate man he was in all things, emotionally and physically. And even without Grey's assistance she could feel it. If he was capable of such passionate anger, she had to believe that he was equally capable of passionate love. And if so, the idea was just as breathtaking as his kiss.

He felt like an immovable thing, like a tree rooted to the spot and refusing to budge . . . and all the while knowing it was strong enough to withstand just about anything. His strength was always so present in him.

Even when he was unsure or battling fear, there was no
doubt that he was anything but a powerful force of life.
She relaxed against him, her hands, trapped between
their bodies, opened and uncurled in order to lay flat
against his chest. He suddenly broke off the kiss, and
hauled her back up against the door. His dark chocolate
eyes were intense, seemingly picking her apart as they
swept over the features of her face.

"I owe you a few things," he said, his words fast on
the back of equally fast breaths. "First"—he touched
his lips to the right corner of her lips, kissing her very
gently—"an apology. I'm beginning to realize I've been
nothing but an ass since we first set eyes on each other.
An ungrateful ass at that. You saved my life, Faith.
Apep would have torn me to shreds, but you saved my
life. Second"—he touched his lips even more slowly and
carefully to the left corner of her lips—"I owe you a
thank you. I thank you for saving my brother's life. You
and I are probably the only ones who will ever know
what the future would have held if we had not succeeded. He is alive and here and able to fill the future
with . . . well, we may never know the scope of the
things that will be affected in the future because we
kept him from dying."

"I—" she said breathlessly, his gentle touches were so
heavily laced with a barely controlled desire that she
could feel it building within the potency of him.

"And third," he interrupted her, holding his mouth
centered to hers, so close that as he spoke, she could
feel his breathy words against her lips. "Third, I owe
you . . ."

He broke off to close the distance between their
mouths. He kissed her slow and deep, as though he
were the chocolate of desire melting into her mouth. It
was just that kiss, his hands braced against the door,
caging her in, preventing her from escape . . . an escape

which she didn't want in any way shape or form anymore. Had she ever? she wondered. Had she ever wanted to run from him when he had radiated this intense desire into her?

No. It had always been him breaking off, pulling away . . . saying no. And what was to say he wouldn't do that again? She couldn't bear it again, she thought in momentary panic. She was too exhausted, too hungry for him, to be able to recover from yet another disappointment.

He must have sensed her resistance, the tension of her anxiety radiating into the kiss.

"What?" he asked gently. There was no anger, no irritation. He was concerned and she felt that even more deeply than she had felt his kiss. The idea that he saw the depths of her outside of the physicality of her needs . . . their needs.

"I can't do this again," she told him in a rushing whisper. "You change like the wind . . . constant one minute, fading the next. But at least the wind shows me the world around me, shows me the path to take and you . . . I never know what to do or say that won't—"

"Hush," he said softly, a finger coming up to brush over her trembling lips. "You're right. I am like the wind. Blowing soft one minute, howling the next. I can only ask that you forgive me for the things I've done that caused the hurt I see in your eyes just now. I never meant to cause you pain, it's just that . . . I'm not used to navigating a world I don't understand. At least before there were rules and responses to everything that I understood . . . that I could predict and react to. But ever since Ch—"

He broke from saying Chatha's name and swallowed. He knew she knew what he was going to say. There was no reason for him to speak such an abhorrent name between them. It didn't belong there. Not in that moment.

"Chatha," he said anyway, determined to keep himself from hiding away from the things he feared. "It is a shortcoming I'm not sure can be fixed anytime soon, but I'm hoping you'll see past that particular deficiency. I promise you, I'll make it up to you," he said, a devilish sort of grin appearing on his lips. He lifted a hand and ran a knuckle gently down the length of her face, stopping at her lips, which he touched with his fingers again. "Your mouth fascinates me," he said, sounding every bit a fascinated man. "Your lower lip is so full, your whole mouth like a succulent blackberry, in color and in taste . . ."—he brushed his mouth gently over hers, making her breath stop in her throat—"Have I ever told you how very much I love blackberries?"

She laughed a short little laugh, part of it humor but the rest of it like a release valve on a steam pipe. She relaxed in his arms once again, and realized she was giving in to him. She would let him do his best, and hope it didn't turn into his worst. She needed and craved him powerfully enough to make her want to take the risk. *No matter what,* she reminded herself, *you have seen the love he is capable of.*

"Are you going to make love to me?" she asked him, as straightforward as ever she was. It made him chuckle.

"But of course I am, little angel. Perhaps even twice. Actually," he said as he let a hand drift warmly down the swell of her breast, shaping and weighing the fullness of it with palm and fingers, "I hate to put limitations on things."

She couldn't help the equally naughty smile that curved across her lips. Then something occurred to her and that smile faltered a little bit. "But in the library . . . you pulled away because . . ." She trailed off. They both knew why he had pulled away. As harsh as it had felt at the time, she agreed with him for doing it. Passion was one thing, responsibility quite another. It was just that . . .

I wanted him to want me beyond caution, beyond fear, beyond everything. It was silly and juvenile, but that had been her desire all the same.

"Ah yes. Well,"—he reached into his back pocket and held up a row of condoms that flipped open like a wallet full of credit cards—"I called in a favor from Jackson. It went like this, 'Hey bud, seeing as how I saved your ass and all that, can a brother get you to dip into your condom supply and hand some over?' "

"You didn't!" She gasped and pressed a hand to her face, her mouth open in breathless shock. What was more, the strip of condoms was like unfurling a world of sensual possibilities. "He's going to know what . . . that you and I . . ."

"Yes, he quite figured that out. But don't worry, he's the soul of discretion if you're worried about your reputation."

"Stop it!"—she laughed and swatted his chest—"You are beyond incorrigible. And it's not my reputation so much as it's . . ." She broke off and laughed, the sound a little uneasy. "Jackson is Menes, the Pharaoh king of the Bodywalkers and a powerful ally for the Night Angels to have. My father would disapprove if my behavior caused him to look at me like . . . like I was somehow . . . less than I should be."

"Less? You mean because you're dallying with a human?" There was no mistaking the sharpness entering his tone. But then he seemed to visibly catch himself and he sighed softly. "No. Of course you wouldn't think that way. You only mean you need his respect and for him to view your behavior as an equal. Well, don't worry. I know Jackson. He would never judge someone too harshly. In fact, his sense of fair play and respect has often allowed him to give people who don't deserve it another chance. He's a good man and a great friend. As long as he's pulling half the weight of what makes Jackson and Menes Pharaoh of his people, he will always make sure Menes views everything with unprejudicial eyes. Which is a hell of a lot more than I can say about myself."

Leo stepped away from her and, taking her hand in his, he walked backward toward the bedroom connected to the living area. He didn't stop until they were standing by the bed and he was dropping his strip of contraception on the bedside table.

When he turned back to her, it was with pure devilment in his eyes. "Looks like we have our work cut out for us. Your new mission, should you decide to accept it, is to achieve upward of one orgasm per use of one condom. I, however, am quite convinced that you are capable of much more than that." He reached to put a hand on the small of her back and used it to yank her forward, bringing them belly to belly and hip to hip. "And frankly, I'm tired of talking about it and not actually doing anything about it. So shut up and give in."

She laughed, her incredulity soft and amazed. "You are so cocksure you think I'm going to say yes?"

"Well, if your answer is no, please allow me the opportunity to change your mind."

He reached to fondle the top button of her dress, the same one with the little blue flowers, his thumb rubbing in a slow circle over it. She had practically ripped off the catsuit the minute they'd been safe at Grey's and put the dress back on. But the suggestive swirl of his thumb on that button made her think of other things well beyond him simply taking her dress off. Faith was pretty positive she wasn't the only one to see the suggestiveness of it. It made her knees weaken and made other parts of her perk up with interest. Slowly, very deliberately as they both watched with full attention, he slipped the first button free.

Leo looked up at her face and features. Her lips were parted, most likely to accommodate the increasing speed with which she was breathing. Her chartreuse eyes were beautiful with anticipation, and he could sense, since he could not see, a warm flush crawling across her cheeks and over her neck.

The next button came free and the way it made her breath hitch made him all the more determined to do it much slower next time.

"Please," she begged him breathlessly when he finally got around to slipping the fourth button free. He was exposing the generous curves of her delectable breasts. The fact that he knew she was braless brought back a heated run of memories about how he had come to the knowledge in Grey's library. But this time would be different. Very different.

"Please what?" he teased her even though they both knew what she was asking for.

"Please, Leo, put your hands on me," she said, reaching to grab hold of his wrist and turning his hand into the open neck of her dress. Her breast was so warm, the feel of it so incredibly full and sweet, he couldn't scold her for ruining the delicious tension that he'd been orchestrating between them.

"Do you have any other requests?" he asked her, his free hand moving to unbutton the next three buttons quickly, letting the fabric part like some kind of biblical miracle, allowing him access to both breasts and the warm expanse of the onyx black skin of her chest and belly.

"I have hundreds of them," she said on a breathy laugh. That made him smile a seductive smile at her, his fingers sweeping and painting across her skin from one warm breast to the next.

"Good. That's very very good." He cupped her in both hands pressing the weight of her breast against her chest, a rough thumb scraping each nipple simultaneously to the other. She let out a low groan of pleasure and again he smiled.

"You know, I think I like this dress," he said, pushing three more buttons out of his way. His hands swept up to her shoulders, catching the fabric of her dress and running them down her arms as he pushed it off her. Gravity played the rest of the act and the dress fell from her body and pooled like a cool blue puddle around her ankles. His fingers continued to scan lightly over her skin, from the yoke of her collarbone to her rapidly rising and falling breast to her belly just above her navel. "I find it so amazing that the only hair you have on your entire body is here." He reached to touch the cream white of her hair at her temple.

"I could say the reverse to you," she said, her hands reaching to pull up his shirt, pushing it up his belly and chest until he obliged her by grabbing his collar and yanking the thing off. It met the same fate as her dress.

It allowed her to run her hands freely over him, her nails scraping through the hair on his chest until she laughed a soft laugh. "I don't think I'll ever take this sensation for granted. It's so new to me . . . so different."

"We have a lot of differences," he noted.

"But none insurmountable," she dared to say as she looked straight into his eyes. "We've proven there's nothing we can't beat."

"Yes," he said, but it was an absent agreement. He still had his demons and it would take time for him to finish wrestling them. But she did not expect any miracles and she did not demand results before he was ready.

Leo was done discussing difficult things and he wanted the same from her. They needed to leave the difficulties of their lives behind for a little while. Or a long while, he amended as he let his eyes roam her bare body. He was definitely going to need some serious time here.

He cupped her shoulders in his hands and slowly turned her around, burning every line and curve of her body into his memory. He was good at that. Topography. He was good at remembering every hill and valley in a determined area. And as he continued to sweep memorizing fingers over every curve of her, his smile drifted away and concentration took root. He touched her. Lightly with a single finger, or heavily with both his palms . . . constantly he touched her. Her skin was so incredibly soft, even when it was pulled snuggly over athletic muscles. Soft and warm . . . and growing ever warmer. All he could hear was the rapidly changing breaths they both breathed, and the sound of his skin brushing over hers.

"Leo, please," she said after several long minutes of letting him touch her everywhere he could immediately reach.

"Another request?" he asked teasingly as he leaned forward to whisper in her ear. "Anything specific?"

He pulled her up against himself, chest to chest once more, a hand on her backside pulling her in hip to hip as well.

"No, I . . . yes. Kiss me," she said. "And then let me undress you."

Leo took a breath trying to control the raging surge of heat that whipped through him, tried to calm the fire that seemed to scorch it's way along the length of his erection. He needed to slow down a little . . . to take it slow . . . because just the feel of her was already making him struggle with uncontrollable impulses. He wanted this to be good for her. He wanted to make up for his dumb-ass maneuvers earlier in Grey's library. Had that only been hours ago? It felt like days. It felt as though he had been starving for her for days.

He kissed her, her lush mouth like melting caramel that spread sweet and warm over his tongue. And once he started, he couldn't seem to stop. Determined to have her way, however, her hands fell to his belt, grabbing hold of the leather and quickly working it free of its buckle. Before he knew it she had popped open the button to his jeans and was slowly sliding her hand down the front of his pants. Her fingers slipped around him, searing like a stripe of heat from a whip as she took his shaft in her hand.

"Christ," he breathed into her delicious mouth as her kisses grew hot and aggressive to match her hot, aggressive caress. "Faith . . . oh Faith, you're killing me," he accused her, reaching to unzip his jeans with fumbling haste. He barely left her mouth long enough to push them down his legs, toe off his boots and kick the tangled mess of it away. It was almost impossible to coordinate it since she wouldn't give up the touch of his mouth or the feel of his cock for even a second.

He was hauling her onto the bed in a sudden sweeping flex of strength, causing her to bounce in among the bedding. She crawled back, elbows and heels, until she was in the dead center of the thing, and he crawled with her until he was braced over her, his thighs between hers, her breasts caught between their chests. She felt so hot, from neck to ankles, and he was almost afraid to let them come into intimate contact . . . afraid that the simple touch of her would set him on fire and have him prematurely ejaculating all over her . . . just because he loved the very idea of it; the idea of painting her with the heat of his seed.

"Faith, I don't think this is going to be very pretty," he said in hard, punctuating words as he slid impatient fingers into the wet, eager folds of her sex. "No, not pretty at all." He groaned at the slick, hot sensation of her around his fingers. She was so ripe. So ready. And he'd hardly done a damn thing to deserve it. "But it is going to be hot . . . and hard . . . and you won't have an instant to wonder about how much I really, really want you. And how fiercely I'm really going to take you."

He thrust his fingers into her, catching her gasp in his mouth. He swept his tongue into the depths of her mouth as his fingers slid into the depths of her hot, tight little channel. *Oh god,* he thought, remembering and understanding why she was so tight, why she would always feel like a woman untried.

It pushed his desire for her into an entirely new stratosphere. Waiting was necessary one moment, impossible the next. He slipped his hand free of her in order to make way for the hard length of his sex. He felt painfully ready for her, as if he'd been longing for her for years instead of the mere days . . . mere hours . . . brief moments it really had been. He slid against her, reveling in her hot gasp, swallowing it up in a fierce, needful kiss.

And once again he found himself in the same instant and dangerous need to have her at all costs, damn all the consequences. But he struggled to quiet himself a little, to think and have a care for her. Not only because he knew why she was so tight for him, but because he had to pay her the respect she deserved.

He reached for the condoms on the nightstand, fumbling with them and groaning as her legs wove around his. Her knees trapped his hips, her hips lifted and undulated in order to rub her sex along the length of his.

"Jesus, Faith, you don't play fair, do you?"

"Mmm . . . no," she admitted without any contrition. "It turns me on to watch you lose control, Leo Alvarez . . . because I know you don't lose control that often or that easily."

He laughed at that and pulled away from her just long enough to dress himself in the condom. "I might have believed that a couple of weeks ago, but I haven't been in control for a while now." He sent her a searing look, "especially as far as you are concerned."

"Let's make love," she encouraged him on a hot breath. "I don't want anything else to matter outside of this bed."

"As always, I'm happy to accommodate your wishes." They both heard him say the word "wish" and both winced at the same time.

"Don't," she laughed.

"Sorry. I'll be careful."

He found his way back to her, his mouth drifting up over her skin, pausing to toy with her berry-colored nipples, devouring her like an impatient child. Her legs wrapped around him again and he felt himself cradled up against her core. He looked down into her eyes, the beauty of passion across her features.

"God, you're beautiful," he ejected on a breath. "And I need to take you right now, okay?"

"I thought you'd never ask," she said with a breathy laugh.

And with a mutual shift of their hips he began to work himself into her. She gasped when the head of his cock popped past the lip of her vagina, and then again when he thrust more deeply into her. Leo thought he would go insane if he didn't get to the root of her. He'd never known such a need like this one. Before he could control himself he found himself lurching into her in ragged, demanding thrusts. She cried out, her back arching, lifting them both off the bed. Jesus God, she was amazing. She felt unbelievable. Tight. Hot. Wet. Everything he could possibly need. And in so many ways.

He began to thrust into her in a hard, punctuating rhythm, their bodies undulating together as if they were one being. She moaned every time he buried himself to the hilt within her, a cadence of sound that grew louder and more present, more real, with every passing instant. She was a passionate creature. He had known this all along, but to see it applied this way . . .

He was lost. She surrounded him in every way possible, both physically and mentally and he had no hope of extricating himself. What was more, he had no desire to extricate himself.

"Faith, you feel . . ." He interrupted himself to groan with a savage wave of pleasure. Then he stopped talking altogether, thrusting into her harder and faster. He wanted to demand she come for him, but he needed all of his breath and all of his focus to keep from losing himself before he was ready. He found her sweet spot. He knew it because of the way she gasped when he moved a certain way across it. It was the beginning of the end for her. He exploited that spot to its fullest, working her into a frenzy. He gloried in the feel of her hands grabbing at his shoulders, grasping at his sides. Eventually her hands rested on his ass, fingers dug in, spurring him on harder and faster.

She locked up suddenly in pleasure, clamping down on him like a vise. He felt the muscles of her vagina contracting in a rolling massage that was determined to milk him. It succeeded famously. He growled as pleasure bucked through him, release jettisoned with unbelievable force. It was as though she was ripping his soul free of its foundations and for that brief moment he thought he could imagine how it must have felt for Jackson to lose hold of his soul.

Only, Jackson never had it so good.

Faith woke up unable to tell if it were day or night at first. Probably because she didn't really care. Leo had used her very well. Very very well. They had made love endlessly, it seemed, until neither could think about moving and they had fallen asleep together.

She lay quietly, taking account of herself and of the room around her. She was sore from head to toe, she realized. It had been quite some time since she'd had a man in her bed and she supposed she was really out of shape. Not used to it for certain. She hadn't found it easy to take lovers in the Night Angel world. There were so many of them grasping for power and position and thinking she would be an excellent method of climbing to the top, and having been down that road before . . . and badly . . . she was cautious about letting it happen again. But Leo didn't care about the things she might inherit one day . . . if she inherited them at all. Her mother or father would have to die before she'd have access to a throne. She was the eldest child for them both, her mother having birthed a son after her and her father having sired another daughter. Since she had lived with her father all of her life, she didn't consider her mother's throne her own. She would leave that to her brother. And anyway, she didn't like to think about these things. She found it maudlin to consider her parent's deaths. Inevitable as it may be, she didn't want it to happen anytime soon at all.

She finally decided to move, lifting her head from the pillow. She rolled toward Leo, snuggling up to him and laying her ear over his heart. She listened to the low, steady beat of it and smiled.

What future is there in this?

Faith pushed that thought away. She didn't want to consider what the ramifications of this night might be. What might become of it. If she started thinking . . . started hoping . . .

Grey had shown them a future that now no longer existed. That future had been contingent on Jackson's death. And while she was grateful she and Leo would not be suffering a death of their child, it disturbed her that it might mean he would never come to love her.

Like she was coming to love him.

Oh, she knew she had barely scratched the surface of him, but ever since they had lived love together she had just . . . known. She had known it could never be any other way for her. That didn't guarantee he saw it even remotely the same way, but for her part . . .

She sighed, closing her eyes and trying to coax herself into just living in the moment. Why couldn't she just take this an instant at a time? She needed to slow down. Leo spooked so easily . . . he could be gone as soon as he was able and she would be left to pick up the tattered remains of her heart.

God, she should not give him that kind of power over her, but she couldn't help herself. And if this is what it would take . . . if leaving herself open for hurt was where this must go, then she would simply take the journey. If she wanted to hope for a reward, then she must be willing to risk everything.

So she closed her eyes and listened to his heart. Listened to the whoosh of his breaths, enjoyed the life in him.

"I have this sense that you are thinking very deep thoughts," he said, his voice a rumble under her ear. It was like a symphony made just for her. It made her smile to think of it that way.

"Why do you say that?"

"I may not be able to read your scroll, but I can hear a forlorn little sigh like the one you just made and know there are deep thoughts behind it."

"Well, you would be right, but I was just telling myself not to think too deeply. To simply enjoy the moment for what it is."

"Hmm. A fine idea, that," he agreed. "Thinking too much causes trouble."

Faith winced. Was that his way of warning her? Was he telling her not to trespass too close to his heart, because he would not consider giving it away? Or was she just reading too deeply into an offhand remark?

"More sighs," he noted, making her realize she'd done so again. She'd have to watch out for that, she thought. "We've had too much to process these past couple of days. You should just relax and enjoy the quiet."

"I plan to. But perhaps that can wait until after I eat. I'm starving."

"Now that you mention it, so am I." And as if to support the statement, she heard his stomach rumble. It made her laugh. He reached out and smacked her bottom, hauling them both out of bed before she could complain or resist. "Get dressed," he said.

"Well, aren't you bossy," she said with a sniff. "I don't like clothes, remember?"

"Hmm. Have I mentioned I enjoy your customs so far?" At her laugh he added, "But do it for me because I know I won't be able to keep my hands off you otherwise."

And, he thought, *I don't want anyone else looking at your bare body. It'll keep me from having to deck someone.* And since most of the males in the house could turn to stone or smite him with supernatural forces, he'd rather not.

"All right," she said, "as a favor to you then."

They got dressed and made their way down to the kitchen.

"I assume you eat all the normal foods?" he said. "Can I make you an omelet?"

"With hot sauce. I like hot sauce."

"Hot sauce?" He chuckled at that. "The hotter the better?"

"I like ghost chili peppers."

"Holy shit. That's serious business."

"Night Angels love hot and spicy foods." She shrugged. "That's just the way it is. I'm just more serious about it than most!"

Leo went about making them breakfast while she went on a hunt for hot sauce. She was victorious, albeit not highly impressed with the hotness of the sauce, but willing to make do in a pinch.

After they finished eating he went to clean up, giving her a nice deep kiss before doing so.

"Mmm, spicy," he said, licking his lips. She laughed at him and pushed away from the table.

"Only just figuring that out?" she countered.

"Seem to be."

"I'm going for a walk. Join me when you're done? I need to feel the wind. And then we have to talk about getting me back to where we saw that lost soul. There's a cusp nearby, she just isn't seeing it. I need to guide her to it."

"Of course we can. We'll go after I'm done here."

"You don't have to come with me, I can just . . ." She brushed her shoulders, indicating her wings. They might be presently hidden, but they were more than able to carry her back to that soul.

"We'll go together, if you don't mind. I'd like to see you do this . . . if it's okay. Will I be able to see it?"

"Well, I'm more used to hiding what I do from humans. I guess there's no real trick to not hiding it. Sure. I'd love it if you could watch."

"Good. I want to understand more about you."

The words made Faith's heart soar recklessly. That and the words striping across his scroll that told her he honestly did want to know more about her, that the actions he was taking were true to his real intentions. He was being so incredibly open . . . whereas before he had tried so hard to shut her down. It was almost as though she were dealing with two different men. She liked to think this more carefree version of Leo was the way it was supposed to be.

Faith went out the front door and onto the porch. She breathed deep of the nighttime desert air and reached out far and wide with her sense of the wind. It was very still, barely a single breeze, and she always found that a little nerve-racking. Without wind there was no way for her to feel everything around herself. No way to know where things were.

She stepped off the porch, took two steps and then stopped. She took another breath and—

The red explosion that hit her was like a bath of fire, and she screamed. The force of it was so hard that she was ruthlessly whipped about, her body spinning down to the ground. Stunned but conscious, she threw up her repulsion shield, covering herself, protecting herself from the next attack.

But the next attack was not of a power she could repel. It was a leap of an incredibly heavy body onto her back and a knife brutally stabbing twice into and out of her side before she could even think of reacting. The message of pain it delivered was agonizing when the shock of the strike began to wear off. Her attacker kept hitting her, the knife sinking into her harder and faster, all the while he was keeping out of her reach. Furious, her wings snapped to full breadth, blue energy lighting the night. But the attacking force barreled into her again before she could take flight. And this time he put the knife right up under her ribs, instantly puncturing a lung.

Faith gasped for breath, but even though she had full use of one of her lungs, it felt as though she couldn't breathe at all. Adrenaline made her body breathe harder, as did panic, and she knew it was hurting her instead of helping her because every breath sent warm rushes of blood spitting out of her wounded body. Then she felt a hand tangling into her hair and she was yanked across the ground. Her attacker had terrifying strength and he dragged her several yards with each pull. She kicked out with her feet, clawed at the hands in her hair. He threw her head down into the hard earth.

"Bad toy!" he spat out at her before kicking her in the head. "Now. Come play. We're going to have so much fun together."

He reached to grab her hair again.

Out of nowhere a dark, fast shape leaped over her and barreled into her attacker, plowing them both into the soil in a tumbling mass of arms and legs. Faith knew instantly it was Leo and knew he didn't stand a chance against Chatha in hand to hand. And now that she'd had a second to focus on him, she knew it was indeed Chatha, his name scrawled in childlike print over one scroll as Andy and the other scroll as Chatha.

"No!" she croaked, forcing herself to scramble toward Leo. Chatha had just bucked Leo off himself and was rearing back, the spell for the Curse of Ra, the fiery red flame, erupting from his lips just as she reached the minimum distance needed to throw up her repulsive shield over him. The red explosion blinded her night acclimated eyes, but it didn't matter. Chatha's attack was deflected back at him, the strike making him scream out in pain and fury. His scrolls lit up in such a confusing, contradicting flurry of responses it hurt to look at them.

Leo skidded over to her, throwing his leg over her, straddling her protectively as he pulled his weapon and aimed for Chatha.

Somehow, against all of what she knew he was feeling, through all the rage and contempt and the fear, he shot Chatha in a leg. Not the heart or the head, but the leg. The psychopathic Bodywalker squealed and screamed, then flung out another volley of the Curse of Ra.

"Slow learning curve, motherfucker?" Leo asked as the attack was repelled again and Chatha was left screaming in pain and fury.

But the Curse wasn't the only weapon in Chatha's arsenal, which was apparent a heartbeat later when he spit out a spell and the ground suddenly went soft beneath them. It was an attack she couldn't repel because it wasn't inherently offensive. The weight of Faith's body began to sink into the soil. Like quicksand it sucked her and Leo down, forcing Leo to shove his weapon into the back waistband of his jeans and grab for Faith. She tried to help him, but she'd lost so much blood so quickly that her whole body had gone weak. She began to panic because she didn't know if she could last much longer, and if she lost consciousness or became too weak she couldn't protect Leo from Chatha's offensive attacks. He would be even more outmatched than he already was.

Luckily the quicksand was only in a small, localized area and Leo was able to grab onto solid ground. But he wasn't strong enough to haul himself and Faith out of the mess at the same time, so he had to let go of her and pull himself up. He dug in and grabbed for her. But as soon as he had her on solid ground Chatha cast the spell again. Leo didn't even have time or energy to waste on swearing the blue streak of words raging through his mind. The quicksand was cold because the soil was cold, and that made him aware of the warm liquid sensation spilling over his arm as he hauled Faith up, yet again, to solid ground.

And Chatha cast the spell again.

"Fuck! Faith, I have to put him down!" he growled in impotent fury.

"Do it!"

He pulled his weapon, the thing filthy with mud and dirt, and aimed it.

Oh, but he wanted to pull the trigger and blow his brain out his nostrils, but part of him screamed that that was the easy way. That Chatha deserved the hard way. He didn't want to listen to himself, but just the same the second bullet hit Chatha in his collarbone. Leo had broken his collarbone once, during parachuting training in the Rangers. And he knew it was the most agonizing pain he could have imagined . . . but that had been before Chatha.

Chatha fell onto the ground screaming, curling up and rocking like a child with a badly skinned knee.

"That should fuck with his concentration long enough for me to get you out of here," he said to Faith, making sure they were both on solid ground before reaching to swing her up into his arms.

"I've got her," a low, masculine voice assured him. Leo looked up into Kamenwati's eyes, the Bodywalker having lowered into a crouch in front of him, graceful hands moving to take hold of Faith. Leo's first instinct was to grab Faith and hold her tighter, more protectively than ever.

"Why don't you worry about that tool from your torturer's emergency kit?" he said, jerking his head toward Chatha. "Because I sure as hell am not giving her to *you*! So keep your hands to yourself before I pick a part of your anatomy for target practice!"

"Give her to me then," Ahnvil said, coming to kneel in front of him. Leo watched a little numbly as the Gargoyle, his slate-gray stone skin gleaming over the contours of his body and his amber eyes glowing with a deep fiery warmth that belied the cold marble look of his skin, lifted Faith while gaining his full height. It was as if he carried a baby, a doll so light and insignificant.

Once he saw them heading to safety, he gained his

feet, whirled around and marched to where Chatha lay on the ground moaning and whimpering. Kamen and Grey were standing over him, guarding to make sure he didn't budge. Kamen looked up at Leo's approach.

"Come," Grey said, pointing down at Chatha. "It's time we put this monster back in the Ether for another hundred years. It is the best we can do, but no one deserves the honor more than you. Perhaps you will find some of the closure you desire."

Leo laughed sardonically. "In order for me to come close to giving him equal payback, I would have to become the same animal that he is. I'll be happy to prove I'm better than him by doing the one thing he refused to do for me. I'll be putting him out of his misery."

Leo pointed the gun at Chatha's head, aiming right between his eyes. The rounded eyes and cheeks of Down syndrome innocence glared up at him, and he had to remind himself that this was the only way. His finger tensed around the trigger, but he did not pull it even though everything inside of him, everything angry and violent and scared to fucking death inside of him was reaching so hard for it that his hand was shaking.

This is a good death, he reminded himself hotly. *It's justice as well as vengeance and a far sight more humane than the other half of Andy deserves.*

"Goddammit!" he ground out, stepping back and turning in a hard about-face. He paced away just three short steps, turned back and pointed the gun at him again.

And still he could not shoot. *Why?* he demanded of himself. *How often had you prayed for this opportunity? Why can't you do it?*

"Here, let me do it," Kamen said quietly reaching to take Leo's weapon from him.

"No!" Leo jerked back from him. "Just . . . just let me think! God!"

He looked toward the direction Faith had been taken, a part of him knowing that she was a source of peace and focus, something he desperately needed right then. If anyone could set him straight, it would be Faith. But she was long gone. That left only one other potential source of comfort and that was Grey. But he hardly knew or understood Grey so the likelihood of finding any solace . . .

Leo stilled, his eyes swinging back to Chatha . . . then back to Grey.

"I want to make a wish," he said with sudden inspiration.

"No," Jackson said, pacing the room in a sharp, tight circuit, ignoring Marissa who followed him every single step as if to catch him should he grow suddenly weak. It wasn't so far-fetched an idea. Leo's friend had looked much better. "It can't be done."

They had bundled Chatha up into the main parlor of the residence, leaving him moaning behind a gag, so he couldn't cast any spells, and tied up so he couldn't physically fight either, although it was clear that there was no physical fight left in him. He, like Faith, had lost a great deal of blood.

"Why not?" Leo demanded of him. "If he can tie a soul down," he pointed to Grey, "and Apep can sever a soul, why can't a wish sever one soul and leave the other intact?"

"That's too simplistic! The souls aren't two independent entities! They've Blended . . ."

"That's not how I understand it," Leo shot back. "As I understand it Templars suppress their hosts, rather then Blend with them."

"He is correct." The arguing men whipped about to look at Kamenwati. He was standing in the parlor entryway, leaning a shoulder against the wall. "We do not Blend. Even now, in spite of the terms I have come to, I have very little awareness of the original soul inside me. He has been beaten down so often, my soul overshadowing his, that I don't think we could ever easily reverse it . . . that we could ever Blend us after so much time. There are times when the host soul 'leaks' out past our more dominant souls, but it's more like a prison break than it is the flip side of the same coin."

"Then that settles it." Leo turned to Grey who had remained quiet and observant all of this time. "Grey, I know what that wish is. The one you said was waiting for me."

"Careful," Jackson hissed, unable to help himself. "Leo, please . . ."

"I wish," Leo repeated, "for the Bodywalker soul, Chatha, to be ejected from Andy's body and sent back into the Ether indefinitely. Once Chatha's soul is purged, I want Andy's soul to remain and I want his memories of all that has happened since Chatha took possession of him to be completely erased so that he doesn't have to suffer with the memories of what Chatha has done. I wish all of this to be done without killing Andy. I want him to be able to lead a normal life once he is free."

Grey took a deep breath and released it in a slow sigh. "That's a very . . . complex wish," Grey noted.

"Can you do it?" Leo asked, his tone hard and his determination evident.

"There will be—"

"A price to pay. Yes, I know. *Can you do it?*"

Grey smiled a very devilish sort of smile. "I'm the Djynn of the Western states who owns a flatulent Pegasus. I can do damn near anything."

Faith opened her eyes, groaned at the heavy weight pressing down on her chest and rolled over. She didn't move more than a half an inch before pain blossomed through her body from several different locations.

"Ow," she whimpered piteously.

"Shh," came the warm rumbling sound of Leo's voice up against her ear. "Don't move too much. Grey said you lost too much blood to properly regenerate using your natural healing abilities. It'll be another day or two before you can start getting around."

"How's Andy?" she asked suddenly, her eyes flying open so she could look into the warm brown of his concerned gaze. He was lying in bed with her, holding her snugly to the right side of his body. She sighed with contentment at the intimate feel of him, at how close it made her feel with him.

"It worked," he assured her, knowing exactly what she meant. She had asked him about it every time she'd woken up since he'd told her about the wish. Apparently every time she fell asleep she thought she had only dreamed it all up. "Andy is a very normal, very stable Down syndrome adult male. Actually"—he cleared his throat—"he's a really cool kid. Completely different than I had expected. I guess I'd expected him to be more like the farce Chatha used to reel his victims in. He's actually quite bright and very mature. I only wish—"

"What is it? What's wrong?" she asked when she saw him frown darkly.

"I wish I didn't feel the way his face still makes me feel. No matter how much I try to explain to myself that Chatha is gone, every time I see Andy's face I'm . . . I still feeling this choking fear . . ."

"Give it some time," Faith soothed him softly, her warm hand reaching out to pet his arm. "You can't expect yourself to just shrug all of your trauma off. Andy's face is a trigger. It's going to bring a lot of memories up for a very long time. You might not ever be able to develop a long-term relationship with Andy."

"I don't want a long-term relationship with anyone, believe me. I am going to find a good place for him that's as far away from this deadly circus as possible."

Faith quieted significantly, enough for him to sense it.

"Are you okay?" he asked.

"You're right. This is no place for an innocent human to be," she said quietly. "And it's best that you stay as far from the dangers of this place as you can possibly manage."

Leo was quiet for several beats of time. "I plan to," he said. "I'm not an idiot, Faith, I know when I'm out-gunned. I've got a life to get back to . . . there are things I can do out in the human world . . . I can help better out there if I stay away from here."

"Then you should go as soon as your responsibilities to Jackson are over," she said, refusing to let even a hint of hurt reflect into her voice. She rolled over, away from him, and pretended to snuggle back into sleep.

"Faith, I . . . I hope we're okay. I mean . . . we're from such different worlds and . . . you have to remember what Grey showed us, that it's no longer a possibility. Things have changed and . . ."

"It's okay," she lied, squeezing her eyes shut tightly against the tears burning into them. "I know what you're saying. It's a different future now. I knew that all along. I mean, you said it yourself, you'd never even consider . . ."

"No, I wouldn't," he agreed. "Even if you were a human female, Faith, I am no good at long-term rela-tionships. Hell, I'm not even good at short-term ones."

"I know," she said softly. "Leo, I'm exhausted."

"Okay," he said, but something sat uneasy with him and he hesitated from moving off the bed. He wanted to prod at her, to make sure she understood his perspec-tive, to make sure she wasn't . . . hurt, but he could tell she was still wiped out. And anyway, he had no real right to ask her for anything. He never really had.

Like he had said, even if she'd been human, he really sucked at relationships. Hell, the only reason Jackson and Docia put up with him was because they'd been anesthetized against his stupidity. They were more like family, and family had to take you in, flaws and all.

Realizing Faith had fallen asleep, Leo got up off the bed and looked around the room. There was hardly anything there outside of a couple of pairs of borrowed jeans and shirts in the room. He'd be giving those back to Jackson. He'd had nothing when he'd got there and would leave with nothing. It was his favorite way to live. No roots, no encumbrances. Even the gun lying on the nightstand wasn't his.

He looked at Faith's sleeping face. She wasn't his either. She was yet another thing he'd borrowed from this strange path he'd been put on, and like everything else she would be left behind. As always, it was for the best.

He wished he could leave right then, rather than a month from now. He was afraid the longer he lingered near Faith the harder it would be when it came time to say goodbye. The longer he lingered the worse it would get. Faith was so remarkable, so damn special . . . he had to admit it was tempting to toy with the what-ifs of life. But that had never served him well. No. He had to keep a distance. Always.

Leo had done a stellar job of avoiding her. She'd been healed now for the past week, so it wasn't as though he had the excuse of her injuries for keeping himself away from her. She could only assume he was thoroughly in the process of putting distance between them. It stung her. Even that moment, it stung tears into her eyes just thinking about it. She had thought that at least . . . at least he might want to take advantage of this last month.

She would have happily lingered for the rest of the month, using the excuse of reinforcing their auras or further defending the house as perfectly plausible reasons for hanging around.

But there was no reason for her to stay, she was realizing. He was taking all of her reasons away, and he was doing it on purpose.

He hadn't even come back to the room he'd been using, the one she'd been healing in, since she'd been well enough to get up out of bed. Faith turned her face up to the wind that was blowing over the New Mexico desert and knew he was inside the house. Of course he was. If she was in, he went out, if she was out, he went in. Without fail he would know where she was and how to avoid her. It was as though he were the one with the preternatural senses.

She had to leave. Yes. She had to leave. Her father would be wondering where she'd gone. He'd want to know how she'd fared. There were a million responsibilities awaiting her and she was letting them all slide just so she could linger around someone who, clearly, wanted nothing to do with her.

So fine. She'd go. She'd strip off yet another borrowed dress and stretch her wings and . . . go.

She turned and marched off the porch, ready to find Jackson and Marissa, ready to gather her tattered pride up and hold her head high, rather than embarrassing herself any more than she already had. She rushed through the door and slammed right into someone.

Leo. Somehow he'd gotten his wires crossed and had actually made the mistake of running into her. His hands circled around her upper arms, holding her tight to help her regain her balance. A look of concern creased over his face. "Are you okay?" he asked.

She knew that he was afraid he'd hurt her since she was still fresh off her injuries.

Her laugh was caustic.

"Oh no, Leo, you haven't hurt me *at all*."

Wow. Subtle Faith, really subtle.

But instead of arguing with her, instead of calling her on it and reiterating why his way was the best way, he frowned deeply and even a little bit darkly. His whiskey-warm eyes were hard and fierce, the expression in them unreadable for several beats. Then, as if he couldn't help himself, his gaze dropped.

To her mouth.

And lingered.

It made Faith's heart turn over in her chest. He wanted her. It was scrawled across his scroll in fiery brilliance. He wanted her. If for no other reason than the physical, he wanted her.

And dammit, she would take what she could get.

She surged up on her toes and crashed their mouths together so hard it should have hurt. And in a way it did. It hurt in poignant, painful ways. Even as heat seared through her, it was a bitter heat, just as consuming as all the other times before when he had kissed her, but painful because in her heart she knew it would be the last time. And that was good. She would pay closer attention this time, now that she knew it was going to be the last. She would remember everything. The way his hands tightened briefly as he considered pushing her away, and then relaxed, just as his mouth went from passive to aggressive against hers. They were on each other like ravenous wolves from that point on. Their mouths remained connected, even as their hands fumbled at each other's clothing and their feet stumbled toward the nearest private room. It was a small sitting room at the front of the house, no locks on the door, no hope for secure privacy. But it didn't matter. Not when she could feel his hot callused hands running up her thighs under her skirt. He was looking for panties, but then laughed when he didn't find any, having forgotten he was lucky she was even wearing a dress. Or maybe he was unlucky at that point, because he was determined to get the dress off her.

She went for his belt, the jingle of the buckle sounding noisy even over their breathing. She was naked by the time she got his fly open. He fished in his back pants pocket for something—a wallet, she realized. It was light, and new, probably didn't hold anything at all in it, but he did come up with a condom, tossing the wallet onto the ground.

She hesitated only for a second, trying to figure out how she should feel about him being prepared like this. Had he been hoping . . . ?

No. She wasn't going to think. This was about feeling, not thinking. It was about holding on to memories, however fast and furtive they were going to be.

"Let me do it," she breathed, holding her hand out for the plastic packet.

Leo found himself hesitating, wondering how the hell he had ended up in this place again. He'd been so determined to give her a wide berth. He'd been hoping, waiting like a coward, for her to just give up on him and leave, but now by doing this he was taking away any headway he might have been making. She was going to think there was going to be more between them when there just couldn't be. He should stop right then and there and tell her he was sorry, that it was just a huge mistake. All of it had been just a huge mistake. But he found himself placing the packet in her hand.

She used her teeth to rip it open then slid the whole of her free hand down the front of his pants, her strong fingers wrapping around his erection one by one until he was groaning and cursing deeply. And just like that they were back onto each other's mouths with tremendous ferocity. Her lips were so damn soft, her tongue like sinfully hot silk. Her fist rolled up the length of his cock, the sensation like lightning straight to the heart of him. His balls ached as if he'd never had her, as if she'd spent this past week teasing him. And in a way she had. She had been in his every thought, worrying at him like Chinese water torture, wearing away at him little by little whether she knew it or not, whether he tried to tell himself otherwise or not.

"Jesus Christ, put it on me already so I can be inside you," he said hotly, gripping at her hip. Then, as if she was forcing him to play dirty, he slid away from her hip and burrowed right between her legs. She gasped in a loud, wide breath and stepped to the side, opening herself up to his invasion. And invade he did. He didn't waste time with a single nicety, as it were, he thrust two fingers right into her, the meat of his palm pressing against her clitoris as he began to thrust them deeply inside of her again and again and again.

"Oh," she laughed breathlessly. "So that's how you want to play?"

"Yeah, that's how I play," he agreed, this time twisting his hand when he thrust into her. She moaned, her eyes fluttering closed for a moment, her body weight dropping down to meet the thrust of his burrowing fingers.

Then suddenly it was all her weight on his hand and he was forced to remove it or snap his wrist. And that was how she came to be on her knees before him, her hands dragging down his jeans before reclaiming her hold on his cock and, before he could even register it was happening, put him into the hot haven of her mouth.

"Oh Jesus Mary and Joseph," he ground out, his hand driving into the cotton white of her hair and fisting tightly. He looked down at her just as she looked up, and he could see the wickedness of her sexual confidence. She knew exactly what kind of hold she had on him right then, and she was going to milk it, and him, for everything he was worth. He felt her swallow around him, felt her run her tongue over that sensitive spot at the base of his cockhead that she had found the first and only night they had made love. She wasn't pulling any punches, and the sudden increasing draw on him made it abundantly clear.

"No! No! Jesus!" He swore in Spanish and English, respectively, and she laughed, a vibration he felt right down the length of his shaft. He gripped her by her chin and pulled himself away, probably with ease because she was laughing. And with eyes dancing she held up the condom and stretched it out over his engorged penis.

"Now up," he commanded of her, dragging her up as though she might not obey. But she was on the same page and with a lunge that put her up on her toes and then, after he reached down for her thighs, had her wrapping her legs high around his waist, she guided him into her eager body, pressing down on him bit by bit, both of them exclaiming in sounds of need as he advanced in one movement . . . two . . . and then finally was seated deep inside her. Then he grabbed hold of her hip with one hand and the wall with the other and began to meet her thrust after thrust after thrust. They probably should have checked the pleasured moans escaping them, but it simply didn't matter to them. They were in the moment for the sake of the moment and not caring about anything else.

And it was because of that focus that they could forget about what might happen. It was because of that focus that they could give in to the wild pleasure coursing through them on such a primal level. He surged into her again and again, as if he were looking to reach a core of her she didn't know she had. Leo couldn't have felt more aroused than he already was. There was no level of excitement beyond this. Not even when riding on the edge of danger, not even when he risked his life, betting it against the worst of odds. Only then had he ever felt truly alive, but in this moment, with the electrical sensation of her running through him, this outshone it by far. *This* was what being alive felt like.

And he never wanted it to end. But the end was coming faster every second. He ought to have slowed down a little, savored it a little, but he couldn't help himself and only went faster and harder the closer the climax came. And then, just like that, he shot over the crest, pleasure ripping through him as he burst inside of her, the glory of the moment dragging everything he had into the orgasm.

His knees gave way and they slid down the wall together, Faith resting in his lap, head thrown back, gasping for breath. Leo realized with shock that he didn't even know if she had come.

"Did you . . . ?" he asked frantically.

"What? Oh! Yes," she laughed breathlessly. "Yes. Very much so."

"Oh. Good." He chuckled. He had completely lost his head. And as he came to better awareness of the world around him, he realized where they were, what they had sounded like, and what the odds were that they had been overheard.

Jesus, what had gotten into him? He'd been avoiding her at all costs, but even running into her like that, he would never have expected it to end like this. But she had kissed him and that had been the end to all of his rational thought.

Just a single kiss and he'd been utterly lost.

Faith could see him working out things in his head, and as he did, tension returned to his body. She could see the writing on the wall . . . and on his scroll. He was realizing what a mistake this had just been. That it had ruined his plans, whatever those might be. All she knew was that his plans didn't include her.

"Wow," she said, forcing her legs to work and hauling herself up off him, trying not to react to the deficit she felt when he slid free of her body. "That was unexpected. But I'm supposed to . . ." She fished for something while trying not to look like she was floundering for an excuse. "Ahnvil wanted me to help him out with something."

"A Gargoyle needing help?"

"Yes," she laughed. "Gargoyles need help, too. I think he's looking for opinions on his new garden. Anyway, I better go, I'm already late."

She had smoothed her dress down and stepped out of his reach before he could react. She went to the door, grasping the knob, forcing him to hastily worry about his state of undress as her exit threatened to expose him to the outside world. Not that he was shy, but he was courteous of Jackson and Marissa's home, and it was bad enough he had played the part of the naughty guest as it was.

"Faith!"

Faith heard him call her at the last minute, but she hurried through and shut the door regardless. After all, what could he possibly have to say. "Don't get any ideas." "This was a mistake." "Nothing has changed."

She didn't want to hear him speak the words aloud, even though all of them were true. It was enough that she was forced to come to that conclusion; she didn't have to feel the wounds of his words as well.

And now she would go. She would huddle over her new memories like a miser huddles over his gold. They were far from being as tender as their previous assignations had been, but they were hers, and no one could take them away from her. She could remember the heat and fire of it all in the future . . . a future she knew was about to get very lonely.

She walked out the front door minutes later, peeled off her borrowed dress, and let it fall to the porch floor. With a deep breath she extended her wings, wriggling them into full extension, sighing with a combination of relief . . . and regret. But she shoved away from the regret as she shoved away from the porch, her body launching into the air.

She ought to have taken her leave of Jackson and his household politely, but perhaps they would understand.

She was leaving the way she had come. Unexpectedly. And she was leaving with what she had arrived with.

Nothing.

Absolutely nothing.

Faith had been home only for an hour before her mother had descended on her, demanding a recounting of all that had happened. Faith hadn't even thought that her father had told her about her mission. She hadn't gone to her father's house specifically so she could avoid too much attention and too many questions. She needed a minute. She needed a minute to mourn what she had lost.

She had been as detailed as was necessary with her mother . . . leaving out the intimacies she had shared with a mortal man. Her mother, in a word, was a snob. Oh, she was a decent person overall, but she was definitely a snob. She had plans for her children, and Faith was very certain they didn't include one of them running off to be lover to a human man.

Fortunate then, that that human man did not want a lover.

"You look simply awful, darling," her mother had cooed, genuine concern in her eyes as she'd examined Faith for the damage she had suffered. "I take it you need to rest before resuming your duties? Is that why you've come here? I know you find it much less taxing here."

"Mother, don't start." Her mother was constantly in a silent competition with her father to be better than he was for her. To offer more, to be more enticing, to possibly deserve more loyalty. Her mother was not petty, merely competitive, and the father of her eldest child was her favorite contestant.

"I'm fine, Mother. I just need a day or two to decompress, then I'll return to Father."

"Yes, of course," her mother agreed gently. "Well, it's entirely up to you, dear. Are you sure you're all right? You seem a little . . . off."

"I'm fine," Faith said. "I'll see you in the evening."

"Oh, I forgot to tell you," her mother said. "Your brother was in some trouble, too." At this her entire visage fell and she began to wring her hands in a rare show of stress. Her mother kept her cool quite well in even the worst of circumstances, which was an excellent quality in the leader of the Australian Night Angels. But when it came to the well-being of her children, most specifically her beloved son who lived with her—as opposed to Faith, who had chosen to live with her father— she worried for him ferociously and tried to protect him at every turn, even though Faith's brother was far and above capable of taking care of himself. "We found him nearly beaten to death in his home."

"Oh no! Is Dax all right?"

"Well, I suppose he is now. Physically, in most respects. But I am not so certain about mentally," her mother said, trailing off at the end and looking very concerned indeed.

"I'll have to go and check up on him."

"But you just got back from the States," her mother said worriedly. But despite her protests, Faith could tell her mother wanted her to do exactly that, and as soon as possible.

"It's no trouble." She would rather stay there and keep busy than set foot in her father's house, back in his domain and on the same continent as . . .

No . . . no, Faith, don't do this to yourself. Otherwise, every time you step into North America you'll want to search for a man who doesn't want anything more to do with you.

There was no explaining just how badly that knowledge hurt. And besides, it wasn't as though she should be shocked. She had known all along that he wouldn't be capable of . . .

That wasn't true. All along she had known he *was* capable. Thanks to Grey she had known almost from the start that he was very much capable of loving her. What hurt was that he didn't seem to want it in spite of what he had seen. In spite of what they had shared. Grey had showed him how deeply they could come to care for each other and still he rejected it. Grey had shown them how amazing life together would be . . .

The future had changed, yes, but did it have to be the entire future? Why couldn't it just be the part where Marissa is driven mad with grief that changes? Why couldn't the rest stay the same? Couldn't he see it could stay the same?

Dax stood staring into the fireplace of his father's home. He had been living with his father ever since . . .

He closed his eyes and sighed. At least he could close his eyes, he thought with gratitude. It had been a week before he had been able to do so without the horror of that night replaying in constant detail. Details he would not share with anyone. Anyone except his closest friend . . . his father.

"Have you been sleeping?" Balthazar asked his son as

he entered the room and found him standing pensively before the fireplace.

"No," he answered truthfully. "I have to do something about this, Father. I can't just let it be."

"I know you feel that way, Dax, but you also know there is nothing that can be done right now."

"I can't just do nothing!" Dax shouted out suddenly, his fist smashing into the mantelpiece and making the objects on it jump in place. "She has stolen from me! I cannot let it go!"

"I think I have some information about this," Balthazar said carefully, watching his son closely. "It involves your sister."

"Faith?"

"Yes," he said. He could hardly begin to understand the pain Dax was in. He could barely empathize. He couldn't cope with the idea of what he had been through, nor did he know how he would have acted had it been himself. Which, from what he was learning, could very easily have been the case. But this deviant who had done this had not risked targeting one of the rulers of the Night Angel world . . . instead he had gone after an heir. Good stock, but not yet enough experience to be able to take on something of that power and magnitude.

Balthazar had only recently learned about what Faith had been through. Slowly he explained to his son how a Bodywalker was not a Bodywalker . . . but a demon god in the guise of a Bodywalker. Every word was like a nail in Dax's hide, a physical pain that was unendurable.

"Faith is coming to check on you. She is concerned for you."

"You didn't tell her—?" Dax turned hard about to look at his father.

"Know me better than that, Dax."

Dax deflated. "Yes. Yes, of course. I'm sorry. I know you wouldn't betray my confidence. But what you are telling me makes this even worse than before. This god is using a part of me to bring terror to this earth. He must be destroyed."

"Before or after the birth of your child, Dax?"

Dax flinched as his father knew he would. But he had to remind his son that there was an innocent life standing between Dax and any vengeance he sought to deliver.

"And there *will* be a child. As a god he can manipulate the workings of his mortal body on all levels. There is no way to doubt that."

"An innocent child," Dax said quietly. "But imbued with the power of an imp god? How innocent will it be for how long a time?"

"That is hard to tell. The future will play its hand as it will. We will keep the heirophants close and await the opportunity we seek. Time for vengeance will come, but it will have to be well thought out."

"Can Faith's sister, Dahlia, come to stay, do you think?" he asked. "She is the most powerful heirophant of all. If anyone will find the right future, it will be her."

"I will ask Faith to make the request once she gets here." Balthazar rested a supportive hand on his son's shoulder. "The right time will come. Believe me when I say that."

"Oh, it will come," Dax assured in return. "It *will* come."

Faith left Dax within an hour of arriving. Dax had told his father only about the true nature of the attack against him, but he had realized while Faith was there that if he were going to get any kind of solution to the dire challenge in front of him, he would very likely need the help of his mother and, perhaps, his sister's father,

Desmond. Or even more than that, he had realized when his sister had explained to him exactly what he was dealing with. Not that he had needed any further explanations. He had known in the moment, as he'd been crushed down into the floor, that he was being molested by a power of sickening proportions.

He had asked Faith to return to her father and to ask Desmond, as a favor to him, for his help and to do so discreetly.

Faith had been unable to deny her brother, not after hearing his no-doubt softened version of what had happened. Dax, though he was younger than she, had always looked on her as though he needed to protect her. Her ability was significant and as a result she needed very little protecting, but his was even more powerful and she supposed that between that and love for her, he had come to feel like he needed to be her protector.

But Dax had just learned that power was subjective. Her defensive power had been able to defeat what his defensive/offensive power had not been able to do. It had no doubt made his bitter pill even more difficult to swallow. So when he asked her to return to her father right away, she couldn't deny him. Whatever her personal feelings, she had to put them aside and go to her father's house. Get to his continent. And even though they resided in Washington state, a good distance from New Mexico, it still felt too close for comfort.

"Oh Faith! I was just coming to look for you! I have a message for you!"

When her sister, the oracle, said message, she knew she didn't just mean the average message.

"Yes? Is there someone who needs ferrying?"

"You need to return to where you came from. You've left something unfinished."

Faith gasped. "Oh my goodness! I did! I forgot about

the woman in the road! Oh, how could I be so thoughtless!"

Chatha's attack and Leo's rejection had completely erased the needy spirit from her mind. The poor creature, she had waited so long already!

"Yes, go to her. And check on the others you left behind as well. You are needed there too."

"Thank you, Dahlia." She put her arms around her sister and hugged her tightly.

"Of course," Dahlia said softly into her ear. "And don't worry about Dax. He's going to be just fine."

"Oh . . . well, I know that," Faith said softly. "He's Dax." She hesitated. "Are you sure . . . that I should go back to the others?"

Odds were that now that it was an entire week past the time that Leo had been required to stay, he had long since left. He had been chafing at the bit a month ago, so by the time he'd been free to leave he must have been halfway out the door already. If she went back she had to prepare herself for the fact that he might not be there . . . and for the fact that he might.

"No," she said to Dahlia with a firm shake of her head. "I'll go back for the soul, but don't ask me to—"

"Faith," she said softly, her warm sunshine-colored eyes were gentle and admonishing at the same time. "I would not ask you to do something without cause."

"But why . . . ?"

"Just go. The rest will work itself out. But you must finish what you've begun."

"I know. I'll go find her. I promise. I'll go right now and I'll be right back."

Faith left her sister hurriedly.

"No," Dahlia said softly to her absent sister, "you won't be back for quite some time."

* * *

Faith landed lightly on the balls of her feet, her wings fluttering with the chill in the air. There was a dark figure sitting on the porch as she approached and it rose to greet her. Expecting Jackson or one of the Gargoyles, she offered up a smile.

The smile faltered when she saw who it was.

Leo.

She hesitated in her progress, even took an involuntary step backward. He came down the steps quickly and stood in front of her. Faced with him so unexpectedly she was flustered and upset, panic gripping her chest. She had been almost positive he would be gone by then! If she had thought he would be there she would never have come . . . or at the very least she would have prepared herself, would have steeled herself for the meeting.

Truth now, Faith. You were hoping he would be here.

Hoping and dreading. *But why didn't he leave?*

"Faith."

"Leo," she greeted him awkwardly. She felt raw and exposed. Her confidence had been in tatters since she had left. So had her peace of mind.

"I came to tell everyone that Andy is in a good home for Down syndrome adults now. He's a real good kid. Funny as hell. He's got a thing for knock-knock jokes. You'd never know . . ."

You'd never know he'd harbored a psychopath.

"I came to finish . . . the lost spirit in the desert . . ." She gestured vaguely behind herself. "I was stopping in. I didn't know you'd be here."

She said the statement hard, so that he would know she hadn't wanted to find him there. She wasn't going to flaunt her feelings, but neither could she hide them in their entirety.

"Faith, come inside. I . . . I have something for you. I

didn't know if you'd ever come back here, but I hoped you would . . . so I . . . I brought you something."

"I really don't need anything," she said, feeling awkward again as he reached out to take her hand and pull her toward the house. He led her upstairs, back into the suite he had used when they'd last been there. She stayed in the living area. She didn't think she could bear looking at the bed where they had made love so thoroughly. Where for a vignette of time, they had meant something intimate to each other.

He went into the room briefly and came back to her.

"I went back and packed up all my things . . . brought them back here. I figured that I need to stay around here. Since I can go out into daylight I can be of real use around here. And I'll be certain to get my adrenaline fixes around here, that's for sure. So anyway, I-I found something . . . something that Docia once gave me when she was a little girl and I guess I could never throw it away."

He handed her a red heart-shaped box with a ribbon around it. She could tell by the heft of it that it was empty, void of all the chocolates that might have been inside of it at one point for some distant Valentine's Day. The box was worn and beaten in along its cardboard rims, the foil embossing flaking and faded.

Utterly puzzled, she pulled the ribbon and opened the box, knowing already there wasn't anything inside. She held the two pieces of the box, one in each hand, and looked up at him in confusion.

"It's my heart," he said quietly. "Old, battered, empty." He reached to run a gentle thumb along the line of her jaw. Everything about him changed in that instant as he drew her closer to himself. "I'm giving it to you so you can fill it up. I know it's going to be hard to do, since I don't make things easy, but I was hoping you'd take on the job. Rescue me, the way you rescued

Jackson. All in." He cleared his throat. "I know it's selfish of me, and I know I have no right to ask. I'm pretty used up and worthless in the emotions department right now, but . . ." He trailed off, but she waited patiently as he searched for his next words, for his cautious feelings.

"I can't promise you anything but this minute, this moment right now," he said softly, pulling her in tight and close. "None of us have anything for certain besides this minute. None of us should promise what we might never be able to give because the next minute after the promise we could be gone, leaving it empty and unfulfilled. And I couldn't do that to you," he said as he pulled her cheek to the fervent, breathy press of his lips. "When you walked out . . . when I realized you'd left me entirely, at first I thought, for just one second I thought, thank God. That will make things easier. And the very next instant I knew I was wrong. I knew . . . I knew I'd been wrong all along. Wrong not to share myself with you, wrong to sell you short, wrong to push you away. I realized the last thing I wanted to do was go on without you. I know you left because I drove you to it, but please, please let me make it up to you. One day at a time. Don't ask me to let you go again because my heart couldn't possibly take it. I love you and I will never betray your trust like that again. Now, my heart is in your hands, Faith," he said, holding her hands where they were holding the silly cardboard box. "Do with it what you will."

Faith felt heated tears burning into her eyes as the intent behind the gesture was suddenly made so clear to her. It was stark in the words he had used, and brilliantly seared across his scroll. That single, glorious word. Love. Then came devotion. Then more and more words, all the same, all running over with his emotions and his feelings toward her. She had never seen anything so bright and beautiful in all of her life. She laughed shakily, a blink of her lashes sending tears haphazardly over her lashes, gluing his gently pressing lips to her cheek. He kissed the salty fluid away.

"Don't," he said, his voice harsh. "Don't cry. I don't mean to hurt you. It's just . . . it's just the best I can do."

She laughed again, this time with more genuine mirth. She pulled back so she could look into his eyes, their warm brown looking troubled and confused. He didn't know how to reconcile her tears with her laughter. He couldn't figure out what she was thinking.

"Leo." It was all she said before walking away. Just his name. And for that instant he thought his chest was going to rip wide open, leaving him bleeding at her feet. To know she was turning her back on him hurt more than he had ever thought it possibly could. Even more than the first time she had left. In all the times he'd given the "It's not you it's me" speech to women as a means of escaping their emotional attachments, he'd never imagined himself ever being on the other end of it. He'd never understood until that instant how horribly painful it was. How cold and callous and unsympathetic he had been when utilizing it.

He should have turned and walked away. Scooped up his shattered pride and ego and cut his losses. But he couldn't move. Couldn't even breathe. He watched her move to the desk in the room, reaching for a stack of Post-it notes and a pen. She wrote something on the Post-it, stuck it onto the inside of the old, ridiculous box, then replaced the cover. Confused and numb, he took the box from her when she held it out to him. Unable to do anything else, he opened the box and read the Post-it.

Faith loves me.

Stunned, he read it twice more before looking up into the luminescent yellow of her eyes.

"See?" she said. "We're off to a very good start."

"I . . ." He was speechless. He was soaring and heart-sore and empty and full all at once. He had never felt anything like this swirling storm of emotion before in his life. He had thought he would never let anything touch him that deeply. The only thing that had ever occupied his heart had been his mother, Jackson, and Docia. It simply didn't know how to function with the enormous emotions being stuffed into it and dragged back out of it.

"Faith, I don't know what I did, or where I did it . . . I don't know how fate could possibly think that I deserve you."

She took the box from his numb fingers and laid it very gently on the table next to her, as if it truly was his heart and must be handled with all due care. And that was when he realized she would always take care of it that thoughtfully. That carefully. Not the stupid cardboard box, but the stupid thing beating in his chest.

She opened her mouth to say something, but he ringed an arm around her waist and dragged her up against his body, squeezing her so tightly a little *meep* squeaked out of her. He covered her mouth with his, anchoring himself in the softness of those plush lips. He drank deeply from her, felt the way she breathed hard against him, felt the way she clutched at the fabric of his shirt at his shoulders, pulling it so tightly he could hear threads popping in protest.

She was so alive. So strong and so damn beautiful it hurt just to think about it, never mind lay his eyes on her. How had he not seen it from the very start? How could he not have felt this feeling the very moment he'd first seen her?

"I realized I needed to stay here. I'm just human, but Jacks and Docia need people around to protect them in daylight. That sounds like a job I can do. And it lets me stay near the people I love. I asked if you could stay

too . . . if . . . if I could get you to, that is. We're building something here, a force of Nightwalkers and humans . . . a force needed if we're going to fight Apep.
You would be a valuable part of that."

Faith laughed at him. He was pitching the idea at her
like he was trying to sell it. As if she would want to go
anywhere where he wasn't.

"I think that's a perfect idea," she said, smiling
through another rush of tears. "Just . . . perfect. Now
make love to me."

"Very well," he said, sweeping her back up against
his body and kissing her so deeply she was breathless.
"Your wish, as always, is granted."

EPILOGUE

Apep was eating banana peppers. For some reason he was craving the hottest, spiciest foods imaginable. It was ridiculously delightful. Cravings meant that his pregnancy was well on its way and was advancing quite properly.

It was a disappointment to have lost Chatha, but there were always more lackeys to be had. The Wraiths, for instance. Although, none would quite have Chatha's special touch. But he would avenge Chatha one day. Actually, Chatha had nothing to do with it. He would set those people down a peg before they got too cocky. Yes, he would. But this time he would take the time to prepare and plan. After all, he couldn't just rush in with him being in such a delicate condition. He might have to wait until after the pregnancy altogether before doing something about it. Then he and his son could lay waste to all of them. They could rout out every Nightwalker on the planet!

In the meantime, he was going to look into how to reverse his curse. Yes. It was a very good idea to be prepared should the need arise.

A very good idea indeed.

Read on for an exciting sneak peek of

FORGED
BY JACQUELYN FRANK

The next book in
The World of Nightwalkers series

"It is *not* an ugly monument of metal with no purpose. It's an ugly monument of metal that's allowing us to carry on this interference-free phone call." That small bit of logic released a tirade of venom about the evils of modern technology from the other end of that lovely connection and Katrina Haynes rolled her eyes heavenward, as if that were going to help deal with her mother for whom logic was a fluid thing. The ugly cell tower they'd just placed on her mother's neighbor's property on the mountain above was a blight and an eyesore and entirely not necessary said she-who-was-infamous-for-bitching-about-dropped-phone-calls and she-who-was-attached-at-the-hip-to-her-barely-understood-smartphone. Her mother had to have the best, whether she could use it to its potential or not.

Katrina's own smartphone had been a gift from her mother for Christmas, otherwise she'd still be making do with her much beloved flip phone, and being quite content with it. Although, she had to admit to an Angry Birds addiction.

"Well Mother, then you'll have to be content with

looking *down* the mountain and not *up* the mountain where the cell tower is. After all, isn't that what a vista is all about? Looking *down* around you?"

She whistled sharply, looking down her own drive to where Karma had disappeared. She exhaled, her breath clouding on the deep sigh. It was cold and crisp, just the way she liked it, and as she looked down at her own vista, a breathtaking view of the valley and the small town of Stone Gorge, Washington, where she lived, she guessed she'd probably be a little pissed off, too, if something marred her view in any direction.

"Momma, Karma's disappeared again. I'm going to have to call you back."

"That dog," her mother tsked. She didn't like the thundering Newfoundland dog. Her mother said it was because the dog reminded her too much of a black bear rather than a dog, and being so close to the wilderness where bears often came down and ravaged her mother's birdfeeders, Katrina could understand the trepidation. Although Karma was a bounding bundle of soft, sweet, slobbering devotion and wouldn't hurt a fly.

Kat said her goodbyes and hung up the phone before moving down the steeply sloping drive whistling again for her dog. But as she came around one of the drive's many curves, she found the dog snuffling into the thick leaf fall left over from that autumn's annual shedding. Karma's big body was blocking her view of whatever it was she had found. Fearing she'd come up with a skunk, Kat hurried forward.

"Karma, come out of there!" she ordered sharply.

And that was when she saw it. Him. It. She couldn't decide and she was frozen in place, rooted with fear and shock, her heart pounding with sudden madness in her chest. He was probably the largest man she had ever seen in her life, and living in nearly-wild mountain country that was saying something. He was almost twice as big as the gigantic dog snuffling at him. But the most shocking thing about him was not that he was clearly nude in the slush of the last snowfall that was half melted yet, but that half his skin was gray, like the coarseness of a stone, and half was dusky, perhaps deeply tanned or maybe racially swarthy with an acre of sculpted muscle. He was lying on his stomach, seemingly dead.

Then he groaned, proving himself alive, and rolled onto his back, and all her fear melted away when she saw a copious amount of bright-red blood. She lurched forward, shoving her dog aside, as she dropped to her knees and reached out to touch him. Her hands fell onto his shoulders, one of which was chilled human skin, the other of which was as rough as stone. But that couldn't be, she thought in some corner of her mind. Skin simply did not turn to stone. Perhaps it was a full thickness burn or some other kind of injury . . . But the sectioning of skin to stone fluctuated under her touch and suddenly the shoulder opposite turned to stone and the other to flesh beneath her trembling hands, robbing her completely of any further excuses.

But with that change came a sudden gush of blood down the ridges of his defined abdomen before it dripped heavily into the snow, much of which was already stained a melting red.

"Don't . . . move," she said, fumbling for her phone. "I'll call for help."

"No!" He reached out to grab her by her front, her thick coat suddenly feeling like nothing in the grip of his fist as he jerked her forward. All of a sudden she felt like something fragile, like he could snap her in two at his whim. "You see what I am. I canna control it. The pain . . . they would see what I am." He looked up then, searching the dark predawn skies. She and her mother had always spoke in the freakishly early hours before dawn, and they always called each other through a cup of tea and coffee, respectively, touching base and bookending their days to the sound of each other's voice. "I need shelter. Please. I canna be caught out in the daylight."

Katrina sat there on her knees, the wet snow melted by her body warmth seeping into her jeans, frozen with fear and indecision. In the end it was the bright red of another gush of blood that galvanized her.

"This is crazy, this is crazy," she said under her breath in a fast, heated whisper. "Okay," she said so he could hear her. "I'll bring you inside. But . . . that doesn't mean I won't call for someone. If you try to hurt me . . . my dog will attack you."

"Oh," he said, his chiseled lips turning into a wry smile, "the dog that was just merrily licking my face?"

Crap. *Damn it, Karma*, she thought with heat.

"W-well . . . I-I'll scream or call for help."

"Thanks for the warning. Once we're inside I'll snap your neck to shut you up." She gasped as he gave her another wry smile. "Doona tell the villain what you're planning tae do when you doona know what he's capable of. I willna hurt you. I need your help. And fast. I'm getting weaker by the second and you willna be able tae move me if I become dead weight. You're far too small."

He mentioned her smallness almost as if it were a terrible failing on her part and that got her back up. People had treated her like this tiny little missish thing all of her life and frankly it just served to piss her off. She was small, no doubt about that, but she could pack a punch if necessary. And after his warning about keeping her plans secret, she bit her lip to keep herself from saying as much.

Instead she reached out to help him up. It was clearly all he could do to gain his feet, and she realized just how critically wounded he was. But she couldn't see the damage just yet with all that blood obscuring her ability to determine the worst of it. Despite his concerns over her diminutive shortcomings, he leaned heavily into her all the same, making the disparateness of their heights seem suddenly more obvious. As they trudged up the sloping drive she began to fear her ability to get him to safety. Her muscles began to burn under the strain of climbing with his significant weight against her just as the house came into view through the thickness of the pines.

"How much . . ."

Farther, he wanted to know. The blood coming from him was soaking the left side of her clothing and she knew why he couldn't speak. He was using all of his focus to stay on his feet.

"It's here. Right here. Not much farther. You can do it," she encouraged him. It seemed to give him strength and he lifted his weight farther onto his own feet and propelled them forward quickly. At the walk of the house, however, he stumbled and went down, staining her stone walkway with his blood. "Come on," she said, fearing he couldn't go farther and, like he had said, she wouldn't be strong enough to get him into the house. She glanced up at the sky, the dawn doing nothing to lighten it because of the bitter cloud cover heavy with snow. Worse still, the wind was picking up, promising a blustering and brutal blizzard.

But the weather was a ways off and it was the least of her worries. Except, a storm could cut her off from any help, and she would be helpless to him . . .

But right then it was he who was helpless to her, and that galvanized her into action.

"Up!" she commanded, yanking at the arm he'd lain across her shoulders. "Get up. Only a little farther. The dawn is coming," she warned him, not knowing why that should trouble him so much. Maybe it was the coming storm that worried him. Rightly so. Washington was known for some mighty mean snowstorms. Especially at this altitude.

She pulled him up and he got his feet under himself in what she suspected was his final act of strength. They stumbled to the door and she hastily juggled him and the doorknob, his weight on her making her fumble at it. Finally it gave way and they staggered into the house.

"Somewhere dark. No light. Protected." His words jolted out of him on groans of obvious pain. Far be it from her to argue.

"I know the feeling," she muttered.

She went for the nearest bedroom, which turned out to be the master suite. All the other rooms were on the second floor and she knew navigating stairs was out of the question for them both. Even without his weight, the burning muscles of her legs couldn't possibly have gotten her up them.

"That's it," she said with a grunt, "I'm getting my fat ass in gear and getting on the treadmill. In the spring it'll be better . . . a few treks up and down the mountain, right?"

After much grunting and bumping into walls, they made it into her bedroom and fell onto the bed together, his weight flattening her until she could barely breathe. She shoved at him, but he was barely conscious and she realized that the weird stone thing was once again shifting in and out of being on his body . . . if that were even possible. Hell, it had to be possible. She was watching it with her own eyes. Feeling it against her own skin. Before he turned to stone completely and she found herself trapped under a ten-ton statue, she strained to push him off her with what remained of her strength. But as much as she shoved at him, she knew it was his help alone that allowed him roll to off her.

She wriggled out from under him and gained her feet by the bed, panting hard for breath. Damn it, she thought inanely as she saw him lying big and bleeding in her bed, she really loved that quilt set and she was never going to be able to get the blood out.

Thinking he was unconscious, she reached out and poked a finger against the stone-looking skin on his arm. She couldn't believe it, but it really was stone! A rough stone like that of an unpolished statue. How in the hell was that possible? It couldn't be . . . but it was. She was feeling it right under her fingertips.

"No outside light. Please," he said, startling her.

Begging her. "The daylight will make it impossible for you to help me, and I will die. I promise you, I *will* die."

She nodded hastily, reaching out to give him an awkward pat of reassurance on the large, curving muscle of his shoulder. "Don't worry. I've already closed the storm shutters." And started a fire in the fireplace that warmed both the master bedroom and the living room with shared sides, its warm light dancing over them both. That and the bedside light was enough.

He exhaled then, a long shuddering breath of his final strength bleeding out of him, and suddenly she remembered what all of that blood meant and forgot about her damaged clothes and quilts. She ran for her bathroom, yanking out the supplies she had squirreled away in dribs and drabs over the years just in case . . . well, just in case. And now, it was in case. She found a basin and loaded it up with gauze, iodine, and 2.0 vicryl sutures. She belatedly washed her hands and snapped on a pair of purple nitrile gloves, even though she was already drenched in his blood. She would work better with clean hands and the traction of the gloves.

She hastened to the bed, moving up to him and hitting both of the bedside lights. She turned him and realized there was no more stone skin on him. He was entirely a flesh-and-blood man. For some reason that comforted her a little. But the idea that that could change at any moment sat heavy in her thoughts. Suddenly she felt the burning presence of her phone in her back pocket. She should call for help, never mind his protestations. He was out like a light and there was nothing he could do about it, he was just that weak. But he had surprised her thus far with his ability to power through his weakness, and even if she called for help, it could take anywhere from thirty minutes to an hour before anyone would make it up the mountain to her. This was what she had feared, and the only thing she had feared, about living alone so remotely. She had imagined things like this, evil men stumbling upon her house and she alone and helpless.

But nothing about him made her sense that he was evil, per se. After all, he had pointed out to her what he *could* do to her . . . inferring the opposite that he *wouldn't* do anything to hurt her.

In the end she decided to leave the phone silent in her pocket, even as she berated herself for probably being stupid and very likely to regret it. But the healer in her jumped to the forefront, and she grabbed gauze and began to wipe at the source of his blood. She gasped when she finally cleared the field and could see the extent of the damage. A cut deep into his side, as if someone had swung a sword into him trying to cleave him in half, and down his side and leg he was violently burned, third degree in most places.

Again, she felt the burn of her phone in her pocket.

"Don't," he rasped, as if he could read her mind.

"I won't," she soothed him. "But you are terribly injured. You need a hospital."

His mouth turned grim and his eyes fluttered open. For the first time the golden topaz of his eyes jumped out at her. They were beautiful, she thought with no little awe, as was the rest of him. He had the darkest, deepest black hair she'd ever seen. Not blue-black . . .

not dark brown . . . but purest black. It had the lightest curl to it as it fell in waves to just above his collar. He had an aquiline nose and deeply sculpted cheeks, the cheekbones wide. His mouth was full, like for a woman, only unmistakably male. She imagined a mouth that large had a smile just as wide. A killer smile, she was sure. He was not pretty or boyish by any stretch of the imagination, but was still strongly handsome.

But there was no time to further enjoy the view. She had to clear her field once again and she grabbed her suture kit. As deep as the wound was, she worried about the contamination of the leaf litter and whatever had caused the injury in the first place. She first used saline to wash it clean until she was satisfied there was no debris in the wound, and then she squeezed the bottle of iodine over him and prayed for the best.

"This is going to hurt. I don't have anything to numb the area." The area? Hell, she was practically going to have to do surgery to put him back together.

"Do it," he rasped. And then, fortunately for him, he passed out completely. She felt it ripple throughout his body, almost like the deflation of sudden death. She worriedly checked his breathing and found it, shallow and weak as it was. She turned her attention to his wound, threaded her needle, and went to work.

FORBIDDEN

From *New York Times* bestselling author Jacquelyn Frank comes the first book in the World of the Nightwalkers – an exciting and sensual new spin-off series in which the Bodywalkers, an ancient race of the night, battle the evil forces who prey on them.

The unexpected happens in an instant. On her way to work, secretary Docia Waverley quickly begins to suspect that things will never be the same when a tall, blond, muscular stranger tells her it is his duty to protect her at all costs. Docia just hopes her saviour doesn't turn out to be a crazed kidnapper.

When Ram finds Docia, he has no doubt that she is his queen. But as this golden warrior sweeps in to protect her, he feels something more than body heat every time they touch. He is overwhelmed by a searing connection that goes deep into the twin souls inside him. A desire rises in him that is forbidden – this woman is his queen, the mate of his king, his leader, his best friend. And yet Docia is so vulnerable and attractive that she awakens a hunger in Ram that is undeniable, a carnal craving he cannot yield to . . . not without risking the very survival of the Bodywalkers.

FOREVER

From *New York Times* bestselling author Jacquelyn Frank
comes the second book in the World of the Nightwalkers –
an exciting and sensual new spin-off series in which
the Bodywalkers, an ancient race of the night,
battle the evil forces who prey on them.

After being brought back from death, police officer Jackson
Waverly receives the shock of his life: he has become
host to a Bodywalker, a spirit that is reborn in flesh
and blood, and part of a proud, ancient race that uses
its extraordinary gifts to battle dark, evil forces.
Jackson's spirit is a powerful one – none other than
the Egyptian pharaoh Menes, who longs to reunite
with his eternal love, the Egyptian queen Hatshepsut.

While Menes is obsessed with finding the perfect vessel for
his queen, Jackson cannot stop thinking about Dr Marissa
Anderson, the gorgeous precinct shrink who keeps pushing
him to confront his grief over the loss of his K-9 partner.
But what Marissa really arouses most in Jackson is intense
desire, which is exactly what Menes is looking for. To fight
a great enemy, pharaoh and queen must join; but to host
Hatshepsut, Marissa will first have to die. Fate has given
Jackson a profound choice: save Marissa from Menes's
plan or keep an entire species from the brink of extinction.

Do you love fiction with a supernatural twist?

Want the chance to hear news about your favourite authors (and the chance to win free books)?

Keri Arthur
S. G. Browne
P.C. Cast
Christine Feehan
Jacquelyn Frank
Thea Harrison
Larissa Ione
Darynda Jones
Sherrilyn Kenyon
Jackie Kessler
Jayne Ann Krentz and Jayne Castle
Martin Millar
Kat Richardson
J.R. Ward
David Wellington
Laura Wright

Then visit the Piatkus website and blog
www.piatkus.co.uk | www.piatkusbooks.net

And follow us on Facebook and Twitter
www.facebook.com/piatkusfiction | www.twitter.com/piatkusbooks

piatkus